Basil King

The High Heart

Basil King

The High Heart

1st Edition | ISBN: 978-3-75238-155-9

Place of Publication: Frankfurt am Main, Germany

Year of Publication: 2020

Outlook Verlag GmbH, Germany.

Reproduction of the original.

THE HIGH HEART

BY

BASIL KING

CHAPTER I

I could not have lived in the Brokenshire circle for nearly a year without recognizing the fact that in the eyes of his family J. Howard, as he was commonly called by the world, was the Great Dispenser; but my first intimation that he meant to act in that capacity toward me came from Larry Strangways, on a bright July morning during the summer of 1913, when we were at Newport.

I was crossing the lawn, going toward the sea, with little Gladys Rossiter, to whom I acted as companion in the hours when she was out of the nursery, with a specific duty to speak French. Larry Strangways was tutor to the Rossiter boy, and in our relative positions we were bound to exercise toward each other a good deal of discretion. We fraternized with constraint. We fraternized because—well, chiefly because we couldn't help it. In the mocking flare of his eye, which contradicted the assumed young gravity of his manner, I read an opinion of the Rossiter household and of the Brokenshire family in general similar to my own. That would have been enough for mutual comprehension had there been no instinctive sympathies between us; but there were. Allowing for the fact that we were of different nationalities, we had the same kind of antecedents; we spoke the same kind of social language; we had the same kind of aims in life. Neither of us regarded the position in the Rossiter establishment as a permanent status. He was a tutor merely for the minute, while feeling his way to that first rung of the ladder which I was convinced would lead him to some high place in American life. I was a nursery governess only on the way to getting married. Matrimony was the continent toward which more or less consciously I had been traveling for five or six years, without having actually descried a port. In this connection I may relate a little incident which had taken place between myself and Mrs. Rossiter after I had accepted my situation in her family. It will retard my meeting with Larry Strangways on the lawn, but it will throw light on it when it comes.

I had met Mrs. Rossiter, who was J. Howard Brokenshire's daughter, in the way that is known as socially. I never understood why she should have taken a house for the summer in our quiet old town of Halifax, unless she was urged to it by the vague restlessness which was one of her characteristics. But there she was in a roomy old brick mansion I had known all my life, with gardens and conservatories and lawns running down to the fiord or back-harbor which we call the Northwest Arm, and a fine English air of seclusion. In our easy, neighborly way she was well received, and made herself agreeable. She flirted with the officers of both Army and Navy enough to create talk without raising scandal; and she was sufficiently good-natured to be civil to us girls, among whom she singled me out for attentions. I attributed this kindness to our recent bereavement and financial crash, which had left me poor after twenty-four years of comfort, and was proportionately grateful. It was partly gratitude, and partly a natural love of children, and partly a special affection for the exquisite thing herself, that drew me to little Gladys Rossiter, to playing with her on the lawns, and rowing her on the Arm, and—as I had been for three or four years at school in Paris—dropping into a habit of lisping French to her. As the child liked me the mother left her more and more to my care, gaining thus the greater scope for her innocuous flirtations.

It was toward the end of the summer that Mrs. Rossiter began to sigh, "I don't know how I shall ever tear Gladys away from you," and, "I do wish you were coming with us."

I wished it in a way myself, since I was rather at a loss as to what to do. I had never expected to have to earn a living; I had expected to get married. My two elder sisters, Louise and Victoria, had married easily enough, the one in the Navy, the other in the Army; but with me suitors seemed to lag. They came and saw—but they never went far enough for conquest. I couldn't understand it. I was not stupid; I was not ugly; and I was generally spoken of as having charm. But there was the fact that I was twenty-four, with scarcely a penny, and drawing nearer and nearer to the end of my expedients. I was not without some social experience, having kept house in a generous way for my widowed father, till his death, some two years before the summer when I met Mrs. Rossiter, brought with it our financial collapse. If he hadn't left a lot of old books—*Canadiana*, the pamphlets were called—and rare first editions of all kinds, which I took over to London and sold at Sothbey's, I shouldn't have had enough on which to dress. This business being settled, I stayed as long as I decently could with Louise at Southsea and Victoria at Gibraltar; but no man asked me to marry him during the course of either visit. Had there been a sign of any such possibility the sisters would have put themselves out to keep me; but as nothing warranted them in doing so they let me go. An uncle and aunt having offered to give me shelter for a time at Halifax, there was nothing left for it but to go back and renew the search for my fortunes in my native town.

When, therefore, Mrs. Rossiter, in her pretty, helpless way said to me one day, "Why shouldn't you come with me, dear Miss Adare?" I jumped inwardly at the opportunity, though I smiled and replied in an offhand manner, "Oh, that would have to be discussed."

Mrs. Rossiter admitted the truth of this observation somewhat pensively. I know now that I took her up with too much promptitude.

"Yes, of course," she returned, absently, and the subject was dropped.

It was taken up again, however, and our bargain made. On Mrs. Rossiter's part it was made astutely, not in the matter of money, but in the way in which she shifted me from the position of a friend into that of a retainer. It was done with the most perfect tact, but it was done. I had no complaint to make. What she wanted was a nursery governess. My own first preoccupations were food and shelter for which I should not be dependent on my kin. We came to the incident I am about to relate very gradually; but when we did come to it I had no difficulty in seeing that it had been in the back of Mrs. Rossiter's mind from the first. It had been the cause of that second thought on the day when I had taken her up too readily.

She began by telling me about her father. Beyond the fact that some man who seemed to be specially well informed would occasionally say with awe, "She's J. Howard Brokenshire's daughter," I knew nothing whatever about him. But I began to see him now as the central sun round whom all the Brokenshires revolved. They revolved round him, not so much from adoration or even from natural affection as from some tremendous rotary force to which there was no resistance.

Up to this time I had heard no more of American life than American life had heard of me. The great country south of our border was scarcely on my map. The Halifax in which I was born and grew up was not the bustling Canadian port, dependent on its hinterland, it is to-day; it was an outpost of England, with its face always turned to the Atlantic and the east. My own face had been turned the same way. My home had been literally a jumping-off place, in that when we left it we never expected to go in any but the one direction. I had known Americans when they came into our midst as summer visitors, but only in the way one knows the stars which dawn and fade and leave no trace of their passage on actual happenings.

In the course of Mrs. Rossiter's confidences I began to see a vast cosmogony beyond my own personal sun, with J. Howard Brokenshire as the pivot of the new universe. With a curious little shock of surprise I discovered that there could be other solar systems besides the one to which I was accustomed, and that Canada was not the whole of North America. It was like looking through a telescope which Mrs. Rossiter held to my eye, a telescope through which I saw the nebular evidence of an immense society, wealthy, confused, more intellectual than our own, but more provincial too, perhaps; more isolated, more timid, more conservative, less instinct with the great throb of national and international impulse which all of us feel who live on the imperial red line and, therefore, less daring, but interesting all the same. I began to glow

4

with the spirit of adventure. My position as a nursery governess presented the opportunities not merely of a Livingstone or a Stanley, but of a Galileo or a Copernicus.

I learned that Mrs. Rossiter's mother had been a Miss Brew, and that the Brews were a great family in Boston. She was the mother of all Mr. Brokenshire's children. By looks and hints and sighs I gathered from Mrs. Rossiter that her father's second marriage had been a trial to his family. Not that there had been any social descent. On the contrary, the present Mrs. Brokenshire had been Editha Billing, of Philadelphia, and there could be nothing better than that. It was a question of fitness, of necessity, of age. "There was no need for him to marry again at all," Mrs. Rossiter complained. "If she'd only been a middle-aged woman," she said to me later, "we might not have felt... . But she's younger than Mildred and only a year or two older than I am." "Oh yes," was another remark, "she's pretty; very pretty ... but I often—wonder."

She described her brothers and her sister by degrees. One day she told me about Mildred, another about Jack, so coming toward her point. Mildred was the eldest of the family, a great invalid. She had been thrown from her horse years before while hunting in England, and had injured her spine. Jack had just gone into business with his father, and had married Pauline Gray, of Baltimore. Though she didn't say it in so many words I judged that it was not a happy marriage in the highest sense—that Jack was somewhat light of love, while Pauline "went her own way" to a degree that made her talked about. It was not till the day before her departure for New York that Mrs. Rossiter mentioned her younger brother, Hugh.

I was helping her to pack—that is, I was helping the maid while Mrs. Rossiter directed. Just at that minute, however, she was standing up, shaking out the folds of an evening dress. She seemed to peep at me round its garnishings as she said, apropos of nothing:

"There's my brother Hugh. He's the youngest of us all—just twenty-six. He has no occupation as yet—he's just studying languages and things. My father wants him to go into diplomacy." As I caught her eye there was a smile in it, but a special kind of smile. It was the smile to go with the sensible, kindly, coaxing inflection with which she said, "You'll leave him alone, won't you?"

I took the dress out of her hand to carry it to the maid in the next room.

"Leave him alone—how?"

She flushed to a lovely pink.

"Oh, you know what I mean. I don't have to explain."

5

"You mean that in my position in the household it will be for me to—to keep out of his way?"

"It's you who put it like that, dear Miss Adare—"

"But it's the way you want me to put it?"

"Well, if I admit that it is?"

"Then I don't think I care for the place."

"What?"

I stated my position more simply.

"If I'm to have nothing to do with your brother, Mrs. Rossiter, I don't want to go."

In the audacity of this response she saw something that amused her, for, snatching the dress from my hand, she ran with it into the next room, laughing.

During the following winter in New York and the early summer of the next year in Newport I saw a good deal of Mr. Hugh Brokenshire, but never with any violent restriction on the part of Mrs. Rossiter. I say violent with intention, for she did intervene when she could do so. Only once did I hear that she knew he was kind to me, and that was from Larry Strangways. It was an observation he had overheard as it passed from Mrs. Rossiter to her husband, and which, in the spirit of our silent *camaraderie*, he thought it right to hand along.

"I can't be responsible for Hugh!" Mrs. Rossiter had said. "He's old enough to look after himself. If he wants a row with father he must have it; and he seems to me in a fair way to get it. If he does it will be his own fault; it won't be Miss Adare's."

Fortified by this acquittal, I went on my way as quietly as I could, though I cannot say I was free from perturbation.

Perturbation caught me like a whiff of wind as I saw Larry Strangways deflect from his course across the lawn and come in my direction. I knew he wouldn't have done that unless he felt himself authorized; and nothing could give him the authorization but something in the way of a message or command. To all observers we were strangers. We should have been strangers even to each other had it not been for that freemasonry of caste, that secret mutual comprehension, which transcends speech and opportunities of meeting, and which, on our part, at least, had little expression beyond smiles and flying glances.

Of course he was good-looking. It has often seemed to me the privilege of ineligible men to be tall and slim and straight, with just such a flash in the eye and just such a beam about the mouth as belonged to Larry Strangways. Instinct had told me from the first that it would be wise for me to avoid him, while prudence, as I have hinted, gave him the same indication to keep at a distance from me. Luckily he didn't live in the house, but in lodgings in the town. We hardly ever met face to face, and then only under the eye of Mrs. Rossiter when each of us marshaled a pupil to lunch or to tea.

As the collie at his heels and the wire-haired terrier at ours made a bee-line for each other the children kept them company, which gave us space for those few minutes of privacy the occasion apparently demanded. Though he lifted his hat formally, and did his best to preserve the decorum of our official situations, the prank in his eye flung out that signal to which I could never do anything but respond.

"I've a message for you, Miss Adare."

I managed to stammer out the word "Indeed?" I couldn't be surprised, and yet I could hardly stand erect from fear.

He glanced at the children to make sure they were out of earshot.

"It's from the great man himself—indirectly."

I was so near to collapse that I could only say, "Indeed?" again, though I rallied sufficiently to add, "I didn't know he was aware of my existence."

"Apparently he wasn't—but he is now. He desires you—I give you the verb as Spellman, the secretary, passed it on to me—he desires you to be in the breakfast loggia here at three this afternoon."

I could barely squeak the words out:

"Does he mean that he's coming to see me?"

"That, it seems, isn't necessary for you to know. Your business is to be there. There's quite a subtle point in the limitation. Being there, you'll see what will happen next. It isn't good for you to be told too much at a time."

My spirit began to revive.

"I'm not his servant. I'm Mrs. Rossiter's. If he wants anything of me why doesn't he say so through her?"

"'Sh, 'sh, Miss Adare! You mustn't dictate to God, or say he should act in this way or in that."

"But he's not God."

7

"Oh, as to that—well, you'll see." He added, with his light laugh, "What will you bet that I don't know what it's all about?"

"Oh, I bet you do."

"Then," he warned, "you're up against it."

I was getting on my mettle.

"Perhaps I am—but I sha'n't be alone."

"No; but you'll be made to feel alone."

"Even so—"

As I was anxious to keep from boasting beforehand, I left the sentence there.

"Yes?" he jogged. "Even so—what?"

"Oh, nothing. I only mean that I'm not afraid of him—that is," I corrected, "I'm not afraid of him fundamentally."

He laughed again. "Not afraid of him fundamentally! That's fine!" Something in his glance seemed to approve of me. "No, I don't believe you are; but I wonder a little why not."

I reflected, gazing beyond his shoulder, down the velvety slopes of the lawn, and across the dancing blue sea to the islets that were mere specks on the horizon. In the end I decided to speak soberly. "I'm not afraid of him," I said at last, "because I've got a sure thing."

"You mean him?"

I knew the reference was to Hugh Brokenshire. "If I mean him," I replied, after a minute's thinking, "it's only as the greater includes the less, or as the universal includes everything."

He whistled under his breath.

"Does that mean anything? Or is it just big talk?"

Half shy and half ashamed of going on with what I had to say, I was obliged to smile ruefully.

"It's big talk because it's a big principle. I don't know how to manage it with anything small." I tried to explain further, knowing that my dark skin flushed to a kind of dahlia-red while I was doing so. "I don't know whether I've read it—or whether I heard it—or whether I've just evolved it—but I seem to have got hold of—of—don't laugh too hard, please—of the secret of success."

"Good for you! I hope you're not going to be stingy with it."

"No; I'll tell you—partly because I want to talk about it to some one, and just at present there's no one else."

"Thanks!"

"The secret of success, as I reason it out, must be something that will protect a weak person against a strong one—me, for instance, against J. Howard Brokenshire—and work everything out all right. There," I cried, "I've said the word."

"You've said a number. Which is the one?"

Anxiety not to seem either young or didactic or a prig made my tone apologetic.

"There's such a thing as Right, written with a capital. If I persist in doing Right—still with a capital—then nothing but right can come of it."

"Oh, can't it!"

"I know it sounds like a platitude—"

"No, it doesn't," he interrupted, rudely, "because a platitude is something obviously true; and this isn't."

I felt some relief.

"Oh, isn't it? Then I'm glad. I thought it must be."

"You won't go on thinking it. Suppose you do right and somebody else does wrong?"

"Then I should be willing to back my way against his. Don't you see? That's the point. That's the secret I'm telling you about. Right works; wrong doesn't."

"That's all very fine—"

"It's all very fine because it's so. Right is—what's the word William James put into the dictionary?"

He suggested pragmatism.

"That's it. Right is pragmatic, which I suppose is the same thing as practical. Wrong must be impractical; it must be—"

"I shouldn't bank too confidently on that in dealing with the great J. Howard."

"But I'm going to bank on it. It's where I'm to have him at a disadvantage. If he does wrong while I do right, why, then I'll get him on the hip."

"How do you know he's going to do wrong?"

"I don't. I merely surmise it. If he does right—"

"He'll get you on the hip."

"No, because there can't be a right for him which isn't a right for me. There can't be two rights, each contrary to the other. That's not in common sense. If he does right then I shall be safe—whichever way I have to take it. Don't you see? That's where the success comes in as well as the secret. It can't be any other way. Please don't think I'm talking in what H. G. Wells calls the tin-pot style—but one must express oneself somehow. I'm not afraid, because I feel as if I'd got something that would hang about me like a magic cloak. Of course for you—a man—a magic cloak may not be necessary; but I assure you that for a girl like me, out in the world on her own—"

He, too, sobered down from his chaffing mood.

"But in this case what is going to be Right—written with a capital?"

I had just time to reply, "Oh, that I shall have to see!" when the children and dogs came scampering up and our conversation was over.

On returning from my walk with Gladys I informed Mrs. Rossiter of the order I had received. I could see her distressed look in the mirror before which she sat doing something to her hair.

"Oh, dear!" she sighed, "it's just what I was afraid of. Now I suppose he'll want you to leave."

"That is, he'll want you to send me away."

"It's the same thing," she said, fretfully, and sat with hands lying idly in her lap.

She stared out of the window. It was a large bow window, with a window-seat cushioned in flowered chintz. Couch, curtains, and easy-chairs reproduced this Enchanted Garden effect, forming a paradisiacal background for her intensely modern and somewhat neurotic prettiness. I had seen her sit by the half-hour like this, gazing over the shrubberies, lawns, and waves, with a yearning in her eyes like that of some twentieth-century Blessed Damozel.

It was her unhappy hour of the day. Between getting up at nine or ten and descending languidly to lunch, life was always a great load to her. It pressed on one too weak to bear its weight and yet too conscientious to throw it off, though, as a matter of fact, this melancholy was only the reaction of her nerves from the mild excitements of the night before. I was generally with her during some portion of this forenoon time, reading her notes and answering them, speaking for her at the telephone, or keeping her company and listening to her confidences while she nibbled without appetite at a bit of toast and sipped her tea.

To put matters on the common footing I said:

"Is there anything you'd like me to do, Mrs. Rossiter?"

She ignored this question, murmuring in a way she had, through half-closed lips, as if mere speech was more than she was equal to: "And just when we were getting on so well—and the way Gladys adores you—"

"And the way I adore Gladys."

"Oh, well, you don't spoil the child, like that Miss Phips. I suppose it's your sensible English bringing up."

"Not English," I interrupted.

"Canadian then. It's almost the same thing." She went on without transition of tone: "Mr. Millinger was there again last night. He was on my left. I do wish they wouldn't keep putting him next to me. It makes everything look so pointed—especially with Harry Scott glowering at me from the other end of the table. He hardly spoke to Daisy Burke, whom he'd taken in. I must say she was a fright. And Mr. Millinger so imprudent! I'm really terrified that Jim will hear gossip when he comes down from New York—or notice something." There was the slightest dropping of the soft fluting voice as she continued: "I've never pretended to love Jim Rossiter more than any man I've ever seen. That was one of papa's matches. He's a born match-maker, you know, just as he's a born everything else. I suppose you didn't think of that. But since I am Jim's wife—"

As I was the confidante of what she called her affairs—a rôle for which I was qualified by residence in British garrison towns—I interposed diplomatically, "But so long as Mr. Millinger hasn't said anything, not any more than Mr. Scott—"

"Oh, if I were to allow men to say things, where should I be? You can go far with a man without letting him come to that. It's something I should think you'd have known—with your sensible bringing up—and the heaps of men you had there in Halifax—and I suppose at Southsea and Gibraltar, too." It was with a hint of helpless complaint that she added, "You remember that I asked you to leave him alone, now don't you?"

"Oh, I remember—quite. And suppose I did—and he didn't leave me alone?"

"Of course there's that, though it won't have any effect on papa. You are unusual, you know. Only one man in five hundred would notice it; but there always is that man. It's what I was afraid of about Hugh from the first. You're different—and it's the sort of thing he'd see."

11

"Different from what?" I asked, with natural curiosity.

Her reply was indirect.

"Oh, well, we Americans have specialized too much on the girl. You're not half as good-looking as plenty of other girls in Newport, and when it comes to dress—"

"Oh, I'm not in their class, I know."

"No; it's what you seem not to know. You aren't in their class—but it doesn't seem to matter. If it does matter, it's rather to your advantage."

"I'm afraid I don't see that."

"No, you wouldn't. You're not sufficiently subtle. You're really not subtle at all, in the way an American girl would be." She picked up the thread she had dropped. "The fact is we've specialized so much on the girl that our girls are too aware of themselves to be wholly human. They're like things wound up to talk well and dress well and exhibit themselves to advantage and calculate their effects—and lack character. We've developed the very highest thing in exquisite girl-mechanics—a work of art that has everything but a soul." She turned half round to where I stood respectfully, my hands resting on the back of an easy-chair. She was lovely and pathetic and judicial all at once. "The difference about you is that you seem to spring right up out of the soil where you're standing—just like an English country house. You belong to your background. Our girls don't. They're too beautiful for their background, too expensive, too produced. Take any group of girls here in Newport—they're no more in place in this down-at-the-heel old town than a flock of parrakeets in a New England wood. It's really inartistic, though we don't know it. You're more of a woman and less of a lovely figurine. But that won't appeal to papa. He likes figurines. Most American men do. Hugh is an exception, and I was afraid he'd see in you just what I've seen myself. But it won't go down with papa."

"If it goes down with Hugh—" I began, meekly.

"Papa is a born match-maker, which I don't suppose you know. He made my match and he made Jack's. Oh, we're—we're satisfied now—in a way; and I suppose Hugh will be, too, in the long run." I wanted to speak, but she tinkled gently on: "Papa has his designs for him, which I may as well tell you at once. He means him to marry Lady Cissie Boscobel. She's Lord Goldborough's daughter, and papa and he are very intimate. Papa knew him when we lived in England before grandpapa died. Papa has done things for him in the American money-market, and when we're in England he does things for us. Two or three of our men have married earls' daughters during the last few years, and it hasn't turned out so badly. Papa doesn't want not to be in the swim."

"Does"—I couldn't pronounce Hugh's name again—"does your brother know of Mr. Brokenshire's intentions?"

"Yes. I told him so. I told him when I began to see that he was noticing you."

"And may I ask what he said?"

"It would be no use telling you that, because, whatever he said, he'd have to do as papa told him in the end."

"But suppose he doesn't?"

"You can't suppose he doesn't. He will. That's all that can be said about it." She turned fully round on me, gazing at me with the largest and sweetest and tenderest eyes. "As for you, dear Miss Adare," she murmured, sympathetically, "when papa comes to see you this afternoon, as apparently he means to do, he'll grind you to powder. If there's anything smaller than powder he'll grind you to that. After he's gone we sha'n't be able to find you. You'll be dust."

CHAPTER II

At five minutes to three, precisely, I took my seat in the breakfast loggia.

The front of the house with the garden looked toward Ochre Point Avenue. The so-called breakfast loggia was thrown out from the dining-room in the direction of the sea. Here the family and their guests could gather on warm evenings, and in fine weather eat in the open air. Paved with red tiles, it was furnished with a long oak table, ornately carved, and some heavy old oak chairs that might have come from a monastery. Steamer chairs and wicker easy-chairs were scattered on the grass outside. On the left the loggia was screened from the neighboring property by a hedge of rambler roses that now ran the gamut of shades from crimson to sea-shell pink, while on the right it commanded a view of the two terraces supporting the house, with their long straight lines of flowers. The house itself had been built piecemeal, and was now a low, rambling succession of pavilions or *corps de logis*, to which a series of rose-colored awnings gave the only unifying principle.

Just now it was a house deserted by every one but the servants and myself. Mrs. Rossiter, having gone out to luncheon, had been careful not to return, and even the children had been sent over to Mrs. Jack Brokenshire, on the pretext of playing with her baby, but really to be out of the way. From Hugh I had had no sign of life since the previous afternoon. As to whether his father was coming as his enemy, his master, or his interpreter I could do nothing but conjecture.

But as far as I could I kept myself from conjecturing; holding my faculties in suspense. I had enough to do in assuring myself that I was not afraid—fundamentally. Superficially I was terrified. I should have been terrified had the great man but passed me in the hall and cast a look at me. He had passed me in the hall on occasions, but as he had never cast the look I had escaped. He had struck me then as a master of that art of seeing without seeing which I had hitherto thought of as feminine. Even when he stopped and spoke to Gladys he seemed not to know that I occupied the ground I stood on. I cannot say I enjoyed this treatment. I was accustomed to being seen. Moreover, I had lived with people who were courteous to inferiors, however cavalier with equals. The great J. Howard was neither courteous nor cavalier toward me, for the reason that where I was he apparently saw nothing but a vacuum.

Out to the loggia I took my work-basket and some sewing. Having no idea from which of the several approaches my visitor would come on me, I drew up one of the heavy arm-chairs and sat facing toward the sea. With the basket on the table beside me and my sewing in my hands I felt indefinably more mistress of myself.

It was a still afternoon and hot, with scarcely a sound but the pounding of the surf on the ledges at the foot of the lawn. Though the sky was blue overhead, a dark low bank rose out of the horizon, foretelling a change of wind with fog. In the air the languorous scent of roses and honeysuckle mingled with the acrid tang of the ocean.

I felt extraordinarily desolate. Not since hearing what the lawyer had told me on the afternoon of my father's funeral had I seemed so entirely alone. The fact that for nearly twenty-four hours Hugh had got no word to me threw me back upon myself. "You'll be made to feel alone," Mr. Strangways had said in the morning; and I was. I didn't blame Hugh. I had purposely left the matter in such a way that there was nothing he could say or do till after his father had spoken. He was probably waiting impatiently; I had, indeed, no doubt about that; but the fact remained that I, a girl, a stranger, in a certain sense a foreigner, was to make the best of my situation without help. J. Howard Brokenshire could grind me to powder—when he had gone away I should be dust.

"If I do right, nothing but right can come of it."

The maxim was my only comfort. By sheer force of repeating it I got strength to thread my needle and go on with my seam, till on the stroke of three the dread personage appeared.

I saw him from the minute he mounted the steps that led up from the Cliff Walk to Mr. Rossiter's lawn. He was accompanied by Mrs. Brokenshire, while a pair of greyhounds followed them. Having reached the lawn, they crossed it diagonally toward the loggia. Because of the heat and the up-hill nature of the way, they advanced slowly, which gave me leisure to observe.

Mrs. Brokenshire's presence had almost caused my heart to stop beating. I could imagine no motive for her coming but one I refused to accept. If the mission was to be unfriendly, she surely would have stayed away; but that it could be other than unfriendly was beyond my strength to hope.

I had never seen her before except in glimpses or at a distance. I noticed now that she was a little thing, looking the smaller for the stalwart six-foot-two beside which she walked. She was in white and carried a white parasol. I saw that her face was one of the most beautiful in features and finish I had ever looked into. Each trait was quite amazingly perfect. The oval was perfect; the coloring was perfect; mouth and nose and forehead might have been made to a measured scale. The finger of personified Art could have drawn nothing more exquisite than the arch of the eyebrows, or more delicately fringed than the lids. It might have been a doll's face, or the face for the cover of an American magazine, had it not been saved by something I hadn't the time to analyze, though I was later to know what it was.

As for him, he was as perfect in his way as she in hers. When I say that he wore white shoes, white-duck trousers, a navy-blue jacket, and a yachting-cap I give no idea of the something noble in his personality. He might have been one of the more ornamental Italian princes of immemorial lineage. A Jove with a Vandyke beard one could have called him, and if you add to that the conception of Jove the Thunderer, Jove with the look that could strike a man dead, perhaps the description would be as good as any. He was straight and held his head high. He walked with a firm setting of his feet that impressed you with the fact that some one of importance was coming.

It is not my purpose to speak of this man from the point of view of the ordinary member of the public. Of that I know next to nothing. I was dimly aware that his wealth and his business interests made him something of a public character; but apart from having heard him mentioned as a financier I could hardly have told what his profession was. So, too, with questions of morals. I have been present when, by hints rather than actual words, he was introduced as a profligate and a hypocrite; and I have also known people of good judgment who upheld him both as man and as citizen. On this subject no opinion of mine would be worth giving. I have always relegated the matter into that limbo of disputed facts with which I have nothing to do. I write of him only as I saw him in daily life, or at least in direct intercourse, and with that my testimony must end. Other people have been curious with regard to those aspects of his character on which I can throw no light. To me he became interesting chiefly because he was one of those men who from a kind of naïve audacity, perhaps an unthinking audacity, don't hesitate to play the part of the Almighty.

When they drew near enough to the loggia I stood up, my sewing in my hand. The two greyhounds, who had outdistanced them, came sniffing to the threshold and stared at me. I felt myself an object to be stared at, though I had taken pains with my appearance and knew that I was neat. Neatness, I may say in passing, is my strong point. Where many other girls can stand expensive dressing I am at my best when meticulously tidy. The shape of my head makes the simplest styles of doing the hair the most distinguished. My figure lends itself to country clothes and the tailor-made. In evening dress I can wear the cheapest and flimsiest thing, so long as it is dependent only on its lines. I was satisfied, therefore, with the way I looked, and when I say I felt myself an object to be stared at I speak only of my consciousness of isolation.

I cannot affirm, however, that J. Howard Brokenshire stared at me. He stared; but only at the general effects in which I was a mere detail. The loggia being open on all sides, he paused for half a second to take it and its contents in. I went with the contents. I looked at him; but nothing in the glance he cast over me recognized me as a human being. I might have been the table; I might have been the floor; for him I was hardly in existence.

I wonder if you have ever stood under the gaze of one who considered you too inferior for notice. The sensation is quite curious. It produces not humiliation or resentment so much as an odd apathy. You sink in your own sight; you go down; you understand that abjection of slaves which kept them from rising against their masters. Negatively at least you concede the right that so treats you. You are meek and humble at once; and yet you can be strong. I think I never felt so strong as when I saw that cold, deep eye, which was steely and fierce and most inconsistently sympathetic all in one quick flash, sweep over me and pay me no attention. *Ecce Femina* I might have been saying to myself, as a pendant in expression to the *Ecce Homo* of the Prætorium.

He moved aside punctiliously at the lower of the two steps that led up to the loggia to let his wife precede him. As she came in I think she gave me a salutation that was little more than a quiver of the lids. Having closed her parasol, she slipped into one of the arm-chairs not far from the table.

Now that he was at close quarters, with his work before him, he proceeded to the task at once. In the act of laying his hat and stick on a chair he began with the question, "Your name is—?"

The voice had a crisp gentleness that seemed to come from the effort to despatch business with the utmost celerity and spend no unnecessary strength on words. The fact that he must have heard my name from Hugh was plainly to play no part in our discussion. I was so unutterably frightened that when I tried to whisper the word "Adare" hardly a sound came forth.

As he raised himself from the placing of his cap and stick he was obliged to utter a sharp, "What?"

"Adare."

"Oh. Adare!"

It is not a bad name as names go; we like to fancy ourselves connected with the famous Fighting Adares of the County Limerick; but on J. Howard Brokenshire's lips it had the undiscriminating commonness of Smith or Jones. I had never been ashamed of it before.

"And you're one of my daughter's—"

"I'm her nursery governess."

"Sit down."

As he took the chair at the end of the table I dropped again into that at the side from which I had risen. It was then that something happened which left me for a second in doubt as to whether to take it as comic or catastrophic. His left eye closed; his left nostril quivered; he winked. To avoid having to face this singular phenomenon a second time I lowered my eyes and began mechanically to sew.

"Put that down!"

I placed the work on the table and once more looked at him. The striking eyes were again as striking as ever. In their sympathetic hardness there was nothing either ribald or jocose.

I suppose my scrutiny annoyed him, though I was unconscious of more than a mute asking for orders. He pointed to a distant chair, a chair in a corner, just within the loggia as you come from the direction of the dining-room.

"Sit there."

I know now that his wink distressed him. It was something which at that time had come upon him recently, and that he could neither control nor understand. A less imposing man, a man to whom personal impressiveness was less of an asset in daily life and work, would probably have been less disturbed by it; but to J. Howard Brokenshire it was a trial in more ways than one. Curiously, too, when the left eye winked the right grew glassy and quite terrible.

Not knowing that he was sensitive in this respect, I took my retreat to the corner as a kind of symbolic banishment.

"Hadn't I better stand up?" I asked, proudly, when I had reached my chair.

"Be good enough to sit down."

I seemed to fall backward. The tone had the effect of a shot. If I had ever felt small and foolish in my life it was then. I flushed to my darkest crimson. Angry and humiliated, I was obliged to rush to my maxim in order not to flash back in some indignant retort.

And then another thing happened of which I was unable at the minute to get the significance. Mrs. Brokenshire sprang up with the words:

"You're quite right, Howard. It's ever so much cooler over here by the edge. I never felt anything so stuffy as the middle of this place. It doesn't seem possible for air to get into it."

While speaking she moved with incomparable daintiness to a chair corresponding to mine and diagonally opposite. With the length and width of the loggia between us we exchanged glances. In hers she seemed to say, "If you are banished I shall be banished too"; in mine I tried to express gratitude. And yet I was aware that I might have misunderstood both movement and look entirely.

My next surprise was in the words Mr. Brokenshire addressed to me. He spoke in the soft, slightly nasal staccato which I am told had on his business associates the effect of a whip-lash.

"We've come over to tell you, Miss—Miss Adare, how much we appreciate your attitude toward our boy, Hugh. I understand from him that he's offered to marry you, and that very properly in your situation you've declined. The boy is foolish, as you evidently see. He meant nothing; he could do nothing. You're probably not without experience of a similar kind among the sons of your other employers. At the same time, as you doubtless expect, we sha'n't let you suffer by your prudence—"

It was a bad beginning. Had he made any sort of appeal to me, however unkindly worded, I should probably have yielded. But the tradition of the Fighting Adares was not in me for nothing, and after a smothering sensation which rendered me speechless I managed to stammer out:

"Won't you allow me to say that—"

The way in which his large, white, handsome hand went up was meant to impose silence upon me while he himself went on:

"In order that you may not be annoyed by my son's folly in the future you will leave my daughter's employ, you'll leave Newport—you'll be well advised, indeed, in going back to your own country, which I understand to be the British provinces. You will lose nothing, however, by this conduct, as I've given you to understand. Three—four—five thousand dollars—I think five ought to be sufficient—generous, in fact—"

"But I've not refused him," I was able at last to interpose. "I—I mean to accept him."

There was an instant of stillness during which one could hear the pounding of the sea.

"Does that mean that you want me to raise your price?"

"No, Mr. Brokenshire. I have no price. If it means anything at all that has to do with you, it's to tell you that I'm mistress of my acts and that I consider your son—he's twenty-six—to be master of his."

There was a continuation of the stillness. His voice when he spoke was the gentlest sound I had ever heard in the way of human utterance. If it were not for the situation it could have been considered kind:

"Anything at all that has to do with me? You seem to attach no importance to the fact that Hugh is my son."

I do not know how words came to me. They seemed to flow from my lips independently of thought.

"I attach importance only to the fact that he's a man. Men who are never anything but their father's sons aren't men."

"And yet a father has some rights."

"Yes, sir; some. He has the right to follow where his grown-up children lead. He hasn't the right to lead and require his grown-up children to follow."

He shifted his ground. "I'm obliged to you for your opinion, but at present it's not to the point—"

I broke in breathlessly: "Pardon me, sir; it's exactly to the point. I'm a woman; Hugh's a man. We're—we're in love with each other; it's all we have to be concerned with."

"Not quite; you've got to be concerned—with me."

"Which is what I deny."

"Oh, denial won't do you any good. I didn't come to hear your denials, or your affirmations, either. I've come to tell you what to do."

"But if I know that already?"

"That's quite possible—if you mean to play your game as doubtless you've played it before. I only want to warn you—"

I looked toward Mrs. Brokenshire for help, but her eyes were fixed on the floor, on which she was drawing what seemed like a design with the tip of her parasol. The greyhounds were stretched at her feet. I could do nothing but speak for myself, which I did with a calmness that surprised me.

"Mr. Brokenshire," I interrupted, "you are a man and I'm a woman. What's more, you're a strong man, while I'm a woman with no protection at all. I ask you—do you think you're playing a man's part in insulting me?"

His tone grew kind almost to affection. "My dear young lady, you misunderstand me. Insult couldn't be further from my thoughts. I'm speaking entirely for your own sake. You're young; you're very pretty; I won't say you've no knowledge of the world because I see you have—"

"I've a good deal of knowledge of the world."

"Only not such knowledge as would warrant you in pitting yourself against me."

"But I don't. If you'd leave me alone—"

"Let us keep to what we're talking of. I'm sorry for you; I really am. You're at the beginning of what might euphemistically—do you know the meaning of the word?—be called a career. I should like to save you from it; that's all. It's why I'm speaking to you very plainly and using language that can't be misunderstood. There's nothing original in your proceeding, believe me. Nearly every family of the standing of mine has had to reckon with something of the sort. Where there are young men, and young women of—what do you want me to say?—young women who mean to do the best they can for themselves—let us put it in that way—"

"I'm a gentleman's daughter," I broke in, weakly.

He smiled. "Oh yes; you're all gentlemen's daughters. Neither is there anything original in that."

"Mrs. Rossiter will tell you that my father was a judge in Canada—"

"The detail doesn't interest me."

"No, but it interests me. It gives me a sense of being equal to—"

"If you please! We'll not go into that."

"But I must speak. If I'm to marry Hugh you must let me tell you who I am."

"It's not necessary. You're not to marry Hugh. Let that be absolutely understood. Once you've accepted the fact—"

"I could only accept it from Hugh himself."

"That's foolish. Hugh will do as I tell him."

"But why should he in this case?"

"That again is something we needn't discuss. All that matters, my dear young lady, is your own interest. I'm working for that, don't you see, against yourself—"

I burst out, "But why shouldn't I marry him?"

He leaned on the table, tapping gently with his hand. "Because we don't want you to. Isn't that enough?"

I ignored this. "If it's because you don't know anything about me I could tell you."

"Oh, but we do know something about you. We know, for example, since you compel me to say it, that you're a little person of no importance whatever."

"My family is one of the best in Canada."

"And admitting that that's so, who would care what constituted a good family in Canada? To us here it means nothing; in England it would mean still less. I've had opportunities of judging how Canadians are regarded in England, and I assure you it's nothing to make you proud."

Of the several things he had said to sting me I was most sensitive to this. I, too, had had opportunities of judging, and knew that if anything could make one ashamed of being a British colonial of any kind it would be British opinion of colonials.

"My father used to say—"

He put up his large, white hand. "Another time. Let us keep to the subject before us."

I omitted the mention of my father to insist on a theory as to which I had often heard him express himself: "If it's part of the subject before us that I'm a Canadian and that Canadians are ground between the upper and lower millstones of both English and American contempt—"

"Isn't that another digression?"

"Not really," I hurried on, determined to speak, "because if I'm a sufferer by it, you are, too, in your degree. It's part of the Anglo-Saxon tradition for those who stay behind to despise those who go out as pioneers. The race has always done it. It isn't only the British who've despised their colonists. The people of the Eastern States despised those who went out and peopled the Middle West; those in the Middle West despised those who went farther West." I was still quoting my father. "It's something that defies reason and eludes argument. It's a base strain in the blood. It's like that hierarchy among servants by which the lady's maid disdains the cook, and the cook disdains the kitchen-maid, and the proudest are those who've nothing to be proud of. For you to look down on me because I'm a Canadian, when the commonest of Englishmen, with precisely the same justification, looks down on you—"

"Dear young lady," he broke in, soothingly, "you're talking wildly. You're speaking of things you know nothing about. Let us get back to what we began with. My son has offered to marry you—"

"He didn't offer to marry me. He asked me—he begged me—to marry him."

"The way of putting it is of no importance."

"Ah, but it is."

22

"I mean that, however he expressed it—however you express it—the result must be the same."

I nerved myself to look at him steadily. "I mean to accept him. When he asked me yesterday I said I wouldn't give him either a Yes or a No till I knew what you and his family thought of it. But now that I do know—"

"You're determined to try the impossible."

"It won't be the impossible till he tells me so."

He seemed for a second or two to study me. "Suppose I accepted you as what you say you are—as a young woman of good antecedents and honorable character. Would you still persist in the effort to force yourself on a family that didn't want you?"

I confess that in the language Mr. Strangways and I had used in the morning, he had me here "on the hip." To force myself on a family that didn't want me would normally have been the last of my desires. But I was fighting now for something that went beyond my desires—something larger—something national, as I conceived of nationality—something human—though I couldn't have said exactly what it was. I answered only after long deliberation.

"I couldn't stop to consider a family. My object would be to marry the man who loved me—and whom I loved."

"So that you'd face the humiliation—"

"It wouldn't be humiliation, because it would have nothing to do with me. It would pass into another sphere."

"It wouldn't be another sphere to him."

"I should have to let him take care of that. It's all I can manage to look out for myself—"

There seemed to be some admiration in his tone.

"Which you seem marvelously well fitted to do."

"Thank you."

"In fact, it's one of the ways in which you betray yourself. An innocent girl —"

I strained forward in my chair. "Wouldn't it be fair for you to tell me what you mean by the word innocent?"

"I mean a girl who has no special ax to grind—"

I could hear my foot tapping on the floor, but I was too indignant to restrain myself. "Even that figure of speech leaves too much to the imagination."

He studied me again. "You're very sharp."

"Don't I need to be," I demanded, "with an enemy of your acumen?"

"But I'm not your enemy. It's what you don't seem to see. I'm your friend. I'm trying to keep you out of a situation that would kill you if you got into it."

I think I laughed. "Isn't death preferable to dishonor?" I saw my mistake in the quickness with which Mrs. Brokenshire looked up. "There are more kinds of dishonor than one," I explained, loftily, "and to me the blackest would be in allowing you to dictate to me."

"My dear young woman, I dictate to men—"

"Oh, to men!"

"I see! You presume on your womanhood. It's a common American expedient, and a cheap one. But I don't stop for that."

"You may not stop for womanhood, Mr. Brokenshire; but neither does womanhood stop for you."

He rose with an air of weary patience. "I'm afraid we sha'n't gain anything by talking further—"

"I'm afraid not." I, too, rose, advancing to the table. We confronted each other across it, while one of the dogs came nosing to his master's hand. I had barely the strength to gasp on: "We've had our talk and you see where I am. I ask nothing but the exercise of human liberty—and the measure of respect I conceive to be due to every one. Surely you, an American, a representative of what America is supposed to stand for, can't think of it as too much."

"If America is supposed to stand for your marrying my son—"

"America stands, so I've been told by Americans, for the reasonable freedom of the individual. If Hugh wants to marry me—"

"Hugh will marry the woman I approve of."

"Then that apparently is what we must put to the test."

I was now so near to tears that I suppose he saw an opening to his own advantage. Coming round the table, he stood looking down at me with that expression which I can only describe as sympathetic. With all the dominating aggressiveness which either forced you to give in to him or urged you to fight him till you dropped, there was that about him which left you with a lingering suspicion that he might be right. It was the man who might be right who was presently sitting easily on the edge of the table, so that his face was on a level with my own, and saying in a kindly voice:

"Now look here! Let's be reasonable. I don't want to be unfair to you, or to say anything a man isn't justified in saying to a woman. I'm willing to throw the whole blame on Hugh—"

"I'm not," I declared, hotly.

"That's generous; but I'm speaking of myself. I'm willing to throw the whole blame on Hugh, because he's my son. I'll absolve you, if you like, because you're a stranger and a girl, and consider you a victim—"

"I'm not a victim," I insisted. "I'm only a human being, asking for a human being's rights."

He shrugged his shoulders. "Oh, rights! Who knows what rights are?"

"I do. That is," I corrected, "I know my own."

"Oh, of course! One always knows one's own. One's own rights are everything one can get. Now you can't get Hugh; but you can get five thousand dollars. That's a lot of money. There are men all over the United States who'd cut off a hand for it. You won't have to cut off a hand. You only need to be a good, sensible little girl and—get out." Perhaps he thought I was yielding, for he tapped his side pocket as he went on speaking. "It won't take a minute. I've got a check-book here—a stroke of the pen—"

My work was lying on the table a few inches away. Leaning forward deliberately I put it into the basket, which I tucked under my arm. I looked at Mrs. Brokenshire, who was leaning forward and looking at me. I inclined my head with a slight salutation, to which she did not respond, and turned away. Of him I took no notice.

"So it's war."

I was half-way to the dining-room when I heard him say that. As I paused to look back he was still sitting sidewise on the edge of the table, swinging a leg and staring after me.

"No, sir," I said, quietly. "It takes two to fight, and I should never think of being one."

"You know, of course, that I shall have no mercy on you."

"No, sir; I don't."

"Then you can know it now. I'm sorry for you; but I can't afford to spare you. Bigger things than you have come in my way—and have been blasted."

Mrs. Brokenshire made a quick little movement behind his back. It told me nothing I understood then, though I was able to interpret it later. I could only say, in a voice that shook with the shaking of my whole body:

"You couldn't blast me, sir, because—because—"

"Yes? Because—what? I should like to know."

There was a robin hopping on the lawn outside and I pointed to it. "You couldn't blast a little bird like that with a bombshell."

"Oh, birds have been shot."

"Yes, sir; with a fowling-piece; but not with a howitzer. The one is too big; the other is too small."

I was about to drop him a little courtesy when I saw him wink. It was a grotesque, amusing wink that quivered and twisted till it finally closed the left eye. If he had been a less handsome man the effect would have been less absurd.

I made my courtesy the deeper, bending my head and lowering my eyes so as to spare him the knowledge that I saw.

CHAPTER III

"He attacked my country. I think I could forgive him everything but that."

It was an hour after Mr. and Mrs. Brokenshire had left me. I was half crying by this time—that is, half crying in the way one cries from rage, and yet laughing nervously, in flashes, at the same time. From the weakness of sheer excitement I had dropped to one of the steps leading down to the Cliff Walk, while Larry Strangways leaned on the stone post. I had met him there as I was going out and he was coming toward the house. We couldn't but stop to exchange a word, especially with his knowledge of the situation. He took what I had to say with the light, gleaming, non-committal smile which he brought to bear on everything. I was glad of that because it kept him detached. I didn't want him any nearer to me than he was.

"Attacked your country? Do you mean England?"

"No; Canada. England is my grandmother; but Canada's my mother. He said you all despised her."

"Oh no, we don't. He was trying to put something over on you."

"Your 'No, we don't' lacks conviction; but I don't mind you. I shouldn't mind him if I hadn't seen so much of it."

"So much of what?"

"Being looked down upon geographically. Of all the ways of being proud," I declared, indignantly, "that which depends on your merely accidental position with regard to land and water strikes me as the most poor-spirited. I can't imagine any one dragging himself down to it who had another rag of a reason for self-respect. As a matter of fact, I don't believe any one ever does. The people I've heard express themselves on the subject—well, I'll give you an illustration: There was a woman at Gibraltar—a major's wife, a big, red-faced woman. Her name was Arbuthnot—her father was a dean or something—a big, red-faced woman, with one of those screechy, twangy English voices that cut you like a saw—you know there are some—a good many—and they don't know it. Well, she was saying something sneering about Canadians. I was sitting opposite—it was at a dinner-party—and so I leaned across the table and asked her why she didn't like them. She said colonials were such dreadful form. I held her with my eye"—I showed him how—"and made myself small and demure as I said, 'But, dear lady, how clever of you! Who would ever have supposed that you'd know that?' My sister Vic pitched into me about it after we got home. She said the Arbuthnot person didn't understand what I meant—nor any one else at the table, they're so awfully thick-skinned—and that it's better to let them alone. But that's the kind of person who—"

He tried to comfort me. "They'll come round in time. One of these days England will see what she owes to her colonists and do them justice."

"Never!" I declared, vehemently. "It will be always the same—till we knock the Empire to pieces. Then they'll respect us. Look at the Boer War. Didn't our men sacrifice everything to go out that long distance—and win battles—and lay down their lives—only to have the English say afterward—especially the army people—that they were more trouble than they were worth? It will be always the same. When we've given our last penny and shed our last drop of blood they'll still tell us we've been nothing but a nuisance. You may live to see it and remember that I said so. If when Shakespeare wrote that it's sharper than a serpent's tooth to have a thankless child he'd gone on to add that it's the very dickens to have a picturesque, self-satisfied old grandmother who thinks her children's children should give her everything and take kicks instead of ha'pence for their pay, he'd have been up to date. Mind you, we don't object to giving our last penny and shedding our last drop of blood; we only hate being abused and sneered at for doing it."

I warmed to my subject as I dabbed fiercely at my eyes.

"I'll tell you what the typical John Bull is like. He's like those men—big, flabby men they generally are—who'll be brutes to you so long as you're civil to them, but will climb down the minute you begin to hit back. Look at the way they treat you Americans! They can't do enough for you—because you snap your fingers in their faces and show them you don't care a hang about them. They come over here, and give you lectures, and marry your girls, and pocket your money, and adopt your bad form as delightful originality—and respect you. Now that earls' daughters are beginning to cast an eye on your millionaires—Mrs. Rossiter told me that—they won't leave you a rag to your back. But with us who've been faithful and loyal they're all the other way. I can hardly tell you the small pin-pricking indignities to which my sisters and I have been subjected for being Canadians. And they'll never change. It will never be otherwise, no matter what we do, no matter what we become, no matter if we give our bodies to be burned, as the Bible says. It will never be otherwise—not till we imitate you and strike them in the face. *Then* you'll see how they'll come round."[1]

He still smiled, with an aloofness in which there was a beam of sweetness. "I had no idea that you were such a little rebel."

"I'm not a rebel. I'm loyal to the King. That is, I'm loyal to the great Anglo-

Saxon ideal of which the King is the symbol—and I suppose he's as good a symbol as any other, especially as he's already there. The English are only partly Anglo-Saxon. 'Saxon and Norman and Dane are they'—didn't Tennyson say that? Well, there's a lot that's Norman, and a lot that's Dane, and a lot that's Scotch and Irish and rag-tag in them. But they're saved by the pure Anglo-Saxon ideal in so far as they hold to it—just as you'll be, with all your mixed bloods—and just as we shall be ourselves. It's like salt in the meat, it's like grace in the Christian religion—it's the thing that saves, and I'm loyal to that. My father used to say that it's the fact that English and Canadians and Australians are all devoted to the same principle that holds us together as an Empire, and not the subservience of distant lands to a Parliament sitting at Westminster. And so it is. We don't always like each other; but that doesn't matter. What does matter is that we should betray the fact that we don't like each other to outsiders—and so give them a handle against us."

"You mean that J. Howard should be in a position to side with the English in looking down on you as a Canadian?"

"Yes, and that the English should give him that position. He's an American and an enemy—every American is an enemy to England *au fond*. Oh yes, he is! You needn't deny it! It's something fundamental, deeper down than anything you understand. Even those of you who like England are hostile to her at heart and would be glad to see her in trouble. So, I say, he's an American and an enemy, and yet they hand me, their child and their friend, over to him to be trampled on. He's had opportunities of judging how Canadians are regarded in England, he says—and he assures me it's nothing to be proud of. That's it. I've had opportunities too—and I have to admit that he's right. Don't you see? That's what enrages me. As far as their liking us and our not liking them is concerned, why, it's all in the family. So long as it's kept in the family it's like the pick that Louise and Vic have always had on me. I'm the youngest and the plainest—"

"Oh, you're the plainest, are you? What on earth are they like?"

"They're quite good-looking, and they're awfully chic. But that's in parentheses. What I mean is that they're always hectoring me because I'm not attractive—"

"Really?"

"I'm not fishing for compliments. I'm too busy and too angry for that. I want to go on talking about what we're talking about."

"But I want to know why they said you were unattractive."

"Well, perhaps they didn't say it. What they have said is this, and it's what Mrs. Rossiter says—she said it to-day—that I'm only attractive to one man in five hundred—"

"But very attractive to him?"

"No; she didn't say that. She merely admitted that her brother Hugh was that man—"

He interrupted with something I wished at the time he hadn't said, and which I tried to ignore:

"He's the man in that five hundred—and I know another in another five hundred, which makes two in a thousand. You'd soon get up to a high percentage, when you think of all the men there are in the world."

As he had never hinted at anything of the kind before, it gave me—how shall I put it?—I can only think of the word fright—it gave me a little fright. It made me uneasy. It was nothing, really. It was spoken with that gleaming smile of his which seemed to put distance between him and me—between him and everything else that was serious—and yet subconsciously I felt as one feels on hearing the first few notes, in an opera or a symphony, of that arresting phrase which is to work up into a great motive. I tried to get back to my original theme, rising to move on as I did so.

"Good gracious!" I cried. "Isn't the world big enough for us all? Why should we go about saying unkind and untrue things of one other, when each of us is an essential part of a composite whole? Isn't it the foot saying to the hand I have no need of thee, and the eye saying the same thing to the nose? We've got something you haven't got, and you've got something we haven't got. Why shouldn't we be appreciative toward each other, and make our exchange with mutual respect as we do with trade commodities?"

It was probably to urge me on to talk that he said, with a challenging smile: "What have you Canadians got that we haven't? Why, we could buy and sell you."

"Oh no, you couldn't; because our special contribution toward the civilization of the American continent isn't a thing for sale. It can be given; it can be inherited; it can be caught; but it can't be purchased."

"Indeed? What is this elusive endowment?"

I answered frankly enough: "I don't know. It's there—and I can't tell you what it is. Ever since I've been living among you I've felt how much we resemble each other—what a difference. I think—mind you, I only think—that what it consists in is a sense of the *comme il faut*. We're simpler than you; and less intellectual; and poorer, of course; and less, much less, self-analytical; and yet we've got a knowledge of what's what that you couldn't command with money. None of the Brokenshires have it at all, and, as far as I can see, none of their friends. They command it with money, and the difference is like having a copy of a work of art instead of the original. It gives them the air of being—I'm using Mrs. Rossiter's word—of being produced. Now we Canadians are not produced. We just come—but we come the right way—without any hooting or tooting or beating of tin pans or self-advertisement. We just are—and we say nothing about it. Let me make an example of what Mrs. Rossiter was discussing this morning. There are lots of pretty girls in my country—as many to the hundred as you have here—but we don't make a fuss about them or talk as if we'd ordered a special brand from the Creator. We grow them as you grow flowers in a garden, at the mercy of the air and sunshine. You grow yours like plants in a hothouse, to be exhibited in horticultural shows. Please don't think I'm bragging—"

He laughed aloud. "Oh no!"

"Well, I'm not," I insisted. "You asked me a question and I'm trying to answer it—and incidentally to justify my own existence, which J. Howard has called into question. You've got lots to offer us, and many of us come and take it thankfully. What we can offer to you is a simpler and healthier and less self-conscious standard of life, with a great deal less talk about it—with no talk about it at all, if you could get yourselves down to that—and a willingness to be instead of an everlasting striving to become. You won't recognize it or take it, of course. No one ever does. Nations seem to me insane, and ruled by insane governments. Don't the English need the Germans, and the Germans the French, and the French the Austrians, and the Austrians the Russians, and so on? Why on earth should the foot be jealous of the nose? But there! You're simply making me say things—and laughing at me all the while—so I'm off to take my walk. We'll get even with J. Howard and all the first-class powers some day, and till then—*au revoir.*"

I had waved my hand to him and gone some paces into the fog that had begun to blow in when he called to me.

"Wait a minute. I've something to tell you."

I turned, without going back.

"I'm—I'm leaving."

I was so amazed that I retraced a step or two toward him. "What?"

His smile underwent a change. It grew frozen and steely instead of being bright with a continuous play suggesting summer lightning, which had been its usual quality.

"My time is up at the end of the month—and I've asked Mr. Rossiter not to expect me to go on."

I was looking for something of the sort sooner or later, but now that it had come I saw how lonely I should be.

"Oh! Where are you going? Have you got anything in particular?"

"I'm going as secretary to Stacy Grainger."

"I've some connection with that name," I said, absently, "though I can't remember what it is."

"You've probably heard of him. He's a good deal in the public eye."

"Have you known him long?" I asked, for the sake of speaking, though I was only thinking of myself.

"Never knew him at all." He came nearer to me. "I've a confession to make, though it won't be of interest to you. All the while I've been here, playing with little Broke Rossiter, I've been—don't laugh—I've been contributing to the press—*moi qui vous parle*!"

"What about?"

"Oh, politics and finance and foreign policy and public things in general. Always had a taste that way. Now it seems that something I wrote for the *Providence Express*—people read it a good deal—has attracted the attention of the great Stacy. Yes, he's great, too—J. Howard's big rival for—"

I began to recall something I had heard. "Wasn't there a story about him and Mr. Brokenshire and Mrs. Brokenshire?"

"That's the man. Well, he's noticed my stuff, and written to the editor—and to me, and I'm to go to him."

I was still thinking of myself and the loss of his *camaraderie*. "I hope he's going to pay you well."

"Oh, for me it will be wealth."

"It will probably be more than that. It will be the first long step up."

He nodded confidently. "I hope so."

I had again begun to move away when he stopped me the second time.

"Miss Adare, what's your first name? Mine's Lawrence, as you know."

If I laughed a little it was to conceal my discomfort at this abrupt approach to the intimate.

"I'm rather sorry for my name," I said, apologetically. "You see my father was one of those poetically loyal Canadians who rather overdo the thing. My eldest sister should have been Victoria, because Victoria was the queen. But the Duchess of Argyll was in Canada at that time—and very nice to father and mother—and so the first of us had to be Louise. He couldn't begin on the queens till there was a second one. That's poor Vic; while I'm—I know you'll shout—I'm Alexandra. If there'd been a fourth she'd have been a Mary; but poor mother died and the series stopped."

He shook hands rather gravely. "Then I shall think of you as Alexandra."

"If you are going to think of me at all," I managed to say, with a little *moue*, "put me down as Alix. That's what I've always been called."

CHAPTER IV

I was glad of the fog. It was cool and refreshing; it was also concealing. I could tramp along under its protection with little or no fear of being seen. Wearing tweeds, thick boots, and a felt hat, I was prepared for wet, and as a Canadian girl I was used to open air in all weathers. The few stragglers generally to be seen on the Cliff Walk having rushed to their houses for shelter, I had the rocks and the breakers, the honeysuckle and the patches of dog-roses, to myself. In the back of my mind I was fortified, too, by the knowledge that dampness curls my hair into pretty little tendrils, so that if I did meet any one I should be looking at my best.

The path is like no other in the world. I have often wondered why the American writer-up of picturesque bits didn't make more of it. Trouville has its *Plage*, and Brighton its King's Road, and Nice its Promenade des Anglais, but in no other kingdom of leisure that I know anything about will you find the combination of qualities, wild and subdued, that mark this ocean-front of the island of Aquidneck. Neither will you easily come elsewhere so near to a sense of the primitive human struggle, of the crude social clash, of the war of the rights of man—Fisherman's Rights, as this coast historically knows them —against encroachment, privilege, and seclusion. As you crunch the gravel, and press the well-rolled turf, and sniff the scent of the white and red clover and Queen Anne's lace that fringe the precipice leaning over the sea, you feel in the air those elements of conflict that make drama.

In clinging to the edge of the cliff, in twisting round every curve of the shore line, in running up hill and down dale, under crags and over them, the path is, of course, not the only one of its kind. You will find the same thing anywhere on the south coast of England or the north coast of France. But in the sum of human interest it sucks into the three miles of its course I can think of nothing else that resembles it. As guaranteeing the rights of the fisherman it is, so I believe, inalienable public property. The fisherman can walk on it, sit on it, fish from it, right into eternity. So much he has secured from the past history of colony and state; but he has done it at the cost of making himself offensive to the gentlemen whose lawns he hems as a seamstress hems a skirt.

It is a hem like a serpent, with a serpent's sinuosity and grace, but also with a serpent's hatefulness to those who can do nothing but accept it as a fact. Since, as a fact, it cannot be abolished it has to be put up with; and since it has to be put up with the means must needs be found to deal with it effectively. Effectively it has been dealt with. Money, skill, and imagination have been spent on it, to adorn it, or disguise it, or sink it out of sight. The architect, the landscape gardener, and the engineer have all been called into counsel. On Fisherman's Rights the smile and the frown are exercised by turns, each with its phase of ingenuity. Along one stretch of a hundred yards bland recognition borders the way with roses or spans the miniature chasms with decorative bridges; along the next shuddering refinement grows a hedge or digs a trench behind which the obtrusive wayfarer may pass unseen. But shuddering refinement and bland recognition alike withdraw into themselves as far as broad lawns and lofty terraces permit them to retire, leaving to the owner of Fisherman's Rights the enjoyment of ocher and umber rocks and sea and sky and grain-fields yellowing on far headlands.

It gave me the nearest thing to glee I ever felt in Newport. It was bracing and open and free. It suggested comparisons with scrambles along Nova-Scotian shores or tramps on the moors in Scotland. I often hated the fine weather; it was oppressive; it was strangling. But a day like this, with its whiffs of wild wind and its handfuls of salt slashing against eyes and mouth and nostrils, was not only exhilarating, it was glorious. I was glad, too, that the prim villas and pretentious châteaux, most of them out of proportion to any scale of housekeeping of which America is capable, could only be descried like castles in a dream through the swirling, diaphanous drift. I could be alone to rage and fume—or fly onward with a speed that was in itself a relief.

I could be alone till, on climbing the slope of a shorn and wind-swept bluff, I saw a square-shouldered figure looming on the crest. It was no more than a deepening of the texture of the fog, but I knew its lines. Skimming up the ascent with a little cry, I was in Hugh's arms, my head on his burly breast.

I think it was his burliness that made the most definite appeal to me. He was so sturdy and strong, and I was so small and desolate. From the beginning, when he first used to come near me, I felt his presence, as the Bible says, like the shadow of a rock in a thirsty land. That was in my early homesick time, before I had seized the new way of living and the new national point of view. The fact, too, that, as I expressed it to myself, I was in the second cabin when I had always been accustomed to the first, inspired a discomfort for which unwittingly I sought consolation. Nobody thought of me as other than Mrs. Rossiter's retainer, but this one kindly man.

I noticed his kindliness almost before I noticed him, just as, I think, he noticed my loneliness almost before he noticed me. He opened doors for me when I went in or out; he served me with things if he happened to be there at tea; he dropped into a chair beside me when I was the only member of a group whom no one spoke to. If Gladys was of the company I was of it too, with a nominal footing but a virtual exclusion. The men in the Rossiter circle were of the four hundred and ninety-nine to whom I wasn't attractive; the women were all civil—from a distance. Occasionally some nice old lady would ask me where I came from and if I liked my work, or talk to me of new educational methods in a way which, with my bringing up, was to me as so much Greek; but I never got any other sign of friendliness. Only this short, stockily built young fellow, with the small, blue eyes, ever recognized me as a human being with the average yearning for human intercourse.

During the winter in New York he never went further than that. I remembered Mrs. Rossiter's recommendation and "let him alone." I knew how to do it. He was not the first man I had ever had to deal with, even if no one had asked me to marry him. I accepted his small, kindly acts with that shade of discretion which defined the distance between us. As far as I could observe, he himself had no disposition to cross the lines I set—not till we moved to Newport.

There was a fortnight between our going there and his—a fortnight which seemed to work a change in him. The Hugh Brokenshire I met on one of my first rambles along the cliffs was not the Hugh Brokenshire I had last seen in Fifth Avenue. Perhaps I was not the same myself. In the new surroundings I had missed him—a little. I will not say that his absence had meant an aching void to me; but where I had had a friend, now I had none—since I was unable to count Larry Strangways. Had it not been for this solitude I should have been less receptive to his comings when he suddenly began to pursue me.

Pursuit is the only word I can use. I found him everywhere, quiet, deliberate, persistent. If he had been ten or even five years older I could have taken his advances without uneasiness. But he was only twenty-six and a dependent. He had no work; apart from his allowance from his father he had no means. And yet when, on the day before my chronicle begins, he stole upon me as I sat in a sheltered nook below the cliffs to which I was fond of retreating when I had time—when he stole upon me there, and kissed me and kissed me and kissed me, I couldn't help confessing that I loved him.

I must leave to some woman who has had to fend for herself the task of telling what it means when a man comes to offer her his heart and his protection. It goes without saying that it means more to her than to the sheltered woman, for it means things different and more wonderful. It is the expected unexpected come to pass; it is the impossible achieved. It is not only success; it is success with an aureole of glory.

I suppose I must be parasitical by nature, for I never have conceived of life as other than dependent on some man who would love me and take care of me. Even when no such man appeared and I was forced out to earn my bread, I looked upon the need as temporary only. In the loneliest of times at Mrs. Rossiter's, at periods when I didn't see a man for weeks, the hero never seemed farther away than just behind the scenes. I confess to minutes when I thought he tarried unnecessarily long; I confess to terrified questionings as to what would happen were he never to come at all; I confess to solitary watches of the night in company with fears and tears; but I cannot confess to anything more than a low burning of that lamp of hope which never went out entirely.

When, therefore, Hugh Brokenshire offered me what he had to offer me I felt for a few minutes—ten, fifteen, twenty perhaps—that sense of the fruition of the being which I am sure comes to us but rarely in this life, and perhaps is a foretaste of eternity. I was like a creature that has long been struggling up to some higher state—and has reached it.

I am ashamed to say, too, that my first consciousness came in pictures to which the dear young man himself was only incidental. Two scenes in particular that for ten years past had been only a little below the threshold of my consciousness came out boldly, like developed photographs. I was the center of both. In one I saw a dainty little dining-room, where the table was laid. The damask was beautiful; the silver rich; the glasses crystalline. Wearing an inexpensive but extremely chic little gown, I was seating the guests. The other picture was more dim, but only in the sense that the room was deliciously darkened. It had white furnishings, a little white cot, and toys. In its very center was a bassinet, and I was leaning over it, wearing a delicate lace peignoir.

Ought I to blush to say that while Hugh stammered out his impassioned declarations I was seeing these two tableaux emerging from the state of only half-acknowledged dreams into real possibility? I dare say. I merely affirm that it was so. Since the dominant craving of my nature was to have a home and a baby, I saw the baby and the home before I could realize a husband or a father, or bring my mind to the definite proposals faltered by poor Hugh.

But I did bring my mind to them, with the result of which I have already given a sufficient indication. Even in admitting that I loved him I thrust and parried and postponed. The whole idea was too big for me to grapple with on the spur of a sudden moment. I suggested his talking the matter over with his father chiefly to gain time.

But to rest in his arms had only a subordinate connection with the great issue I had to face. It was a joy in itself. It was a pledge of the future, even if I were never to take anything but the pledge. After my shifts and struggles and anxieties I could feel the satisfaction of knowing it was in my power to let them all roll off. If I were never to do it, if I were to go back to my uncertainties, this minute would mitigate the trial in advance. I might fight for existence during all the rest of my life, and yet I should still have the bliss of remembering that some one was willing to fight for me.

He released me at last, since there might be people in Newport as indifferent to weather as ourselves.

"What happened?" he asked then, with an eagerness which almost choked the question in its utterance. "Was it awful?"

I was too nearly hysterical to enter on anything like a recital. "It might have been worse," I half laughed and half sobbed, trying to recover my breath and dry my eyes.

His spirit seemed to leap at the answer. "Do you mean to say you got concessions from him—or anything like that?"

I couldn't help clinging to the edge of his raincoat. "Did you expect me to?"

"I didn't know but what, when he saw you—"

"Oh, but he didn't see me. That was part of the difficulty. He looked where I was—but he didn't find anything there."

He laughed, with a hint of disappointment. "I know what you mean; but you mustn't be surprised. He'll see you yet." He clasped me again. "I didn't see you at first, little girl; I swear I didn't. You're like that. A fellow must look at you twice before he knows that you're there; but when he begins to take notice—" I struggled out of his embrace, while he continued: "It's the same with all the great things—with pictures and mountains and cathedrals, and so on. Often thought about it when we've been abroad. See something once and pass it by. Next time you look at it a little. Third time it begins to grow on you. Fourth time you've found a wonder. You're a wonder, little Alix, do you know it?"

"Oh no, I'm not. I must warn you, Hugh darling, that I'm very prosaic and practical and ordinary. You mustn't put me on a pedestal—"

"Put you on a pedestal? You were born on a pedestal. You're the woman I've seen in hopes and dreams—"

We began to walk on, coming to a little hollow that dipped near enough to the shore to allow of our scrambling over the rocks to where we could sit down among them. As we were here below the thickest belt of the fog line, I could see him in a way that had been impossible on the bluff.

If he was good-looking it was only in the handsome-ugly sense. Mrs. Rossiter often said he was the one member of the family who inherited from the Brews of Boston, a statement I could verify from the first Mrs. Brokenshire's portrait by Carolus-Duran. Hugh's features were not ill-formed so much as they were out of proportion to each other, becoming thus a mere jumble of organs. The blue eyes were too small and too wide apart; the forehead was too broad for its height; the nose, which started at the same fine angle as his father's, changed in mid-course to a knob; the upper lip was intended to be long, but half-way in its descent took a notion to curve upward, making a hollow for a tender, youthful, fair mustache that didn't quite meet in the center and might have been applied with a camel's-hair brush; the lower lip turned outward with a little fullness that spilled over in a little fall, giving to the whole expression something lovably good-natured.

Because the sea boiled over the ledges and scraped on the pebbles with a screechy sound we were obliged to sit close together in order to make ourselves heard. His arm about me was amazingly protective. I felt safe.

The account of his interview with his father was too incoherent to give me more than the idea that they had talked somewhat at cross-purposes. To Hugh's statement that he wished to marry Miss Adare, the little nursery governess at Ethel's, his father had responded by reading a letter from Lord Goldborough inviting Hugh to his place in Scotland for the shooting.

"It would be well for you to accept," the father commented, as he folded the letter. "I've cabled to Goldborough to say you'd sail on—"

"But, father, how can I sail when I've asked Miss Adare to marry me?"

To this the reply was the mention of the steamer and the date. He went on to say, however: "If you've asked any one to marry you it's absurd, of course. But I'll take care of that. If you go by that boat you'll reach London in plenty of time to fit out at your tailor's and still be at Strath-na-Cloid by the twelfth. In case you're short of money—"

Apparently they got no further than that. To Hugh's assertions and objections his father had but one response. It was a response, as I understood, which confronted the younger man like a wall he had neither the force to break down nor the agility to climb over, and left him staring at a blank.

Then followed another outburst which to my unaccustomed ear was as wild, sweet music. It wasn't merely that he loved me, he adored me; it wasn't merely that I was young and pretty and captivating with a sly, unobtrusive fascination that held you enchanted when it held you at all. I was mistress of the wisdom of the ages. Among the nice expensively dressed young girls with whom he danced and rode and swam and flirted, Hugh had never seen any one who could "hold a candle" to me in knowledge of human nature and the world. It wasn't that I had seen more than they or done more than they; it was that I had a mind through which every impression filtered and came out as something of my own. It was what he had always been looking for in a woman, and had given up the hope of finding. He spoke as if he was forty. He was serious himself, he averred; he had reflected, and held original convictions. Though a rich man's son, with corresponding prospects, his heart was with the masses and he labeled himself a Socialist.

It was not the same thing to be a Socialist now, he explained to me, as it had been twenty years before, since so many men of education and position had adopted this system of opinion. In fact, his own conversion had been partly due to young Lord Ernest Hayes, of the British Embassy, who had spent the preceding summer at Newport, though his inclinations had gone in this direction ever since he had begun to think. It was because I was so open-eyed and so sincere that he had been drawn to me as soon as he had started in to notice me. It was true that he had noticed me first of all because I was in a subordinate position and alone, but, having done so, he had found a queen disguised as a working girl. I was a queen of the vital things in life, a queen of intelligence, of sympathy, of the defiance of convention, of everything that was great. I was the woman a Socialist could love, of whom a Socialist could make his star.

"If father would only give me credit for being twenty-six and a man," the dear boy went on earnestly, "with a man's responsibility to society and the human race! But he doesn't. He thinks I ought to quit being a Socialist because he tells me to—or else he doesn't think at all. Nine times out of ten, when I begin to say what I believe, he talks of something else—just as he did last night in bringing up the Goldboroughs."

I found the opportunity for which I had been looking during his impassioned rhapsody. The mention of the Goldboroughs gave me that kind of chill about the heart which the mist imparted to the hands and face.

"You know them all very well," I said, when I found an opening in which I could speak.

"Oh yes," he admitted, indifferently. "Known them all my life. Father represented Meek & Brokenshire in England till my grandfather died. Goldborough used to be an impecunious chap, land poor, till he and father began to pull together. Father's been able to give him tips on the market, and he's given father— Well, dad's always had a taste for English swells. Never could stand the Continental kind—gilt gingerbread he's called 'em—and so, well, you can see."

I admitted that I could see, going on to ask what the Goldborough family consisted of.

There was Lord Leatherhead, the eldest son; then there were two younger sons, one in the army and one preparing for the Church; and there were three girls.

"Any of the daughters married?" I ventured, timidly.

There was nothing forced in the indifference with which he made his explanations. Laura was married to a banker named Bell; Janet, he thought he had heard, was engaged to a chap in the Inverness Rangers; Cecilia—Cissie they usually called her—was to the best of his knowledge still wholly free, but the best of his knowledge did not go far.

I pumped up my courage again. "Is she—nice?"

"Oh, nice enough." He really didn't know much about her. She was generally away at school when he had been at Goldborough Castle. When she was there he hadn't seen more than a long-legged, gawky girl, rather good at tennis, with red hair hanging down her back.

Satisfied with these replies, I went on to tell him of my interview with his father an hour or two before. Of this he seized on one point with some ecstasy.

"So you told him you'd take me! Oh, Alix—gosh!"

The exclamation was a sigh of relief as well as of rapture. I could smile at it because it was so boyish and American, especially as he clasped me again and held me in a way that almost stopped my breath. When I freed myself, however, I said, with a show of firmness:

"Yes, Hugh; it's what I said to him; but it's not what I'm going to repeat to you."

"Not what you're going to repeat to me? But if you said it to him—"

"I'm still not obliged to accept you—to-day."

"But if you mean to accept me at all—"

"Yes, I mean to accept you—if all goes well."

"But what do you mean by that?"

"I mean—if your family should want me."

I could feel his clasp relax as he said: "Oh, if you're going to wait for that!"

"Hugh, darling, how can I not wait for it? I told him I couldn't stop to consider a family; but—but I see I must."

"Oh, but why? We shall lose everything if you do that. To wait for my family to want you to marry me—"

I detached myself altogether from his embrace, pretending to arrange my skirts about my feet. He leaned forward, his fingers interlocked, his elbows on his knees, his kind young face disconsolate.

"When I talked to your father," I tried to explain, "I saw chiefly the individual's side of the question of marriage. There is that side; but there's another. Marriage doesn't concern a man and a woman alone; it concerns a family—sometimes two."

His cry came out with the explosive force of a slowly gathering groan. "Oh, rot, Alix!" He went on to expostulate: "Can't you see? If we were to go now and buy a license—and be married by the first clergyman we met—the family couldn't say a word."

"Exactly; it's just what I do see. Since you want it I could force myself on them—the word is your father's—and they'd have no choice but to accept me."

"Well, then?"

"Hugh, dear, I—I can't do it that way."

"Then what way could you do it?"

"I'm not sure yet. I haven't thought of it. I only know in advance that even if I told you I'd marry you against—against all their wishes, I couldn't keep my promise in the end."

"That is," he said, bitterly, "you think more of them than you do of me."

I put my hand on his clasped fingers. "Nonsense. I—I love you. Don't you see I do? How could I help loving you when you've been so kind to me? But marriage is always a serious thing to a woman; and when it comes to marriage into a family that would look on me as a great misfortune—Hugh, darling, I don't see how I could ever face it."

"I do," he declared, promptly. "It isn't so bad as you think. Families come round. There was Tracy Allen. Married a manicure. The Allens kicked up a row at first—wouldn't see Tracy and all that; but now—"

"Yes, but, Hugh, I'm not a manicure."

"You're a nursery governess."

"By accident—and a little by misfortune. I wasn't a nursery governess when I first knew your sister."

"But what difference does that make?"

"It makes this difference: that a manicure would probably not think of herself as your equal. She'd expect coldness at first, and be prepared for it."

"Well, couldn't you?"

"No, because, you see, I'm your equal."

He hunched his big shoulders impatiently. "Oh, Alix, I don't go into that. I'm a Socialist. I don't care what you are."

"But you see I do. I don't want to expose myself to being looked down upon, and perhaps despised, for the rest of my life, because my family is quite as good as your own."

He turned slowly from peering into the fog-bank to fix on me a look of which the tenderness and pity and incredulity seemed to stab me. I felt the helplessness of a sane person insisting on his sanity to some one who believes him mad.

"Don't let us talk about those things, darling little Alix," he begged, gently. "Let's do the thing in style, like Tracy Allen, without any flummery or fluff. What's family—once you get away from the idea? When I sink it I should think that you could afford to do it too. If I take you as Tracy Allen took Libby Jaynes—that was her name, I remember now—not a very pretty girl—but if I take you as he took her, and you take me as she took him—"

"But, Hugh, I can't. If I were Libby Jaynes, it's possible I could; but as it is —"

And in the end he came round to my point of view. That is to say, he appreciated my unwillingness to reward Mrs. Rossiter's kindness to me by creating a scandal, and he was not without some admiration for what he called my "magnanimity toward his old man" in hesitating to drive him to extremes.

And yet it was Hugh himself who drove him to extremes, over questions which I hardly raised. That was some ten days later, when Hugh refused point-blank to sail on the steamer his father had selected to take him on the way to Strath-na-Cloid. I was, of course, not present at the interview, but having heard of it from Hugh, and got his account corroborated by Ethel Rossiter, I can describe it much as it took place.

I may say here, perhaps, that I still remained with Mrs. Rossiter. My marching orders, expected from hour to hour, didn't come. Mrs. Rossiter herself explained this delay to me some four days after that scene in the breakfast loggia which had left me in a state of curiosity and suspense.

"Father seems to think that if he insisted on your leaving it would make Hugh's asking you to marry him too much a matter of importance."

"And doesn't he himself consider it a matter of importance?"

Mrs. Rossiter patted a tress of her brown hair into place. "No, I don't think he does."

Perhaps nothing from the beginning had made me more inwardly indignant than the simplicity of this reply. I had imagined him raging against me in his heart and forming deep, dark plans to destroy me.

"It would be a matter of importance to most people," I said, trying not to betray my feeling of offense.

"Most people aren't father," Mrs. Rossiter contented herself with replying, still occupied with her tress of hair.

It was the confidential hour of the morning in her big chintzy room. The maid having departed, I had been answering notes and was still sitting at the desk. It was the first time she had broached the subject in the four days which had been to me a period of so much restlessness. Wondering at this detachment, I had the boldness to question her.

"Doesn't it seem important to you?"

She threw me a glance over her shoulder, turning back to the mirror at once. "What have I got to do with it? It's father's affair—and Hugh's."

"And mine, too, I suppose?" I hazarded, interrogatively.

To this she said nothing. Her silence gave me to understand what so many other little things impressed upon me—that I didn't count. What Hugh did or didn't do was a matter for the Brokenshires to feel and for J. Howard Brokenshire to deal with. Ethel Rossiter herself was neither for me nor against me. I was her nursery governess, and useful as an unofficial companion-secretary. As long as it was not forbidden she would keep me in that capacity; when the order came she would send me away. As for anything I had to suffer, that was my own lookout. Hugh would be managed by his father, and from that fate there was no appeal. There was nothing, therefore, to worry Mrs. Rossiter. She could dismiss the whole matter, as she presently did, to discuss her troubles over the rival attentions of Mr. Millinger and Mr. Scott, and to protest against their making her so conspicuous. She had the kindness to say, however, just as she was leaving the house for Bailey's Beach:

"I don't talk to you about this affair of Hugh's because I really don't see much of father. It's his business, you see, and nothing for me to interfere with. With that woman there I hardly ever go to their house, and he doesn't often come here. Her mother's with them, too, just now—that's old Mrs. Billing—a harpy if ever there was one—and with all the things people are saying! If father only knew! But, of course, he'll be the last one to hear it."

She was getting into her car by this time and I seized no more; but at lunch I had a few minutes in which to bring my searchings of heart before Larry Strangways.

It was not often we took this repast alone with the children, but it had to happen sometimes. Mrs. Rossiter had telephoned from Bailey's that she had accepted the invitation of some friends and we were not to expect her. We should lunch, however, she informed me, in the breakfast loggia, where the open air would act as chaperon and insure the necessary measure of propriety.

So long as Broke and Gladys were present we were as demure as if we had met by chance in the restaurant car of a train. With the coffee the children begged to be allowed to play with the dogs on the grass, which left us for a few minutes as man and woman.

"How is everything?" he asked at once, taking on that smile which seemed to put him outside the sphere of my interests.

I shrugged my shoulders and looked down at the spoon with which I was dabbling in my cup. "Oh, just the same," I glanced up to say. "Tell me. Have people in this country no other measure of your standing but that of money?"

"Have they any such measure in any country?"

I was beginning with the words, "Why, yes," when he interrupted me.

"Think."

"I am thinking," I insisted. "In England and Canada and the British Empire generally—"

"You attach some importance to birth. Yes; so do we here—when it goes with money. Without the basis of that support neither you nor we give what is so deliciously called birth the honor of a second thought."

"Oh yes, we do—"

"When it's your only asset—yes; but you do it alone. No one else pays it any attention."

I colored. "That's rather cruel—"

"It's not a bit more cruel than the fact. Take your case and mine as an illustration. As the estimate of birth goes in this country, I'm as well born as the majority. My ancestors were New-Englanders, country doctors and lawyers and ministers—especially the ministers. But as long as I haven't the cash I'm only a tutor, and eat at the second table. Jim Rossiter's forebears were much the same as mine; but the fact that he has a hundred thousand dollars a year and I've hardly got two is the only thing that would be taken into consideration, by any one in either the United Kingdom or the United States. It would be the same if I descended from Crusaders. If I've got nothing but that and my character to recommend me—" He raised his hand and snapped his fingers with a scornful laugh. "Take your case," he hurried on as I was about to speak. "You're probably like me, sprung of a line of professional men—"

"And soldiers," I interrupted, proudly. "The first of my family to settle in Canada was a General Adare in the middle of the seventeen hundreds. He'd been in the garrison at Halifax and chose to remain in Nova Scotia." Perhaps there was some boastfulness in my tone as I added, "He came of the famous Fighting Adares of the County Limerick."

"And all that isn't worth a row of pins—except to yourself. If you were the daughter of a miner who'd struck it rich you'd be a candidate for the British peerage. You'd be received in the best houses in London; you could marry a duke and no one would say you nay. As it is—"

"As it is," I said, tremulously, "I'm just a nursery governess, and there's no getting away from the fact."

"Not until you get away from the condition."

"So that when I told Hugh Brokenshire the other day that in point of family I was his equal—"

"He probably didn't believe you."

The memory of Hugh's look still rankled in me. "No, I don't think he did."

"Of course he didn't. As the world counts—as we all count—no poor family, however noble, is the equal of any rich family, however base." There was that transformation of his smile from something sunny to something hard which I had noticed once before, as he went on to add, "If you want to marry Hugh Brokenshire—"

"Which I do," I interposed, defiantly.

"Then you must enter into his game as he enters into it himself. He thinks of himself as doing the big romantic thing. He's marrying a poor girl who has nothing but herself as guaranty. That your great-grandfather was a general and one of the—what did you call them?—Fighting Adares of the County Cork would mean no more to him than if you said you were descended from the Lacedæmonians and the dragon's teeth. As far as that goes, you might as well be an immigrant girl from Sweden; you might as well be a cook. He's stooping to pick up his diamond from the mire, instead of buying it from a jeweler's window. Very well, then, you must let him stoop. You mustn't try to underestimate his condescension. You mustn't tell him you were once in a jeweler's window, and only fell into the mire by chance—"

"Because," I smiled, "the mire is where I belong, until I'm taken out of it."

"We belong," he stated, judicially, "where the world puts us. If we're wise we'll stay there—till we can meet the world's own terms for getting out."

CHAPTER V

I come at last to Hugh's defiance of his father. It took place not only without my incitement, but without my knowledge. No one could have been more sick with misgiving than I when I learned that the boy had left his father's house and gone to a hotel. If I was to blame at all it was in mentioning from time to time his condition of dependence.

"You haven't the right to defy your father's wishes," I said to him. "so long as you're living on his money. What it comes to is that he pays you to do as he tells you. If you don't do as he tells you, you're not earning your allowance honestly."

The point of view was new to him. "But if I was making a living of my own?"

"Ah, that would be different."

"You'd marry me then?"

I considered this. "It would still have to depend," I was obliged to say at last.

"Depend on what?"

"On the degree to which you made yourself your own master."

"I should be my own master if I earned a good income."

I admitted this.

"Very well," he declared, with decision. "I shall earn it."

I didn't question his power to do that. I had heard so much of the American man's ability to make money that I took it for granted, as I did a bird's capacity for flight. As far as Hugh was concerned, it seemed to me more a matter of intention than of opportunity. I reasoned that if he made up his mind to be independent, independent he would be. It would rest with him. It was not of the future I was thinking so much as of the present; and in the present I was chiefly dodging his plea that we settle the matter by taking the law into our own hands.

"It won't be as bad as you think," he kept urging. "Father would be sure to come round to you if you were my wife. He never quarrels with the accomplished fact. That's been part of the secret of his success. He'll fight a thing as long as he can; but when it's carried over his head no one knows better than he how to make the best of it."

"But, Hugh, I don't want to have him make the best of it that way—at least, so long as you're not your own master."

One day at the Casino he pointed out Libby Jaynes to me. I was there in charge of the children, and he managed to slip over from the tennis he was playing for a word:

"There she is—that girl with the orange-silk sweater."

The point of his remark was that Libby Jaynes was one of a group of half a dozen people, and was apparently received at Newport like anybody else. The men were in flannels; the women in the short skirts and easy attitudes developed by a sporting life. The silk sweater in its brilliant hues was to the Casino grounds as the parrot to Brazilian woods. Libby Jaynes wasn't pretty; her lips were too widely parted and her teeth too big; but her figure was adapted to the costume of the day, and her head to the slouching panama. She wore both with a decided *chic*. She was the orange spot where there was another of purple and another of pink and another of bright emerald-green. As far as I could see no one remembered that she had ever rubbed men's finger-nails in the barber's room of a hotel, and she certainly betrayed no sign of it. It was what Hugh begged me to observe. If I liked I could within a year be a member of this privileged troop instead of an outsider looking on. "You'd be just as good as she is," he declared with a naïveté I couldn't help taking with a smile.

I was about to say, "But I don't feel inferior to her as it is," when I recalled the queer look of incredulity he had given me on the beach.

And then one morning I heard he had quarreled with his father. It was Hugh who told me first, but Mrs. Rossiter gave me all the details within an hour afterward.

It appeared that they had had a dinner-party in honor of old Mrs. Billing which had gone off with some success. The guests having left, the family had gathered in Mildred's sitting-room to give the invalid an account of the entertainment. It was one of those domestic reunions on which the household god insisted from time to time, so that his wife should seem to have that support from his children which both he and she knew she didn't have. The Jack Brokenshires were there, and Hugh, and Ethel Rossiter.

It was exactly the scene for a tragi-comedy, and had the kind of setting theatrical producers liked before the new scene-painters set the note of allegorical simplicity. Mildred had the best corner room up-stairs, though, like the rest of the house, her surroundings suffered from her father's taste for the Italianate and over-rich. Heavy dark cabinets, heavy dark chairs, gilt candelabra, and splendidly brocaded stuffs threw the girl's wan face and weak figure into prominence. I think she often sighed for pretty papers and cretonnes, for Sèvres and colored prints, but she took her tapestries and old masters and majolica as decreed by a power she couldn't question. When everything was done for her comfort the poor thing had nothing to do for herself.

The room had the further resemblance to a scene on the stage since, as I was given to understand, no one felt the reality of the friendliness enacted. To all J. Howard's children it was odious that he should worship a woman who was younger than Mildred and very little older than Ethel. They had loved their mother, who had been plain. They resented the fact that their father had got hold of her money for himself, had made her unhappy, and had forgotten her. That he should have become infatuated with a girl who was their own contemporary would have been a humiliation to them in any case; but when the story of his fight for her became public property, when it was the joke of the Stock Exchange and the subject of leading articles in the press, they could only hold their heads high and carry the situation with bravado. It was a proof of his grip on New York that he could put Editha Billing where he wished to see her, and find no authority, social or financial, bold enough to question him; it was equally a proof of his dominance in his family that neither son nor daughter could treat his new wife with anything but deference. She was the *maîtresse en titre* to whom even the princes and princesses had to bow.

They were bowing on this evening by treating old Mrs. Billing as if they liked her and counted her one of themselves. As the mother of the favorite she could reasonably claim this homage, and no one refused it but poor Hugh. He turned his back on it. Mildred being obliged to lie on a couch, he put himself at her feet, refusing thus to be witness of what he called a flattering hypocrisy that sickened him. That went on in the dimly, richly lighted room behind him, where the others sat about, pretending to be gay.

Then the match went into the gunpowder all at once.

"I'm the more glad the evening has been pleasant," J. Howard observed, blandly, "since we may consider it a farewell to Hugh. He's sailing on—"

Hugh merely said over his shoulder, "No, father; I'm not."

The startled silence was just long enough to be noticed before the father went on, as if he had not been interrupted:

"He's sailing on—"

"No, father; I'm not."

There was no change in Hugh's tone any more than in his parent's. I gathered from Mrs. Rossiter that all present held their breaths as if in expectation that

50

this blasphemer would be struck dead. Mentally they stood off, too, like the chorus in an opera, to see the great tragedy acted to the end without interference of their own. Jack Brokenshire, who was fingering an extinct cigar, twiddled it nervously at his lips. Pauline clasped her hands and leaned forward in excitement. Mrs. Brokenshire affected to hear nothing and arranged her five rows of pearls. Mrs. Billing, whom Mrs. Rossiter described as a condor with lace on her head and diamonds round her shrunken neck, looked from one to another through her lorgnette, which she fixed at last on her son-in-law. Ethel Rossiter kept herself detached. Knowing that Hugh had been riding for a fall, she expected him now to come his cropper.

It caused some surprise to the lookers-on that Mr. Brokenshire should merely press the electric bell. "Tell Mr. Spellman to come here," he said, quietly, to the footman who answered his ring.

Mr. Spellman appeared, a smooth-shaven man of indefinite age, with dark shadows in the face, and cadaverous. His master instructed him with a word or two. There was silence during the minute that followed the man's withdrawal, a silence ominous with expectation. When Spellman had returned and handed a long envelope to his employer and withdrawn again, the suspended action was renewed.

Hugh, who was playing in seeming unconcern with the tassel of Mildred's dressing-gown, had given no attention to the small drama going on behind him.

"Hugh, here's father," Mildred whispered.

Her white face was drawn; she was fond of Hugh; she seemed to scent the catastrophe. Hugh continued to play with the tassel without glancing upward.

It was not J. Howard's practice to raise his voice or to speak with emphasis except when the occasion demanded it. He was very gentle now as his hand slipped over Hugh's shoulder.

"Hugh, here's your ticket and your letter of credit. I asked Spellman to see to them when he was in New York."

The young man barely turned his head. "Thank you, father; but I don't want them. I can't go over—because I'm going to marry Miss Adare."

As it was no time for the chorus of an opera to intervene, all waited for what would happen next. Old Mrs. Billing, turning her lorgnette on the rebellious boy, saw nothing but the back of his head. The father's hand wavered for a minute over the son's shoulder and let the envelope fall. Hugh continued to play with the tassel.

For once Howard Brokenshire was disconcerted. Having stepped back a pace or two, he said in his quiet voice, "What did you say, Hugh?"

The answer was quite distinct. "I said I was going to marry Miss Adare."

"Who's that?"

"You know perfectly well, father. She's Ethel's nursery governess. You've been to see her, and she's told you she's going to marry me."

"Oh, but I thought that was over and done with."

"No, you didn't, father. Please don't try to come that. I told you nearly a fortnight ago that I was perfectly serious—and I am."

"Oh, are you? Well, so am I. The Goldboroughs are expecting you for the twelfth—"

"The Goldboroughs can go to—"

"Hugh!" It was Mildred who cut him short with a cry that was almost a petition.

"All right, Milly," he assured her under his breath. "I'm not going to make a scene."

That J. Howard expected to become the principal in a duel, under the eyes of excited witnesses, I do not think. If he had chosen to speak when witnesses were present, it was because of his assumption that Hugh's submission would be thus more easily secured. As it was his policy never to enter into a conflict of authorities, or of will against will, he was for the moment nonplussed. I have an idea he would have retired gracefully, waiting for a more convenient opportunity, had it not been for old Mrs. Billing's lorgnette.

It will, perhaps, not interrupt my narrative too much if I say here that of all the important women he knew he was most afraid of her. She had coached him when he was a beginner in life and she an established young woman of the world. She must then have had a certain *beauté du diable* and that nameless thing which men find exciting in women. I have been told that she was an example of the modern Helen of Troy, over whom men fight while she holds the stakes, and I can believe it. Her history was said to be full of dramatic episodes, though I never knew what they were. Even at sixty, which was the age at which I saw her, she had that kind of presence which challenges and dares. She was ugly and hook-nosed and withered; but she couldn't be overlooked. To me she suggested that Madame Poisson who so carefully prepared her daughter to become the Marquise de Pompadour. Stacy Grainger, I believe, was the Louis XV. of her earlier plans, though, like a born strategist, she changed her methods when reasons arose for doing so. I shall return to this later in my story. At present I only want to say that I do not believe that Mr. Brokenshire would have pushed things to an issue that night had her lorgnette not been there to provoke him.

"Has it occurred to you, Hugh," he asked, in his softest tones, on reaching a stand before the chimney which was filled with dwarfed potted palms, "that I pay you an allowance of six thousand dollars a year?"

Hugh continued to play with the tassel of Mildred's gown. "Yes, father; and as a Socialist I don't think it right. I've been coming to the decision that—"

"You'll spare us your poses and let the Socialist nonsense drop. I simply want to remind you—"

"I can't let the Socialist nonsense drop, father, because—"

The tartness of the tone betrayed a rising irritation.

"Be good enough to turn round this way. I don't understand what you're saying. Perhaps you'll take a chair, and leave poor Mildred alone."

Mildred whispered: "Oh, Hugh, be careful. I'll do anything for you if you won't get him worked up. It'll hurt his face—and his poor eye."

Hugh slouched—the word is Mrs. Rossiter's—to a nearby chair, where he sat down in a hunched position, his hands in his trousers pockets and his feet thrust out before him. The attitude was neither graceful nor respectful to the company.

"It's no use talking, father," he declared, sulkily, "because I've said my last word."

"Oh no, you haven't, for I haven't said my first."

In the tone in which Hugh cried out there must have been something of the plea of a little boy before he is punished:

"Please don't give me any orders, father, because I sha'n't be able to obey them."

"Hugh, your expression 'sha'n't be able to obey' is not in the vocabulary with which I'm familiar."

"But it's in the one with which I am."

"Then you've probably learnt it from Ethel's little servant—I've forgotten the name—"

Hugh spoke with spirit. "She's not a servant; and her name is Alexandra Adare. Please, dad, try to fix it in your memory. You'll find you'll have a lot of use for it."

"Don't be impertinent."

"I'm not impertinent. I'm stating a fact. I ask every one here to remember that name—"

"We needn't bring any one else into this foolish business. It's between you and me. Even so, I wish to have no argument."

"Nor I."

"Then in that case we understand each other. You'll be with the Goldboroughs for the twelfth—"

Hugh spoke very distinctly: "Father—I'm—not—going."

In the silence that followed one could hear the ticking of the mantelpiece clock.

"Then may I ask where you are going?"

Hugh raised himself from his sprawling attitude, holding his bulky young figure erect. "I'm going to earn a living."

Some one, perhaps old Mrs. Billing, laughed. The father continued to speak with great if dangerous courtesy.

"Ah? Indeed! That's interesting. And may I ask at what?"

"At what I can find."

"That's more interesting still. Earning a living in New York is like the proverbial looking for the needle in the haystack. The needle is there, but it takes—"

"Very good eyesight to detect it. All right, dad. I shall be on the job."

"Good! And when do you propose to begin?"

It had not been Hugh's intention to begin at any time in particular, but, thus challenged, he said, boldly, "To-morrow."

"That's excellent. But why put it off so long? I should think you'd start out—to-night."

Mrs. Billing's "Ha-a!" subdued and prolonged, was like that tense exclamation which the spectators utter at some exiting moment of a game. It took no sides, but it did justice to a sporting situation. As Hugh told me the story on the following day he confessed that more than any other occurrence it put the next move "up to him." According to Ethel Rossiter he lumbered heavily to his feet and crossed the room toward his father. He began to speak as he neared the architectural chimneypiece, merely throwing the words at J.

Howard as he passed.

"All right, father. Since you wish it—"

"Oh no. My wishes are out of it. As you defy those I've expressed, there's no more to be said."

Hugh paused in his walk, his hands in the pockets of his dinner-jacket, and eyed his father obliquely. "I don't defy your wishes, dad. I only claim the right, as a man of twenty-six, to live my own life. If you wouldn't make yourself God—"

The handsome hand went up. "We'll not talk about that, if you please. I'd no intention of discussing the matter any longer. I merely thought that if I were in the situation in which you've placed yourself, I should be—getting busy. Still, if you want to stay the night—"

"Oh, not in the least." Hugh was as nonchalant as he had the power to make himself. "Thanks awfully, father, all the same." He looked round on the circle where each of the chorus sat with an appropriate expression of horror—that is, with the exception of the old lady Billing, who, with her lorgnette still to her eyes, nodded approval of so much spirit. "Good night, every one," Hugh continued, coolly, and made his way toward the door.

He had nearly reached it when Mildred cried out: "Hugh! Hughie! You're not going away like that!"

He retraced his steps to the couch, where he stooped, pressed his sister's thin fingers, and kissed her. In doing so he was able to whisper:

"Don't worry, Milly dear. Going to be all right. Shall be a man now. See you soon again." Having raised himself, he nodded once more. "Good night, every one."

Mrs. Rossiter said that he was so much like a young fellow going to his execution that she couldn't respond by a word.

Hugh then marched up to his father and held out his hand. "Good night, dad. We needn't have any ill-feeling even if we don't agree."

But the Great Dispenser didn't see him. An imposing figure standing with his hands behind his back, he kept his fingers clasped. Looking through his son as if he was no more than air, he remarked to the company in general:

"I don't think I've ever seen Daisy Burke appear better than she did to-night. She's usually so badly dressed." He turned with a little deferential stoop to where Mrs. Brokenshire—whom Ethel Rossiter described as a rigid, exquisite thing staring off into vacancy—sat on a small upright chair. "What do you think, darling?"

Hugh could hear the family trying to rally to the hint that had thus been given them, and doing their best to discuss the merits and demerits of Daisy Burke, as he stood in the big, square hall outside, wondering where he should seek shelter.

CHAPTER VI

What Hugh did in the end was simple. Finding the footman who was accustomed to valet him, he ordered him to bring a supply of linen and some suits to a certain hotel early on the following morning. He then put on a light overcoat and a cap and left the house.

The first few steps from the door he closed behind him gave him, so he told me next day, the strangest feeling he had ever experienced. He was consciously venturing forth into life without any of his usual supports. What those supports had been he had never realized till then. He had always been stayed by some one else's authority and buoyed all round by plenty of money. Now he felt, to change the simile as he changed it himself, as if he had been thrown out of the nest before having learnt to fly. As he walked resolutely down the dark driveway toward Ochre Point Avenue he was mentally hovering and balancing and trembling, with a tendency to flop. There was no longer a downy bed behind him; no longer a parent bill to bring him his daily worm. The outlook which had been one thing when he was within that imposing, many-lighted mansion became another now that he was turning his back on it permanently and in the dark.

This he confessed when he had surprised me by appearing at the breakfast loggia, where I was having my coffee with little Gladys Rossiter somewhere between half past eight and nine. He was not an early riser, except when the tide enticed him to get up at some unusual hour to take his dip, and even then he generally went back to bed. To see him coming through the shrubbery now, carefully dressed, pallid and grave, half told me his news before he had spoken.

Luckily Gladys was too young to follow anything we said, so that after having joyfully kissed her uncle Hugh she went on with her bread and milk. Hugh took a cup of coffee, sitting sidewise to the table of which only one end was spread, while I was at the head. It was the hour of the day when we were safest. Mrs. Rossiter never left her room before eleven at earliest, and no one else whom we were afraid of was likely to be about.

"Well, the fat's all in the fire, little Alix," were the words in which he announced his position. "I'm out on my own at last."

I could risk nothing in the way of tenderness, partly because of the maid who was coming and going, and partly because that was something Gladys would understand. I tried to let him see by my eyes, however, the sympathy I felt. I knew he was taking the new turn of events soberly, and soberly, with an immense semi-maternal yearning over him, I couldn't help taking it myself.

He told his tale quietly, with almost no interruption on my part. I was pleased to note that he expressed nothing in the way of recrimination toward his father. With the exception of an occasional fling at old Mrs. Billing, whom he seemed to regard as a joss or a bottle imp, he was temperate, too, in his remarks about everybody else. I liked his sporting attitude and told him so.

"Oh, there's nothing sporting in it," he threw off with a kind of serious carelessness. "I'm a man; that's all. As I look back over the past I seem to have been a doll."

I asked him what were his plans. He said he was going to apply to his cousin, Andrew Brew, of Boston, going on to tell me more about the Brews than I had ever heard. He was surprised that I knew nothing of the important house of Brew, Borrodaile & Co., of Boston, who did such an important business with England and Europe in general. I replied that in Canada all my connections had been with the law, and with Service people in England. I noticed, as I had noticed before in saying things like that, that, in common with most American business men, he looked on the Army and Navy as inferior occupations. There was no money in either. That in itself was sufficient to condemn them in the eyes of a gentleman.

I forgot to be nettled, as I sometimes had been, because of finding myself so deeply immersed in his interests. Up to that minute, too, I had had no idea that he had so much pride of birth. He talked of the Brews and the Brokenshires as if they had been Bourbons and Hohenzollerns, making me feel a veritable Libby Jaynes never to have heard of them. Of the Brews in particular he spoke with reverence. There had been Brews in Boston, he said, since the year one. Like all other American families, as I came to know later, they were descended from three brothers. In Norfolk and Suffolk they had been, so I guessed—though Hugh passed the subject over with some vagueness—of comparatively humble stock, but under the American flag they had acquired money, a quasi-nobility and coats of arms. To hear a man boasting, however modestly—and he was modest—of these respectable nobodies, who had simply earned money and saved it, made me blush inwardly in such a way that I vowed never to mention the Fighting Adares again.

I could do this with no diminution of my feeling for poor Hugh. His artless glory in a line of ancestry of which the fame had never gone beyond the shores of Massachusetts Bay was, after all, a harmless bit of vanity. It took nothing away from his kindness, his good intentions, or his solid worth. When he asked me how I should care to live in Boston I replied that I should like it very much. I had always heard of it as a pleasant city of English characteristics and affiliations.

Wherever he was, I told him, I should be at home—if I made up my mind to marry him.

"But you have made up your mind, haven't you?" he asked, anxiously.

I was obliged to reply with frankness, "Not quite, Hugh, because—"

"Then what's the use of my getting into this hole, if it isn't to be with you?"

"You mean by the hole the being, as you call it, out on your own? But I thought you did that to be a Socialist—and a man."

"I've done it because father won't let me marry you any other way."

"Then if that's all, Hugh—"

"But it isn't all," he interrupted, hastily. "I don't say but what if father had given us his blessing, and come down with another six thousand a year—we could hardly scrub along on less—I'd have taken it and been thankful. But now that he hasn't—well, I can see that it's all for the best. It's—it's brought me out, as you might say, and forced me to a decision."

I harked back to the sentence in which he had broken in on me. "If it was all, Hugh, then that would oblige me to make up my mind at once. I couldn't be the means of compelling you to break with your family and give up a large income."

He cried out impatiently, "Alix, what the dickens is a family and a large income to me in comparison with you?"

I must say that his intensity touched me. Tears sprang into my eyes. I risked Gladys's presence to say: "Hugh, darling, I love you. I can't tell you what your generosity and nobleness mean to me. I hadn't imagined that there was a man like you in the world. But if you could be in my place—"

He pushed aside his coffee-cup to lean with both arms on the table and look me fiercely in the eyes. "If I can't be in your place, Alix, I've seen women who were, and who didn't beat so terribly about the bush. Look at the way Libby Jaynes married Tracy Allen. She didn't talk about his family or his giving up a big income. She trusted him."

"And I trust you; only—" I broke off, to get at him from another point of view. "Do you know Libby Jaynes personally?"

He nodded.

"Is she—is she anything like me?"

"No one is like you," he exclaimed, with something that was almost bitterness in the tone. "Isn't that what I'm trying to make you see? You're the one of your kind in the world. You've got me where a woman has never got a man before. I'd give up everything—I'd starve—I'd lick dust—but I'd follow you to the ends of the earth, and I'd cling to you and keep you." He, too, risked Gladys's presence. "But you're so damn cool, Alix—"

"Oh no, I'm not, Hugh, daring," I pleaded on my own behalf. "I may seem like that on the outside, because—oh, because I've such a lot to think of, and I have to think for us two. That's why I'm asking you if you found Libby Jaynes like me."

He looked puzzled. "She's—she's decent." he said, as if not knowing what else to say.

"Yes, of course; but I mean—does she strike you as having had my kind of ways? Or my kind of antecedents?"

"Oh, antecedents! Why talk about them?"

"It's what you've been doing, isn't it, for the past half-hour?"

"Oh, mine, yes; because I want you to see that I've got a big asset in Cousin Andrew Brew. I know he'll do anything for me, and if you'll trust me, Alix —"

"I do trust you, Hugh, and as soon as you have anything like what would make you independent, and justified in braving your family's disapproval—"

He took an apologetic tone. "I said just now that we couldn't scrape along on less than twelve thousand a year—"

To me the sum seemed ridiculously enormous. "Oh, I'm sure we could."

"Well, that's what I've been thinking," he said, wistfully. "That figure was based on having the Brokenshire position to keep up. But if we were to live in Boston, where less would be expected of us, we could manage, I should think, on ten."

Even that struck me as too much. "On five, Hugh," I declared, with confidence. "I know I could manage on five, and have everything we needed."

He smiled at my eagerness. "Oh, well, darling, I sha'n't ask you to come down to that. Ten will be the least."

To me this was riches. I saw the vision of the dainty dining-room again, and the nursery with the bassinet; but I saw Hugh also in the background, a little shadowy, perhaps, a little like a dream as an artist embodies it in a picture, and yet unmistakably himself. I spoke reservedly, however, far more reservedly than I felt, because I hadn't yet made my point quite clear to him.

"I'm sure we could be comfortable on that. When you get it—"

I hadn't realized that this was the detail as to which he was most sensitive.

"There you go again! When I get it! Do you think I sha'n't get it?"

I felt my eyebrows going up in surprise. "Why, no, Hugh, dear. I suppose you know what you can get and what you can't. I was only going to say that when you do get it I shall feel as if you were free to give yourself away, and that I shouldn't have"—I tried to smile at him—"and that I shouldn't have the air of —of stealing you from your family. Can't you see, dear? You keep quoting Libby Jaynes at me; but in my opinion she did steal Tracy Allen. That the Allens have made the best of it has nothing to do with the original theft."

"Theft is a big word."

"Not bigger than the thing. For Libby Jaynes it was possibly all right. I'm not condemning her. But it wouldn't be all right for me."

"Why not? What's the difference?"

"I can't explain it to you, Hugh, if you don't see it already. It's a difference of tradition."

"But what's difference of tradition got to do with love? Since you admit that you love me, and I certainly love you—"

"Yes, I admit that I love you, but love is not the only thing in the world."

"It's the biggest thing in the world."

"Possibly; and yet it isn't necessarily the surest guide in conduct. There's honor, for instance. If one had to take love without honor, or honor without love, surely one would choose the latter."

"And what would you call love without honor in this case?"

I reflected. "I'd call it doing this thing—getting engaged or married, whichever you like—just because we have the physical power to do it, and making the family, especially the father, to whom you're indebted for everything you are, unhappy."

"He doesn't mind making you and me unhappy."

"But that's his responsibility. We haven't got to do what's right for him; we've only got to do what's right for ourselves." I fell back on my maxim, "If we do right, only right will come of it, whatever the wrong it seems to threaten now."

"But if I made ten thousand a year of my own—"

"I should consider you free. I should feel free myself. I should feel free on less than so big an income."

His spirits began to return.

"I don't call that big. We should have to pinch like the devil to keep our heads above water—no motor—no butler—"

"I've never had either," I smiled at him, "nor a lot of the things that go with them. Not having them might be privations to you—"

"Not when you were there, little Alix. You can bet your sweet life on that."

We laughed together over the expression, and as Broke came bounding out to his breakfast, with the cry, "Hello, Uncle Hughie!" we lapsed into that language of signs and nods and cryptic things which we mutually understood to elude his sharp young wits. By this method of *double entendre* Hugh gave me to understand his intention of going to Boston by an afternoon train. He thought it possible he might stay there. The friendliness of Cousin Andrew Brew would probably detain him till he should go to work, which was likely to be in a day or two. Even if he had to wait a week he would prefer to do so at Boston, where he had not only ties of blood, but acquaintances and interests dating back to his Harvard days, which had ended three years before.

In the mean time, my position might prove to be precarious. He recognized that, making it an excuse for once more forcing on me his immediate protection. Marriage was not named by word on Broke's account, but I understood that if I chose we could be marred within an hour or two, go to Boston together, and begin our common life without further delays.

My answer to this being what it had been before, we discussed, over the children's heads, the chances that could befall me before night. Of these the one most threatening was that I might be sent away in disgrace. If sent away in disgrace I should have to go on the instant. I might be paid for a month or two ahead; it was probable I should be. It was J. Howard's policy to deal with his cashiered employees with that kind of liberality, so as to put himself more in the right. But I should have to go with scarcely the time to pack my boxes, as Hugh had gone himself, and must know of a place where I could take shelter.

I didn't know of any such refuge. My sojourn under Mrs. Rossiter's roof had been remarkably free from contacts or curiosities of my own. Hugh knew no more than I. I could, therefore, only ask his consent to my consulting Mr. Strangways, a proposal to which he agreed. This I was able to do when Larry came for Broke, not many minutes after Hugh had taken his departure.

I could talk to him the more freely because of his knowledge of my relation to Hugh. With the fact that I was in love with another man kept well in the foreground between us, he could acquit me of those ulterior designs on himself the suspicion of which is so disturbing to a woman's friendship with a man. As the maid was clearing the table, as Broke had to go to his lessons, as Gladys had to be remanded to the nursery while I attended to Mrs. Rossiter's telephone calls and correspondence, our talk was squeezed in during the seconds in which we retreated through the dining-room into the main part of the house.

"The long and short of it is," Larry Strangways summed up, when I had confided to him my fears of being sent about my business as soon as Hugh had left for Boston—"the long and the short of it is that I shall have to look you up another job."

It is almost absurd to point out that the idea was new to me. In going to Mrs. Rossiter I had never thought of starting out on a career of earning a living professionally, as you might say. I clung to the conception of myself as a lady, with all sorts of possibilities in the way of genteel interventions of Providence coming in between me and a lifetime of work. I had always supposed that if I left Mrs. Rossiter I should go back to my uncle and aunt at Halifax. After all, if Hugh was going to marry me, it would be no more than correct that he should do it from under their wing. Larry Strangways's suggestions of another job threw open a vista of places I should fill in the future little short of appalling to a woman instinctively looking for a man to come and support her.

I shelved these considerations, however, to say, as casually as I could: "Why should you do it? Why shouldn't I look out for myself?"

"Because when I've gone to Stacy Grainger it may be right in my line."

"But I'd rather you didn't have me on your mind."

He laughed—uneasily, as it seemed to me. "Perhaps it's too late for that."

It was another of the things I was sorry to hear him say. I could only reply, still on the forced casual note: "But it's not too late for me to look after my own affairs. What I'm chiefly concerned with is that if I have to leave here—to-night, let us say—I sha'n't in the least know where to go."

He was ready for me in the event of this contingency. I suspected that he had already considered it. He had a married sister in New York, a Mrs. Applegate, a woman of philanthropic interests, a director on the board of a Home for Working-Girls. Again I shied at the word. He must have seen that I did, for he went on, with a smile in which I detected a gleam of mockery:

"You are a working-girl, aren't you?"

I answered with the kind of humility I can only describe as spirited, and which was meant to take the wind out of his sails:

"I suppose so—as long as I'm working." But I gave him a flying upward glance as I asked the imprudent question, "Is that how you've thought of me?"

I was sorry to have said it as soon as the words were out. I didn't want to know what he thought of me. It was something with which I was so little concerned that I colored with embarrassment at having betrayed so much futile curiosity. Apparently he saw that, too, hastening to come to my relief.

"I've thought of you," he laughed, when we had reached the main stairway, "as a clever little woman, with a special set of aptitudes, who ought to be earning more money than she's probably getting here; and when I'm with Stacy Grainger—"

Grateful for this turning of the current into the business-like and commonplace, I called Gladys, who was lagging in the dining-room with Broke, and went on my way up-stairs.

Mrs. Rossiter was sitting up in bed, her breakfast before her on a light wicker tray that stood on legs. It was an abstemious breakfast, carefully selected from foods containing most nutrition with least adipose deposit. She had reached the age, within sight of the thirties, when her figure was becoming a matter for consideration. It was almost the only personal detail as to which she had as yet any cause for anxiety. Her complexion was as bright as at eighteen; her brown hair, which now hung in a loose, heavy coil over her left shoulder, was thick and silky and long; her eyes were clear, her lips ruby. I always noticed that she waked with the sleepy softness of a flower uncurling to the sun. In the great walnut bed, of which the curves were gilded à la Louis Quinze, she made me think of that Jeanne Bécu who became Comtesse du Barry, in the days of her indolence and luxury.

Having no idea as to how she would receive me, I was not surprised that it should be as usual. Since I had entered her employ she was never what I should call gracious, but she was always easy and familiar. Sometimes she was petulant; often she was depressed; but beyond a belief that she inspired tumultuous passions in young men there was no pose about her nor any haughtiness. I was not afraid of her, therefore; I was only uneasy as to the degree in which she would let herself be used against me as a tool.

"The letters are here on the bed," was her response to my greeting, which I was careful to make in the form in which I made it every day.

Taking the small arm-chair at the bedside, I sorted the pile. The notes she had not glanced at for herself I read aloud, penciling on the margins the data for the answers. Some I replied to by telephone, which stood within her reach on the *table de nuit*; for a few I sat down at the desk and wrote. I was doing the latter, and had just scribbled the words "Mrs. James Worthington Rossiter will have much pleasure in accepting—" when she said, in a slightly querulous tone:

"I should think you'd do something about Hugh—the way he goes on."

I continued to write as I asked, "How does he go on?"

"Like an idiot."

"Has he been doing anything new?"

My object being to get a second version of the story Hugh had told me, I succeeded. Mrs. Rossiter's facts were practically the same as her brother's, only viewed from a different angle. As she presented the case Hugh had been merely preposterous, dashing his head against a stone wall, with nothing he could gain by the exercise.

"The idea of his saying he'll not go to the Goldboroughs for the twelfth! Of course he'll go. Since father means him to do it, he will."

I was addressing an envelope, and went on with my task. "But I thought you said he'd left home?"

"Oh, well, he'll come back."

"But suppose he doesn't? Suppose he goes to work?"

"Pff! The idea! He won't keep that up long."

I was glad to be sitting with my back to her. To disguise the quaver in my voice I licked the flap of the envelope as I said:

"But he'll have to if he means to support a wife."

"Support a wife? What nonsense! Father means him to marry Cissie Boscobel, as I've told you already—and he'll fix them up with a good income."

"But apparently Hugh doesn't see things that way. He's told me—"

"Oh, he'd tell you anything."

"He's told me," I persisted, boldly, "that he—he loves me; and he's made me say that—that I love him."

"And that's where you're so foolish, dear Miss Adare. You let him take you in. It isn't that he's not sincere; I don't say that for a minute. But people can't

65

go about marrying every one they love, now can they? I should think you'd have seen that—with the heaps of men you had there at Halifax—hardly room to step over them."

I said, slyly, "I never saw them that way."

"Oh, well, I did. And by the way, I wonder what's become of that Captain Venables. He was a case! He could take more liberties in a half-hour—don't you think?"

"He never took any liberties with me."

"Then that must have been your fault. Talk about Mr. Millinger! Our men aren't in it with yours—not when it comes to the real thing."

I got back to the subject in which I was most interested by saying, as I spread another note before me:

"It seems to be the real thing with Hugh."

"Oh, I dare say it is. It was the real thing with Jack. I don't say"—her voice took on a tender tremolo—"I don't say that it wasn't the real thing with me. But that didn't make any difference to father. It was the real thing with Pauline Gray—when she was down there at Baltimore; but when father picked her out for Jack, because of her money and his relations with old Mr. Gray—"

I couldn't help half turning round, to cry out in tones of which I was unable to conceal the exasperation: "But I don't see how you can all let yourselves be hooked by the nose like that—not even by Mr. Brokenshire!"

Her fatalistic resignation gave me a sense of helplessness.

"Oh, well, you will before father has done with you—if Hugh goes on this way. Father's only playing with you so far."

"He can't touch me," I declared, indignantly.

"But he can touch Hugh. That's all he needs to know, as far as you're concerned." She asked, in another tone, "What are you answering now?"

I told her it was the invitation to Mrs. Allen's dance.

"Then tear it up and say I can't go. Say I've a previous engagement. I'd forgotten that they had that odious Mrs. Tracy Allen there."

I tore up the sheet slowly, throwing the fragments into the waste-paper basket.

"Why is she odious?"

"Because she is." She dropped for a second into the tone of the early friendly days in Halifax. "My dear, she was a shop-girl—or worse. I've forgotten what she was, but it was awful, and I don't mean to meet her."

I began to write the refusal.

"She goes about with very good people, doesn't she?"

"She doesn't go about with me, nor with some others I know, I can tell you that. If she did it would queer us."

In the hope of drawing out some such repudiation as that which I felt myself, I said, dryly: "Hugh tells me that if I married him I could be as good as she is —by this time next year."

I got nothing for my pains.

"That wouldn't help you much—not among the people who count."

There was white anger underneath my meekness.

"But perhaps I could get along with the people who don't count."

"Yes, you might—but Hugh wouldn't."

She dismissed the subject as one in which she took only a secondary interest to say that old Mrs. Billing was coming to lunch, and that Gladys and I should have to take that repast up-stairs. She was never direct in her denunciations of her father's second marriage. She brought them in by reference and innuendo, like a prisoner who keeps in mind the fact that walls have ears. She gave me to understand, however, that she considered Mrs. Billing a witch out of "Macbeth" or a wicked old vulture—I could take my choice of comparisons —and she hated having her in the house. She wouldn't do it only that, in ways she could hardly understand, Mrs. Billing was the power behind the throne. She didn't loathe her stepmother, she said in effect, so much as she loathed her father's attitude toward her. I have never forgotten the words she used in this connection, dropping her voice and glancing about her, afraid she might be overheard. "It's as if God himself had become the slave of some silly human woman just because she had a pretty face." The sentence not only betrayed the Brokenshire attitude of mind toward J. Howard, but sent a chill down my back.

Having finished my notes and addressed them I rose to return to Gladys; but there was still an unanswered question in my mind. I asked it, standing for a minute beside the bed:

"Then you don't want me to go away?"

She arched her lovely eyebrows. "Go away? What for?"

"Because of the danger of my marrying Hugh."

She gave a little laugh. "Oh, there's no danger of that."

"But there is," I insisted. "He's asked me a number of times to go with him to the nearest clergyman, and settle the question once for all."

"Only you don't do it. There you are! What father doesn't want doesn't happen; and what he does want does. That's all there is to be said."

CHAPTER VII

As a matter of fact, that was all Mrs. Rossiter and I did say. I was so relieved at not being thrown out of house and home on the instant that I went back to Gladys and her lisping in French almost cheerily. You will think me pusillanimous—and I was. I didn't want to go to Mrs. Applegate and the Home for Working-Girls. As far as food and shelter were concerned I liked them well enough where I was. I liked Mrs. Rossiter too. I should be sorry to give the impression that she was supercilious or unkind. She was neither the one nor the other. If she betrayed little sentiment or sympathy toward me, it was because of admitting me into that feminine freemasonry in which the emotional is not called for. I might suffer while she remained indifferent; I might be killed on the spot while she wouldn't shed a tear; and yet there was a heartless, good-natured, live-and-let-live detachment about her which left me with nothing but good-will.

Then, too, I knew that when I married Hugh she would do nothing of her own free will against me. She would not brave her father's decree, but she wouldn't be intolerant; she might think Hugh had been a fool, but when she could do so surreptitiously she would invite him and me to dinner.

As this was a kind of recognition in advance, I could not be otherwise than grateful.

It made waiting for Hugh the easier. I calculated that if he entered into some sort of partnership with his cousin Andrew Brew—I didn't in the least know what—we might be married within a month or two. At furthest it might be about the time when Mrs. Rossiter removed to New York, which would make it October or November. I could then slip quietly back to Halifax, be quietly married, and quietly settle with Hugh in Boston. In the mean time I was glad not to be disturbed.

I spent, therefore, a pleasant morning with my pupil, and ate a pleasant lunch, watching from the gable window of the school-room the great people assemble in the breakfast loggia in honor of the Marquise de Pompadour's mother. I am not sure that old Madame Poisson ever went to court; but if she did I know the courtiers must have shown her just such deference as that which Mrs. Rossiter's guests exhibited to this withered old lady with the hooked nose and the lorgnette.

I was curious about the whole entertainment. It was not the only one of the kind I had seen from a distance since coming to Mrs. Rossiter, and I couldn't help comparisons with the same kind of thing as done in the ways with which I was familiar. Here it was less a luncheon than it was an exquisite thing on the stage, rehearsed to the last point. In England, in Canada, luncheon would be something of a friendly haphazard, primarily for the sake of getting food, secondly as a means to a scrambling, jolly sort of social intercourse, and hardly at all a ceremonial. Here the ceremonial came first. Hostess and guests seemed alike to be taking part in a rite of seeing and being seen. The food, which was probably excellent, was a matter of slight importance. The social intercourse amounted to nothing, since they all knew one another but too well, and had no urgent vitality of interests in any case. The rite was the thing. Every detail was prepared for that. Silver, porcelain, flowers, doilies, were of the most expensive and the most correct. The guests were dressed to perfection—a little too well, according to the English standard, but not too well for a function. As a function it was beautiful, an occasion of privilege, a proof of attainment. It was the best thing of its kind America could show. Those who had money could alone present the passport that would give the right of admission.

If I had a criticism to make, it was that the guests were too much alike. They were all business men, and the wives or widows of business men. The two or three who did nothing but live on inherited incomes were business men in heart and in blood. Granted that in the New World the business man must be dominant, it was possible to have too much of him. Having too much of him lowered the standard of interest, narrowed the circle of taste. In the countries I knew the business man might be present at such a festivity, but there would be something to give him color, to throw him into relief. There would be a touch of the creative or the intellectual, of the spiritual or the picturesque. The company wouldn't be all of a gilded drab. There would be a writer or a painter or a politician or an actor or a soldier or a priest. There would be something that wasn't money before it was anything else. Here there was nothing. Birds of a feather were flocking together, and they were all parrots or parrakeets. They had plumage, but no song. They drove out the thrushes and the larks and the wild swans. Their shrill screeches and hoarse shouts came up in a not wholly pleasant babel to the open window where I sat looking down and Gladys hovered and hopped, wondering if Thomas, the rosy-cheeked footman, would remember to bring us some of the left-over ice-cream.

I thought it was a pity. With elements as good as could be found anywhere to form a Society—that fusion of all varieties of achievement to which alone the word written with a capital can be applied—there was no one to form it. It was a woman's business; and for the rôle of hostess in the big sense the American woman, as far as I could judge, had little or no aptitude. She was too timid, too distrustful of herself, too much afraid of doing the wrong thing

70

or of knowing the wrong people. She was so little sure of her standing that, as Mrs. Rossiter expressed it, she could be "queered" by shaking hands with Libby Jaynes. She lacked authority. She could stand out in a throng by her dress or her grace, but she couldn't lead or combine or co-ordinate. She could lend a charming hand where some one else was the Lady Holland or the Madame de Staël, but she couldn't take the seemingly heterogeneous types represented by the writer, the painter, the politician, the actor, the soldier, the priest, and the business man and weld them into the delightful, promiscuous, entertaining whole to be found, in its greater or lesser degree, according to size or importance of place, almost anywhere within the borders of the British Empire. I came to the conclusion that this was why there were few "great houses" in America and fewer women of importance.

It was why, too, the guests were subordinated to the ceremonial. It couldn't be any other way. With flint and steel you can get a spark; but where you have nothing but flint or nothing but steel, friction produces no light. The American hostess, in so far as she exists, rarely hopes for anything from the clash of minds, and therefore centers her attention on her doilies. It must be admitted that she has the most tasteful doilies in the world. There is a pathos in the way in which, for want of the courage to get interesting human specimens together, she spends her strength on the details of her rite. It is like the instinct of women who in default of babies lavish their passion on little dogs. One can say that it is *faute de mieux*. *Faute de mieux* was, I am sure, the reason why Ethel Rossiter took her table appointments with what seemed to me such extraordinary seriousness. When all was said and done it was the only real thing to care about.

I repeat that I thought it was a pity. I had dreams, as I looked down, of what I could do with the same use of money, the same position of command. I had dreams that the Brokenshires accepted me, that Hugh came into the means that would be his in the ordinary course. I saw myself standing at the head of the stairway of a fine big house in Washington or New York. People were streaming upward, and I was shaking hands with a delightful, smiling *désinvolture*. I saw men and women of all the ranks and orders of conspicuous accomplishment, each contributing a gift—some nothing but beauty, some nothing but wit, some nothing but money, some nothing but position, some nothing but fame, some nothing but national importance. The Brokenshire clan was there, and the Billings and the Grays and the Burkes; but statesmen and diplomatists, too, were there, and those leaders in the world of the pen and the brush and the buskin of whom, oddly enough, I saw Larry Strangways, with his eternal defensive smile, emerging from the crowd as chief. I was wearing diamonds, black velvet, and a train, waving in my disengaged hand a spangled fan.

From these visions I was roused by Gladys, who came prancing from the stair-head.

"V'là, Mademoiselle! V'là Thomas et le ice-cream!"

Having consumed this dainty, we watched the company wander about the terraces and lawns and finally drift away. I was getting Gladys ready for her walk when Thomas, with a pitying expression on his boyish face, came back to say that Mr. Brokenshire would like to speak with me down-stairs.

I was never so near fainting in my life. I had barely the strength to gasp, "Very well, Thomas, I'll come," and to send Gladys to her nurse. Thomas watched me with his good, kind, sympathetic eyes. Like the other servants, he must have known something of my secret and was on my side. I called him the *bouton de rose*, partly because his clean, pink cheeks suggested a Killarney breaking into flower, and partly because in his waiting on Gladys and me he had the yearning, care-taking air of a fatherly little boy. Just now he could only march down the passage ahead of me, throw open the door of my bedroom as if he was lord chamberlain to a queen, and give me a look which seemed to say, "If I can be your liege knight against this giant, pray, dear lady, command me." I threw him my thanks in a trumped-up smile, which he returned with such sweet encouragement as to nearly unman me.

I stayed in my room only long enough to be sure that I was neat, smoothing my hair and picking one or two threads from my white-linen suit. The suit had scarlet cuffs and a scarlet belt, and as there was a scarlet flush beneath my summer tan, like the color under the glaze of a Chinese jar, I could see for myself that my appearance was not ineffective.

The *bouton de rose* was in waiting at the foot of the stairs as I came down. Through the hall and the dining-room he ushered me royally; but as I came out on the breakfast loggia my royalty stopped with what I can only describe as a bump.

The guests had gone, but the family remained. The last phase of the details of the rite were also on the table. All the doilies were there, and the magnificent lace centerpiece which Mrs. Rossiter had at various times called on me to admire. The old Spode dessert service was the more dimly, anciently brilliant because of the old polished oak, and so were the glasses and finger-bowls picked out in gold.

Mr. Brokenshire, whom I had seen from my window strolling with some ladies on the lawn, had returned to the foot of the table, opposite to the door by which I came out, where he now sat in a careless, sidewise attitude, fingering his cigar. Old Mrs. Billing, who was beside him on his right, put up her lorgnette immediately I appeared in the entrance. Mrs. Rossiter had dropped into a chance chair half-way down the table on the left; but Mrs. Brokenshire, oddly enough, was in that same seat in the far corner to which she had retreated on the occasion of my summoning ten days before. I wondered whether this was by intention or by chance, though I was presently to know.

Terrified though I was, I felt salvation to lie in keeping a certain dignity. I made, therefore, something between a bow and a courtesy, first to Mr. Brokenshire, then to Mrs. Billing, then to Mrs. Rossiter, and lastly to Mrs. Brokenshire, to whom I raised my eyes and looked all the way diagonally across the loggia. I took my time in making these four distinct salutations, though in response I was only stared at. After that there was a space of some seconds in which I merely stood, in my pose of *Ecce Femina*!

"Sit down!"

The command came, of course, from J. Howard. The chair to which I had once before been banished being still in its corner, I slipped into it.

"I wished to speak to you, Miss—a—Miss—"

He glanced helplessly toward his daughter, who supplied the name.

"Ah yes. I wished to speak to you, Miss Adare, because my son has been acting very foolishly."

I made my tone as meek as I could, scarcely daring to lift my eyes from the floor. "Wouldn't it be well, sir, to talk to him about that?"

Mrs. Billing's lorgnette came down. She glanced toward her son-in-law as though finding the point well taken.

He went on imperturbably. "I've said all I mean to say to him. My present appeal is to you."

"Oh, then this is an—appeal?"

He seemed to hesitate, to reflect. "If you choose to take it so," he admitted, stiffly.

"It surely isn't as I choose to take it, sir; it's as you choose to mean."

"Don't bandy words."

"But I must use words, sir. I only want to be sure that you're making an appeal to me, and not giving me commands."

He spoke sharply. "I wish you to understand that you're inducing a young man to act in a way he is going to find contrary to his interests."

I could barely nerve myself to look up at him. "If by the 'young man' you mean Mr. Hugh Brokenshire, then I'm inducing him to do nothing whatever; unless," I added, "you call it an inducement that I—I"—I was bound to force the word out—"unless you call it an inducement that I love him."

"But that's it," Mrs. Rossiter broke in. "That's what my father means. If you'd stop caring anything about him you wouldn't give him encouragement."

I looked at her with a dim, apologetic smile. It was a time, I felt, to speak not only with more courage, but with more sentiment than I was accustomed to use in expressing myself.

"I'm afraid I can't give my heart, and take it back, like that."

"I can," she returned, readily. She spoke as if it was a matter of cracking her knuckles or wagging her ears. "If I don't want to like a person I don't do it. It's training and self-command."

"You're fortunate," I said, quietly. Why I should have glanced again at Mrs. Brokenshire I hardly know; but I did so, as I added: "I've had no training of that kind—and I doubt if many women have."

Mrs. Brokenshire, who was gazing at me with the same kind of fascinated stare as on the former occasion, faintly, but quite perceptibly, inclined her head. In this movement I was sure I had the key to the mystery that seemed to surround her.

"All this," J. Howard declared, magisterially, "is beside the point. If you've told my son that you'd marry him—"

"I haven't."

"Or even given him to understand that you would—"

"I've only given him to understand that I'd marry him—on conditions."

"Indeed? And would it be discreet on my part to inquire the terms you've been kind enough to lay down?"

I pulled myself together and spoke firmly. "The first is that I'll marry him—if his family come to me and express a wish to have me as a sister and a daughter."

Old Mrs. Billing emitted the queer, cracked cackle of a hen when it crows, but she put up her lorgnette and examined me more closely. Ethel Rossiter gasped audibly, moving her chair a little farther round in my direction. Mrs. Brokenshire stared with concentrated intensity, but somehow, I didn't know why, I felt that she was backing me up.

The great man contented himself with saying, "Oh, you will!"

I ignored the tone to speak with a decision and a spirit I was far from feeling.

"Yes, sir, I will. I shall not steal him from you—not so long as he's dependent."

"That's very kind. And may I ask—"

"You haven't let me tell you my other condition."

"True. Go on."

I panted the words out as best I could. "I've told him I'd marry him—if he rendered himself independent; if he earned his own money and became a man."

"Ah! And you expect one or the other of these miracles to take place?"

"I expect both."

Though the words uttered themselves, without calculation or expectation on my part, they gave me so much of the courage of conviction that I held up my head. To my surprise Mrs. Billing didn't crow again or so much as laugh. She only gasped out that long "Ha-a!" which proclaims the sporting interest, of which both Hugh and Ethel Rossiter had told me in the morning.

Mr. Brokenshire seemed to brace himself, leaning forward, with his elbow on the table and his cigar between the fingers of his raised right hand. His eyes were bent on me—fine eyes they were!—as if in kindly amusement.

"My good girl," he said, in his most pitying voice, "I wish I could tell you how sorry for you I am. Neither of these dreams can possibly come true—"

My blood being up, I interrupted with some force. "Then in that case, Mr. Brokenshire, you can be quite easy in your mind, for I should never marry your son." Having made this statement, I followed it up by saying, "Since that is understood, I presume there's no object in my staying any longer." I was half rising when his hand went up.

"Wait. We'll tell you when to go. You haven't yet got my point. Perhaps I haven't made it clear. I'm not interested in your hopes—"

"No, sir; of course not; nor I in yours."

"I haven't inquired as to that—but we'll let it pass. We're both apparently interested in my son."

I gave a little bow of assent.

"I said I wished to make an appeal to you."

I made another little bow of assent.

"It's on his behalf. You could do him a great kindness. You could make him understand—I gather that he's under your influence to some degree; you're a clever girl, I can see that—but you could make him understand that in fancying he'll marry you he's starting out on a task in which there's no hope whatever."

"But there is."

"Pardon me, there isn't. By your own showing there isn't. You've laid down conditions that will never be fulfilled."

"What makes you say that?"

"My knowledge of the world."

"Oh, but would you call that knowledge of the world?" I was swept along by the force of an inner indignation which had become reckless. "Knowledge of the world," I hurried on, "implies knowledge of the human heart, and you've none of that at all." I could see him flush.

"My good girl, we're here to speak of you, not of me—"

"Surely we're here to speak of us both, since at any minute I choose I can marry your son. If I don't marry him it's because I don't choose; but when I do choose—"

Again the hand went up. "Yes, of course; but that's not what we want specially to hear. Let us assume, as you say, that you can marry my son at any time you choose. You don't choose, for the reason that you're astute enough to see that your last state would be worse than the first. To enter a family that would disown you at once—"

I kept down my tone, though I couldn't master my excitement. "That's not my reason. If I don't marry him it's precisely because I have the power. There are people—cowards they are at heart, as a rule—who because they have the power use it to be insolent, especially to those who are weaker. I'm not one of those. There's a *noblesse oblige* that compels one in spite of everything. In dealing with an elderly man, who I suppose loves his son, and with a lady who's been so kind to me as Mrs. Rossiter—"

"You've been hired, and you're paid. There's no special call for gratitude."

"Gratitude is in the person who feels it; but that isn't what I specially want to say."

"What you specially want to say apparently is—"

"That I'm not afraid of you, sir; I'm not afraid of your family or your money or your position or anything or any one you can control. If I don't marry

76

Hugh, it's for the reason that I've given, and for no other. As long as he's dependent on your money I shall not marry him till you come and beg me to do it—and that I shall expect of you."

He smiled tolerantly. "That is, till you've brought us to our knees."

I could barely pipe, but I stood to my guns. "If you like the expression, sir— yes. I shall not marry Hugh—so long as you support him—till I've brought you to your knees."

If I expected the heavens to fall at this I was disappointed. All J. Howard did was to lean on his arm toward Mrs. Billing and talk to her privately. Mrs. Rossiter got up and went to her father, entering also into a whispered colloquy. Once or twice he glanced backward to his wife, but she was now gazing sidewise in the direction of the house and over the lines of flowers that edged the terraces.

When Mrs. Rossiter had gone back to her seat, and J. Howard had raised himself from his conversation with Mrs. Billing, he began again to address me tranquilly:

"I hoped you might have sympathized with my hopes for Hugh, and have helped to convince him how useless his plans for a marriage between him and you must be."

I answered with decision: "No; I can't do that."

"I should have appreciated it—"

"That I can quite understand."

"And some day have shown you that I'm acting for your good."

"Oh, sir," I cried, "whatever else you do, you'll let my good be my own affair, will you not?"

I thought I heard Mrs. Billing say, "Brava!" At any rate, she tapped her fingers together as if in applause. I began to feel a more lenient spirit toward her.

"I'm quite willing to do that," my opponent said, in a moderate, long-suffering tone, "now that I see that you refuse to take Hugh's good into consideration. So long as you encourage him in his present madness—"

"I'm not doing that."

He took no notice of the interruption. "—I'm obliged to regard him as nothing to me."

"That must be between you and your son."

"It is. I'm only asking you to note that you—ruin him."

"No, no," I began to protest, but he silenced me with a movement of his hand.

"I'm not a hard man naturally," he went on, in his tranquil voice, "but I have to be obeyed."

"Why?" I demanded. "Why should you be obeyed more than any one else?"

"Because I mean to be. That must be enough—"

"But it isn't," I insisted. "I've no intention of obeying you—"

He broke in with some haste: "Oh, there's no question of you, my dear young lady. I've nothing to do with you. I'm speaking of my son. He must obey me, or take the consequences. And the consequences will last as long as he lives. I'm not one to speak rashly, or to speak twice. So that's what I'm putting to you. Do you think—do you honestly think—that you're improving your position by ruining a man who sooner or later—sooner rather than later—will lay his ruin at your door and loathe you? Come now! You're a clever girl. The case is by no means beyond you. Think, and think straight."

"I am thinking, sir. I'm thinking so straight that I see right through you. My father used to say—"

"No reminiscence, please."

"Very well, then; we'll let the reminiscence go. But you're thinking of committing a crime, a crime against Hugh, a crime against yourself, a crime against love, every kind of love—and that's the worst crime of all—and you haven't the moral courage to shoulder the guilt yourself; you're trying to shuffle it off on me."

"My good woman—"

But nothing could silence me now. I leaned forward, with hands clasped in my lap, and merely looked at him. My voice was low, but I spoke rapidly:

"You're talking to bewilder me, to throw dust in my eyes, to snare me into taking the blame for what you're doing of your own free act. It's a kind of reasoning which some girls would be caught by, but I'm not one of them. If Hugh is ruined in the sense you mean, it's his father who will ruin him—but even that is not the worst. What's worst, what's dastardly, what's not merely unworthy of a man like you but unworthy of any man—of anything that calls itself a male—is that you, with all your resources of every kind, should try to foist your responsibilities off on a woman who has no resources whatever. That I shouldn't have believed of any of your sex—if it hadn't happened to myself."

But my eloquence left him as unmoved as before. He whispered with Mrs. Billing. The old lady was animated, making beats and lunges with her lorgnette.

"So that what it comes to," he said to me at last, lifting himself up and speaking in a tired voice, "is that you really mean to pit yourself against me."

"No, sir; but that you mean to pit yourself against me." Something compelled me to add: "And I can tell you now that you'll be beaten in the end."

Perhaps he didn't hear me, for he rose and, stooping, carried on his discussion with Mrs. Billing. There was a long period in which no one paid any further attention to my presence; in fact, no one paid any attention to me any more. To my last words I expected some retort, but none came. Ethel Rossiter joined her father at the end of the table, and when Mrs. Billing also rose the conversation went on à trois. Mrs. Brokenshire alone remained seated and aloof.

But the moment came when her husband turned toward her. Not having been dismissed, I merely stood and looked on. What I saw then passed quickly, so quickly that it took a minute of reflection before I could put two and two together.

Having taken one step toward his wife, Howard Brokenshire stood still, abruptly, putting his hand suddenly to the left side of his face. His wife, too, put up her hand, but palm outward and as if to wave him back. At the same time she averted her face—and I knew it was his eye.

It was over before either of the other two women perceived anything. Presently, all four were out on the grass, strolling along in a little chattering group together. My dismissal having come automatically, as you might say, I was free to go.

CHAPTER VIII

An hour later I had what up to then I must call the greatest surprise of my life.

I was crying by myself on the shore, in that secluded corner among the rocks where Hugh had first told me that he loved me. As a rule, I don't cry easily. I did it now chiefly from being overwrought. I was desolate. I missed Hugh. The few days or few weeks that must pass before I could see him again stretched before me like a century. All whom I could call my own were so far away. Even had they been near, they would probably, with the individualism of our race, have left me to shift for myself. Louise and Victoria had always given me to understand that, though they didn't mind lending me an occasional sisterly hand, my life was my own affair. It would have been a relief to talk the whole thing out philosophically with Larry Strangways. As I came from the house I tried, for the first time since knowing him, to throw myself in his path; but, as usual when one needs a friend, he was nowhere to be seen.

I could, therefore, only scramble down to my favorite corner among the rocks. Not that it was really a scramble. As a matter of fact, the path was easy if you knew where to find it; but it was hidden from the ordinary passer on the Cliff Walk, first by a boulder, round which you had to slip, and then by a tangle of wild rosebines, wild raspberries, and Queen Anne's lace. It was something like a secret door, known only to the Rossiter household, their servants, and their friends. Once you had passed it you had a measure of the public privacy you get in a box at the theater or the opera. You had space and ease and a wide outlook, with no fear of intrusion.

I cannot say that I was unhappy. I was rather in that state of mind which the American people, with its gift for the happy, unexpected word, have long spoken of as "mad." I was certainly mad. I was mad with J. Howard Brokenshire first of all; I was mad with his family for having got up and left me without so much as a nod; I was mad with Hugh for having made me fall in love with him; I was mad with Larry Strangways for not having been on the spot; and I was most of all mad with myself. I had been boastful and bumptious; I had been disrespectful and absurd. It was foolish to make worse enemies than I had already. Mrs. Rossiter wouldn't keep me now. There would be no escape from Mrs. Applegate and the Home for Working-Girls.

The still summer beauty of the afternoon added to my wretchedness. All round and before me there was luxury and joyousness and sport. The very sea was in a playful mood, lapping at my feet like a tamed, affectionate leviathan, and curling round the ledges in the offing with delicate lace-like spouts of spume. Sea-gulls swooped and hovered with hoarse cries and a lovely effect of silvery wings. Here and there was a sail on the blue, or the smoke of a steamer or a war-ship. Eastons Point, some two or three miles away, was a long, burnished line of ripening wheat. To right and to left of me were broken crags, red-yellow, red-brown, red-green, where lovers and happy groups could perch or nestle carelessly, thrusting trouble for the moment to a distance. I had to bring my trouble with me. If it had not been for trouble I shouldn't have been there. There wasn't a soul in the world who would fight to take my part but Hugh, and I was, in all my primary instincts, a clinging, parasitic thing that hated to stand alone.

There was nothing for it then but crying, and I did that to the best of my ability; not loudly, of course, or vulgarly, but gently and sentimentally, with an immense pity for myself. I cried for what had happened that day and for what had happened yesterday. I cried for things long past, which I had omitted to cry for at the time. When I had finished with these I went further back to dig up other ignominies, and I cried for them. I cried for my father and mother and my orphaned condition; I cried for the way in which my father—who was a good, kind man, *du reste*—had lived on his principal, and left me with scarcely a penny to my name; I cried for my various disappointments in love, and for the girl friends who had predeceased me. I massed all these motives together and cried for them in bulk. I cried for Hugh and the brilliant future we should have on the money he would make. I cried for Larry Strangways and the loneliness his absence would entail on me. I cried for the future as well as for the past and if I could have thought of a future beyond the future I should have cried for that. It was delicious and sad and consoling all at once; and when I had no more tears I felt almost as if Hugh's strong arm had been about me, and I was comforted.

I was just wiping my eyes and wondering whether at the moment of going homeward my nose would be too red, when I heard a quiet step. I thought I must be mistaken. It was so unlikely that any one would be there at this hour of the day—the servants generally came down at night—that for a minute I didn't turn. It was the uncomfortable sense that some one was behind me that made me look back at last, when I caught the flutter of lace and the shimmer of pale-rose taffeta. Mrs. Brokenshire had worn lace and pale-rose taffeta at the lunch.

Fear and amazement wrestled in my soul together. Struggling to my feet, I turned round as slowly as I could.

"Don't get up," she said in a sweet, quiet voice. "I'll come and sit down beside you, if I may." She had already seated herself on a low flat rock as she said, "I saw you were crying, so I waited."

I am not usually at a loss for words, but I was then. I stuttered and stammered and babbled, without being able to say anything articulate. Indeed, I had nothing articulate to say. The mind had suspended its action.

My impressions were all subconscious, but registered exactly. She was the most exquisite production I had ever seen in human guise. Her perfection was that of some lovely little bird in which no color fails to shade harmoniously into some other color, in which no single feather is out of place. The word I used of her was *soignée*—that which is smoothed and curled and polished and caressed till there is not an eyelash which hasn't received its measure of attention. I don't mean that she was artificial, or that her effects were too thought out. She was no more artificial than a highly cultivated flower is artificial, or a many-faceted diamond, or a King Charles spaniel, or anything else that is carefully bred or cut or shaped. She was the work of some specialist in beauty, who had no aim in view but to give to the world the loveliest thing possible.

When I had mastered my confusion sufficiently I sat down with the words, rather lamely spoken:

"I didn't know any one was here. I hope I haven't kept you standing long."

"No; but I was watching you. I came down only a few minutes after you did. You see, I was afraid—when we came away from Mrs. Rossiter's—that you might be unhappy."

"I'm not as unhappy as I was," I faltered, without knowing what I said, and was rewarded to see her smile.

It was an innocent smile, without glee, a little sad in fact, but full of unutterable things like a very young child's. I had never seen such teeth, so white, so small, so regular.

"I'm glad of that," she said, simply. "I thought if some—some other woman was near you, you mightn't feel so—so much alone. That's why I watched round and followed you."

I could have fallen at her feet, but I restricted myself to saying:

"Thank you very much. It does make a difference." I got courage to add, however, with a smile of my own, "I see you know."

"Yes, I know. I've thought about you a good deal since that day about a fortnight ago—you remember?"

"Oh yes, I remember. I'm not likely to forget, am I? Only, you see, I had no idea—if I had, I mightn't have felt so—so awfully forlorn."

Her eyes rested upon me. I can only say of them that they were sweet and lovely, which is saying nothing at all. Sweet and lovely are the words that come to me when I think of her, and they are so lamentably overworked. She seemed to study me with a child-like unconsciousness.

"Yes," she said at last, "I suppose you do feel forlorn. I didn't think of that or —or I might have managed to come to you before."

"That you should have come now," I said, warmly, "is the kindest thing one human being ever did for another."

Again there was the smile, a little to one side of the mouth, wistful, wan.

"Oh no, it isn't. I've really come on my own account." I waited for some explanation of this, but she only went on: "Tell me about yourself. How did you come here? Ethel Rossiter has never really said anything about you. I should like to know."

Her manner had the gentle command that queens and princesses and very rich women unconsciously acquire. I tried to obey her, but found little to say. Uttered to her my facts were so meager. I told her of my father and mother, of my father's mania for old books, of Louise and Victoria and their husbands, of my visits abroad; but I felt her attention wandering. That is, I felt she was interested not in my data, but in me. Halifax and Canada and British army and navy life and rare first editions were outside the range of her ken. Paris she knew; and London she knew; but not from any point of view from which I could speak of them. I could see she was the well-placed American who knows some of the great English houses and all of the great English hotels, but nothing of that Britannic backbone of which I might have been called a rib. She broke in presently, not apropos of anything I was saying, with the words:

"How old are you?"

I told her I was twenty-four.

"I'm twenty-nine."

I said I had understood as much from Mrs. Rossiter, but that I could easily have supposed her no older than myself. This was true. Had there not been that something mournful in her face which simulates maturity I could have thought of her as nothing but a girl. If I stood in awe of her it was only of what I guessed at as a sorrow.

She went on to give me two or three details of her life, with nearly all of which I was familiar through hints from Hugh and Ethel Rossiter.

"We're really Philadelphians, my mother and I. We've lived a good deal in New York, of course, and abroad. I was at school in Paris, too, at the Convent des Abeilles." She wandered on, somewhat inconsequentially, with facts of this sort, when she added, suddenly: "I was to have married some one else."

I knew then that I had the clue to her thought. The marriage she had missed was on her mind. It created an obsession or a broken heart, I wasn't quite sure which. It was what she wanted to talk about, though her glance fell before the spark of intelligence in mine.

THE MARRIAGE SHE HAD MISSED WAS ON HER MIND. IT CREATED AN OBSESSION OR A BROKEN HEART, I WASN'T QUITE SURE WHICH

Since there was nothing I could say in actual words, I merely murmured sympathetically. At the same time there came to me, like the slow breaking of a dawn, an illuminating glimpse of the great J. Howard's life. I seemed to be admitted into its secret, into a perception of its weak spot, more fully than his wife had any notion of. She would never, I was sure, see what she was betraying to me from my point of view. She would never see how she was giving him away. She wouldn't even see how she was giving away herself— she was so sweet, and gentle, and child-like, and unsuspecting.

I don't know for how many seconds her quiet, inconsequential speech trickled on without my being able to follow it. I came to myself again, as it were, on hearing her say:

"And if you do love him, oh, don't give him up!"

I grasped the fact then that I had lost something about Hugh, and did my best to catch up with it.

"I don't mean to, if either of my conditions is fulfilled. You heard what they were."

"Oh, but if I were you I wouldn't make them. That's where I think you're wrong. If you love him—"

"I couldn't steal him from his family, even if I loved him."

"Oh, but it wouldn't be stealing. When two people love each other there's nothing else to think about."

"And yet that might sometimes be dangerous doctrine."

"If there was never any danger there'd never be any courage. And courage is one of the finest things in life."

"Yes, of course; but even courage can carry one very far."

"Nothing can carry us so far as love. I see that now. It's why I'm anxious about poor Hugh. I—I know a man who—who loves a woman whom he—he couldn't marry, and—" She caught herself up. "I'm fond of Hugh, you see, even though he doesn't like me. I wish he understood, that they all understood —that—that it isn't my fault. If I could have had my way—" She righted herself here with a slight change of tense. "If I could have my way, Hugh would marry the woman he's in love with and who's in love with him."

I tried to enroll her decisively on my side.

"So that you don't agree with Mr. Brokenshire."

Her immediate response was to color with a soft, suffused rose-pink like that of the inside of shells. Her eyes grew misty with a kind of helplessness. She looked at me imploringly, and looked away. One might have supposed that she was pleading with me to be let off answering. Nevertheless, when she spoke at last, her words brought me to a new phase of her self-revelation.

"Why aren't you afraid of him?"

"Oh, but I am."

"Yes, but not like—" Again she saved herself. "Yes, but not like—so many people. You may be afraid of him inside, but you fight."

"Any one fights for right."

There was a repetition of the wistful smile, a little to the left corner of the mouth.

"Oh, do they? I wish I did. Or rather I wish I had."

"It's never too late," I declared, with what was meant to be encouragement.

There was a queer little gleam in her eye, like that which comes into the pupil of a startled bird.

"So I've heard some one else say. I suppose it's true—but it frightens me."

I was quite strangely uneasy. Hints of her story came back to me, but I had never heard it completely enough to be able to piece the fragments together. It was new for me to imagine myself called on to protect any one—I needed protection so much for myself!—but I was moved with a protective instinct toward her. It was rather ridiculous, and yet it was so.

"Only one must be sure one is right before one fights, mustn't one?" was all I could think of saying.

She responded dreamily, looking seaward.

"Don't you think there may be worse things than wrong?"

This being so contrary to my pet principles, I answered, emphatically, that I didn't think so at all. I brought out my maxim that if you did right nothing but right could come of it; but she surprised me by saying, simply, "I don't believe that."

I was a little indignant.

"But it's not a matter of believing; it's one of proving, of demonstration."

"I've done right, and wrong came of it."

"Oh, but it couldn't—not in the long run."

"Well, then I did wrong. That's what I've been afraid of, and what—what some one else tells me." If a pet bird could look at you with a challenging expression it was the thing she did. "Now what do you say?"

I really didn't know what to say. I spoke from instinct, and some common sense.

"If one's done wrong, or made a mistake, I suppose the only way one can rectify it is to begin again to do right. Right must have a rectifying power."

"But if you've made a mistake the mistake is there, unless you go back and unmake it. If you don't, isn't it what they call building on a bad foundation?"

"I dare say it is; and yet you can't push a material comparison too far when you're thinking of spiritual things. This is spiritual, isn't it? I suppose one can't really do evil and expect good to come of it; but one can overcome evil with good."

She looked at me with a sweet mistiness.

"I've no doubt that's true, but it's very deep. It's too deep for me." She rose with an air of dismissing the subject, though she continued to speak of it allusively. "You know so much about it. I could see you did from the first. If I

87

was to tell you the whole story—but, of course, I can't do that. No, don't get up. I have to run away, because we're expecting people to tea; but I should have liked staying to talk with you. You're awfully clever, aren't you? I suppose it must be living round in those queer places—Gibraltar, didn't you say? I've seen Gibraltar, but only from the steamer, on the way to Naples. I felt that I was with you from that very first time I saw you. I'd seen you before, of course, with little Gladys, but not to notice you. I never noticed you till I heard that Hugh was in love with you. That was just before Mr. Brokenshire took me over—you remember!—that day. He wanted me to see how easily he could deal with people who opposed him; but I didn't think he succeeded very well. He made you go and sit at a distance. That was to show you he had the power. Did you notice what I did? Oh, I'm glad. I wanted you to understand that if it was a question of love I was—I was with you. You saw that, didn't you? Oh, I'm glad. I must run away now. We've people to tea; but some time, if I can manage it, I'll come again."

She had begun slipping up the path, like a great rose-colored moth in the greenery, when she turned to say:

"I can never do anything for you, I'm too afraid of him; but I'm on your side."

After she had gone I began putting two and two together. What her visit did for me especially was to distract my mind. I got a better perspective on my own small drama in seeing it as incidental to a larger one. That there was a large one here I had no doubt, though I could neither seize nor outline its proportions. As far as I could judge of my visitor I found her dazed by the magnitude of the thing that had happened to her, whatever that was. She was good and kind; she hadn't a thought that wasn't tender; normally she would have been the devoted, clinging type of wife I longed to be myself; and yet some one's passion, or some one's ambition, or both in collusion, had caught her like a bird in a net.

It was perhaps because she was a woman and I was a woman and J. Howard was a man that my reactions concerned themselves chiefly with him. I thought of him throughout the afternoon. I began to get new views of him. I wondered if he knew of himself what I knew. I supposed he did. I supposed he must. He couldn't have been married two or three years to this sweet stricken creature without seeing that her heart wasn't his. Furthermore, he couldn't have beheld, as he and I had beheld that afternoon, the hand that went up palm outward, without divining a horror of his person that was more than a shrinking from his poor contorted eye. For love the contorted eye would have meant more love, since it would have been love with its cognate of pity; but not so that uplifted hand and that instinctive waving of him back.

There was more than an involuntary repulsion in that, more than an instant of abhorrence. What there was he must have discovered, he must have tasted, from the minute he first took her in his arms.

I was sorry for him. I could throw enough of the masculine into my imagination to know how he must adore a creature of such perfected charm. She was the sort of woman men would adore, especially the men whose ideal lies first of all in the physical. For them it would mean nothing that she lacked mentality, that the pendulum of her nature had only a limited swing; that she was as good as she looked would be enough, seeing that she looked like an angel straight out of heaven. In spite of poor J. Howard's kingly suavity I knew he must have minutes of sheer animal despair, of fierce and bitter suffering.

Mrs. Rossiter spoke to me that evening with a suggestion of reprimand, which was letting me off easily. I was so sure of my dismissal, that when I returned to the house from the shore I expected some sort of *lettre de congé*; but I found nothing. I had had supper with Gladys and put her to bed when the maid brought me a message to say that Mrs. Rossiter would like me to come down and see her dress, as she was going out to dinner.

I was admiring the dress, which was a new one, when she said, rather fretfully:

"I wish you wouldn't talk like that to father. It upsets him so."

I was adjusting a slight fullness at the back, which made it the easier for me to answer.

"I wouldn't if he didn't talk like that to me. What can I do? I have to say something."

She was peering into the cheval glass over her shoulder, giving her attention to two things at once.

"I mean your saying you expected both of those preposterous things to happen. Of course, you don't—nor either of them—and it only rubs him up the wrong way."

I was too meek now to argue the point. Besides, I was preoccupied with the widening interests in which I found myself involved. To probe the security of my position once more, I said:

"I wonder you stand it—that you don't send me away."

She was still twisting in front of the cheval glass.

"Don't you think that shoulder-strap is loose? It really looks as if the whole thing would slip off me. If he can stand it I can," she added, as a matter of secondary concern.

"Oh, then he can stand it." I felt the shoulder-strap. "No, I think it's all right, if you don't wriggle too much."

"I'm sure it's going to come down—and there I shall be. He has to stand it, don't you see, or let you think that you wound him?"

I was frankly curious.

"Do I wound him?"

"He'd never let you know it if you did. The fact that he ignores you and lets you stay on with me is the only thing by which I can judge. If you didn't hurt him at all he'd tell me to send you about your business." She turned from the glass. "Well, if you say that strap is all right I suppose it must be, but I don't feel any too sure." She was picking up her gloves and her fan which the maid had laid out, when she said, suddenly: "If you're so keen on getting married, for goodness' sake why don't you take that young Strangways?"

My sensation can only be compared to that of a person who has got a terrific blow on the head from a trip-hammer. I seemed to wonder why I hadn't been crushed or struck dead. As it was, I felt that I could never move again from the spot on which I stood. I was vaguely conscious of something outraged within me and yet was too stunned to resent it. I could only gasp, feebly, after what seemed an interminable time: "In the first place, I'm not so awfully keen on getting married—"

She was examining her gloves.

"There, that stupid Séraphine has put me out two lefts. No, she hasn't; it's all right. Stuff, my dear! Every girl is keen on getting married."

"And then," I stammered on, "Mr. Strangways has never given me the chance."

"Oh, well, he will. Do hand me my wrap, like a love." I was putting the wrap over her shoulders as she repeated: "Oh, well, he will. I can tell by the way he looks at you. It would be ever so much more suitable. Jim says he'll be a first-class man in time—if you don't rush in like an idiot and marry Hugh."

"I may marry Hugh," I tried to say, loftily, "but I hope I sha'n't do it like an idiot."

She swept toward the stairway, but she had left me with subjects for thought not only for that evening, but for the next day and the next. Now that the first shock was over I managed to work up the proper sense of indignity. I told myself I was hurt and offended. She shouldn't have mentioned such a thing. I wouldn't have stood it from one of my own sisters. I had never thought of

Larry Strangways in any such way, and to do so disturbed our relations. To begin with, I wasn't in love with him; and to end with, he was too poor. Not that I was looking for a rich husband; but neither was I a lunatic. It would be years before he could think of marrying, if there were no other consideration; and in the mean time there was Hugh.

There was Hugh with his letters from Boston, full of high ambitious hopes. Cousin Andrew Brew had written from Bar Harbor that he was coming to town in a day or two and would give him the interview he demanded. Already Hugh had his eye on a little house on Beacon Hill—so like a corner of Mayfair, he wrote, if Mayfair stood on an eminence—in which we could be as snug as two love-birds. I was composing in my mind the letter I should write to my aunt in Halifax, asking to be allowed to come back for the wedding.

I filled in the hours wondering how Larry Strangways looked at me when there was only Mrs. Rossiter as spectator. I knew how he looked at me when I was looking back—it was with that gleaming smile which defied you to see behind it, as the sun defies you to see behind its rays. But I wanted to know how he looked at me when my head was turned another way; to know how the sun appears when you view it through a telescope that nullifies its defensive. For that I had only my imagination, since he had obtained two or three days' leave to go to New York to see his new employer. He had warned me to betray no hint as to the new employer's name, since there was a feud between the Brokenshire clan and Stacy Grainger which I connected vaguely with the story I had heard of Mrs. Brokenshire.

Then on the fourth day Hugh came back. He appeared as he had on saying good-by, while I was breakfasting with Gladys in the open air and Broke was with his mother. Hugh was more pallid than when he went away; he was positively woe-begone. Everything that was love in me leaped into flame at sight of his honest, sorry face.

I think I can tell his story best by giving it in my own words, in the way of direct narration. He didn't tell it to me all at once, but bit by bit, as new details occurred to him. The picture was slow in printing itself on my mind, but when I got it it was with satisfactory exactitude.

He had been three days at the hotel in Boston before learning that Cousin Andrew Brew was actually in town and would see him at the bank at eleven on a certain morning. Hugh was on the moment. The promptitude with which his relative sprang up in his seat, somewhat as if impelled by a piece of mechanism, was truly cordial. Not less was the handshake and the formula of greeting. The sons of J. Howard Brokenshire were always welcome guests among their Boston kin, on whom they shed a pleasant luster of metropolitan glory. While the Brews and Borrodailes prided themselves on what they called their Boston provinciality and didn't believe to be provinciality at all, they enjoyed the New York connection.

"Hello, Hugh! Glad to see you. Come in. Sit down. Looking older than when I saw you last. Growing a mustache. Not married yet? Sit down and tell us all about it. What can I do for you? Sit down."

Hugh took the comfortable little upright arm-chair that stood at the corner of his cousin's desk, while the latter resumed the seat of honor. Knowing that the banker's time was valuable, and feeling that he would reveal his aptitude for business by going to the point at once, the younger man began his tale. He had just reached the fact that he had fallen in love with a little girl on whose merits he wouldn't enlarge, since all lovers had the same sort of things to say, though he was surer of his data than others of his kind, when there was a tinkle at the desk telephone.

"Excuse me."

During the conversation in which Cousin Andrew then engaged Hugh was able to observe the long-established, unassuming comfort of this friendly office, which suggested the cozy air that hangs about the smoking-rooms of good old English inns. There was a warm worn carpet on the floor; deep leather arm-chairs showed the effect of contact with two generations of moneyed backs; on the walls the lithographed heads of Brews and Borrodailes bore witness to the firm's respectability. In the atmosphere a faint odor of tobacco emphasized the human associations.

Cousin Andrew emphasized them, too. "Now!" He put down the receiver and turned to Hugh with an air of relief at being able to give him his attention. He was a tall, thin man with a head like a nut. It would have been an expressionless nut had it not been for a facile tight-lipped smile that creased his face as stretching creases rubber. Coming and going rapidly, it gave him the appearance of mirth, creating at each end of a long, mobile mouth two concentric semicircles cutting deep into the cheeks that would have been of value to a low comedian. A slate-colored morning suit, a white piqué edge to the opening of the waistcoat, a slate-colored tie with a pearl in it, emphasized the union of dignity and lightness which were the keynotes to Cousin Andrew's character. Blended as they were, they formed a delightfully debonair combination, bringing down to your own level a man who was somebody in the world of finance. It was part of his endearing quality that he liked you to see him as a jolly good fellow no whit better than yourself. He was fond of gossip and of the lighter topics of the moment. He was also fond of dancing, and frequented most of the gatherings, private and public, for the cultivation of that art which was the vogue of the year before the Great War. With his tall, limber figure he passed for less than his age of forty-three till you got him at close quarters.

On the genial "Now!" in which there was an inflection of command Hugh went on with his tale, telling of his breach with his father and his determination to go into business for himself.

"I ought to be independent, anyhow, at my age," he declared. "I've my own views, and it's only right to confess to you that I'm a bit of a Socialist. That won't make any difference, however, to our working together, Cousin Andrew, for, to make a long story short, I've looked in to tell you that I've come to the place where I should like to accept your kind offer."

The statement was received with cheerful detachment, while Cousin Andrew threw himself forward with his arms on his desk, rubbing his long, thin hands together.

"My kind offer? What was that?"

Hugh was slightly dashed.

"About my coming to you if ever I wanted to go into business."

"Oh! You're going into business?"

Hugh named the places and dates at which, during the past few years, Cousin Andrew had offered his help to his young kinsman if ever it was needed.

Cousin Andrew tossed himself back in his chair with one of his brisk, restless movements.

"Did I say that? Well, if I did I'll stick to it." There was another tinkle at the telephone. "Excuse me."

Hugh had time for reflection and some irritation. He had not expected to be thrust into the place of a petitioner, or to have to make explanations galling to his pride. He had counted not only on his cousinship, but on his position in the world as J. Howard Brokenshire's son. It seemed to him that Cousin Andrew was disposed to undervalue that.

"I don't want to hold you to anything you don't care for, Cousin Andrew," he began, when his relative had again put the receiver aside, "but I understood —"

"Oh, that's all right. I've no doubt I said it. I do recall something of the sort, vaguely, at a time when I thought your father might want— In any case we can fix you up. Sure to be something you can do. When'd you like to begin?"

Hugh expressed his willingness to be put into office at once.

"Just so. Turn you over to old Williamson. He licks the young ones into shape. Suppose your father'll think it hard of us to go against him. But on the other hand he may be pleased—he'll know you're in safe hands."

It was a delicate thing for Hugh to attempt, but as he was going into business not from an irresistible impulse toward a financial career, but in order to make enough money to marry on, he felt obliged to ask, in such terms as he could command, how much money he should make.

"Just so!" Cousin Andrew took up the receiver again. "Want to speak to Mr. Williamson.... Oh, Williamson, how much is Duffers getting now? ... And how much before that? ... Good! Thanks!"

The result of these investigations was communicated to Hugh. He should receive Duffers's pay, and when he had earned it should come in for Duffers's promotion. The immediate effect was to make him look startled and blank. "What?" was his only question; but it contained several shades of incredulity.

Cousin Andrew took this dismay in good part.

"Why, what did you expect?"

Hugh could only stammer:

"I thought it would be more."

"How much more?"

Hugh sought an answer that wouldn't betray the ludicrous figure of his hopes.

"Well, enough to live on as a married man at least."

The banker's good nature was proved by the creases of his rubber smile.

"What did you think you'd be worth to us—with no backing from your father?"

The question was of the kind commonly called a poser. Hugh had not, so I understood from him, hitherto thought of his entering his kinsfolks' banking-house as primarily a matter of earning capacity. It wasn't to be like working for "any old firm." He had prefigured it as becoming a component part of a machine that turned out money of which he would get his share, that share being in proportion to the dignity of the house itself and bearing a relation to his blood connection with the dominating partners. When Cousin Andrew had repeated his question Hugh was obliged to reply:

"I wasn't thinking of that so much as of what you'd be worth to me."

"We could be worth a good deal to you in time."

There was a ray of hope.

"How long a time?"

"Oh, twenty or thirty years, perhaps, if you work and save. Of course, if you had capital to bring in—but you haven't, have you? Didn't Cousin Sophy, your mother, leave everything to your father? I thought so. Mind you, I'm putting out of the question all thought of your father's coming round and putting money in for you. I'm talking of the thing on the ground on which you've put it."

Hugh had no heart to resent the quirks and grimaces in Cousin Andrew's smile. He had all he could do in taking his leave in a way to save his face and cast the episode behind him. The banker lent himself to this effort with good-humored grace, accompanying his relative to the door of the room, where he shook him by the shoulder as he turned the knob.

"Thought you'd go right in as a director? Not the first youngster who's had that idea, and you'll not be the last. Good-by. Let me hear from you if you change your mind." He called after him, as the door was about to close: "Best try to fix it up with your father, Hugh. As for the girl—well, there'll be others, and more in your line."

CHAPTER IX

On that first morning I got no more than the gist of what had happened during Hugh's visit to his cousin Andrew Brew. Hugh announced it in fact by a metaphor as soon as we had exchanged greetings and he had sat down at the table with his arm over Gladys's shoulder.

"Well, little Alix, I got it where the chicken got the ax."

"Where was that?" I asked, innocently, for the figure of speech was new to me.

"In the neck."

Neither of us laughed. His tone was so lugubrious as to preclude laughing. But I understood. I may say that by the time he had given me the outline of what he had to say I understood more than he. I might have seen poor Hugh's limitations before; but I never had. During the old life in Halifax I had known plenty of young men brought up in comfort who couldn't earn a living when the time came to do it. If I had never classed Hugh among the number, it was because the Brokenshires were all so rich that I supposed they must have some secret prescription for wringing money from the air. Besides, Hugh was an American; and American and money were words I was accustomed to pronounce together. I never questioned his ability to have any reasonable income he named—till now. Now I began to see him as he must have seen himself during those first few minutes after turning his back on the parental haven, alone and in the dark.

I cannot say that for the moment I had any of the qualms of fear. My yearning over him was too motherly for that. I wanted to comfort and, as far as possible, to encourage him. Something within me whispered, too, the words, "It's going to be up to me." I meant—or that which spoke in me meant—that the whole position was reversed. I had been taking my ease hitherto, believing that the strong young man who had asked me to marry him would do the necessary work. It was to be up to him. My part was to be the passive bliss of having some one to love me and maintain me. That Hugh loved me I knew; that in one way or another he would be able to maintain me I took for granted. With a Brokenshire, I assumed, that would be the last of cares. And now I saw in a flash that I was wrong; that I who was nothing but a parasite by nature would somehow have to give my strong young man support.

When all was said that he could say at the moment I took the responsibility of sending Gladys indoors with the maid who was waiting on the table, after which I asked Hugh to walk down the lawn with me. A stone balustrade ran above the Cliff Walk, and here was a bit of shrubbery where no one could observe us from the house, while passers on the Cliff Walk could see us only by looking upward. At that hour in the morning even they were likely to be rare.

"Hugh, darling," I said, "this is becoming very, very serious. You're throwing yourself out of house and home and your father's good-will for my sake. We must think about it, Hugh—"

His answer was to seize me in his arms—we were sufficiently screened from view—and crush his lips against mine in a way that made speech impossible.

Again I must make a confession. It was his doing that sort of thing that paralyzed my judgment. You will blame me, perhaps, but, oh, reader, have you any idea of what it is never to have had a man wild to kiss you before? Never before to have had any one adore you? Never before to have been the greatest of all blessings to so much as the least among his brethren? The experience was new to me. I had no rule of thumb by which to measure it. I could only think that the man who wanted me with so mad a desire must have me, no matter what reserves I might have preferred to make on my own account.

I struggled, however, and with some success. For the first time I clearly perceived that occasions might arise in which, between love and marriage, one might have to make a distinction. Ethel Rossiter's dictum came back to me: "People can't go about marrying every one they love, now can they?" It came to me as a terrible possibility that I might be doomed to love Hugh all my life, and equally doomed to refuse him. If I didn't, the responsibilities would be "up to me." If besides loving him I were to accept him and marry him, it would be for me to see that the one possible condition was fulfilled. I should have to bring J. Howard to his knees.

When he got breath to say anything it was with a mere hot muttering into my face, as he held me with my head thrown back:

"I know what I'm doing, little Alix. You mustn't ask me to count the cost. The cost only makes you the more precious. Since I have to suffer for you I'll suffer, but I'll never give you up. Do you take me for a fellow who'd weigh money or comfort in the balances with you?"

"No, Hugh," I whispered. His embrace was enough to strangle me.

"Well, then, never ask me to think about this thing again, I've thought all I'm going to. As I mean to get you anyhow, little Alix, you may as well promise now, this very minute, that whatever happens you'll be my wife."

But I didn't promise. First I got him to release me on the ground that some bathers, after a dip at Eastons Beach, were going by, with their heads on a level with our feet. Then I asked the natural question:

"What do you think of doing now?"

He said he was going to let no mushrooms spring in his footsteps, and that he was taking a morning train for New York. He talked about bankers and brokers and moneyed things in general in a way I couldn't follow, though I could see that in spite of Cousin Andrew Brew's rejection he still expected great things of himself. Like me, he seemed to feel that there was a faculty for conjuring money in the very name of Brokenshire. Never having known what it was to be without as much money as he wanted, never having been given to suppose that such an eventuality could come to pass, it was perhaps not strange that he should consider his power of commanding a large income to be in the nature of things. Bankers and brokers would be glad to have him as their associate from the mere fact that he was his father's son.

I endeavored to throw a cup of cold water on too much certainty, by saying:

"But, Hugh, dear, won't you have to begin at the beginning? Wasn't that what your cousin Andrew Brew—?"

"Cousin Andrew Brew is an ass. He's one great big Boston stick-in-the-mud. He wouldn't know which side his bread was buttered on, not if it was buttered on both."

"Still," I persisted, "you'll have to begin at the beginning."

"Well, I shouldn't be the first."

"No, but you might be the first to do it with a clog round his feet in the shape of a person like me. How many years did your cousin say—twenty or thirty, wasn't it?"

"R-rot, little Alix!" He brought out the interjection with a contemptuous roll. "It might be twenty or thirty years for a numskull like Duffers, but for me! There are ways by which a man who's in the business already, as you might say, goes skimming over the ground the common herd have to tramp. Look at the gentlemen-rankers in your own army. They enlist as privates, and in two or three years they're in the officers' mess with a commission. That comes of their education and—"

"That's often true, I admit. I've known of several cases in my own experience. But even two or three years—"

"Wouldn't you wait for me?"

He asked the question with a sharpness that gave me something like a stab.

"Yes, of course, Hugh, if I promised you. And yet to bind you by such a promise doesn't seem to me fair."

"I'll take care of that," he declared, manfully. "As a matter of fact, when father sees how determined I am, he'll only be too happy to do the handsome thing and come down with the brass."

"You think he's bluffing then?" I threw some conviction into my tone as I added, "I don't."

"He's not bluffing to his own knowledge; but he is—"

"To yours. But isn't it his knowledge that we've got to go by? We must expect the worst, even if we hope for the best."

"And what it all comes to is—"

"Is that you're facing a very hard time, Hugh, and I don't feel that I can accept the responsibility of encouraging you to do it."

"But, good Lord, Alix, you're not encouraging me. It's the other way round. You're a perfect wet blanket; you're an ice-water shower. I'm doing this thing on my own—"

"You know, Hugh, I've seen your father since you went away."

His face brightened.

"Good! And did he show any signs of tacking to the wind?"

"Not a bit. He said you would be ruined, and that I should ruin you."

"The deuce you will! That's where he's got the wrong number, poor old dad! I hope you told him you would marry me—and let him have it straight."

I made no reply to that, going on to tell him all that was said as to bringing J. Howard to his knees.

He roared with ironic laughter.

"You did have the gall!"

"Then you think they'll never, never accept me?"

"Not that way; not beforehand."

Hot rage rose within me, against him and them and this scorn of my personality.

"I think they will."

"Not on your life! Dad wouldn't do it, not if I was on my death-bed and needed you to come and raise me up. Milly is the only one; and even she thinks I'm the craziest idiot—"

"Very well, then, Hugh," I said, quickly; "I'm afraid we must consider it all —"

He gathered me into his arms as he had done before, and once more stopped my protests. Once more, too, I yielded to this masculine argument.

"For you and me there's nothing but love," he murmured, with his cheek pressed close against mine.

"Oh no, Hugh," I managed to say, when I had struggled free. "There's honor —and perhaps there's pride." It gave some relief to what I conceived of as the humiliation he unconsciously heaped on me to be able to add: "As a matter of fact, pride and honor, in me, are as inseparable as the oxygen and hydrogen that go to make up water."

He was obliged to leave it there, since he had no more than the time to catch his train for New York. It was, however, the sense of pride and honor that calmed my nerves when Mrs. Rossiter asked me to take little Gladys to see her grandfather in the afternoon. I had done it from time to time all through the summer, but not since Hugh had declared his love for me. If I went now, I reasoned, it would have to be on a new footing; and if it was on a new footing something might come of the visit in spite of my fears.

We started a little after three, as Gladys had to be back in time for her early supper and bed. Chips, the wire-haired terrier, was nominally at our heels, but actually nosing the shrubbery in front of us, or scouring the lawns on our right with a challenging bark to any of his kind who might be within earshot to come down and contest our passage.

"*Qu'il est drôle, ce Chips! N'est-ce-pas, mademoiselle?*" Gladys would exclaim from time to time, to which I would make some suitable and instructive rejoinder.

Her hand was in mine; her eyes as they laughed up at me were of the color of the blue convolvulus. In her little smocked liberty silk, with a leghorn hat trimmed with a wreath of tiny roses, she made me yearn for that bassinet between which and myself there were such stormy seas to cross. Everything was to be up to me. That was the great solemnity from which my mind couldn't get away. I was to be the David to confront Goliath, without so much as a sling or a stone. What I was to do, and how I was to do it, I knew no more than I knew of commanding an army. I could only take my stand on the maxim of which I was making a foundation-stone. I went so far as to believe that if I did right more right would unfold itself. It would be like following a trail through a difficult wood, a trail of which you observe all the notches and steps and signs, sometimes with misgivings, often with the fear that you're astray, but on which a moment arrives when you see with delight that you're coming out to the clearing. So I argued as I prattled with Gladys of such things as were in sight, of ships and lobster-pots and little dogs, giving her a new word as occasion served, and trying to keep my mind from terrors and remote anticipations.

If you know Newport at all you know J. Howard Brokenshire's place in the neighborhood of Ochre Point. Anyone would name it as you passed by. J. Howard didn't build the house; he bought it from some people who, it seemed, hadn't found in Newport the hospitality of which they were in search. It is gloomy and fortress-like, as if the architect had planned a Palazzo Strozzi which he hadn't the courage to carry out. That it is incongruous with its surroundings goes without saying; but then it is not more incongruous than anything else. I had been long enough in America to see that for the man who could build on American soil a house which would have some relation to its site—as they can do in Mexico, and as we do to a lesser degree in Canada— fame and fortune would be in store.

The entrance hall was baronial and richly Italianate. One's first impressions were of gilding and red damask. When one's eye lighted on a chest or settle, one could smell the stale incense in a Sienese or Pisan sacristy. At the foot of the great stairway ebony slaves held gilded torches in which were electric lights.

Both the greyhounds came sniffing to meet Chips, and J. Howard, who had seen our approach across the lawn as we came from the Cliff Walk, emerged from the library to welcome his grandchild. He wore a suit of light-gray check, and was as imposingly handsome as usual. Gladys ran to greet him with a childish cry. On seizing her he tossed her into the air and kissed her.

I stood in the middle of the hall, waiting. On previous occasions I had done the same thing; but then I had not been, as one might say, "introduced." I wondered if he would acknowledge the introduction now or give me a glance. But he didn't. Setting Gladys down, he took her by the hand and returned to the library.

There was nothing new in this. It had happened to me before. Left like an empty motor-car till there was need for me again, I had sometimes seated myself in one of the huge ecclesiastical hall chairs, and sometimes, if the door chanced to be open, had wandered out to the veranda. As it was open this afternoon, I strolled toward the glimpse of green lawn, and the sparkle of blue sea which gleamed at the end of the hall.

It was a possibility I had foreseen. Mrs. Brokenshire might be there. I might get into further touch with the mystery of her heart.

Mrs. Brokenshire was not on the veranda, but Mrs. Billing was. She was seated in a low easy-chair, reading a French novel, and had been smoking cigarettes. An inlaid Oriental taboret, on which were a gold cigarette-case and ash-tray, stood beside her on the red-tiled floor.

I had forgotten all about her, as seemingly she had forgotten about me. Her surprise in seeing me appear was not greater than mine at finding her. Instinctively she took up her lorgnette, which was lying in her lap, but put it down without using it.

"So it's you," was her greeting.

"I beg your pardon, madam," I stammered, respectfully. "I didn't know there was anybody here."

I was about to withdraw when she said, commandingly:

"Wait." I waited, while she went on: "You're a little spitfire. Did you know it?"

The voice was harsh, with the Quaker drawl I have noticed in the older generation of Philadelphians; but the tone wasn't hostile. On the contrary, there was something in it that invited me to play up. I played up, demurely, however, saying, with a more emphatic respectfulness:

"No, madam; I didn't."

"Well, you can know it now. Who are you?" She made the quaint little gesture with which I have seen English princesses summon those they wished to talk to. "Come over here where I can get a look at you."

I moved nearer, but she didn't ask me to sit down. In answer to her question I said, simply, "I'm a Canadian."

"Oh, a Canadian! That's neither fish, flesh, nor fowl. It's nothing."

"No, madam, nothing but a point of view."

"What do you mean by that?"

I repeated something of my father's:

"The point of view of the Englishman who understands America or of the American who understands England, as one chooses to put it. The Canadian is the only person who does both."

"Oh, indeed? I'm not a Canadian—and yet I flatter myself I know my England pretty well."

I made so bold as to smile dimly.

"Knowing and understanding are different things, madam, aren't they? The Canadian understands America because he is an American; he understands England because he is an Englishman. It's only of him that that can be said. You're quite right when you label him a point of view rather than a citizen or a subject."

"I didn't label him anything of the kind. I don't know anything about him, and I don't care. What are you besides being a Canadian?"

"Nothing, madam," I said, humbly.

"Nothing? What do you mean?"

"I mean that there's nothing about me, that I have or am, that I don't owe to my country."

"Oh, stuff! That's the way we used to talk in the United States forty years ago."

"That's the way we talk in Canada still, madam—and feel."

"Oh, well, you'll get over it as we did—when you're more of a people."

"Most of us would prefer to be less of a people, and not get over it."

She put up her lorgnette.

"Who was your father? What sort of people do you come from?"

I tried to bring out my small store of personal facts, but she paid them no attention. When I said that my father had been a judge of the Supreme Court of Nova Scotia I might have been calling him a voivode of Montenegro or the president of a zemstvo. It was too remote from herself for her mind to take in. I could see her, however, examining my features, my hands, my dress, with the shrewd, sharp eyes of a connoisseur in feminine appearance.

She broke into the midst of my recital with the words:

"You can't be in love with Hugh Brokenshire."

Fearing attack from an unexpected quarter, I clasped my hands with some emotion.

"Oh, but, madam, why not?"

The reply nearly knocked me down.

"Because you're too sensible a girl. He's as stupid as an owl."

"He's very good and kind," was all I could find to say.

"Yes; but what's that? A girl like you needs more than a man who's only good and kind. Heavens above, you'll want some spice in your life!"

I maintained my meek air as I said:

"I could do without the spice if I could be sure of bread and butter."

"Oh, if you're marrying for a home let me tell you you won't get it. Hugh'll never be able to offer you one, and his father wouldn't let him if he was."

I decided to be bold.

"But you heard what I said the other day, madam. I expect his father to come round."

She uttered the queer cackle that was like a hen when it crows.

"Oh, you do, do you? You don't know Howard Brokenshire. You could break him more easily than you could bend him—and you can't break him. Good Lord, girl, I've tried!"

"But I haven't," I returned, quietly. "Now I'm going to."

"How? What with? You can't try if you've nothing to try on."

"I have."

"For Heaven's sake—what?"

I was going to say, "Right"; but I knew it would sound sententious. I had been sententious enough in talking about my country. Now I only smiled.

"You must let me keep that as a secret," I answered, mildly.

She gave herself what I can only call a hitch in her chair.

"Then may I be there to see."

"I hope you may be, madam."

"Oh, I'll come," she cackled. "Don't worry about that. Just let me know. You'll have to fight like the devil. I suppose you know that."

I replied that I did.

"And when it's all over you'll have got nothing for your pains."

"I shall have had the fight."

She looked hard at me before speaking.

"Good girl!" The tone was that of a spectator who calls out, "Good hit!" or, "Good shot!" at a game. "If that's all you want—"

"No; I want Hugh."

"Then I hope you won't get him. He's as big a dolt as his father, and that's saying a great deal." Terrified, I glanced over my shoulder at the house, but she went on imperturbably: "Oh, I know he's in there; but what do I care? I'm not saying anything behind his back that I haven't said to his face. He doesn't bear me any malice, either, I'll say that for him."

"Nobody could—" I began, deferentially.

"Nobody had better. But that's neither here nor there. All I'm telling you is to have nothing to do with Hugh Brokenshire. Never mind the money; what you need is a husband with brains. Don't I know? Haven't I been through it? My husband was kind and good, just like Hugh Brokenshire—and, O Lord! The sins of the father are visited on the children, too. Look at my daughter—pretty as a picture and not the brains of a white mouse." She nodded at me fiercely, "You're my kind. I can see that. Mind what I say—and be off."

She turned abruptly to her book, hitching her chair a little away from me. Accepting my dismissal, I said in the third person, as though I was speaking to a royalty:

"Madam flatters me too much; but I'm glad I intruded, for the minute, just to hear her say that."

I had made my courtesy and reached the door leading inward when she called after me:

"You're a puss. Do you know it?"

Not feeling it necessary to respond in words, I merely smiled over my shoulder and entered the house.

In one of the big chairs I waited a half-hour before J. Howard came out of the library with his grandchild. He had given her a doll which she hugged in her left arm, while her right hand was in his. The farewell scene was pretty, and took place in the middle of the hall.

"Now run away," he said, genially, after much kissing and petting, "and give my love to mamma."

He might have been shooing the sweet thing off into the air. There was no reference whatever to any one to take care of her. His eyes rested on me, but only as they rested on the wall behind me. I must say it was well done—if one has to do that sort of thing at all. Feeling myself, as his regard swept me, no more than a part of the carved ecclesiastical chair to which I stood clinging, I wondered how I was ever to bring this man to seeing me.

I debated the question inwardly while I chatted with Gladys on the way homeward. I was obliged, in fact, to brace myself, to reason it out again that right was self-propagating and wrong necessarily sterile. Right I figured as a way which seemed to finish in a blind alley or cul-de-sac, but which, as one neared what seemed to be its end, led off in a new direction. Nearing the end of that there would be still a new lead, and so one would go on.

And, sure enough, the new lead came within the next half-hour, though I didn't recognize it for what it was till afterward.

CHAPTER X

As we passed the Jack Brokenshire cottage, Larry Strangways and Broke, with Noble, the collie, bounding beside them, came racing down the lawn to overtake us. It was natural then that for the rest of the way Chips and Noble should form one company, Broke and his sister another, while we two elders strolled along behind them.

It was the hour of the day for strolling. The mellow afternoon light was of the kind that brings something new into life, something we should be glad to keep if we knew how to catch it. It was not merely that grass and leaf and sea had a shimmer of gold on them. There was a sweet enchantment in the atmosphere, a poignant wizardry, a suggestion of emotions both higher and lower than those of our poor mortal scale. They made one reluctant to hurry one's footsteps, and slow in the return to that sheerly human shelter we call home. All along the path, down among the rocks, out in the water, up on the lawns, there were people, gentle and simple alike, who lingered and idled and paused to steep themselves in this magic.

I have to admit that we followed their example. Anything served as an excuse for it, the dogs and the children doing the same from a similar instinct. I got the impression, too, that my companion was less in the throes of the discretion we had imposed upon ourselves, for the reason that his term as a mere educational lackey was drawing to a close. It had, in fact, only two more days to run. Then August would come and he would desert us.

As it might be my last opportunity to surprise him into looking at me in the way Mrs. Rossiter had observed, I kept my eye on him pretty closely. I cannot say that I detected any change that flattered me. Tall and straight and splendidly poised, he was as smilingly impenetrable as ever. Like Howard Brokenshire, he betrayed no wound, even if I had inflicted one. It was a little exasperating. I was more than piqued.

I told him I hadn't heard of his return from New York and asked how he had fared. His reply was enthusiastic. He had seen Stacy Grainger and was eager to be his henchman.

"He's got that about him," he declared, "that would make anybody glad to work for him."

He described his personal appearance, brawny and spare with the attributes of race. It was an odd comment on the laws of heredity that his grandfather was said to have begun life as a peddler, and yet there he was a *grand seigneur* to the finger-tips. I said that Howard Brokenshire was also a *grand seigneur*, to which he replied that Howard Brokenshire was a monument. American conditions had raised him, and on those conditions he stood as a statue on its pedestal. His position was so secure that all he had to do was stand. It was for this reason that he could be so dictatorial. He was safely fastened to his base; nothing short of seismic convulsion of the whole economic world was likely to knock him off. In the course of that conversation I learned more of the origin of the Brokenshire fortunes than I had ever before heard.

It was the great-grandfather of J. Howard who apparently had laid the foundation-stone on which later generations built so well. That patriarch, so I understood, had been a farmer in the Connecticut Valley. His method of finance was no more esoteric than that of lending out small sums of money at a high rate of interest. Occasionally he took mortgages on his neighbors' farms, with the result that he became in time something of a landed proprietor. When the suburbs of a city had spread over one of the possessions thus acquired, the foundation-stone to which I have referred might have been considered well and truly laid.

About the year 1830, his son migrated to New York. The firm of Meek & Brokenshire, of which the fame was to go through two continents, was founded when Van Buren was in the presidential seat and Victoria just coming to the throne. It seems there was a Meek in those days, though at the time of which I am writing nothing remained of him but a syllable.

It was after the Civil War, however, when the grandson of the Connecticut Valley veteran was in power, that the house of Meek & Brokenshire forged to the front rank among financial agencies. It formed European affiliations. It became the financial representative of a great European power. John H. Brokenshire, whose name was distinguished from that of his more famous son only by a distribution of initials, had a house at Hyde Park Corner as well as one in New York. He was the first American banker to become something of an international magnate. The development of his country made him so. With the vexed questions of slavery and secession settled, with the phenomenal expansion of the West, with the freer uses of steam and electricity, with the tightening of bonds between the two hemispheres, that pedestal was being raised on which J. Howard was to pose with such decorative effectiveness.

His posing began on his father's death in the year 1898. Up to that time he had represented the house in England, the post being occupied now by his younger brother James. Polished manners, a splendid appearance, and an authoritative air imported to New York a touch of the Court of St. James's. Mrs. Billing had called him a dolt. Perhaps he was one. If so he was a dolt raised up and sustained by all that was powerful in the United States. It was with these vast influences rather than with the man himself that, as Larry Strangways talked, I began to see I was in conflict.

In Stacy Grainger, I gathered, the contemporaneous development of the country had produced something different, just as the same piece of ground will grow an oak or a rose-bush, according to the seed. People with a taste for social antithesis called him the grandson of a peddler. Mr. Strangways considered this description below the level of the ancestral Grainger's occupation. In the days of scattered farms and difficult communications throughout Illinois, Wisconsin, and Minnesota he might better have been termed an itinerant merchant. He was the traveling salesman who delivered the goods. His journeys being made by river boats and ox-teams, he began to see the necessity of steam. He was of the group who projected the system of railways, some of which failed and some of which succeeded, through the regions west of Lake Superior. Later he forsook the highways for a more feverish life in the incipient Chicago. His wandering years having given him an idea of the value of this focal point, he put his savings into land. The phoenix rise of the city after the great fire made him a man of some wealth. Out of the financial crash of 1873 he became richer. His son grew richer still on the panic of 1893, when he, too, descended on New York. It was he who became a power on the Stock Exchange and bought the big house with which parts of my narrative will have to do.

All I want to say now is that as I strolled with Larry Strangways along that sunny walk, and as he ran on about Brokenshires and Graingers, I got my first bit of insight into the immense American romance which the nineteenth century unfolded. I saw it was romance, gigantic, race-wide. For the first time in my life I realized that there were other tales to make men proud besides the story of the British Empire.

I could see that Larry Strangways was proud—proud and anxious. I had never seen this side of him before. Pride was in the way in which he held his fine young head; there was anxiety in his tone, and now and then in the flash of his eye, in spite of his efforts not to be too serious.

It was about the country that he talked—its growth, its vastness. Even as recently as when he was a boy it was still a manageable thing, with a population reckoned at no more than seventy or eighty millions. It had been homogeneous in spirit if not in blood, and those who had come from other lands, and been welcomed and adopted, accepted their new situation with some gratitude. Patriotism was still a word with a meaning, and if it now and then became spread-eagleism it was only as the waves when thrown too far inland become froth. The wave was the thing and it hadn't ebbed.

"And do you think it has ebbed now?" I asked.

He didn't answer this question directly.

"We're becoming colossal. We shall soon count our people by the hundred million and more. Of these relatively few will have got our ideals. Some will reject them. There are mutterings already of other standards to which we must be taught to conform. Some of our own best people of pure Anglo-Saxon descent are losing heart and renouncing and denouncing the democratic tradition, though they've nothing to put in its place. And we're growing so huge—with a hugeness that threatens to make us lethargic."

I tried to be encouraging.

"You seem to me anything but that."

"National lethargy can easily exist side by side with individual energy. Take China, for instance. There are few peoples in the world more individually diligent than the Chinese; and yet when it comes to national stirring it's a country as difficult to move as an unwieldy overfed giant. It's flabby and nerveless and inert. It's spread half over Asia, and it has the largest and most industrious population in the world; and yet it's a congeries of inner weaknesses, and a prey to any one who chooses to attack it."

"And you think this country is on the way to being the China of the west?"

"I don't say on the way. There's danger of it. In proportion as we too become unwieldy and overfed, the circulation of that national impulse which is like blood grows slower. The elephant is a heavily moving beast in comparison with the lion."

"But it's the more intelligent," I argued, still with a disposition to be encouraging.

"Intelligence won't save it when the lion leaps on its back."

"Then what will?"

"That's what we want to find out."

"And how are you going to do it?"

"By men. We've come to a time when the country is going to need stronger men than it ever had, and more of them."

I suppose it is because I am a woman that I have to bring all questions to the personal.

"And is your Stacy Grainger going to be one?"

He walked on a few paces without replying, his head in the air.

110

"No," he said, at last, "I don't think so. He's got a weakness."

"What kind of weakness?"

"I'm not going to tell you," he laughed. "It's enough to say that it's one which I think will put him out of commission for the job." He gave me some inkling, however, of what he meant when he added: "The country's coming to a place where it will need disinterested men, and whole-hearted men, and clean-hearted men, if it's going to pull through. It's extraordinary how deficient we've been in leaders who've had any of these characteristics, to say nothing of all three."

"Is the United States singular in that?"

He spoke in a half-jesting tone probably to hide the fact that he was so much in earnest.

"No; perhaps not. But it's got to have them if it's going to be saved. Moreover," he went on, "it must find them among the young men. The older men are all steeped and branded and tarred and feathered with the materialism of the nineteenth century. They're perfectly sodden. They see no patriotism except in loyalty to a political machine; and no loyalty to a political machine except for what they can get out of it. From our Presidents down most of them will sacrifice any law of right to the good of a party. They don't realize that nine times out of ten the good of a party is the evil of the common weal; and our older men will never learn the fact. If we can't wake the younger men, we're done for."

"And are you going to wake them?"

"I'm going to be awake myself. That's all I can be responsible for. If I can find another fellow who's awake I'll follow him."

"Why not lead him? I should think you could."

He turned around on me. I shall never forget the gleam in his eye.

"No one is ever going to get away with this thing who thinks of leadership. There are times in the history of countries when men are called on to give up everything and be true to an ideal. I believe that time is approaching. It may come into Europe in one way and to America in another; but it's coming to us all. There'll be a call for—for—" he hesitated at the word, uttering it only with an apologetic laugh—"for consecration."

I was curious.

"And what do you mean by that—by consecration?"

He reflected before answering.

"I suppose I mean knowing what this country stands for, and being true to it oneself through thick and thin. There'll be thin and there'll be thick—plenty of them both—but it will be a question of the value of the individual. If there had been ten righteous men in Sodom and Gomorrah, they wouldn't have been destroyed. I take that as a kind of figure. A handful of disinterested, whole-hearted, clean-hearted, and perhaps I ought to add stout-hearted Americans, who know what they believe and live by it, will hold the fort against all efforts, within and without, to pull it down." He paused in his walk, obliging me to do the same. "I've been thinking a good deal," he smiled, "during the past few weeks of your law of Right—with a capital. I laughed at it when you first spoke of it—"

"Oh, hardly that," I interposed.

"But I've come to believe that it will work."

"I'm so glad."

"In fact, it's the only thing that will work."

"Exactly," I exclaimed, enthusiastically.

"We must stand by it, we younger men, just as the younger men of the late fifties stood by the principles represented by Lincoln. I believe in my heart that the need is going to be greater for us than it was for them, and if we don't respond to it, then may the Lord have mercy on our souls."

I give this scrap of conversation because it introduced a new note into my knowledge of Americans. I had not supposed that any Americans felt like that. In the Rossiter circle I never saw anything but an immense self-satisfaction. Money and what money could do was, I am sure, the only topic of their thought. Their ideas of position and privilege were all spuriously European. Nothing was indigenous. Except for their sense of money, their aims were as foreign to the soil as their pictures, their tapestries, their furniture, and their clothes. Even stranger I found the imitation of Europe in tastes which Europe was daily giving up. But in Larry Strangways, it seemed to me, I found something native, something that really lived and cared. It caused me to look at him with a new interest.

His jesting tone allowed me to take my cue in the same vein.

"I'm tremendously flattered, Mr. Strangways, that you should have found anything in my ideas that could be turned to good account."

He laughed shortly and rather hardly.

"Oh, if it was only that!"

It was another of the things I wished he hadn't said, but with the words he

112

started on again, walking so fast for a few paces that I made no effort to keep up with him. When he waited till I rejoined him we fell again to talking of Stacy Grainger. At the first opportunity I asked the question that was chiefly on my mind.

"Wasn't there something at one time between him and Mrs. Brokenshire?"

He marched on with head erect.

"I believe so," he admitted, reluctantly, but not till some seconds had passed.

"There was a big fight, wasn't there," I persisted, "between him and Mr. Brokenshire—over Editha Billing—on the Stock Exchange—or something like that?"

Again he allowed some seconds to go by.

"So I've heard."

I fished out of my memory such tag ends of gossip as had reached me, I could hardly tell from where.

"Didn't Mr. Brokenshire attack his interests—railways and steel and things—and nearly ruin him?"

"I believe there was some such talk."

I admired the way in which he refused to lend himself to the spread of the legend; but I insisted on going on, because the idea of this conflict of modern giants, with a beautiful maiden as the prize, appealed to my imagination.

"And didn't old Mrs. Billing shift round all of a sudden from the man who seemed to be going under to—?"

He cut the subject short by giving it another twist.

"Grainger's been unlucky. His whole family have been unlucky. It's an instance of tragedy haunting a race such as one reads of in mythology and now and then in modern history—the house of Atreus, for example, and the Stuarts, and the Hapsburgs, and so on."

I questioned him as to this, only to learn of a series of accidents, suicides, and sudden deaths, leaving Stacy as the last of his line, lonely and picturesque.

At the foot of the steps leading up to the Rossiter lawn Larry Strangways paused again. The children and dogs having preceded us and being safe on their own grounds, we could consider them off our minds.

"What do you know about old books?" he asked, suddenly.

The question took me so much by surprise that I could only say:

"What makes you think I know anything?"

"Didn't your father have a library full of them? And didn't you catalogue them and sell them in London?"

I admitted this, but added that even that undertaking had left me very ignorant of the subject.

"Yes; but it's a beginning. If you know the Greek or Russian alphabet it's a very good point from which to go on and learn the language."

"But why should I learn that language?"

"Because I know a man who's going to have a vacancy soon for a librarian. It's a private library, rather a famous one in New York, and the young lady at present in command is leaving to be married."

I smiled pleasantly.

"Yes; but what has that got to do with me?"

"Didn't I tell you I was going to look you up another job?"

"Oh! And so you've looked me up this!"

"No, I didn't. It looked me up. The owner of the library mentioned the fact as a great bore. It was his father who made the collection in the days of the first great American splurge. Stacy Grainger has added a rug or a Chinese jar from time to time, but he doesn't give a hang for the lot."

"Oh, so it's his."

"Yes; it's his. He says he feels inclined to shut the place up; but I told him it was a pity to do that since I knew the very young lady for the post."

I dropped the subject there, because of a new inspiration.

"If Mr. Grainger has places at his command, couldn't he do something for poor Hugh?"

"Why poor Hugh? I thought he was—"

I gave him a brief account of the fiasco in Boston, venturing to betray Hugh's confidence for the sake of some possible advantage. Mr. Strangways only shrugged his shoulders.

"Of course," he said. "What could you expect?" I was sure he was looking down on me with the expression Mrs. Rossiter had detected, though I didn't dare to lift an eye to catch him in the act. "You really mean to marry him?"

"Mean to marry him is not the term," I answered, with the decision which I felt the situation called for. "I mean to marry him only—on conditions."

"Oh, on conditions! What kind of conditions?"

I named them to him as I had named them to others. First that Hugh should become independent.

He repeated his short, hard laugh.

"I don't believe you had better bank on that."

"Perhaps not," I admitted. "But I've another string to my bow. His family may come and ask me."

He almost shouted.

"Never!"

It was the tone they all took, and which especially enraged me. I kept my voice steady, however, as I said, "That remains to be seen."

"It doesn't remain to be seen, because I can tell you now that they won't."

"And I can tell you now that they will," I said, with an assurance that, on the surface at least, was quite as strong as his own.

He laughed again, more shortly, more hardly.

"Oh, well!"

The laugh ended in a kind of sigh. I noted the sigh as I noted the laugh, and their relation to each other. Both reached me, touching something within me that had never yet been stirred. Physically it was like the prick of the spur to a spirited animal, it sent me bounding up the steps. I was off as from a danger; and though I would have given much to see the expression with which he stood gazing after me, I would not permit myself so much as to glance back.

CHAPTER XI

The steps by which I came to be Stacy Grainger's librarian could easily be traced, though to do so with much detail would be tedious.

After Hugh's departure for New York my position with Mrs. Rossiter soon became untenable. The reports that reached Newport of the young man's doings in the city were not merely galling to the family pride, but maddening to his father's sense of pre-eminence. Hugh was actually going from door to door, as you might say, in Wall Street and Broad Street, only to be turned away.

"He's making the most awful fool of himself," Mrs. Rossiter informed me one morning, "and papa's growing furious. Jim writes that every one is laughing at him, and, of course, they know it's all about some girl."

I held my tongue at this. That they should be laughing at poor Hugh was a new example of the world's falsity. His letters to me were only a record of half-promises and fair speeches, but he found every one of them encouraging. Nowhere had he met with the brutal treatment he had received at the hands of Cousin Andrew Brew. The minute his card went in to never so great a banker or broker, he was received with a welcome. If no one had just the right thing to offer him, no one had turned him down. It was explained to him that it was largely a matter of the off season—for his purpose August was the worst month in the year—and of the lack of an opening which it would be worth the while of a man of his quality to fill. Later, perhaps! The two words, courteously spoken, gave the gist of all his interviews. He had every reason to feel satisfied.

In the mean while he was comfortable at his club—his cash in hand would hold out to Christmas and beyond—and in the matter of energy, he wrote, not a mushroom was springing in his tracks. He was on the job early and late, day in and day out. The off season which was obviously a disadvantage in some respects had its merits in others, since it would be known, when things began to look up again, that he was available for any big house that could get him. That there would be competition in this respect every one had given him to understand. All this he told me in letters as full of love as they were of business, written in a great, sprawling, unformed, boyish hand, and with an occasional bit of phonetic spelling which made his protestations the more touching.

But Jim Rossiter's sources of information were of another kind.

"Get your father to do something to stop him," he wrote to his wife. "He's making the whole house of Meek & Brokenshire a laughing-stock."

There came, in fact, a Saturday when Mr. Rossiter actually appeared for the week-end.

"He wouldn't be doing that," Mrs. Rossiter almost sobbed to me, on receipt of the telegram announcing his approach, "unless things were pretty bad."

Though I dreaded his coming, I was speedily reassured. Whatever the object of Mr. Rossiter's visit, I, in my own person, had nothing to do with it. On the afternoon of his arrival he came out to where I was knocking the croquet balls about with Gladys on the lawn, and was as polite as he had been through the winter in New York. He was always polite even to the maids, to whom he scrupulously said good-morning. His wistful desire to be liked by every one was inspired by the same sort of impulse as the jovial *bonhomie* of Cousin Andrew Brew. He was a little, weazened man, with face and legs like a jockey, which I think he would gladly have been. Racin' and ridin', as he called them, were the amusements in which he found most pleasure, while his health was his chief preoccupation. He took pills before and after all his meals and a variety of medicinal waters. During the winter under his roof my own conversation with him had been entirely on the score of his complaints.

In just the same way he sauntered up now. He talked of his lack of appetite and the beastly cooking at clubs. Expecting him to broach the subject of Hugh, I got myself ready; but he did nothing of the kind. He was merely amiable and, as far as I could judge, indifferent. Within ten minutes he had sauntered away again, leading Gladys by the hand.

I saw then that in common with the other Brokenshires he considered that I didn't count. Hugh could be dealt with independently of me. So long as I was useful to his wife, there was no reason why I should be disturbed. I was too light a thing to be weighed in their balances.

Next day there was a grand family council and on Monday Jack Brokenshire accompanied his brother-in-law to New York. Hugh wrote me of their threats and flatteries, their beseechings and cajoleries. He was to come to his senses; he was to be decent to his father; he was to quit being a fool. I gathered that for forty-eight hours they had put him through most of the tortures known to fraternal inquisition; but he wrote me he would bear it all and more, for the sake of winning me.

Nor would he allow them to have everything their own way. That he wrote me, too. When it came to the question of marriage he bade them look at home. Each of them was an instance of what J. Howard could do in the matrimonial line, and what a mess he and they had made of it! He asked Jack in so many words how much he would have been in love with Pauline Gray if she hadn't had a big fortune, and, now that he had got her money and her, how true he was to his compact. Who were Trixie Delorme and Baby Bevan, he demanded, with a knowledge of Jack's affairs which compelled the elder brother to tell him to mind his own business.

Hugh laughed scornfully at that.

"I can mind my own business, Jack, and still keep an eye on yours, seeing that you and Pauline are the talk of the town. If she doesn't divorce you within the next five years, it will be because you've already divorced her. Even that won't be as big a scandal as your going on living together."

Mr. Rossiter intervened on this and did his best to calm the younger brother down:

"Ah, cut that out now, Hugh!"

But Hugh rounded on him, shaking off the hand that had been laid on his arm.

"You're a nice one, Jim, to come with your mealy-mouthed talk to me. Look at Ethel! If I'd married a woman as you married her—or if I'd been married as she married you—just because your father was a partner in Meek & Brokenshire and it was well to keep the money in the family—if I'd done that I'd shut up. I'd consider myself too low-down a cur to be kicked. What kind of a wife is Ethel to you? What kind of a husband are you to her? What kind of a father do you make to the children who hardly know you by sight? And now, just because I'm trying to be a man, and decent, and true to the girl I love, you come sneaking round to tell me she's not good enough. What do I care whether she's good enough or not, so long as she isn't like Ethel and Pauline? You can go back and tell them so."

Jack Brokenshire came back, but I think he kept this confidence to himself. What he told, however, was enough to produce a good deal of gloom in the family. Though Mrs. Rossiter didn't cease to be nice to me in her non-committal way, I began to reason that there were limits even to indifference. I had made up my mind to go and was working out some practical way of going, when an incident hastened my departure.

Doing an errand one day for Mrs. Rossiter in the shopping part of Bellevue Avenue, I saw old Mrs. Billing going by in an open motor landaulette. She signaled to me to stop, and, poking the chauffeur in the back through the open window, made him draw up at the curb.

"I've got something for you," she said, without other form of greeting. She began to stir things round in her bag. "I thought you'd like it. I've been carrying it about with me for the last three or four days—ever since Jack

Brokenshire got back from New York. Where the dickens is the thing? Ah, here!" She handed me out a crumpled card. "That's all, Antoine," she continued to the man. "Drive on."

I was left with the card in my hand, finding it to be an advertisement for the Hotel Mary Chilton, a place of entertainment for women alone, in a central and reputable part of New York.

By the time I got back to Mrs. Rossiter's I had solved what had at first been a puzzle, and, having reported on my errand, I gave my resignation verbally. I saw then—what old Mrs. Billing had also seen—that it was time. Mrs. Rossiter expressed no relief, but she made no attempt to dissuade me. That she was sorry she allowed me to see. She didn't speak of Hugh; but on the morning when I went she gave up her engagements to stay at home with me. As I said good-by she threw her arms round my neck and kissed me. I could feel on my cheek tears of hers as well as tears of my own, as I drew down my veil.

Hugh met me at the station in New York, and we dined at a restaurant together. He came for me next morning, and we lunched and dined at restaurants again. When we did the same on the third day that sense of being in a false position which had been with me from the first, and which argument couldn't counteract, began to be disquieting. On the fourth day I tried to make excuses and remain at the hotel, but when he insisted I was obliged to let him take me out once more. The people at the Mary Chilton were kindly, but I was afraid they would regard me with suspicion. I was afraid of some other things, besides.

For one thing I was afraid of Hugh. He began again to plead with me to marry him. Even he admitted that we couldn't continue to "go round together like that." We went to the most expensive restaurants, he argued, where there were plenty of people who would know him. When they saw him every day with a girl they didn't know, they would draw their own conclusions. As in a situation similar to theirs I would have drawn my own, I brought my bit of Bohemianism to a speedy end.

There followed some days during which it seemed to me I was deprived of any outlook. I could hardly see what I was there for. I could hardly see what I was living for. Never till then had I realized how, in normal conditions, each day is linked to the day before as well as to the morrow. Here the link was gone. I left nothing undone when I went to bed; I had nothing to get up for in the morning. My reason for existing had suddenly been snuffed out.

It was a time for the testing of my faith. I was near the end of my *cul-de-sac*, and yet I saw no further development ahead. If the continuous unfolding of right on which, to use Larry Strangways's expression, I had banked, were to come to a stop, I should be left not only without a duty, but without a law. Of the two possibilities it was the latter I dreaded most. One can live if one has a motive theory within one; without it— And then, just as I was coming to the last stretches of what seemed a blind alley and no more, my confidence was justified. Larry Strangways called on me.

I have not said that on coming to New York I had decided to let my acquaintance with him end. He made me uneasy. I was terrified by the thought that he might be in love with me. Why I was terrified I didn't know; I only knew I was. I did not tell him, therefore, when I left Mrs. Rossiter; and in the whirlpool of New York I considered that I was swallowed up. But here was his card, and he himself waiting in the drawing-room below.

Naturally my first question was as to how he had found me out. This he laughed off, pretending to be annoyed with me for coming to the city without telling him. I could see, however, that he was in spirits much too high to allow of his being seriously annoyed with anything. Life promised well with him. He enjoyed his work, and for his employer he had that eager personal devotion which is always a herald of success. After having run away from him, as it were, I was now a little irritated at seeing that he hadn't missed me.

But he did not take his leave without a bit of information that puzzled me beyond expression. He was going out of Mr. Grainger's office that morning, he said, with a bundle of letters which he was to answer, when his master observed, casually:

"The young lady of whom you spoke to me as qualified to take Miss Davis's place is at the Hotel Mary Chilton. Go and see her and get her opinion as to accepting the job!"

I was what the French call *atterrée*—knocked flat.

"But how on earth could he know?"

Larry Strangways laughed.

"Oh, don't ask me. He knows anything he wants to know. He's got the flair of a detective. I don't try to fathom him. But the point is that the position is there for you to take or to leave."

I tried to bring my mind back from the fact that this important man, a total stranger to me, was in some way interested in my destiny.

"What can I do but leave it, when I know no more about it than I do of sailing a ship?"

"Oh yes, you do. You know what books are, and you know what rare books are. For the rest, all you'd have to do would be to consult the catalogue. I don't know what the duties are; but if Miss Davis is up to them I guess you would be, too. She's a sweet, pretty kitten of a thing—daughter of one of Stacy Grainger's old pals who came to grief—but I don't believe she knows much more about a book than the cover from the print. Anyhow, I've given you the message with neither more nor less than he said. Look here!" he exclaimed, suddenly. "Why shouldn't you put on your hat and walk down the street with me, so that I could show you where the library is? It's not ten minutes away. I've never been inside it, but every one knows what it looks like."

Consulting my wrist-watch, I objected that it was but twenty minutes to the time when Hugh was due to come and take me to walk in Central Park, returning to the hotel to tea.

"Oh, let him go to the deuce! We can be there and back in twenty minutes, and you can leave a message for him at the office."

So we started. The Mary Chilton is in one of the cross-streets between Fifth and Sixth Avenues. I discovered that Stacy Grainger's house was on the corner of Fifth Avenue and a corresponding cross-street a little farther down-town. It is a big brownstone house, in the eighteen-seventy style, of the type which all round it has been turned into offices and shops. All its many windows were blinded in a yellowish holland staff, giving to the whole building an aspect sealed and dead.

I shuddered.

"I hope I shouldn't have to work there."

"No. The house has been shut up for years." He named the hotel overlooking the Park at which Stacy Grainger actually lived. "Anybody else would have sold the place; but he has a lot of queer sentiment about him. Of the two or three devotions in his life one of the most intense is to his father's memory. I believe the old fellow committed suicide in that house, and the son hallows it as he would a grave."

"Cheerful!"

"Oh, cheerful isn't the word one would associate with him first—"

"Or last, apparently."

"No, or last; but he's got other qualities to which cheerfulness is as small change to gold. All I want you to see is that he keeps this property, which is worth half a million at the least, from motives which the immense majority wouldn't understand. It gives you a clue to the man."

"But what I want," I said, with nervous flippancy, for I was afraid of meeting Hugh, "is a clue to the library."

"There it is."

"That?"

He had pointed to a small, low, rectangular building I had seen a hundred times, without the curiosity to wonder what it was. It stood behind the house, in the center of a grass-plot, and was approached from the cross-street, through a small wrought-iron gate. Built of brownstone, without a window, and with no other ornament than a frieze in relief below the eave, it suggested a tomb. At the back was a kind of covered cloister connecting with the house.

"If I had to sit in there all day," I commented, as we turned back toward the hotel, "I should feel as if I were buried alive. I know that strange things would happen to me!"

"Oh no, they wouldn't. It's sure to be all right or a pretty little thing like Miss Davis couldn't have stood it for three years. It's lighted from the top, and there are a lot of fine things scattered about."

He gave me a brief history of how the collection had been formed. The elder Grainger on coming to New York had bought up the contents of two or three great European sales *en bloc*. He knew little about the objects he had thus acquired, and cared less. His motive was simply that of the rich American to play the nobleman.

He was still talking of this when Hugh passed us and turned round. Between the two men there was a stiff form of greeting. That is, it was stiff on Larry Strangways's side, while on Hugh's it was the nearest thing to no greeting at all. I could see he considered the tutor of his sister's son beneath him.

"What the devil were you walking with that fellow for?" he asked, after Mr. Strangways had left us and while we were continuing our way up-town. He spoke, wonderingly rather than impatiently.

"Because he had come from a gentleman who had offered me employment. I had just gone down with him to look at the outside of the house."

I could hardly be surprised that Hugh should stop abruptly, forcing the stream of foot-passengers to divide into two currents about us.

"The impertinent bounder! Offer employment—to you—my—my wife!"

I walked on with dignity.

"You mustn't call me that, Hugh. It's a word only to be used in its exact signification." He began to apologize, but I interrupted. "I'm not only not your wife, but as yet I haven't even promised to marry you. We must keep that fact unmistakably clear before us. It will prevent possible complications in the end."

He spoke humbly:

"What sort of complications?"

"I don't know; but I can see they might arise. And as for the matter of employment, I must have it for a lot of reasons."

"I don't see that. Give me two or three months, Alix!"

"But it's precisely during those two or three months, Hugh, that I should be left high and dry. Unless I have something to do I have no motive for staying here in New York."

"What about me?"

"I can't stay just to see you. That's the difference between a woman and a man. The situation is awkward enough as it is; but if I were to go on living here for two or three months, merely for the sake of having a few hours every day with you—"

Before we reached the Park he saw the justice of my argument. Remembering what Larry Strangways had once said as to Hugh's belief that he was stooping to pick his diamond out of the mire, I reasoned that since he was marrying a working-girl it would best preserve the decencies if the working-girl were working. For this procedure Hugh himself was able to establish precedent, since we were in sight of the very hotel where Libby Jaynes had rubbed men's nails up to within an hour or two of her marriage to Tracy Allen. He pointed it out as if it was an historic monument, and in the same spirit I gazed at it.

That matter settled, I attacked another as we advanced farther into the Park.

"And Mr. Strangways is not a bounder, Hugh, darling. I wish you wouldn't call him that."

His response was sufficiently good-natured, but it expressed that Brokenshire disdain for everything that didn't have money which specially enraged me.

"Well, I won't," he conceded. "I don't care a hang what he is."

"I do," I declared, with some tartness. "I care that he's a gentleman and that he's treated as one."

"Oh, every one's a gentleman."

"No, Hugh, every one isn't. I know men right here in New York who could buy and sell Mr. Strangways a thousand times, perhaps a million times over, and who wouldn't be worthy to valet him."

His small wide-apart blue eyes were turned on me questioningly.

"You don't know many men right here in New York. Who do you mean?"

I saw that he had me there and, not wishing to be driven into a corner, I beat a shuffling retreat.

"I don't mean any one in particular. I'm speaking in general." As we had reached an empty bench and the afternoon was hot, I suggested that we sit down.

We had been silent a little while, when he asked the question I had been expecting.

"Who was the person who offered you the—the—" I saw how he hated the word—"the employment?"

I had already decided to betray no knowledge of matters which didn't concern me.

"It's a Mr. Grainger," I said, as casually as I could.

As he sat close to me I could feel him start.

"Not Stacy Grainger?"

I maintained my tone of indifference.

"I think that is his name. Do you know him? He seems to be some one of importance."

"Oh, he is."

"Mr. Strangways has gone to him as secretary and, I suppose, knowing that I was out of a situation, he must have mentioned me."

"For what?"

"As I understand it, it's librarian. It seems that this Mr. Grainger has quite a collection—"

"Oh yes, I know." As he remained silent for some time I waited for him to raise objections, but he only said at last: "In that case you wouldn't have much to do with him. He's never there."

"No, I fancy not," I hastened to agree, and Hugh said no more.

He said no more, but I could see that it was because he was wrestling with a subject of which he couldn't perceive the bearings. As far as I was concerned he plainly considered it wise not to tell me that which, as a stranger and a foreigner, I wouldn't be likely to know. He consequently dropped the topic, and when he talked again it was of trivial things.

A half-hour later, as we were on our way homeward, he exclaimed, suddenly, and apropos of nothing at all:

"Little Alix, if you were to love anybody else I'd—I'd shoot myself."

His innocent, boyish, inexperienced face wore such a look of misery that I laughed. I laughed to conceal the fact that I was near to crying.

"Oh no, you wouldn't, Hugh. Besides, you don't see any likelihood of my doing it."

"I'm not so sure about that," he grumbled.

"Well, I am, Hugh, dear." I laughed again. "I've no intention of loving any one else—till I've settled my account with your father."

CHAPTER XII

Nearly a week later, in the middle of a hot afternoon, I came back from some shopping to wait for Hugh at the hotel. Though it was a half-hour before I expected him, I was too tired to go up-stairs and so went directly to the reception-room. It was not only cool and restful there, but after the glare of the streets outside, it was so dim that I took the place to be empty. Having gone to a mirror for a moment to straighten my hat and smooth the wayward tendrils of my hair, so that I shouldn't look disheveled when Hugh arrived, I threw myself into an arm-chair.

I remember that my attitude was anything but graceful, and that I sighed. I sighed more than once and somewhat loudly. I was depressed, and as usual when depressed I felt small and desolate. It would have been a relief to cry; but I couldn't cry when I was expecting Hugh. I could only toss about in my big chair and give utterance to my pent-up heart a little too explosively.

It was five or six days since Larry Strangways's call, and no real development of my blind alley was in sight. He had not returned, nor had I heard from him. On the previous evening Hugh had said, "I thought nothing would come of that," in a tone which carried conviction. It wasn't that I was eager to be Stacy Grainger's librarian; it was only that I wanted something to happen, something that would justify my staying in New York. August had passed, and with the coming in of September I saw the stirring of a new life in the streets; but there was no new life for me.

Nor, for the matter of that, did I see any new life for Hugh. He had entered now on that stage of waiting on the postman which a good many people have found sickening. Bankers and brokers having promised to write when they knew of anything to suit him, he was expecting a summons by every delivery of letters. On his dear face I began to read the evidence of hope deferred. He was cheery enough; he could find fifty explanations to account for the fact that he hadn't yet been called; but brave words couldn't counteract the look of disquietude that was creeping day by day into his kindly eyes. On the previous evening he had informed me, too, that he had left his club and installed himself in a small hotel, not far from my own neighborhood. When I asked him why he had done that he said it was "to get away from a lot of the fellows who were always chewing the rag," but I suspected the motive of economy. For the motive of economy I should have had nothing but respect, if it hadn't been so incongruous with everything I had known of him.

It was probably because my eyes had grown accustomed to the gloom in the reception-room that I noticed, suddenly, two other eyes. They were in a distant corner and seemed to be looking at me with the detached and burning stare of motor-lamps at night. For a minute I could discern no personality, the eyes themselves were so lustrous.

I was about to be frightened when a man arose and restlessly moved toward the chimneypiece, not because there was anything there he desired to see, but because he couldn't continue to sit still. He was a striking figure, tall, spare, large-boned and powerful. The face was of the type which for want of a better word I can only speak of as masculine. It was long and lean and strong; if it was handsome it was only because every feature and line was cut to the same large pattern as the frame. Sweeping mustaches, of the kind school-girls are commonly supposed to love, concealed a mouth which I could have wagered would be hard, while the luminosity of the gaze suggested a rather hungry set of human qualities and passions.

We were now two restless persons instead of one, and I was about to leave the room when a page came in.

"Sorry, sir," said the honest-faced little boy, with an amusingly uncouth accent I find it impossible to transcribe, "but number four-twenty-three ain't in, so I guess she must be out."

Startled, I rose to my feet.

"But I'm number four-twenty-three."

The boy turned toward me nonchalantly.

"Didn't know you was here! That gentleman wants you."

With this introduction he dashed away, and I was once more conscious of the luminous eyes bent upon me. The tall figure, too, advanced a few paces in my direction.

"I asked for Miss Adare." The voice was deep and grave and harsh and musical all at once.

"That's my name."

"Mine's Grainger."

I gasped silently, like a dying fish, before I could stammer the words—

"Won't you sit down?"

As he seated himself near me and in a good light, I saw that his skin was tanned, as if he lived on the sea or in the open air. I learned later from Larry Strangways that he had just come from a summer's yachting. His gaze studied me—not as a man studies a woman, but as a workman inspects a tool.

"You probably know my errand."

"Mr. Strangways—"

"Yes, I told him to sound you."

"But I'm afraid I wouldn't do."

"Why do you think so?"

"Because I don't know anything about the work."

"There's no work to know anything about. All you'd have to do would be to sit still. You'd never have more than two or three visitors in a day—and most days none at all."

"But what should I do when visitors came?"

"Show them what they asked to see. You'd find that in the catalogue. You'd soon get the hang of the place. It's small. There's not much in it when you come to sum it up. Miss Davis will show you the ropes before she leaves on the first of October. I'll give you the same salary I've been paying her."

He named a sum the munificence of which almost took my breath away.

"Oh, but I shouldn't be worth that."

"It's the salary," he said, briefly, as he rose. "You can arrange with my secretary, Strangways, when you would like to begin. The sooner the better, as I understand that Miss Davis would like to get off."

He was on his way to the door when, thinking of the tomb-like aspect of the place, I asked, desperately:

"Should I be all alone?"

He turned.

"There's a man and his wife in the house. One of them would be always within call. The woman will bring you tea at half past four."

I could hardly believe my ears. I had never heard of such solicitude. "But I shouldn't need tea!" I began to assure him.

He paused for a moment, looking at me searchingly.

"You'll have callers—"

"Oh no, I sha'n't."

"You'll have callers," he repeated, as if I hadn't spoken, "and there'll be tea every day at four-thirty."

He was gone before I could protest further, or ask any more questions.

Hugh's explanation, when I laid the matter before him, was that Mr. Grainger was trying to play into the hands of that fellow, Strangways.

"But why?" I demanded.

"He thinks there's something between him and you."

"But there isn't."

"I should hope not; but, evidently, Strangways has made him think—"

"Oh no, he hasn't, Hugh. Mr. Strangways is not that kind of man. Mr. Grainger has some other reason for wanting me there, but I can't think what it is."

"Then I shouldn't go till I knew," Hugh counseled, moodily.

But I did. I went the next week. Larry Strangways made the arrangements, and, after a fortnight under Miss Davis's instructions, I found myself alone.

It was not so trying as I feared, though it was monotonous. It was monotonous because there was so little to do. I was there each morning at half past nine. From one to two I had an hour for lunch. At six I came away. On Saturdays I had the afternoon. It was a little like being a prisoner, but a prisoner in a palace, a prisoner who is well paid.

The place consisted of one big, handsome room, some sixty feet by thirty, resembling the libraries of great houses I had seen abroad. That in this case it was detached from the dwelling was, I suppose, a matter of architectural convenience. Book-shelves lined the walls right up to the cornice. The dull reds and browns and blues and greens of the bindings carried out the mellow effects of the Oriental rugs on the floor. Under the shelves there were cupboards, some of them empty, others stocked with portfolios of prints, European and Japanese. There were no pictures, but a few large pieces of old porcelain and faïence, Persian, Spanish, and Chinese, stood on the mantelpiece and tables. For the rest, the furnishings consisted of a bust or two, a desk or two, and some decorative tables and chairs.

My chief objection to the life was its seeming pointlessness. I was hard at work doing nothing. The number of visitors was negligible. Once during the autumn an old gentleman brought some engravings to compare with similar examples in Mr. Grainger's collection; once a lady student of Shakespeare came to examine his early editions; perhaps as often as twice a week some wandering tourist in New York would enter and stare vacantly, and go as he arrived. To while away the time I read and wrote and did knitting and fancy-work, and at half past four every day, as regularly as the hands of the clock came round, I solemnly had my tea. It was very good tea, with cake and bread and butter in the orthodox style, and was brought by Mrs. Daly, the motherly old Irish caretaker of the house, who stumped in and stumped out, giving me, while she stayed, a good deal of detail as to her "sky-attic" nerves and swollen "varikiss" veins.

I am bound to admit that the tea ceremony oppressed me—not that I didn't enjoy it in its way but because its generosity seemed overdone. It was not in the necessities of the case; it was, above all, not American. On both the occasions when Mr. Grainger honored the library with a call I tried to screw up my courage to ask him to let me off this hospitality, but I couldn't reach the point. I was not so much afraid of him as I was overawed. He was perfectly civil; he never treated me as the dust beneath his feet, like Howard Brokenshire; but any one could see that he was immensely and perhaps tragically preoccupied.

I was having tea all alone on a cold afternoon in November, when the sound of the opening of the outer door attracted my attention. At first one came into a vestibule from which there was no entrance, till on my side I touched the spring of a closed wrought-iron grille. I had gone forward to see who was there and, if necessary, give the further admission, when to my astonishment I saw Mrs. Brokenshire.

She was in a walking-dress with furs. The color in her cheeks might have been due to the cold wind, but the light in her eyes was that of excitement.

"I heard you were here," she whispered, as she fluttered in, "and I've come to see you."

My sense of the imprudence of this step was such that I could hardly welcome her. That feeling of protection which I had once before on her behalf came back to me.

"Who told you?" I asked, as soon as she was seated and I was pouring her out a cup of tea. For the first time since taking the position I was glad the ceremony had not been suppressed.

She answered, while glancing into the shadows about her.

"Mildred told me. Hugh wrote it to her. He does write to her, you know. She's the only one with whom he is still in communication. She seems to think the poor boy is in trouble. I came to—to see if there was anything I could do."

I told her I was living at the Hotel Mary Chilton and that, if necessary at any time, she could see me there.

She repeated the address, but I knew it took no hold on her memory.

"Ah yes; the Hotel Mary Chilton. I think I've heard of it. But I haven't many minutes, and you must tell me all you can about dear Hugh."

As my anxiety on Hugh's account was deepening, I was the more eager to do as I was bid. I said he had found no employment as yet, and that in my opinion employment would be hard to secure. If he was willing to work for a year or two for next to nothing, as he would consider the salary, he might eventually learn the financial trade; but to expect that his name would be a key to open the door of any bank at which he might present himself was preposterous. I hadn't been able to convince him of that, however, and he was still hoping. But he was hoping with a sad, worried face that almost broke my heart.

"And how is he off for money?"

I said I thought his bank-account was running low. He made no complaint of that to me, but I noticed that he rarely now went to any of his clubs, and that he took his meals at the more inexpensive places. In taxis, too, he was careful, and in tickets for the theater. These were the signs by which I judged.

Her eyes had the sweet mistiness I remembered from our last meeting.

"I can let him have money—as much as he needs."

I considered this.

"But it would be Mr. Brokenshire's money, wouldn't it?"

"It would be money Mr. Brokenshire gives me."

"In that case I don't think Hugh could accept it. You see, he's trying to make himself independent of his father, so as to do what his father doesn't like."

"But he can't starve."

"He must either starve, or earn a living, or go back to his father and—give up."

"Does that mean that you won't marry him unless he has money of his own?"

"It means what I've said more than once before—that I can't marry him if he has no money of his own, unless his family come and ask me to do it."

There was a little furrow between her brows.

"Oh, well, they won't do that. I would," she hastened to add, "because—"she smiled, like an angel—"because I believe in love; but they wouldn't."

"I think Mrs. Rossiter would," I argued, "if she was left free."

"She might; and, of course, there's Mildred. She'd do anything for Hugh,

though she thinks ... but neither Jack nor Pauline would give in; and as for Mr. Brokenshire—I believe it would break his heart."

"Why should he feel toward me like that?" I demanded, bitterly. "How am I inferior to Pauline Gray, except that I have no money?"

"Well, I suppose in a way that's it. It's what Mr. Brokenshire calls the solidarity of aristocracies. They have to hold together."

"But aristocracy and money aren't one."

As she rose she smiled again, distantly and dreamily. "If you were an American, dear Miss Adare, you'd know."

Before she said good-by she looked deliberately about the room. It was not the hasty inspection I should have expected; it was tranquil, and I could even say that it was thorough. She made no mention of Mr. Grainger, but I couldn't help thinking he was in her mind.

At the door to which I accompanied her, however, her manner changed. Before trusting herself to the few paces of walk running from the entrance to the wrought-iron gate, she glanced up and down the street. It was dark by this time, and the lamps were lit, but not till the pavement was tolerably clear did she venture out. Even then she didn't turn toward Fifth Avenue, which would have been her natural direction; but rapidly and, as I imagined, furtively, she walked the other way.

I mentioned to no one that she had come to see me. Her kind thought of Hugh I was sorry to keep to myself; but I knew of no purpose to be served in divulging it. With my maxim to guide me it was not difficult to be sure that in this case right lay in silence.

A few days later I got Hugh's doings from a new point of view. As I was going back to my lunch at the hotel, Mrs. Rossiter called to me from her motor and made me get in. The distance I had to cover being slight, she drove me up to Central Park and back again to have the time to talk.

"My dear, he's crazy. He's going round to all the offices that practically turned him out six or eight weeks ago and begging them to find a place for him. Two or three of papa's old friends have written to ask what they could really do for him—for papa, that is—and he's sent them word that he'd take it as a favor if they'd show Hugh to the door."

"Of course, if his father makes himself his enemy—"

"He only makes himself his enemy in order to be his friend, dear Miss Adare. He's your friend, too, papa is, if you only saw it."

"I'm afraid I don't," I said, dryly.

"Oh, you will some day, and do him justice. He's the kindest man when you let him have his own way."

"Which would be to separate Hugh and me."

"But you'd both get over that; and I know he'd do the handsome thing by you, as well as by him."

"So long as we do the handsome thing by each other—"

"Oh, well, you can see where that leads to. Hugh'll never be in a position to marry you, dear Miss Adare."

"He will when your father comes round."

"Nonsense, my dear! You know you're not looking forward to that, not any more than I am."

Later, as I was getting out at my door, she said, as if it was an afterthought:

"Oh, by the way, you know papa has made me write to Lady Cissie Boscobel?"

I looked up at her from the pavement.

"What for?"

"To ask her to come over and spend a month or two in New York. She says she will if she can. She's a good deal of a girl, Cissie is. If you're going to keep your hold on Hugh— Well, all I can say is that Cissie will give you a run for your money. Of course, it's nothing to me. I only thought I'd tell you."

This, too, I kept from Hugh; but I seized an early opportunity to paint the portrait of the imaginary charming girl he could have for a wife, with plenty of money to support himself and her, if he would only give me up. This was as we walked home one night from the theater—I was obliged from time to time to let him take me so that we might have a pretext for being together— and we strolled in the shadows of the narrow cross-streets.

"Little Alix," he declared, fervently, "I could no more give you up than I could give up my breath or my blood. You're part of me. You're the most vital part of me. If you were to fail me I should die. If I were to fail you—But that's not worth thinking of. Look here!" He paused in a dark spot beside a great silent warehouse. "Look here. I'm having a pretty tough time. I'll confess it. I didn't mean to tell you, but I will. When I go to see certain people now—men I've met dozens of times at my father's table—what do you think happens? They have me shown to the door, and not too politely. These are the chaps who two months ago were squirming for joy at the thought of getting me. What do you think of that? How do you suppose it makes me feel?" I was about to break in with some indignant response when he continued, placidly: "Well, it all turns to music the minute I think of you. It's as if I'd drunk some glowing cordial. I'm kicked out, let us say—and it's not too much to say— and I'm ready to curse for all I'm worth, but I think of you. I remember I'm doing it for you and bearing it for you, so that one day I may strike the right thing and we may be together and happy forever afterward, and I swear to you it's as if angels were singing in the sky."

I had to let him kiss me there in the shadow of the street, as if we were a footman and a housemaid. I had to let him kiss away my tears and soothe me and console me. I told him I wasn't worthy of such love, and that, if he would consider the fitness of things, he would go away and leave me, but he only kissed me the more.

Again I was having my tea. It had been a lifeless day, and I was wondering how long I could endure the lifelessness. Not a soul had come near the place since morning, and my only approach to human intercourse had been in discussing Mrs. Daly's "varikiss" veins. Even that interlude was over, for the lady would not return for the tea things till after my departure. I was so lonely —I felt the uselessness of what I was doing so acutely—that in spite of the easy work and generous pay I was thinking of sending my resignation in to Mr. Grainger and looking for something else.

The outer door opened swiftly and silently, and I knew some one was inside. I knew, too, before rising from my place, that it was Mrs. Brokenshire. Subconsciously I had been expecting her, though I couldn't have said why. Her lovely face was all asparkle.

"I've come to see you again," she whispered, as I let her in. "I hope you're alone."

I replied that I was and, choosing my words carefully, I said it was kind of her to keep me in mind.

"Oh yes, I keep you in mind, and I keep Hugh. What I've really come for is to beg you to hand him the money of which I spoke the other day."

She seated herself, but not before glancing about the room, either expectantly or fearfully. As I poured out her tea I repeated what I had said already on the subject of the money. She wasn't listening, however. When she made replies they were not to the point. All the while she sipped her tea and nibbled her cake her eyes had the shifting alertness of a watchful little bird's.

"Oh, but what does it all matter when it's a question of love?" she said, somewhat at a venture. "Love is the only thing, don't you think? It must make its opportunities as it can."

"You mean that love can be—unscrupulous?"

"Oh, I shouldn't use that word."

"It isn't the word I'm thinking of. It's the act."

"Love is like war, isn't it? All's fair!"

"But is it?"

Her eyes rested on mine, not boldly, but with a certain daring.

"Why—yes."

"You believe that?"

She still kept her eyes on mine. Her tone was that of a challenge.

"Why—yes." She added, perhaps defiantly, "Don't you?"

I said, decidedly:

"No, I don't."

"Then you don't love. You can't love. Love is reckless. Love—" There was a long pause before she dropped the two concluding words, spacing them apart as if to emphasize her deliberation. "Love—risks—all."

"If it risks all it may lose all."

The challenge was renewed.

"Well? Isn't that better than—?"

"It's not better than doing right," I hastened to say, "however hard it may be."

"Ah, but what is right? A thing can't be right if—if—" she sought for a word —"if it's killing you."

As she said this there was a sound along the corridor leading from the house. I thought Mrs. Daly had forgotten something and was coming back. But the tread was different from her slow stump, and my sense of a danger at hand was such as the good woman never inspired.

Mrs. Brokenshire made no attempt to play a part or to put me off the scent. She acted as if I understood what was happening. Her teacup resting in her lap, she sat with eyes aglow and lips slightly apart in a look of heavenly expectation. I could hardly believe her to be the dazed, stricken little creature I had seen three months ago. As the footsteps approached she murmured, "He's coming!" or, "Who's coming?" I couldn't be sure which.

Mr. Grainger entered like a man who is on his own ground and knows what he is about to find. There was no uncertainty in his manner and no apparent sense of secrecy. His head was high and his walk firm as he pushed his way amid tables and chairs to where we were sitting in the glow of a shaded light.

I stood up as he approached, but I had time to appraise my situation. I saw all its little mysteries illumined as by a flash. I saw why Stacy Grainger had kept track of me; I saw why, in spite of my deficiencies, he had taken me on as his librarian; but I saw, too, that the Lord had delivered J. Howard Brokenshire into my hands, as Sisera into those of Jael, the wife of Heber the Kenite.

CHAPTER XIII

I was relieved of some of my embarrassment by the fact that Mr. Grainger took command.

Having bowed over Mrs. Brokenshire's hand with an empressement he made no attempt to conceal, he murmured the words, "I'm delighted to see you again." After this greeting, which might have been commonplace and was not, he turned to me. "Perhaps Miss Adare will give me some tea."

I could carry out this request, listen to their scraps of conversation, and think my own thoughts all at the same time.

Thinking my own thoughts was the least easy of the three, for the reason that thought stunned me. The facts knocked me on the head. Since before my engagement as Mr. Grainger's librarian this situation had been planned! Mrs. Brokenshire had chosen me for my part in it! She had given Mr. Grainger my address, which she could have learned from her mother, and recommended me as one with whom they would be safe!

Their talk was only of superficial things; but it was not the clue to their emotions. That was in the way they talked—haltingly, falteringly, with glances that met and shifted and fell, or that rested on each other with long, mute looks, and then turned away hurriedly, as if something in the spirit reeled. As she gave him bits of information concerning the summer at Newport, she stumbled in her words, because there was no correlation between the sentences she formed and her fundamental thought. The same was true of his account of yachting on the coast of Maine, of Gloucester, Islesboro, and Bar Harbor. He stuttered and stammered and repeated himself. It was like one of those old Italian duets in which stupid words are sung to a passionate, heartbreaking melody. Nevertheless, I had enough sympathy with love, even with a guilty love, to have some mercy in my judgments.

Not that I believed it to be a guilty love—as yet. That, too, I was obliged to think over and form my opinion about it. It was not a guilty love as yet; but it might easily become a guilty love. I remembered that Larry Strangways, with all his admiration for his employer, had refused him a place in his list of whole-hearted, clean-hearted men because he had a weakness; and I reflected that on the part of Mrs. Billing's daughter there might be no rigorous concept of the moralities. What I saw, therefore, was a man and a woman so consumed with longing for each other that guilt would be chiefly a matter of opportunity. To create that opportunity I had been brought upon the scene.

I SAW A MAN AND A WOMAN CONSUMED WITH LONGING FOR EACH OTHER

I could see, of course, how admirably I was suited to the purpose I was meant to serve. In the first place, I was young, and might but dimly perceive—might not perceive at all—what was being done with me. In the next place, I was presumably too inexperienced to take a line of my own even if I suspected what was not for me to know. Then, I was poor and a stranger, and too glad of the easy work for which I was liberally paid not to be willing to take its bitter with its sweet. Lastly, I, too, was in love; and I, too, was a victim of Howard Brokenshire. If I couldn't approve of what I might see and hear, at least I might be reckoned on not to speak of it. Once more I was made to feel that, though I might play a subordinate rôle of some importance, my own wishes and personality didn't count.

It was obviously a minute at which to bring my maxim into operation. I had to do what was Right—with a capital. For that I must wait for inspiration, and presently I got it.

That is, I got it by degrees. I got it first by noting in a puzzled way the glances which both my companions sent in my direction. They were sidelong glances, singularly alike, whether they came from Stacy Grainger's melancholy brown eyes or Mrs. Brokenshire's sweet, misty ones. They were timid glances, pleading, uneasy. They asked what words wouldn't dare to ask, and what I was too dense to understand. I sat sipping my tea, running hot and cold as the odiousness of my position struck me from the various points of view; but I made no attempt to move.

They were still talking of people of whom I knew nothing, but talking brokenly, futilely, for the sake of hearing each other's voice, and yet stifling the things which it would have been fatal to them both to say, when Mr. Grainger got up and brought me his cup.

"May I have another?"

I looked up to take the cup, but he held it in his hands. He held it in his hands and gazed down at me. He gazed down at me with an expression such as I have never seen in any eyes but a dog's. As I write I blush to remember that, with such a mingling of hints and entreaties and commands, I didn't know what he was trying to convey to me. I took the cup, poured out his tea, handed the cup back to him—and sat.

But after he had reached his seat the truth flashed on me. I was in the way; I was *de trop*. I had done part of my work in being the pretext for Mrs. Brokenshire's visit; now I ought, tactfully, to absent myself. I needn't go far; I needn't go for long. There was an alcove at the end of the room where one could be out of sight; there was also the corridor leading to the house. I could easily make an excuse; I could get up and move without an excuse of any kind. But I sat.

I hated myself; I despised myself; but I sat. I drank my tea without knowing it; I ate my cake without tasting it—and I sat.

The talk between my companions grew more fitful. Silence was easier for them—silence and that dumb interchange of looks which had the sympathy of something within myself. I knew that in their eyes I was a nuisance, a thing to be got rid of. I was so in my own—but I went on eating and drinking stolidly —and sat.

It was in my mind that this was my chance to be avenged on Howard Brokenshire; but I didn't want my vengeance that way. I have to confess that I was so poor-spirited as to have little or no animosity against him. I could see how easy it was for him to think of me as an adventuress. I wanted to convince and convert him, but not to make him suffer. If in any sense I could be called the guardian of his interests I would rather have been true to the trust than not. As I sat, therefore, gulping down my tea as if I relished it, it was partly because of my protective instinct toward the exquisite creature before me who might not know how to protect herself—and partly because I couldn't help it. Mr. Grainger could order me to go, but until he did I meant to go on eating.

Probably because of the insistence of my presence Mrs. Brokenshire felt obliged to begin to talk again. I did my best not to listen, but fragments of her sentences came to me.

"My mother spent a few weeks with us in August. I—I don't think she and—and Mr. Brokenshire get on so well."

Almost for the first time he was interested in what she said rather than in her.

"What's the trouble?"

"Oh, I don't know—the whole thing." A long pause ensued, during which their eyes rested on each other in mute questioning. "She's changed, mamma is."

"Changed in what way?"

"Oh, I don't know. I—I suppose she sees that she—she—miscalculated."

It was his turn to ruminate silently, and when he spoke at last it was as if throwing up to the surface but one of a deep undercurrent of thoughts.

"After the pounding I got three years ago she didn't believe I'd come back."

She accepted this without comment. Before speaking again she sent me another of her frightened, pleading looks.

"She always liked you better than any one else."

He seconded the glance in my direction as he said, with a grim smile:

"Which didn't prevent her going to the highest bidder."

She colored and sighed.

"You wouldn't be so hard on her if you knew what a fight she had to make during papa's lifetime. We were always in debt. You knew that, didn't you? Poor mamma used to say she'd save me from that if she never—"

I lost the rest of the sentence by deliberately rattling the tea things in pouring myself a third or a fourth cup of tea. Nothing but disconnected words reached me after that, but I caught the name of Madeline Pyne. I knew who she was, having heard her story day by day as it unfolded itself during my first weeks with Mrs. Rossiter. It was a simple tale as tales go in the twentieth century. Mrs. Pyre had been Mrs. Grimshaw. While she was Mrs. Grimshaw she had spent three days at a seaside resort with Mr. Pyne. The law having been invoked, she had changed her residence from the house of Mr. Grimshaw in Seventy-fifth Street to that of Mr. Pyne in Seventy-seventh Street, and likewise changed her name. Only a very discerning eye could now have told that in the opinion of society there was a difference between her and Cæsar's wife. The drama was sufficiently recent to make the topic a natural one for an interchange of confidences. That confidences were being interchanged I could see; that from those confidences certain terrifying, passionate deductions were being drawn silently I could also see. I could see without hearing; I didn't need to hear. I could tell by her pallor and his embarrassment how each read the mind of the other, how each was tempted and how each recoiled. I knew that neither pointed the moral of the parable, for the reason that it stared them in the face.

Because that subject, too, was exhausted, or because they had come to a place where they could say no more, they sat silent again. They looked at each other; they looked at me; neither would take the responsibility of giving me a further hint to go. Much as they desired my going, I was sure they were both afraid of it. I might be a nuisance and yet I was a safeguard. They were too near the brink of danger not to feel that, after all, there was something in having the safeguard there.

A few minutes later Mrs. Brokenshire flew to shelter herself behind this protection. She fluttered softly to my side, beginning again to talk of Hugh. Knowing by this time that her interest in him was only a blind for her frightened essays in passion, I took up the subject but half-heartedly.

"I've the money here," she confided to me, "if you'll only take charge of it."

When I had declined to do this, for the reasons I had already given, her face brightened.

"Then we can talk it over again." She rose as she spoke. "I can't stay any longer now—but we'll talk it over again. Let me see! This is Tuesday. If I came—"

"I'm always at the Hotel Mary Chilton after six," I said, significantly.

I smiled inwardly at the way in which she took this information.

"Oh, I'll come before that—and I sha'n't keep you—just to talk about Hugh —and see he won't take the money—perhaps on—on Thursday."

As nominally she had come to see me, nominally it was my place to accompany her to the door. In this at least I got my cue, walking the few paces with her, while she held my hand. I gathered that, the minutes of temptation being past, she bore me some gratitude for having helped her over them. At any rate, she pressed my fingers and gave me wistful, teary smiles, till at last she was out in the lighted street and I had closed the door behind her.

It was only half past five, and I had still thirty minutes to fill in. As I turned back into the room I found Mr. Grainger walking aimlessly up and down, inspecting a bit of lustrous faïence or the backs of a row of books, and making me feel that there was something he wished to say. His movements were exactly those of a man screwing up his courage or trying to find words.

The simplest thing I could do was to sit down at my desk and make a feint at writing. I seemed to be ignoring my employer's presence, but in reality, as I watched him from under my lids, I was getting a better impression of him than on any previous occasion.

There was nothing Olympian about him as there was about Howard Brokenshire. He was too young to be Olympian, being not more than thirty-eight. He struck me, indeed, as just a big, sinewy man of the type which fights and hunts and races and loves, and has dumb, uncomprehended longings which none of these pursuits can satisfy. In this he was English more than American, and Scottish more than English. He was certainly not the American business man as seen in hotel lobbies and on the stage. He might have been classed as the American romantic—an explorer, a missionary, or a shooter of big game, according to taste and income. Larry Strangways said that among Americans you most frequently met his like in East Africa, Manchuria, or Brazil. That he was in business in New York was an accident of tradition and inheritance. Just as an Englishman who might have been a soldier or a solicitor is a country gentleman because his father has left him landed estates, so Stacy Grainger had become a financier.

As a financier, I understood he helped to furnish the money in undertakings in which other men did the work. In this respect the direction his interests took was what might have been expected of so virile a character—steel, iron, gunpowder, shells, the founding of cannon, the building of war-ships; the forceful, the destructive. I gathered from Mr. Strangways that he was forever making journeys to Washington, to Pittsburg, to Cape Breton, wherever money could be invested in mighty conquering things. It was these projects that Howard Brokenshire had attacked so savagely as almost to bring him to ruin, though he had now re-established himself as strongly as before.

Being as terrified of him as of his rival, I prayed inwardly that he would go away. Once or twice in marching up and down he paused before my desk, and the pen almost dropped from my hand. I knew he was trying to formulate a hint that when Mrs. Brokenshire came again—But even on my part the thought would not go into words. Words made it gross, and it was what he must have discovered each time he approached me. Each time he approached me I fancied that his poetic eye grew apologetic, that his shoulders sagged, and that his hard, strong mouth became weak before syllables that would not pass the lips. Then he would veer away, searching doubtless some easier phrase, some more delicate suggestion, only to fail again.

It was a relief when, after a last attempt, he passed into the corridor leading to the house. I could breathe, I could think; I could look back over the last half-hour and examine my conduct. I was not satisfied with it, because I had frustrated love—even that kind of love; and yet I asked myself how I could have acted differently.

In substance I asked the same of Larry Strangways when he came to dine with me next day. Hugh being in Philadelphia on one of his pathetic cruises after work, I had invited Mr. Strangways by telephone, begging him to come on the ground that, having got me into this trouble, he must advise me as to getting out.

"I didn't get you into the trouble," he smiled across the table. "I only helped to get you the job."

"But when you got me the job, as you call it—"

"I knew you would be able to do the work."

"And did you think the work would be—this?"

"I couldn't tell anything about that. I simply knew you could do the work—from all the points of view."

"And do you think I've done it?"

"I know you've done it. You couldn't do anything else. I won't go back of that."

If my heart gave a sudden leap at these words it was because of the tone. It betrayed that quality behind the tone to which I had been responding, and of which I had been afraid, ever since I knew the man. By a great effort I kept my words on the casual, friendly plane, as I said:

"Your confidence is flattering, but it doesn't help me. What I want to know is this: Assuming that they love each other, should I allow myself to be used as the pretext for their meetings?"

"Does it do you any harm?"

"Does it do them any good?"

"Couldn't you let that be their affair?"

"How can I, when I'm dragged into it?"

"If you're only dragged into it to the extent of this afternoon—"

"Only! You can use that word of a situation—"

"In which you played propriety."

"Oh, it wasn't playing."

"Yes, it was; it was playing the game—as they only play it who aren't quitters but real sports."

"But I'm not a sport. I've the quitter in me. I'm even thinking of flinging up the position—"

"And leaving them to their fate."

I smiled.

"Couldn't I let that be their affair?"

He, too, smiled, his head thrown back, his white teeth gleaming.

"You think you've caught me, don't you? But you've got the shoe on the wrong foot. I said just now that it might be their affair as to whether or not it did them any good to have you as the pretext of their meetings; but it's surely your affair when you say they sha'n't. Their meetings will be one thing so long as they have you; whereas without you—"

"Then you think they'll keep meeting in any case?"

"I've nothing to say about that. I limit myself to believing that in any situation that requires skilful handling your first name is resourcefulness."

I shifted my ground.

"Oh, but when it's such an odious situation!"

"No situation is odious in which you're a participant, just as no view is ugly where there's a garden full of flowers."

He went on with his dinner as complacently as if he had not thrown me into a state of violent inward confusion. All I could do was to summon Hugh's image from the shades of memory into which it had withdrawn, and beg it to keep me true to him. The thought of being false to the man to whom I had actually owned my love outraged in me every sentiment akin to single-heartedness. In a kind of desperation I dragged Hugh's name into the conversation, and yet in doing so I merely laid myself open to another shock.

"You can't be in love with him!"

The words were the same as Mrs. Billing's; the emphasis was similar.

"I am," I declared, bluntly, not so much to contradict the speaker as to fortify myself.

"You may think you are—"

"Well, if I think I am, isn't it the same thing as—"

"Lord, no! not with love! Love is the most deceptive of the emotions—to people who haven't had much experience of its tricks."

"Have you?"

He met this frankly.

"No; nor you. That's why you can so easily take yourself in."

I grew cold and dignified.

"If you think I'm taking myself in when I say that I'm in love with Hugh Brokenshire—"

"That's certainly it."

Though I knew my cheeks were flaming a dahlia red, I forced myself to look him in the eyes.

"Then I'm afraid it would be useless to try to convince you—"

He nodded.

"Quite!"

"So that we can only let the subject drop."

He looked at me with mock gravity.

"I don't see that. It's an interesting topic."

"Possibly; but as it doesn't lead us any further—"

"But it does. It leads us to where we see straighter."

"Yes, but if I don't need to see straighter than I do?"

"We all need to see as straight as we can."

"I'm seeing as straight as I can when I say—"

"Oh, but not as straight as I can! I can see that a noble character doesn't always distinguish clearly between love and kindness, or between kindness and loyalty, or between loyalty and self-sacrifice, and that the higher the heart, the more likely it is to impose on itself. No one is so easily deceived as to love and loving as the man or the woman who's truly generous."

"If I was truly generous—"

"I know what you are," he said, shortly.

"Then if you know what I am you must know, too, that I couldn't do other than care for a man who's given up so much for my sake."

"You couldn't do other than admire him. You couldn't do other than be grateful to him. You probably couldn't do other than want to stand by him through thick and thin—"

"Well, then?"

"But that's not love."

"If it isn't love it's so near to it—"

"Exactly—which is what I'm saying. It's so near it that you don't know the difference, and won't know the difference till—till the real thing affords you the contrast."

I did my best to be scornful.

"Really! You speak like an expert."

"Yes; an expert by intuition."

I was still scornful.

"Only that?"

"Only that. You see," he smiled, "the expert by experience has learnt a little; but the expert by intuition knows it all."

"Then, when I need information on the subject, I'll come to you."

"And I'll promise to give it to you frankly."

"Thanks," I said, sweetly. "But you'll wait till I come, won't you? And in the mean time, you'll not say any more about it."

"Does that mean that I'm not to say any more about it ever—or only for to-night?"

I knew, suddenly, what the question meant to me. I took time to see that I was shutting a door which my heart cried out to have left open. But I answered, still sweetly and with a smile:

"Suppose we make it that you won't say any more about it—ever?"

He gazed at me; I gazed at him. A long half-minute went by before he uttered the words, very slowly and deliberately:

"I won't say any more about it—for to-night."

CHAPTER XIV

On Thursday Mr. Grainger came to the library to tea, but notwithstanding her suggestion Mrs. Brokenshire did not. She came, however, on Friday when he did not. For some time after that he came daily.

Toward me his manner had little variation; he was courteous and distant. I cannot say that he ever had tea with me, for even if he accepted a cup, which he did from time to time, as if keeping up a rôle, he carried it to some distant corner of the room where he was either examining the objects or making their acquaintance. He came about half past four and went about half past five, always appearing from the house and retiring by the same way. In the house itself, as I understood from Mrs. Daly, he displayed an interest he had not shown for years.

"It's out of wan room and into another, and raisin' the shades and pushin' the furniture about, till you'd swear he was goin' to be married."

I thought of Mr. Pyne, wondering if, before his trip to Atlantic City with Mrs. Grimshaw, he, too, had wandered about his house, appraising its possibilities from the point of view of a new mistress.

On the Friday when Mrs. Brokenshire came and Mr. Grainger did not she made no comment on his non-appearance. She even sustained with some success the fiction that her visit was on my account. Only her soft eyes turned with a quick light toward the door leading to the house at every sound that might have been a footstep.

When she talked it was chiefly about Mr. Brokenshire.

"It's telling on him—all this trouble about Hugh."

I was curious.

"Telling on him in what way?"

"It's made him older—and grayer—and the trouble with his eye comes oftener."

It seemed to me that I saw an opportunity.

"Then why doesn't he give in?"

"Give in? Mr. Brokenshire? Why, he never gave in in his life."

"But if he suffers?"

"He'd rather suffer than give in. He's not an unkind man, not really, so long as he has his own way; but once he's thwarted—"

"Every one has to be thwarted some time."

"He'd agree to that; but he'd say every one but him. That's why, when he first met—met me—and my mother at that time meant to have me—to have me marry some one else— You knew that, didn't you?"

I reminded her that she had told me so among the rocks at Newport.

"Did I? Perhaps I did. It's—it's rather on my mind. I had to change so—so suddenly. But what I was going to say was that when Mr. Brokenshire saw that mamma meant me to marry some one else, and that I—that I wanted to, there was nothing he didn't do. It was in the papers—and everything. But nothing would stop him till he'd got what he wanted."

I pumped up my courage to say:

"You mean, till you gave it to him."

She bit her lip.

"Mamma gave it to him. I had to do as I was told. You'd say, I suppose, that I needn't have done it, but you don't know." She hesitated before going on. "It —it was money. We—we had to have it. Mamma thought that Mr.—the man I was to have married first—would never have any more. It was all sorts of things on the Stock Exchange—and bulls and bears and things like that. There was a whole week of it—and every one knew it was about me. I nearly died; but mamma didn't mind. She enjoyed it. It's the sort of thing she would enjoy. She made me go with her to the opera every night. Some one always asked us to sit in their box. She put me in the front where the audience watched me through their opera-glasses more than they did the stage—and I was a kind of spectacle. There was one night—they were singing the 'Meistersinger'— when I felt just like Eva, put up as a prize for whoever could win me. But I was talking of Mr. Brokenshire, wasn't I? Do you think his eye will ever be any better?"

She asked the question without change of tone. I could only reply that I didn't know.

"The doctor says—that is, he's told me—that in a way it's mental. It's the result of the strain he's put upon his nerves by overwork and awful tempers. Of course, his responsibilities have been heavy, though of late years he's been able to shift some of them to other people's shoulders. And then," she went on, in her sweet, even voice, "what happened about me—coming to him so late in life—and—and tearing him to pieces more violently than if he'd been a younger man—young men get over things—that made it worse. Don't you see it would?"

I said I could understand that that might be the effect.

"Of course, if I could really be a wife to him—"

"Well, can't you?"

She shuddered.

"He terrifies me. When he's there I'm not a woman any more; I'm a captive."

"But since you've married him—"

"I didn't marry him; he married me. I was as much a bargain as if I had been bought. And now mamma sees that—that she might have got a better price."

I thought it enough to say:

"That must make it hard for her."

A sigh bubbled up, like that of a child who has been crying.

"It makes it hard for me." She eyed me with a long, oblique regard. "Don't you think it's awful when an elderly man falls in love with a young girl who herself is in love with some one else?"

I could only dodge that question.

"All unhappiness is awful."

"Ah, but this! An elderly man!—in love! Madly in love! It's not natural; it's frightful; and when it's with yourself—"

She moved away from me and began to inspect the room. In spite of her agitation she did this more in detail than when she had been there before, making the round of the book-shelves much as Mr. Grainger himself was in the habit of doing, and gazing without comment on the Persian and Italian potteries. It was easy to place her as one of those women who live surrounded by beautiful things to which they pay no attention. Mr. Brokenshire's richly Italianate dwelling was to her just a house. It would have been equally just a house had it been Jacobean or Louis Quinze or in the fashion of the Brothers Adam, and she would have seen little or no difference in periods and styles. The books she now looked at were mere backs; they were bindings and titles. Since they belonged to Stacy Grainger she could look at them with soft, unseeing eyes, thinking of him. That was all. Without comment of my own I accompanied her, watching the quick, bird-like turnings of her head whenever she thought she heard a step.

"It's nice for you here," she said, when at last she gave signs of going. "I—I

149

love it. It's so quiet—and—and safe. Nobody knows I come to—to see you."

Her stammering emboldened me to take a liberty.

"But suppose they found out?"

She was as innocent as a child as she glanced up at me and said:

"It would still be to see you. There's no harm in that."

"Even so, Mr. Brokenshire wouldn't approve of it."

"But he'll never know. It's not the sort of thing any one would think of. I leave the motor down at Sixth Avenue, and this time of year it's so dark. As soon as I heard Miss Davis was leaving I thought how nice the place would be for you."

Since it was useless to make the obvious correction here, I thanked her for her kindness, going on to add:

"But I don't want to get into any trouble."

"No, of course not." She began moving toward the door. "What kind of trouble were you thinking of?"

I wondered whether or not, having taken one liberty, I could take another.

"When I see my boat being caught in the rapids I'm afraid there's a cataract ahead."

It took her some thirty seconds to seize the force of this. Having got it her eyes fell.

"Oh, I see! And does that mean," she went on, her bosom heaving, "that you're afraid of the cataract on your own account—or on mine?"

I paused in our slow drifting toward the door. She was a great lady in the land, and I was nobody. I had much to risk, and I risked it.

"Should I offend you," I asked, deferentially, "if I said—on yours?"

For an instant she became as haughty as so sweet a nature knew how to be, but the prompting passed.

"No; you don't offend me," she said, after a brief pause. "We're friends, aren't we, in spite of—"

As she hesitated I filled in the phrase.

"In spite of the difference between us."

Because she was pursuing her own thoughts she allowed that to pass.

"People have gone over cataracts—and still lived."

"Ah, but there's more to existence than life," I exclaimed, promptly.

"There was a friend of my own," she continued, without immediate reference to my observation; "at least she was a friend—I suppose she is still—her name was Madeline Grimshaw—"

"Yes, Mrs. Pyne; but she wasn't Mrs. Brokenshire."

"No; she never was so unhappy." She pressed her handkerchief against the two great tears that rolled down her cheeks. "She did love Mr. Grimshaw at one time, whereas I—"

"But you say he's kind."

"Oh yes. It isn't that. He's more than kind. He'd smother me with things I'd like to have. It's—it's when he comes near me—when he touches me—and—and his eye!"

I knew enough of physical repulsion to be able to change my line of appeal. "But do you think you'd gain anything if you made him unhappy—now?"

She looked at me wonderingly.

"I shouldn't think you'd plead for him."

I had ventured so far that I could go a little farther.

"I don't think I'm pleading for him so much as for you."

"Why do you plead for me? Do you think I should be—sorry?"

"If you did what I imagine you're contemplating—yes."

She surprised me by admitting my implication.

"Even if I did, I couldn't be sorrier than I am."

"Oh, but existence is more than joy and sorrow."

"You said just now that it was more than life. I suppose you mean that it's love."

"I should say that it's more than love."

"Why, what can it be?"

I smiled apologetically.

"Mightn't it be—right?"

She studied me with an air of angelic sweetness.

"Oh no, I could never believe that."

And she went more resolutely toward the door.

Hugh returned in good spirits from Philadelphia. He had been well received. His name had secured him much the same welcome as that accorded him on his first excursions into Wall Street. I didn't tell him I feared that the results would be similar, for I saw that he was cheered.

To verify the love I had acknowledged to him more than once, I was eager to look at him again. I found a man thinner and older and shabbier than the Hugh who first attracted my attention by being kind to me. I could have borne with his being thinner and older; but that he should be shabbier wrung my heart.

I considered myself engaged to him. That as yet I had not spoken the final word was a detail, in my mind, considering that I had so often rested in his arms and pillowed my head on his shoulder. The fact, too, that when I had first allowed myself those privileges I had taken him to be a strong character —the shadow of a rock in a thirsty land, I had called him—and that I now saw he was a weak one, bound me to him the more closely. I had gone to him because I needed him; but now that I saw he needed me I was sure I could never break away from him.

He dined with me at the Mary Chilton on the evening of his return, sitting where Larry Strangways had sat only forty-eight hours previously. I was sorry then that I had not changed the table. To be face to face with two men, on exactly the same spot, on occasions so near together, in conditions so alike, gave me a sense of faithlessness. Though I wanted nothing so much as to be honest with them both, I was afraid of being so with neither; and yet for this I hardly knew where to place the blame. I suffered for Hugh because of Larry Strangways, and I suffered for Larry Strangways because of Hugh. If I suffered for myself I was scarcely aware of it, having to give so much thought to them.

Nevertheless, I regretted that I had not chosen another table, and all the more when Hugh brought the matter up. He had finished telling me of his experiences in Philadelphia. "Now what have you been doing?" he demanded, a smile lighting up his tired face.

"Oh, nothing much—the same old thing."

"Seen anybody in particular?"

I weighed my answer carefully.

"Nobody in particular, except Mr. Strangways."

He frowned.

"Where did you see that fellow?"

"Right here."

"Right here? What do you mean by that?"

"He came to dine with me."

"Dine with you! And sat where I'm sitting now?"

I tried to take this pleasantly.

"It's the only place I've got to ask any one I want to talk to."

"But why should you want to talk to—to—" I saw him struggling with the word, but it came out—"to that bounder?"

"He's a friend of mine, Hugh. I've asked you already to remember that he's a gentleman."

"Gentleman! O Lord!" He became kindly and coaxing, leaning across the table with an ingratiating smile. "Look here, little Alix! Don't you think that for my sake it's time you were beginning to drop that lot?"

Though I revolted against the expression, I pretended to see nothing amiss.

"You mean just as Libby Jaynes had to drop the barbers and the pages in the hotel when she became Mrs. Tracy Allen."

He laughed nervously.

"Oh, I don't go as far as that. And yet if I did—"

"It wouldn't be too far." I gave him the impression that I was thinking the question out. "But you see, Hugh, dear, I don't see any difference between Mr. Strangways—"

"And me?"

"I wasn't going to say you, but between Mr. Strangways and the people you'd like me to know. Or rather, if I do see a difference it's that Mr. Strangways is so much more a man of the world than—than—"

Perceiving my embarrassment, he broke in:

"Than who?"

I took my courage in both hands.

"Than Mr. Rossiter, for example, or your brother, Mr. Jack Brokenshire, or any of the men I met when I was with your sister. If I hadn't seen you—the truest gentleman I ever knew—I shouldn't have supposed that any of them belonged to the real great world at all."

To my relief he took this good-naturedly.

"That's what we call social inexperience, little Alix. It's because you don't know how to distinguish."

"That is, I don't know a good thing when I see it."

"You don't know that sort of good thing—the American who counts. But you can learn. And if you learn you've got to take as a starting-point the fact that, just as there are things one does and things one doesn't do, so there are people one knows and people one doesn't know—and no one can tell you the reason why."

"But if one asked for a reason—"

"It would queer you with the right people. They don't want a reason. If people do want a reason—well, they've got to stay out of it. It was one of the things Libby Jaynes picked up as if she'd been born to it. She knew how to cut; she knew how to cut dead; and she cut as dead as she knew how."

"But, Hugh, darling, I don't know how."

He was all forbearance.

"You'll learn, sweet." As for the moment the waitress was absent, he put out his hand and locked his fingers within mine. "You've got it in you. Once you've had a chance you'll knock Libby Jaynes into a cocked hat."

I shook my head.

"I'm not sure that you're right."

"I know I'm right, if you do as I tell you: and to begin with you've got to put that fellow Strangways in his place."

I let it go at that, having so many other things to think of that any mere status of my own became of no importance. I was willing that Hugh should marry me as Tracy Allen married Libby Jaynes, or in any other way, so long as I could play my part in the rest of the drama with right-mindedness. But it was precisely that that grew more difficult.

When Mrs. Brokenshire and Mr. Grainger next met under what I can only call my chaperonage they were distinctly more at ease. The first stammering, shamefaced awkwardness was gone. They knew by this time what they had to say and said it. They had also come to understand that if I could not be moved I might be outwitted. By the simple expedient of wandering away on the plea of looking at this or that decorative object they obtained enough solitude to serve their purposes. Without taking themselves beyond my range of vision they got out of earshot.

As far as that went I was relieved. I was not responsible for what they did, but only for what I did myself. I was not their keeper; I didn't want to be a spy on them. When, at a certain minute, as they returned toward me, I saw him pass a letter to her, it was entirely by chance. I reflected then that, while she ran no risk in using the mails in writing to him, it was not so with him in writing to her, and that communications of importance might have to pass between them. It was nothing to me. I was sorry to have surprised the act and tried to dismiss it from my mind.

It was repeated, however, the next time they came and many times after that. Their comings settled into a routine of being twice a week, with fair regularity. Tuesdays and Fridays were their days, though not without variation. It was indeed this variation that saved the situation on a certain afternoon when otherwise all might have been lost.

CHAPTER XV

We had come to February, 1914. During the intervening months the conditions in which I lived and worked underwent little change. My days and nights were passed between the library and the Mary Chilton, with few social distractions, though I had some. Larry Strangways's sister, Mrs. Applegate, had called on me, and her house, a headquarters of New York philanthropies, had opened to me its kindly doors. Through Mrs. Applegate one or two other women came to relieve my loneliness, and now and then old Halifax friends visiting New York took me to theaters and to dinners at hotels. Ethel Rossiter was as friendly as fear of her father and of social conventions permitted her to be, and once or twice when she was quite alone I lunched with her. On each of these occasions she had something new to tell me.

The first was that Hugh had met his father accidentally face to face, and that the parent had cut the son. Of that Hugh had told me nothing. According to Ethel, he was more affected by the incident than by anything else since the beginning of his cares. He felt it too deeply to speak of it even to me, to whom he spoke of everything.

It happened, I believe at the foot of the steps of a club. Hugh, who was passing, saw his father coming down, and waited. Howard Brokenshire brought into play his faculty of seeing without seeing, and went on majestically, while Hugh stared after him with tears of vexation in his eyes.

"He felt it the more," Mrs. Rossiter stated in her impartial way, "because I doubt if he had the price of his dinner in his pocket."

It was then that she gave me to understand that if it were not that Mildred was lending him money he would have nothing to subsist on at all. Mildred had a little from her grandfather Brew, being privileged in this respect because she was the only one of the first Mrs. Brokenshire's children born at the time of the grandfather's demise. The legacy had been a trifle, but from this fund, which had never been his father's, Hugh consented to take loans.

"Hugh, darling," I said to him the next time I had speech with him, "don't you see now that he's irreconcilable? He'll either starve you into surrender—"

"Never," he cried, thumping the table with his hand.

"Or else you must take such work as you can get."

"Such work as I can get! Do you know how much that would bring me in a week?"

"Even so," I reasoned, "you'd have work and I should have work, and we'd live."

He was hurt.

"Americans don't believe in working their women," he declared, loftily. "If I can't give you a life in which you'll have nothing at all to do—"

"But I don't want a life in which I'll have nothing at all to do," I cried. "Your idle women strike me as a weak point in your national organization. It's like the dinner-parties I've seen at some of your restaurants and hotels—a circle of men at one table and a circle of women at another. You revolve too much in separate spheres. Your women have too little to do with business and politics and your men with society and the fine arts. I'm not used to such a pitiless separation of the sexes. Don't let us begin it, Hugh, darling. Let me share what you share—"

"You won't share anything sordid, little Alix, I can tell you that. When you're my wife you'll have nothing to think of but having a good time and looking your prettiest—"

"I should die of it," I exclaimed but this he took as a joke.

That had passed in January. What Ethel Rossiter told me the next time I lunched with her was that Lady Cecilia Boscobel had accepted her invitation and was expected within a few weeks. She repeated what she had already said of her, in exactly the same words.

"She's a good deal of a girl, Cissie is." My heart leaped and fell almost simultaneously. If I could only give up Hugh in such a way that he would have to give me up, this girl might help us out of our impasse. Had Mrs. Rossiter stopped there I might have made some noble vow of renunciation; but she went on: "If she wants Hugh she'll take him. Don't be under any illusion about that."

Though my quick mettle was up, I said, docilely:

"Oh no, I'm not. But if you mean taking him away from me—well, a good many people have tried it, haven't they?"

"Cissie Boscobel hasn't tried it."

But I was peaceably inclined.

"Oh, well," I said, "perhaps she won't. She may not think it worth her while."

"If you want to know my opinion," Mrs. Rossiter insisted, as she helped herself to the peas which the rosebud Thomas was passing, "I think she will.

Men aren't so plentiful over there as you seem to suppose—that is, men of the kind they'd marry. Lord Goldborough has no money at all, as you might say, and yet the girls have to be set up in big establishments. You've only got to look at them to see it. Cissie marrying a subaltern with a thousand pounds a year isn't thinkable. It wouldn't dress her. She's coming over here to take a look at Hugh, and if she likes him— Well, I told you long ago that you'd be wise to snap up that young Strangways. He's much better-looking than Hugh, and more in your own— Besides, Jim says that now that he's with"—she balked at the name of Grainger—"now that he's where he is he's beginning to make money. It doesn't take so long when people have the brains for it."

All this gave me a feeling of mingled curiosity and fear when, a few weeks later, I came on Mrs. Rossiter and Lady Cecilia Boscobel looking into a shop window in Fifth Avenue. It was a Saturday afternoon, the day which I had off and on which I made my modest purchases. It was a cold, brisk day, with light snow whirling in tiny eddies on the ground. I was going northward on the sunny side. At a distance of some fifty yards I recognized Mrs. Rossiter's motor standing by the curb, and cast my eyes about for a possible glimpse of her. Moving away from the window of the jeweler's whence she had probably come out, she saw me approach, and turned at once with a word or two to the lady beside her, who also looked in my direction. I knew by intuition who Mrs. Rossiter's companion was, and that my connection with the family had been explained to her.

Mrs. Rossiter made the presentation in her usual offhand way.

"Oh, Miss Adare! I want to introduce you to Lady Cecilia Boscobel."

We exchanged civil, remote, and non-committal salutations, each of us with her hands in her muff. My immediate impression was one of color, as it is when you see old Limoges enamels. There was more color in Lady Cissie's personality than in that of any one I have ever looked at. Her hair was red— not auburn or copper, but red—a decorative, flaming red. I have often noticed how slight is the difference between beautiful red hair and ugly. Lady Cissie's was of the shade that is generally ugly, but which in her case was rendered glorious by the introduction of some such pigment, gleaming and umber, as that which gives the peculiar hue to Australian gold. I had never seen such hair or hair in such quantities, except in certain pictures of the pre-Raphaelite brotherhood, for which I should have supposed there could have been no earthly model had my father not known Eleanor Siddall. Lady Cissie's eyes were gray, with a greenish light in them when she turned her head. Her complexion could only be compared to the kind of carnation which the whitest of whites is flecked in just the right spots by the rosiest rose. In the lips, which were full and firm, also like Eleanor Siddall's, the rose became carmine, to melt away into coral-pink in the shell-like ears. Her dress of seal-brown broadcloth, on which there was a sheen, was relieved by occasional touches of sage-green, and the numerous sable tails on her boa and muff blew this way and that way in the wind. In the small black hat, perched at what I can only describe as a triumphant angle, an orange wing became at the tip of each tiny topmost feather a daring line of scarlet. Nestling on the sage-green below the throat a row of amber beads slumbered and smoldered with lemon and orange and ruby lights that now and then shot out rays of crimson or scarlet fire.

I thought of my own costume—naturally. I was in gray, with inexpensive black furs. An iridescent buckle, with hues such as you see in a pigeon's neck, at the side of my black-velvet toque was my only bit of color. I was poor Jenny Wren in contrast to a splendid bird-of-paradise. So be it! I could at least be a foil to this healthy, vigorous young beauty who was two inches taller than I, and might have my share of the advantages which go with all antithesis.

The talk was desultory, and in it the English girl took no part. Mrs. Rossiter asked me where I was going, what I was going for, and whether or not she couldn't take me to my destination in her car. I declined this offer, explained that my errands were trivial, and examined Lady Cissie through the corner of my eye. On her side Lady Cissie examined me quite frankly—not haughtily, but distantly and rather sympathetically. She had come all this distance to take a look at Hugh, and I was the girl he loved. I counted on the fact to give poor Jenny Wren her value, and I think it did. At any rate, when I had answered all Mrs. Rossiter's questions and was moving off to continue my way up-town, Lady Cissie's rich lips quivered in a sort of farewell smile.

But Hugh showed little interest when I painted her portrait verbally.

"Yes, that's the girl," he observed indifferently, "red-headed, long-legged, slashy-colored, laid on a bit too thick."

"She's beautiful, Hugh."

"Is she? Well, perhaps so. Wouldn't be my style; but every one to his taste."

"It you saw her now—"

"Oh, I've seen her often enough, just as she's seen me."

"She hasn't seen you as you are to-day, and neither have you seen her. A few years makes a difference."

He looked at me quizzically.

"Look here, little Alix, what are you giving us? Do you think I'd turn you

159

down now—for all the Lady Cissies in the British peerage? Do you, now?"

"Not, perhaps, if you put it as turning me down—"

"Well, as you turning me down, then?"

"Our outlook is pretty dark, isn't it?"

"Just wait."

I ignored his pathetic boastfulness to continue my own sentence.

"And this prospect is so brilliant. You'd have a handsome wife, a big income, a good position, an important family backing on both sides of the Atlantic—all of which would make you the man you ought to be. Now that I've seen her, and rather guess that she'd take you, I don't see how I can let you forfeit so much. I don't want to make you regret the day you ever saw me—"

"Or regret yourself the day you ever saw me."

If I took up this challenge it was more for his sake than my own.

"Then suppose I accept that way of putting it?"

He looked at me solemnly, for a second or two, after which he burst out laughing. That I might have hesitations as to connecting myself with the Brokenshires was more than he could grasp. He might have minutes of jealousy of Larry Strangways, but his doubt could go no further. It went no further, even after he had seen Lady Cecilia and they had renewed their early acquaintance. Ethel Rossiter had managed that, of course with her father's connivance.

"Fine big girl," Hugh commended, "but too showy."

"She's not showy," I contradicted. "A thing isn't necessarily showy because it has bright colors. Tropical birds are not showy, nor roses, nor rubies—"

"I prefer pearls," he said, quietly. "You're a pearl, little Alix, the pearl of great price for which a man sells all that he has and buys it." Before I could respond to this kindly speech he burst out: "Good Lord! don't you suppose I can see what it all means? Cissie's the gay artificial fly that's to tempt the fish away from the little silvery minnow. Once I've darted after the bit of red and yellow dad will have hooked me. That's his game. Don't you think I see it? What dad wants is not that I shall have a wife I can love, but that he shall have a daughter-in-law with a title. You'd have to be, well, what I hope you will be some day, to know what that means to a man like dad. A son-in-law with a title—that's as common as beans to rich Americans; but a daughter-in-law with a title—a real, genuine British title, as sound as the Bank of England—that's something new. You can count on the fingers of one hand the American families that have got 'em"—he named them, one in Philadelphia, one in Chicago, one or two in New York—"and dad's as mad as blazes that he didn't think of the thing first. If he had, he'd have put Jack on to it, in spite of all Pauline's money; but since it's too late for that I must toe the mark. Well, I'm not going to, do you see? I'm going to choose my own wife, and I've chosen her. Birth and position mean nothing to me, for I'm as much of a Socialist as ever—or almost."

With such resolution as this there was no way of reasoning, so that I could only go on, wondering and hoping and doing what I could for the best.

What I could do for the best included watching over Mrs. Brokenshire. As winter progressed the task became harder and I grew the more anxious. So far no one suspected her visits to Mr. Grainger's library, and to the best of my knowledge her imprudence ended there. Further than to wander about the room the lovers never tried to elude me, though now and then I could see, without watching them, that he took her hand. Once or twice I thought he kissed her, but of that I was happily not sure. It was a relief, too, that as the days grew longer occasional visitors dropped in while they were there. The old gentleman interested in prints and the lady who studied Shakespeare came not infrequently. There were couples, too, who wandered in, seeking for their own purposes a half-hour of privacy. After all, the place was almost a public one to those who knew how to find it; and I was quick enough to see that in this very publicity lay a measure of salvation.

Mrs. Brokenshire was as quick to perceive this as I. When there were other people there she was more at ease. Nothing was simpler then than for Mr. Grainger and herself to be visitors like the rest, strolling about or sitting in shady corners, and keeping themselves unrecognized. There was thus a Thursday in the early part of March when I didn't expect them, because it was a Thursday. They came, however, only to find the old gentleman interested in prints and the lady who studied Shakespeare already on the spot. I was never so glad of anything as of this accidental happening when a surprising thing occurred to me next day.

It was between half past five and six on the Friday. As the lovers had come on the preceding day, I knew they would not appear on this, and was beginning to make my preparations for going home. I was actually pinning on my hat when the soft opening of the outer door startled me. A soft step sounded in the little inner vestibule, and then there came an equally soft, breathless standing still.

My hands were paralyzed in their upward position at my hat; my heart pounded so that I could hear it; my eyes were wide with terror as they looked back at me from the splendid Venetian mirror before which I stood. I was always afraid of robbers or murderers, even though I had the wrought-iron grille between me and them, and Mr. or Mrs. Daly within call.

Knowing that there was nothing for it but to go and see who was there, and suspecting that it might be Mrs. Brokenshire, after all, I dragged my feet across the few intervening paces. It was not Mrs. Brokenshire. It was a man, a man who looked inordinately big and majestic in this little decorative pen. I needed a few seconds in which to gaze, a few seconds in which to adjust my faculties, before grasping the fact that I saw Mrs. Brokenshire's husband. On his side, he needed something of the sort himself. Of all people in the world with whom he expected to find himself face to face I am sure I must have been the last.

I touched the spring, however, and the little portal opened. It opened and he stepped in. He stepped in and stood still. He stood still and looked round him. If I dare to say it of one who was never timid in his life, he looked round him timidly. His eyes showed it, his attitude showed it. He had come on a hateful errand; his feet were on hateful ground. He expected to see something more than me—and emptiness.

I got back some of my own self-control by being sorry for him, giving no indication of ever having met him before.

"You'd like to see the library, sir," I said, as I should have said it to any chance visitor.

He dropped into a large William and Mary chair, one of the show pieces, and placed his silk hat on the floor.

"I'll sit down," he murmured less to me than to himself. His stick he dandled now across and now between his knees.

The tea things were still on the table.

"Would you like a cup of tea?" I asked, in genuine solicitude.

"Yes—no." I think he would have liked it, but he probably remembered whose tea it was. "No," he repeated, with decision.

He breathed heavily, with short, puffy gasps. I recalled then that Mrs. Brokenshire had said that his heart had been affected. As a matter of fact, he put his gloved left hand up to it, as people do who feel something giving way within.

To relieve the embarrassment of the situation I said:

"I could turn on all the lights and you could see the library without going round it."

162

Withdrawing the hand at his heart, he raised it in the manner with which I was familiar.

"Sit down," he commanded, as sternly as his shortness of breath allowed.

The companion William and Mary chair being near, I slipped into it. Having him in three-quarters profile, I could study him without doing it too obviously, and could verify Mrs. Brokenshire's statements that Hugh's affairs were "telling on him." He was perceptibly older, in the way in which people look older all at once after having long kept the semblance of youth. The skin had grown baggy, the eyes tired; the beard and mustache, though as well cared for as ever, more decidedly mixed with gray. It was indicative of something that had begun to disintegrate in his self-esteem, that when his poor left eye screwed up he turned the terrifying right one on me with no effort to conceal the grimace.

As it was for him to break the silence, I waited in my huge ornamental chair, hoping he would begin.

"What are you doing here?"

The voice had lost none of its soft staccato nor of its whip-lash snap.

"I'm Mr. Grainger's librarian," I replied, meekly.

"Since when?" he panted.

"Since not long after I left Mrs. Rossiter."

He took his time to think another question out.

"How did your employer come to know about you?"

I explained, as though he had had no knowledge of the fact, that Mrs. Rossiter had employed for her boy, Brokenshire, a tutor named Strangways. This Mr. Strangways had attracted Mr. Grainger's attention by some articles he had written for the financial press. An introduction had followed, after which Mr. Grainger had engaged the young man as his secretary. Hearing that Mr. Grainger had need of a librarian, Mr. Strangways had suggested me.

I could see suspicion in the way in which he eyed me as well as in his words.

"Had you no other recommendation?"

"No, sir," I said, simply, "none that Mr. Grainger ever told me of."

He let that pass.

"And what do you do here?"

"I show the library to visitors. If any one wishes a particular book, or to look at engravings, I help him to find what he wants." I thought it well to keep up the fiction that he had come as a sight-seer. "If you'd care to go over the place now, sir—"

His hand went up in a majestic waving aside of this courtesy.

"And have you many visitors to the—to the library?"

Though I saw the implication, I managed to elude it.

"Yes, sir, taking one day with another. It depends a little on the weather and the time of year."

"Are they chiefly strangers—or—or do you ever see any one you've—you've seen before?"

His difficulty in phrasing this question made me even more sorry for him than I was already. I decided, both for his sake and my own, to walk up frankly and take the bull by the horns. "They're generally strangers; but sometimes people come whom I know." I looked at him steadily as I continued. "I'll tell you something, sir. Perhaps I ought not to, and it may be betraying a secret; but you might as well know it from me as hear it from some one else." The expression of the face he turned on me was so much that of Jove, whose look could strike a man dead, that I had all I could do to go on. "Mrs. Brokenshire comes to see me."

"To see—you?"

"Yes, sir, to see me."

The staccato accent grew difficult and thick. "What for?"

"Because she can't help it. She's sorry for me."

There was a new attempt to ignore me and my troubles as he said:

"Why should she be sorry for you?"

"Because she sees that you're hard on me—"

"I haven't meant to be hard on you, only just."

"Well, just then; but Mrs. Brokenshire doesn't know anything about justice when she can be merciful. You must know that yourself, sir. I think she's the most beautiful woman God ever made; and she's as kind as she's beautiful. I'll tell you something else, sir. It will be another betrayal, but it will show you what she is. One day at Newport—after you'd spoken to me—and she saw that I was so crushed by it that all I could do was to creep down among the rocks and cry—she watched me, and followed me, and came and cried with me. And so when she heard I was here—"

164

"Who told her?"

There was a measure of accusation in the tone of the question, but I pretended not to detect it.

"Mrs. Rossiter, perhaps—she knows—or almost anybody. I never asked her."

"Very well! What then?"

"I was only going to say that when she heard I was here she came almost at once. I begged her not to—"

"Why? What were you afraid of?"

"I knew you wouldn't like it. But I couldn't stop her. No one could stop her when it comes to her doing an act of kindness. She obeys her own nature because she can't do anything else. She's like a little bird that you can keep from flying by holding it in your hand, but as soon as your grasp is relaxed— it flies."

Something of this was true, in that it was true potentially. She had these qualities, even if they were nipped in her as buds are nipped in a backward spring. I could only calm my conscience as I went along by saying to myself that if I saved her she would have to bear me out through being true to the picture I was painting, and living up to her real self.

Praise of the woman he adored would have been as music to him had he not had something on his mind that turned music into poignancy. What it was I could surmise, and so be prepared for it. Not till he had been some time silent, probably getting his question into the right words, did he say:

"And are you always alone when Mrs. Brokenshire comes?"

"Oh no, sir!" I made the tone as natural as I could. "But Mrs. Brokenshire doesn't seem to mind. Yesterday, for instance—"

"Was she here yesterday? I thought she came on—"

I broke in before he could betray himself further.

"Yes, she was here yesterday; and there was—let me see!—there was an old gentleman comparing his Japanese prints with Mr. Grainger's, and a middle-aged lady who comes to study the old editions of Shakespeare. But Mrs. Brokenshire didn't object to them. She sat with me and had a cup of tea."

I knew I had come to dangerous ground, and was ready for my part in the adventure. Had he asked the question: "Was there anybody else?" I was resolved, in the spirit of my maxim, to tell the truth as harmlessly as I knew how. But I didn't think he would ask it. I reckoned on his unwillingness to take me into his confidence or to humiliate himself more than he could help.

165

That he guessed at something behind my words I could easily suspect; but I was so sure he would have torn out his tongue rather than force his pride to cross-examine me too closely, that I was able to run my risk.

As a matter of fact, he became pensive, and through the gloom of the half-lighted room I could see that his face was contorted twice, still with no effort on his part to hide his misfortune. As he took the time to think I could do the same, with a kind of intuition in following the course of his meditations. I was not surprised, therefore, when he said, with renewed thickness of utterance:

"Has Mrs. Brokenshire any—any other motive in coming here than just—just to see you?"

I hung my head, perhaps with a touch of that play-acting spirit which most women are able to command, when the time comes.

"Yes, sir."

He waited again. I never heard such overtones of despair as were in the three words which at last he tried to toss off easily.

"What is it?"

I still hung my head.

"She brings me money for poor Hugh."

He started back, whether from anger or relief I couldn't tell, and his face twitched for the fourth time. In the end, I suppose, he decided that anger was the card he could play most skilfully.

"So that that's what enables him to keep up his rebellion against me!"

"No, sir," I said, humbly, "because he never takes it." I went on with that portrait of Mrs. Brokenshire which I vowed she would have to justify. "That doesn't make any difference, however, to her wonderful tenderness of heart in wanting him to have it. You see, sir, when any one's so much like an angel as she is they don't stop to consider how justly other people are suffering or how they've brought their troubles on themselves. Where there's trouble they only ask to help; where there's suffering their first instinct is to heal. Mrs. Brokenshire doesn't want to sustain your son against you; that never enters her head: she only wants him not—not"—my own voice shook a little—"not to have to go without his proper meals. He's doing that now, I think—sometimes, at least. Oh, sir," I ventured to plead, "you can't blame her, not when she's so—so heavenly." Stealing a glance at him, I was amazed and shocked, and not a little comforted, to see two tears steal down his withered cheeks. Knowing then that he would not for some minutes be able to control himself sufficiently to speak, I hurried on. "Hugh doesn't take the money, because he knows that this is something he must go through with on his own strength. If he can't do that he must give in. I think I've made that clear to him. I'm not the adventuress you consider me—indeed I'm not. I've told him that if he's ever independent I will marry him; but I shall not marry him so long as he isn't free to give himself away. He's putting up a big fight, and he's doing it so bravely, that if you only knew what he's going through you'd be proud of him as your son."

Resting my case there, I waited for some response, but I waited in vain. He reflected, and sat silent, and crossed and uncrossed his knees. At last he picked up his hat from the floor and rose. I, too, rose, waiting beside my chair, while he flicked the dust from the crown of his hat and seemed to study its glossy surface as he still reflected.

I was now altogether without a clue to what was passing in his mind, though I could guess at the age-long tragedy of December's love for May. Having seen Ibsen's "Master Builder," at Munich, and read one or two books on the theme with which it deals, I could, in a measure, supplement my own experience. It was, however, the first time I had seen with my own eyes this desperate yearning of age for youth, or this something that is almost a death-blow which youth can inflict on age. My father used to say that fundamentally there is no such period as age, that only the outer husk grows old, while the inner self, the vital *ego*, is young eternally. Here, it seemed to me, was an instance of the fact. This man was essentially as young as he had been at twenty-five; he had the same instincts and passions; he demanded the same things. If anything, he demanded them more imperiously because of the long, long habit of desire. Denial which thirty years ago he could have taken philosophically was now a source of anguish. As I looked at him I could see anguish on his lips, in his eyes, in the contraction of his forehead—the anguish of a love ridiculous to all, and to the object of it frightful and unnatural, for the reason that at sixty-two the skin had grown baggy and the heart was supposed to be dead.

167

From the smoothing of the crown of his hat he glanced up suddenly. The whip-lash inflection was again in the timbre of the voice.

"How much do you get here?"

I was taken aback, but I named the amount of my salary.

"I will give you twice as much as that for the next five years if—if you go back to where you came from."

It took me a minute to seize all the implications contained in this little speech. I saw then that if I hoped I was making an impression, or getting further ahead with him, I was mistaken. Neither had my interpretation of Mrs. Brokenshire's character put him off the scent concerning her. I was so far indeed from influencing him in either her favor or my own that he believed that if he could get rid of me an obstacle would be removed.

Tears sprang into my eyes, though they didn't fall.

"So you blame me, sir, for everything."

He continued to watch his gloved hand as it made the circle of the crown of his hat.

"I'll make it twice what you're getting here for ten years. I'll put it in my will." It was no use being angry or mounting my high horse. The struggle with tears kept me silent as he glanced up from the rubbing of his hat and said in a jerky, kindly tone: "Well? What do you say?"

I didn't know what to say; and what I did say was foolish. I should have known enough to suppress it before I began.

"Do you remember, sir, that once when you were speaking to me severely, you said you were my friend? Well, why shouldn't I be your friend, too?"

The look he bent down on me was that of a great personage positively dazed by an inferior's audacity.

"I could be your friend," I stumbled on, in an absurd effort to explain myself. "I should like to be. There are—there are things I could do for you."

He put on his tall hat with the air of a Charlemagne or a Napoleon crowning himself. This increase of authority must have made me desperate. It is only thus that I can account for my *gaffe*—the French word alone expresses it—as I dashed on, wildly:

"I like you, sir—I can't help it. I don't know why, but I do. I like you in spite of—in spite of everything. And, oh, I'm so sorry for you—"

He moved away. There was noble, wounded offense in his manner of passing through the wrought-iron grille, which he closed with a little click behind him. He stepped out of the place as softly as he had stepped in.

For long minutes I stood, holding to the side of the William and Mary chair, regretting that the interview should have ended in this way. I didn't cry; I had, in fact, no longer any tendency to tears. I was thoughtful—wondering what it was that dug the gulf between this man and his family and me. Ethel Rossiter had never—I could see it well enough now—accepted me as an equal, and even to Hugh I was only another type of Libby Jaynes. I was as intelligent as they, as well born, as well mannered, as thoroughly accustomed to the world. Why should they consider me an inferior? Was it because I had no money? Was it because I was a Canadian? Would it have made a difference if I had been an Englishwoman like Cissie Boscobel, or rich like any of themselves? I couldn't tell. All I knew was that my heart was hot within me, and since Howard Brokenshire wouldn't have me as a friend I wanted to act as his enemy. I could see how to do it. Indeed, without doing anything at all I could encourage, and perhaps bring about, a situation that would send the name of the family ringing through the press of two continents and break his heart. I had only to sit still—or at most to put in a word here and there. I am not a saint; I had my hour of temptation.

It was a stormy hour, though I never moved from the spot where I stood. The storm was within. That which, as the minutes went by, became rage in me saw with satisfaction Howard Brokenshire brought to a desolate old age, and Mildred and Ethel and Jack and Pauline, in spite of their bravado and their high heads, all seared by the flame of notorious disgrace. I went so far as to gloat over poor Hugh's discomfiture, taking vengeance on his habit of rating me with the socially incompetent. As for Mrs. Brokenshire, she would be over and done with, a poor little gilded outcast, whose fall would be such that even as Mrs. Stacy Grainger she would never rise again. Like another Samson, I could pull down this house of pride, though, happier than Samson, I should not be overwhelmed in the ruin of it. From that I should be safe—with Larry Strangways.

Nearly half an hour went by while I stood thus indulging in fierce day-dreams. I was racked and suffering. I suffered, indeed, from the misfortunes I saw descending on people whom at bottom of my heart I cared for. It was not till I began to move, till I had put on my jacket and was turning out the lights, that my maxim came back to me. I knew then that whatever happened I should stand by that, and having come to this understanding with myself, I was quieted.

CHAPTER XVI

Having made up my mind to adhere, however imperfectly, to the principle that had guided me hitherto, I was obliged to examine my conscience as to what I had said to Mr. Brokenshire. This I did in the evening, coming to the conclusion that I had told him nothing but the truth, even if it was not all the truth. Though I hated duplicity, I couldn't see that I had a right to tell him all the truth, or that to do so would be wise. If he could be kept, for everybody's sake, from knowing more than he knew already, however much or little that was, it seemed to me that diplomatic action on my part would be justified.

In the line of diplomatic action I had before all things to inform Mrs. Brokenshire of the visit I had received. This was not so easy as it may seem. I could not trust to a letter, through fear of its falling into other hands than hers. Neither could I wait for her coming on the following Tuesday, since that was what I wanted to prevent. There was no intermediary whom I could intrust with a message, unless it was Larry Strangways, who knew something of the facts; but even with him the secret was too much to share.

In the end I had recourse to the telephone, asking to be allowed to speak to Mrs. Brokenshire. I was told that she never answered the telephone herself, and was requested to transmit my message. Not to arouse suspicion, I didn't ask that she should break her rule, but begged that during the day she might find a minute in which to see Miss Adare, who was in a difficulty that involved her work. That this way of putting it was understood I gathered from the reply that came back to me. It was to the effect that as Mr. Brokenshire would be lunching with some men in the lower part of New York Mrs. Brokenshire would be alone and able to receive Miss Adare at two. Fortunately, it was a Saturday, so that my afternoon was free.

Almost everybody familiar with New York knows the residence of J. Howard Brokenshire not far above the Museum. Built of brick with stone facings, it is meant to be in the style of Louis Treize. It would be quite in the style of Louis Treize were the stonework not too heavy and elaborate, and the façade too high for its length. Inside, with an incongruity many rich people do not mind, it is sumptuously Roman and Florentine—the Brokenshire villa at Newport on a larger and more lavish scale. Having gone over the house with Ethel Rossiter during the winter I spent with her, I had carried away the impression of huge unoccupied rooms, of heavily carved or gilded furniture, of rich brocades, of dim old masters in elaborate gold frames, of vitrines and vases and mirrors and consoles, all supplied by some princely dealer in *objets d'art* who had received *carte blanche* in the way of decoration. The Brokenshire family, with the possible exception of Mildred, cared little for the things with which they lived. Ethel Rossiter, in showing me over the house, hardly knew a Perugino from a Fragonard, and still less could she distinguish, between the glorious fading softness of a Flemish fifteenth-century tapestry and a smug and staring bit of Gobelins. Hugh went in and out as indifferently as in a hotel, while Jack Brokenshire's taste in art hardly reached beyond racing prints. Mildred liked pretty garlanded things *à la* Marie Antoinette, which the parental habit of deciding everything would never let her have. J. Howard alone made an effort at knowing the value, artistic and otherwise, of his possessions, and would sometimes, when strangers were present, point to this or that object with the authority of a connoisseur, which he was not.

It was a house for life in perpetual state, with no state to maintain. Stafford House, Holland House, Bridgewater House, to name but a few of the historic mansions in London, were made spacious and splendid to meet a definite necessity. They belonged to days when the feudal tradition still obtained and there were no comfortable hotels. Great lords came to them with great families and great suites of retainers. Accommodation being the first of all needs, there was a time when every corner of these stately residences was lived in. But now that in England the great lord tends more and more to be only a simple democratic individual, and the wants of his relatives are easily met on a public or co-operative principle, the noble Palladian or Georgian dwelling either becomes a museum or a club, or remains a white elephant on the hands of some one who would gladly be rid of it. Princes and princesses of the blood royal rent numbered houses in squares and streets, next door to the Smiths and the Joneses, in preference to the draughty grandeurs of St. James's and Buckingham Palace, while a villa in the suburbs, with a few trees and a garden, is often the shelter sought by the nobility.

But in proportion as civilization in England, to say nothing of the rest of Europe, puts off the burdensome to enjoy simplicity, America, it strikes me, chases the tail of an antiquated, disappearing stateliness. Rich men, just because they have the money, take upon their shoulders huge domestic responsibilities in which there is no object, and which it is probable the next generation will refuse to carry. In New York, in Washington, in Newport, in Chicago, they raise palaces and châteaux where they often find themselves lonely, and which they can rarely fill more than two or three times a year. In the case of the Howard Brokenshires it had ceased to be as often as that. After Ethel was married Mr. Brokenshire seldom entertained, his second wife having no heart for that kind of display. Now and then, in the course of a winter, a great dinner was given in the great dining-room, or the music-room was filled for a concert; but this was done for the sake of "killing off" those to whom some attention had to be shown, and not because either host or hostess cared for it. Otherwise the down-stairs rooms were silent and empty, and whatever was life in the house went on in a corner of the mansard.

Thither the footman took me in a lift. Here were the rooms—a sort of flat—which the occupants could dominate with their personalities. They reminded me of those tiny chambers at Versailles to which what was human in poor Marie Antoinette fled for refuge from her uncomfortable gorgeousness as queen.

Not that these rooms were tiny. On the contrary, the library or living-room into which I was ushered was as large as would be found in the average big house, and, notwithstanding its tapestries and massive furniture, was bright with sunshine and flowers. Books lay about, and papers and magazines, and after the tomb-like deadness of the lower floors one got at least the impression of life.

From the far end of the room Mrs. Brokenshire came forward, threading her way between arm-chairs and taborets, and looking more exquisite, and also more lost, than ever. She wore what might be called a glorified *negligée*, lilac and lavender shading into violet, the train adding to her height. Fear had to some degree blotted out her color and put trouble into the sweetness of her eyes.

"Something has happened," she said at once, as she took my hand.

I spoke as directly as she did, though a little pantingly.

"Yes; Mr. Brokenshire came to the library yesterday."

"Ah-h!" The exclamation was no more than a long, frightened breath. "Then that explains things. I saw when he came home to dinner that he was unhappy."

"Did he say anything?"

"No; nothing. He was just—unhappy. Sit down and tell me."

Staring wide-eyed at each other, we seated ourselves on the edge of two huge arm-chairs. Having half expected my companion to fling the gauntlet in her husband's face, I was relieved to find in her chiefly the dread of detection.

As exactly as I could I gave her an account of what had passed between Mr. Brokenshire and myself, omitting only those absurd suggestions of my own that had sent him away in dudgeon. She listened with no more interruption than a question or two, after which she said, simply:

"Then, I suppose, I can't go any more."

"On the contrary," I corrected, "you must come just the same as ever, only not on the same days, or at the same hours—or—or when there's any one else there besides the visitors and me. If you stopped coming all of a sudden Mr. Brokenshire would think—"

"But he thinks that already."

"Of course, but he doesn't know—not after what I said to him." I seized the opportunity to beg her to play up. "You are all the things I told him you were, dear Mrs. Brokenshire, don't you see you are?"

But my appeal passed unheeded.

"What made him suspect? I thought that would be the last thing."

"I don't know. It might have been a lot of things. Once or twice I've rather fancied that some of the people who came there—"

Her features contracted in a spasm of horror.

"You don't mean detect—" She found the word difficult to pronounce. "You don't mean de-detectives watching—me?"

"I don't say as much as that; but I've never liked Mr. Brokenshire's man, Spellman."

"No, nor I. He's out now. I made sure of that before you came."

"So he might have sent some one; or— But it's no use speculating, is it? when there are so many ways. What we've specially got to know is how to act, and I think I've told you the best method. If you don't keep coming—judiciously —you'll show you're conscious of having done wrong."

She sighed plaintively.

"I don't want to do wrong unless I can't help it. If I can't—"

"Oh, but you can." I tried once more to get in my point. "You wouldn't be all I told Mr. Brokenshire you were if your first instinct wasn't to do right."

"Oh, right!" She sighed again, but impatiently. "You're always talking about that."

"One has to, don't you think, when it's so important—and so easy to do wrong?"

She grew mildly argumentative.

"I don't see anything so terrible about wrong, when other people do it and are none the worse."

"May not that be because you've never tried it on your own account? It depends a little on the grain of which one's made. The finer the grain, the more harm wrong can do to it—just as a fragile bit of Venetian glass is more easily broken than an earthenware jug, and an infinitely greater loss."

But the simile was wasted. From long contemplation of her hands she looked up to say in a curiously coaxing tone:

"You live at the Hotel Mary Chilton, don't you?"

I caught her suggestion in a flash, and decided that I could let it go no further.

"Yes, but you couldn't come there—unless it was only to see me."

"But what shall I do?"

It was a kind of cry. She twisted her ringed fingers, while her eyes implored me to help her.

"Do nothing," I said, gently, and yet with some severity. "If you do anything do just as I've said. That's all we've got to know for the present."

"But I must see him. Now that I've got used to doing it—"

"If you must see him, dear Mrs. Brokenshire, you will."

"Shall I? Will you promise me?"

"I don't have to promise you. It's the way life works. If we only trust to events—and to whatever it is that guides events—and—and do right—I must repeat it—then the thing that ought to be will shape its course—"

"Ah, but if it doesn't?"

"In that case we can know that it oughtn't to be."

"I don't care whether it ought to be or not, so long as I can go on seeing him —somewhere."

I had enough sympathy with her to say:

"Yes, but don't plan for it. Let it take care of itself and happen in some natural way. Isn't it by mapping out things for ourselves that we often thwart the good that would otherwise have come to us? I remember reading somewhere of a lady who wrote of herself that she had been healed of planning, and spoke of it as a real cure. That struck me as so sensible. Life—not to use a greater word—knows much better what's good for us than we do ourselves."

She allowed this theme to lapse, while she sat pensive.

"What shall I say," she asked at last, "if he brings the subject up?"

I saw another opportunity.

"What can you say other than what I've said already? You came to me because you were sorry for me, and you wanted to help Hugh. He might regret that you should do both, but he couldn't blame you for either. They're only kindnesses—and we're all at liberty to be kind. Oh, don't you see? That's your—how shall I put it?—that's your line if Mr. Brokenshire ever speaks to you."

"And suppose he tells me not to go to see you any more?"

"Then you must stop. That will be the time. But not now when the mere stopping would be a kind of confession—"

And so, after many repetitions and some tears on both our parts, the lesson was urged home. She was less docile, however, when in the spirit of our new compact she came on the following Monday morning.

"I must see him," was the burden of what she had to say. She spoke as if I was forbidding her and ought to lift my veto. I might even have inferred that in my position in Mr. Grainger's employ it was for me to arrange their meetings.

"You will see him, dear Mrs. Brokenshire—if it's right," was the only answer I could find.

"You don't seem to remember that I was to have married him."

"I do, but we both have to remember that you didn't."

"Neither did I marry Mr. Brokenshire. I was handed over to him. When Lady Mary Hamilton was handed over in that way to the Prince of Monaco the Pope annulled the marriage. We knew her afterward in Budapest, married to some one else. If there's such a thing as right, as you're so fond of saying, I ought to be considered free."

I was holding both her hands as I said:

"Don't try to make yourself free. Let life do it."

"Life!" she cried, with a passionate vehemence I scarcely knew to be in her. "It's life that—"

"Treat life as a friend and not as an enemy. Trust it; wait for it. Don't hurry it, or force it, or be impatient with it. I can't believe that essentially it's hard or cruel or a curse. If it comes from God, it must be good and beautiful. In proportion as we cling to the good and beautiful we must surely get the thing we ought to have."

Though I cannot say that she accepted this doctrine, it helped her over a day or two, leaving me free for the time being to give my attention to my own affairs. Having no natural stamina, the poor, lovely little creature lived on such mental and spiritual pick-me-ups as I was able to administer. Whenever she was specially in despair, which was every forty-eight or sixty hours, she came back to me, and I did what I could to brace her for the next short step of her way. I find it hard to explain the intensity of her appeal to me. I suppose I must have submitted to that spell of the perfect face which had bewitched Stacy Grainger and Howard Brokenshire. I submitted also to her child-like helplessness. God knows I am not a heroine. Any little fright or difficulty upsets me. As compared with her, however, I was a giant refreshed with wine. When her lip quivered, or when the sudden mist drifted across her eyes, obscuring their forget-me-not blue with violet, my yearning was exactly that which makes any woman long to take any suffering baby in her arms. For this reason she didn't tax my patience, nor had I that impulse to scold or shake her to which another woman of such obvious limitations would have driven me. Touched as I was by the aching heart, I was captivated by the perfect face; and I couldn't help it.

Thus through the rest of February and into March my chief occupation was in keeping Howard Brokenshire's wife as true to him as the conditions rendered possible. In the intervals I comforted Hugh, and beat off Larry Strangways, and sat rigidly still while Stacy Grainger prowled round me with fierce, suspicious, melancholy eyes, like those of a cowed tiger. Afraid of him as I was, it filled me with grim inward amusement to discover that he was equally afraid of me. He came into the library from time to time, when he happened to be at his house, and like Mrs. Brokenshire gave me the impression that the frustration of their love was my fault. As I sat primly and severely at my desk, and he stalked round and round the room, stabbing the old gentleman who classified prints and the lady who collated the early editions of Shakespeare with contemptuous glances, I knew that in his sight I represented—poor me! —that virtuous respectability the sinner always holds in scorn. He could not be ignorant of the fact that if it hadn't been for me Mrs. Brokenshire would have been meeting him elsewhere, and so he held me as an enemy. Had he not known that I was something besides an enemy he would doubtless have sent me about my business.

In one of the intervals of this portion of the drama I received a visit that took me by surprise. Early in the afternoon of a day in March, Mrs. Billing trotted into the library, followed by Lady Cecilia Boscobel. It was the sort of occasion on which I should have been nervous enough in any case, but it became terrifying when Mrs. Billing marched up to my desk and pointed at me with her lorgnette, saying over her shoulder, "There she is," as though I was a portrait.

I struggled to my feet with what was meant to be a smile.

"Lady Cecilia Boscobel," I stammered, "has seen me already."

"Well, she can look at you again, can't she?"

The English girl came to my rescue by smiling back, and murmuring a faint "How do you do?" She eased the situation further by saying, with a crisp, rapid articulation, in which every syllable was charmingly distinct: "Mrs. Billing thought that as we were out sight-seeing we might as well look at this. It's shown every day, isn't it?"

She went on to observe that when places were shown only on certain days it was so tiresome. One of her father's places, Dillingham Hall, in Nottinghamshire, an old Tudor house, perfectly awful to live in, was open to the public only on the second and fourth Wednesdays, and even the family couldn't remember when those days came round. It was so awkward to be doing your hair, or worse, and have tourists stumbling in on you.

I counted it to the credit of her tact and kindliness that she chatted in this way long enough for me to get my breath, while Mrs. Billing turned her lorgnette on the room with which she must have once been familiar. If there was to be anything like rivalry between Lady Cissie and me I gathered that she wouldn't stoop to petty feminine advantages. Dressed in dark green, with a small hat of the same color worn dashingly, she had that air of being the absolutely finished thing which the tones of her voice announced to you. My heart grew faint at the thought that Hugh would have to choose between this girl, so certain of herself, and me.

As we were all standing, I invited my callers to sit down. To this Lady Cecilia acceded, though old Mrs. Billing strolled off to renew her acquaintance with the room. I may say here that I call her old because to be old was a kind of pose with her. She looked old and "dressed old" so as to enjoy the dictatorial privileges that go with being old, when as a matter of fact she was only sixty, which nowadays is young.

"You're English, aren't you?" Lady Cecilia began, as soon as we were alone. "I can tell by the way you speak."

I said I was a Canadian, that I was in New York more or less by accident, and might go back to my own country again.

"How interesting! It belongs to us, Canadia, doesn't it?"

With a slightly ironic emphasis on the proper noun I replied that Canadia naturally belonged to the Canadians, but that the King of Great Britain and Ireland was our king, and that we were very loyal to all that we represented.

"Fancy! And isn't it near here?"

All of Canada, I stated, was north of some of the United States, and some of it was south of others of the United States, but none of the more settled parts was difficult of access from New York.

"How very odd!" was her comment on these geographical indications. "I think I remember that a cousin of ours was governor out there—or something —though perhaps it was in India."

I named the series of British noblemen who had ruled over us since the confederation of the provinces in 1867, but as Lady Cecilia's kinsman was not among them we concluded that he must have been Viceroy of India or Governor-General of Australia.

The theme served to introduce us to each other, and lasted while Mrs. Billing's tour of inspection kept her within earshot.

I am bound to admit that I admired Lady Cecilia with an envy that might be qualified as green. She was not clever and she was not well educated, but her high breeding was so spontaneous. She so obviously belonged to spheres where no other rule obtained. Her manner was the union of polish and simplicity; each word she pronounced was a pleasure to the ear. In my own case life had been a struggle with that American-Canadian crudity which stamps our New World carriage and speech with commonness; but you could no more imagine this girl lapsing from the even tenor of the exquisite than you could fancy the hermit thrush failing in its song.

When Mrs. Billing was quite at the other end of the room my companion's manner underwent a change. During a second or two of silence her eyes fell, while the shifting of color over the milk-whiteness of her skin was like the play of Canadian northern lights. I was prepared for the fact that beneath her poise she might be shy, and that, being shy, she would be abrupt.

"You're engaged to Hugh Brokenshire, aren't you?"

The words were whipped out fast and jerkily, partly to profit by the minute during which Mrs. Billing was at a distance, and partly because it was a matter of now-or-never with their utterance.

I made the necessary explanations, for what seemed to me must be the hundredth time. I was not precisely engaged to him, but I had said I would marry him if either of two conditions could be carried out. I went on to state what those conditions were, finishing with the information that of the two I had practically abandoned one.

She nodded her comprehension.

"You see that—that they won't come round."

"No," I replied, with some incisiveness; "they will come round—especially Mr. Brokenshire. It's the other condition I no longer expect to see fulfilled."

If the hermit thrush could fail in its song it did it then. Lady Cecilia stared at me with a blankness that became awe.

"That's the most extraordinary thing I ever heard. Ethel Rossiter must be wrong."

I had a sudden suspicion.

"Wrong about what?"

The question put Lady Cecilia on her guard.

"Oh, nothing I need explain." But her face lighted with quick enthusiasm. "I call it magnificent."

"Call what 'magnificent'?"

"Why, that you should have that conviction. When one sees any one so sporting—"

I began to get her idea.

"Oh, I'm not sporting. I'm a perfect coward. But a sheep will make a stand when it's put to it."

With her hands in her sable muff, her shapely figure was inclined slightly toward me.

"I'm not sure that a sheep that makes a stand isn't braver than a lion. The man my sister Janet is engaged to—he's in the Inverness Rangers—often says that no one could be funkier than he on going into action; but that," she continued, her face aglow, "didn't prevent his being ever so many times mentioned in despatches and getting his D. S. O."

"Please don't put me into that class—"

"No; I won't. After all a soldier couldn't really funk things, because he's got everything to back him up. But you haven't. And when I think of you sitting here all by yourself, and expecting that great big rich Mr. Brokenshire and Ethel, and all of them, to come to your terms—"

To get away from a view of my situation that both consoled and embarrassed me, I said:

"Thank you, Lady Cecilia, very, very much; but it isn't what you meant to say when you began, is it?"

With some confusion she admitted that it wasn't.

"Only," she went on, "that isn't worth while now."

A hint in her tone impelled me to insist.

"It may be. You don't know. Please tell me what it was."

"But what's the use? It was only something Ethel Rossiter said—and she was wrong."

"What makes you so sure she was wrong?"

"Because I am. I can see." She added, reluctantly, "Ethel thought there was some one—some one besides Hugh—"

"And what if there was?"

Though startled by the challenge, she stood her ground.

"I don't believe in people making each other any more unhappy than they can help, do you?" She had a habit of screwing up her small gray-green eyes into two glimmering little slits of light, with an effect of shyness showing through amusement and *diablerie*. "We're both girls, aren't we? I'm twenty, and you can't be much older. And so I thought—that is, I thought at first—that if you had any one else in mind, there'd be no use in our making each other miserable—but I see you haven't; and so—"

"And so," I laughed, nervously, "the race must be to the swift and the battle to the strong. Is that it?"

"N-no; not exactly. What I was going to say is that since—since there's nobody but Hugh—you won't be offended with me, will you?—I won't step in—"

It was my turn to be enthusiastic.

"But that's what I call sporting!"

"Oh no, it isn't. I haven't seen Hugh for two or three years, and whatever little thing there was—"

I strained forward across my desk. I know my eyes must have been enormous.

"But was there—was there ever—anything?"

"Oh no; not at all. He—he never noticed me. I was only in the school-room, and he was a grown-up young man. If his father and mine hadn't been great friends—and got plans into their heads—Laura and Janet used to poke fun at me about it. And then we rode together and played tennis and golf, and so— but it was all—just nothing. You know how silly a girl of seventeen can be. It was nonsense. I only want you to know, in case he ever says anything about it —but then he never will—men see so little—I only want you to know that

that's the way I feel about it—and that I didn't come over here to— I don't say that if in your case there had been any one else—but I see there isn't—Ethel Rossiter is wrong—and so if I can do anything for Hugh and yourself with the Brokenshires. I—I want you to make use of me."

With a dignity oddly in contrast to this stammering confession, which was what it was, she rose to her feet as Mrs. Billing came back to us.

The hook-nosed face was somber. Curiosity as to other people's business had for once given place in the old lady's thoughts to meditations that turned inward. I suppose that in some perverse fashion of her own she loved her daughter, and suffered from her unhappiness. There was enough in this room to prove to her how cruelly mere self-seeking can overreach itself and ruin what it tries to build.

"Well, what are you talking about?" she snapped, as she approached us. "Hugh Brokenshire, I'll bet a dime."

"Fancy!" was the stroke with which the English girl, smiling dimly, endeavored to counter this attack.

Mrs. Billing hardly paused as she made her way toward the door.

"Don't let her have him," she threw at Lady Cecilia. "He's not good enough for her. She's my kind," she went on, poking at me with her lorgnette. "Needs a man with brains. Come along, Cissie. Don't mind what she says. You grab Hugh the first chance you get. She'll have bigger fish to fry. Do come along. We've had enough of this."

Lady Cissie and I shook hands with the over-acted listlessness of two daughters of the Anglo-Saxon race trying to carry off an emotional crisis as if they didn't know what it meant. But after she had gone I thought of her—I thought of her with her Limoges-enamel coloring, her luscious English voice, her English air of race, her dignity, her style, her youth, her naïveté, her combination of all the qualities that make human beings distinguished, because there is nothing else for them to be. I dragged myself to the Venetian mirror and looked into it. With my plain gray frock, my dark complexion, and my simply arranged hair. I was a poor little frump whom not even the one man in five hundred could find attractive. I wondered how Hugh could be such a fool. I asked myself if he could go on being such a fool much longer. And with the thought that he would—and again with the thought that he wouldn't—I surprised myself by bursting into tears.

CHAPTER XVII

In similar small happenings April passed and we had reached the middle of May. Easter and the opera were over; as the warm weather was coming on people were already leaving town for the country, the seaside or Europe. Personally, I had no plans beyond spending the month of August, which Mr. Grainger informed me I was to have "off," in making a visit to my old home in Halifax. Hugh had ceased to talk of immediate marriage, since he had all he could do to live on what he earned in selling bonds.

He had taken that job when Mildred could lend him no more without dipping into funds that had been his father's. He was still resolute on that point. He was resolute, too, in seeing nothing in the charms of Cissie Boscobel. He hated red hair, he said, making no allowance for the umber-red of Australian gold, and where I saw the lights of Limoges enamel he found no more than the garish tints of a chromolithograph. When I hinted that he might be the hero of some young romance on Cissie's part, he was contented to say "R-rot!" with a contemptuous roll of the first consonant.

Larry Strangways was industrious, happy, and prospering. He enjoyed the men with whom his work brought him into contact, and I gathered that his writing for daily, weekly, and monthly publications was bringing him into view as a young man of originality and power. From himself I learned that his small inherited capital was doubling and tripling and quadrupling itself through association with Stacy Grainger's enterprises. For Stacy Grainger himself he continued to feel an admiration not free from an uneasiness, with regard to which he made no direct admissions.

Of Mrs. Brokenshire I was seeing less. Either she had grown used to doing without her lover or she was meeting him in some other way. She still came to see me as often as once a week, but she was not so emotional or excitable. She might have been more affectionate than before, and yet it was with a dignity that gradually put me at a distance.

Cissie Boscobel I didn't meet during the whole of the six weeks except in the company of Mrs. Rossiter. That happened when once or twice I went to the house to see Gladys when she was suffering from colds, or when my former employer drove me round the Park. Just once I got the opportunity to hint that Lady Cissie hadn't taken Hugh from me as yet, to which Mrs. Rossiter replied that that was obviously because she didn't want him.

We were all, therefore, at a standstill, or moving so slowly that I couldn't perceive that we were moving at all, when in the middle of a May forenoon I was summoned to the telephone. I was not surprised to find Mr. Strangways at the other end, since he used any and every excuse to call me up; but his words struck me as those of a man who had taken leave of his senses. He plunged into them without any of the usual morning greetings or preliminary remarks.

"Are you game to go to Boston by the five-o'clock train to-day?"

I naturally said, "What?" but I said it with some emphasis.

He repeated the question a little more anxiously.

"Could you be ready to go to Boston by the five-o'clock train this afternoon?"

"Why should I be?"

He seemed to hesitate before replying.

"You'd know that," he said at last, "when you got on the train."

"Is it a joke?" I inquired, with a light laugh.

"No; it's not a joke. It's serious. I want you to take that train and go."

"But what for?"

"I've told you you'd know that when you got on the train—or before you had gone very far."

"And do you think that's information enough?"

"It will be information enough for you when I say that a great deal may depend on your doing as I ask."

I raised a new objection.

"How can I go when I've my work to attend to here?"

"You must be ready to give that up. If any one makes any trouble, you must say you've resigned the position."

As far as was possible over the wire I got the impression of earnestness on his part and perhaps excitement; but I was not yet satisfied.

"What shall I do when I get to Boston? Where shall I go?"

"You'll see. You'll know. You'll have to act for yourself. Trust your own judgment as I trust it."

"But, Mr. Strangways, I don't understand a bit," I was beginning to protest, when he broke in on me.

"Oh, don't you see? It will all explain itself as you go on. I can't tell you about it in advance. I don't know. All I can say is that whatever happens you'll be needed, and if you're needed you'll be able to play the game."

He went on with further directions. It would be possible to take my seat in the train at twenty minutes before the hour of departure. I was to be early on the spot so as to be among the first to be in my place. I was to take nothing but a suit-case; but I was to put into it enough to last me for a week, or even for a week or two. I was to be prepared for roughing it, if necessary, or for anything else that developed. He would send me my ticket within an hour and provide me with plenty of money.

"But what is it?" I implored again. "It sounds like spying, or the secret service, or something melodramatic."

"It's none of those things. Just be ready. Wait where you are till you get your ticket and the money."

"Will you bring them yourself?"

"No. I can't; I'm too busy. I'm calling from a pay-station. Don't ring me up for any more questions. Just do as I've asked you, and I know you'll not regret it—not as long as you live."

He put up the receiver, leaving me bewildered. My ignorance was such that speculation was shut out. I kept saying to myself: "It must be this," or, "It must be that," but with no conviction in my guesses. One dreadful suspicion came to me, but I firmly put it away.

A little after twelve a special messenger arrived, bringing my ticket and five hundred dollars in bank-notes. I knew then that I was in for a genuine adventure. At one I put on my hat and coat, locked the door behind me, and went off to my hotel. Mentally I was leaving a work to which, from certain points of view, I was sorry to say good-by, but I could afford no backward looks.

At the hotel I packed my belongings and left them so that they could be sent after me in case I should not return. I might be back the next morning; but then I might never come back at all. I thought of those villagers who from idle curiosity followed the carriage of Louis XVI. and Marie Antoinette as it drove out of Varennes, some of them never to see their native town again till they had been dragged over half the battle-fields of Europe. Like them I had no prevision as to where I was going or what was to become of me. I knew only —gloatingly, and with a kind of glory in the fact—that I was going at the call of Larry Strangways, to do his bidding, because he believed in me. But that thought, too, I tried to put out of my mind. In as far as it was in my mind I did my best to express it in terms of prose, seeing myself not as the heroine of a mysterious romance—a view to which I was inclined—but as a practical business woman, competent, up-to-date, and unafraid. I was afraid, mortally afraid, and I was neither up-to-date nor competent; but the fiction sustained me while I packed my trunks and sent a telegram to Hugh.

This last I did only when it was too late for him to answer or intercept me.

"Called suddenly out of town," I wrote. "May lead to a new place. Will write or wire as soon as possible." Having sent this off at half past four, I took a taxicab for the station.

My instructions were so far carried out successfully that, with a colored porter wearing a red cap to precede me, I was the first to pass the barrier leading to the train, and the first to take my seat in the long, narrow parlor-car. My chair was two from the end toward the entrance and exit. Once enthroned within its upholstered depths I watched for strange occurrences.

But I watched in vain. For a time I saw nothing but the straight, empty cavern of the car. Then a colored porter, as like to my own as one pea to another, came puffing his way in, dragging valises and other impedimenta, and followed by an old gentleman and his wife. These the porter installed in chairs toward the middle of the car, and, touching his cap on receipt of his tip, made hastily for the door. Similar arrivals came soon after that, with much stowing of luggage into overhead racks, and kisses, and injunctions as to conduct, and farewells. Within my range of vision were two elderly ladies, a smartly dressed young man, a couple in the disillusioned, surly stage, a couple who had recently been married, a clergyman, a youth of the cheap sporting type. To one looking for the solution of a mystery the material was not promising.

The three chairs immediately in front of mine remained unoccupied. I kept my eye on them, of course, and presently got some reward. Shortly before the train pulled out of the station a shadow passed me which I knew to be that of Larry Strangways. He went on to the fourth seat, counting mine as the first, and, having reached it, turned round and looked at me. He looked at me gravely, with no sign of recognition beyond a shake of the head. I understood then that I was not to recognize him, and that in the adventure, however it turned out, we were to be as strangers.

One more thing I saw. He had never been so pale or grim or determined in all the time I had known him. I had hardly supposed that it was in him to be so determined, so grim, or so pale. I gathered that he was taking our mission more to heart than I had supposed, and that, prompt in action as I had been, I was considering it too flippantly. Inwardly I prayed for nerve to support him, and for that presence of mind which would tell me what to do when there was anything to be done.

Perhaps it increased my zeal that he was so handsome. Straight and slim and upright, his features were of that lean, blond, regular type I used to consider Anglo-Saxon, but which, now that I have seen it in so many Scandinavians, I have come to ascribe to the Norse strain in our blood. The eyes were direct; the chin was firm; the nose as straight as an ancient Greek's. The relatively small mouth was adorned by a relatively small mustache, twisted up at the ends, of the color of the coffee-bean, and, to my admiring feminine appreciation, blooming on his face like a flower.

His neat spring suit was also of the color of the coffee-bean, and so was his soft felt hat. In his shirt there were lines of tan and violet, and tan and violet appeared in the tie beneath which a soft collar was pinned with a gold safety pin. The yellow gloves that men have affected of late years gave a pleasant finish to this costume, which was quite complete when he pulled from his bag an English traveling-cap of several shades of tan and put it on. He also took out a book, stretching himself in his chair in such a way that the English traveling-cap was all I could henceforth see of his personality.

I give these details because they entered into the mingled unwillingness and zest with which I found myself dragged on an errand to which I had no clue. Still less had I a clue when the train began to move, and I had nothing but the view of the English traveling-cap to bear me company. But no, I had one other detail. Before sitting down Mr. Strangways had carefully separated his own hand-luggage from that of the person who would be behind him, and which included an ulster, a walking-stick, and a case of golf-clubs. I inferred, therefore, that the wayfarer who owned one of the two chairs between Mr. Strangways and myself must be a man. The chair directly in front of mine remained empty.

As we passed into the tunnel my mind lashed wildly about in search of explanations, the only one I could find being that Larry Strangways was kidnapping me. On arriving in Boston I might find myself confronted by a marriage license and a clergyman. If so, I said to myself, with an extraordinary thrill, there would be nothing for it but submission to this *force majeure*, though I had to admit that the averted head, the English traveling-cap, and the intervening ulster, walking-stick, and golf-clubs worked against my theory. I was dreaming in this way when the train emerged from the tunnel and stopped so briefly at One Hundred and Twenty-fifth Street that, considering it afterward, I concluded that the pause had been arranged for. It was just long enough for an odd little bundle of womanhood to be pulled and shoved on the car and thrown into the seat immediately in front of mine. I choose my verbs with care, since they give the effect produced on me. The little woman, who was swathed in black veils and clad in a long black shapeless coat, seemed not to act of her own volition and to be more dead than alive. The porter who had brought her in flung down her two or three bags and waited, significantly, though the train was already creeping its way onward. She was plainly unused to fending for herself, and only when, as a reminder, the man had touched his hat a second time did it occur to her what she had to do. Hastily unfastening a small bag, she pulled out a handful of money and thrust it at him. The man grinned and was gone, after which she sagged back helplessly into her seat, the satchel open in her lap.

That dreadful suspicion which had smitten me earlier in the day came back again, but the new-comer was so stiflingly wrapped up that even I could not be sure. She reminded me of nothing so much as of the veiled Begum of Bhopal as she sat in the durbar with the other Indian potentates, her head done up in a bag, as seen in the pictures in the illustrated London papers. For a lady who wished to pass unperceived it was perfect—for every eye in the car was turned on her. I myself studied her, of course, searching for something to confirm my fears, but finding nothing I could take as convincing. For the matter of that, as she sat huddled in the enormous chair I could see little beyond a swathing of veils round a close-fitting hat and the folds of the long black coat. The easiest inference was that she might be some poor old thing whom her relatives were anxious to be rid of, which was, I think, the conclusion most of our neighbors drew. Speaking of neighbors, I had noticed that in spite of the disturbance caused by this curious entrance, Larry Strangways had not turned his head.

I could only sit, therefore, and wait for enlightenment, or for an opportunity. Both came when, some half-hour later, the ticket-collectors passed slowly down the aisle. Other passengers got ready for them in advance, but the little begum in front of me did nothing. When at last the collectors were before her she came to herself with a start.

She came to herself with a start, seizing her satchel awkwardly and spilling its contents on the floor. The tickets came out, and some money. The collectors picked up the tickets and began to pencil and tear them; the youth of the cheap sporting type and I went after the coins. Since I was a young woman and the lady with her head in a bag might be taken for an old one, I had no difficulty in securing his harvest, which he handed over to me with an ingratiating leer. Returning the leer as much in his own style as I could render it, I offered the handful of silver and copper to its owner. To do this I stood as directly as might be in front of her, and when, inadvertently, she raised her head I tried to look her in the eyes.

I couldn't see them. The shimmer I caught behind the two or three veils might have been any one's eyes. But in the motion of the hand that took the money, and in the silvery tinkle of the voice that made itself as low as possible in murmuring the words, "Thank you!" I couldn't be mistaken. It was enough. If I hadn't seen her she at least had seen me, and so I went back to my seat.

I had got the first part of my revelation. With the aid of the ulster, the walking-stick, and the golf-clubs I could guess at the rest. I knew now why Larry Strangways wanted me there, but I didn't know what I was to do. By myself I could do nothing. Unless the little begum took the initiative I shouldn't know where to begin. I could hardly tear off a disguise she had chosen to assume, nor could I take it for granted that she was not on legitimate business.

But she had seen me, and there was something in that. If the owner of the vacant chair turned up he, too, would see me, and he wouldn't wear a veil. We should look each other in the eyes, and he would know that I knew what he was about to do. The situation would not be pleasant for me; but it would conceivably be much less pleasant for anybody else.

I waited, therefore, watching the beautiful green country go tearing by. The smiling freshness of spring was over the hillsides on the left, while the setting sun gilded the tiny headlands on the right and turned the rapid succession of creeks and inlets and marshy pools into sheets of orange and red. Fire illumined the windows of many a passing house, to be extinguished instantaneously, and touched with occasional flames the cold spring-tide blue of the sea. Clumps of forsythia were in blossom, and here and there an apple-tree held out toward the sun a branch of early flowers.

When the train stopped at New Haven I was afraid that the owner of the ulster and the golf-clubs would appear, and that my work, whatever it was to be, would be rendered the more difficult. But no new arrival entered. On the other hand, the passengers began to thin out as the time came for going to the dining-car. In the matter of food I determined to stay at my post if I died of starvation, especially on seeing that the English traveling-cap was equally courageous.

Twilight gradually filtered into the world outside; the marshes, inlets, and creeks grew dim. Dim was the long, burnished line of the Sound, above which I could soon make out a sprinkling of wan yellow stars. Wan yellow lights appeared in windows where no curtains were drawn, and what a few minutes earlier had been twilight became quickly the night. It was the wistful time, the homesick, heart-searching time. If the little lady in front of me were to have qualms as to what she was doing they would come then.

And indeed as I watched her it seemed to me that she inserted her handkerchief under her series of coverings as if to wipe away a tear. Presently she lifted two unsteady hands and began to untie her outer veil. When it came to finding the pins by which it was adjusted she fumbled so helplessly that I took it on myself to lean forward with the words, "Won't you allow me?" I could do this without moving round to where I should have been obliged to look her in the face; and it was so when I helped her take off the veil underneath.

"I'm smothering," she said, very much as it might have been said by a little child in distress.

She wore still another veil, but only that which was ordinarily attached to her hat. The car being not very brightly lighted, and most of our fellow-travelers having gone to dinner, she probably thought she had little to fear. As she gave no sign of recognition on my rendering my small services I subsided again into my chair.

But I knew she was as conscious of my presence as I was of hers. It was not wholly surprising, then, that some twenty minutes later she should swing round in the revolving-chair and drop all disguises. She did it with the words, tearfully yet angrily spoken:

"What are you doing here?"

"I'm going to Boston, Mrs. Brokenshire," I replied, meekly. "Are you doing the same?"

"You know what I'm doing, and you've come to spy on me."

There is something about the wrath of the sweet, mild, gentle creature, not easily provoked, which is far more terrible than the rage of an irascible old man accustomed to furies. I quailed before it now, but not so much that I couldn't outwardly keep my composure.

"If I know what you're doing, Mrs. Brokenshire," I said, gently, "it isn't from any information received beforehand. I didn't know you were to be on this train till you got in; and I haven't been sure it was you till this minute."

"I've a right to do as I please," she declared, hoarsely, "without having people to dog me."

"Do I strike you as the sort of person who'd do that? You've had some opportunity of knowing me; and have I ever done anything for which you didn't first give me leave? If I'm here this evening and you're here, too, it's pure accident—as far as I'm concerned." I added, with some deepening of the tone, and speaking slowly so that she should get the meaning of the words: "I'll only venture to surmise that accidents of that kind don't happen for nothing."

189

I could just make out her swimming eyes as they stared at me through the remaining veil, which was as black and thick as a widow's.

"What do you mean?"

"Wouldn't that depend on what you mean?"

"If you think you're going to stop me—"

"Dear Mrs. Brokenshire, I don't think anything at all. How can I? We're both going to Boston. By a singular set of circumstances we're seated side by side on the same train. What can I see more in the situation than that?"

"You do see more."

"But I'm trying not to. If you insist on betraying more, when perhaps I'd rather you wouldn't, well, that won't be my fault, will it?"

"Because I've given you my confidence once or twice isn't a reason why you should take liberties all the rest of your life."

To this, for a minute, I made no reply.

"That hurts me," I said at last, "but I believe that when you've considered it you'll see that you've been unjust to me."

"You've suspected me ever since I knew you."

"I've only suspected you of a sweetness and kindness and goodness which I don't think you've discovered in yourself. I've never said anything of you, and never thought anything, but what I told Mr. Brokenshire two months ago, that you seem to me the loveliest thing God ever made. That you shouldn't live up to the beauty of your character strikes me as impossible. I'll admit that I think that; and if you call it suspicion—"

Her anger began to pass into a kind of childish rebellion.

"You've always talked to me about impossible things—"

"I wasn't aware of it. One has to have standards of life, and do one's best to live up to them."

"Why should I do my best to live up to them when other people— Look at Madeline Pyne, and a lot of women I know!"

"Do you think we can ever judge by other people, or take their actions as an example for our own? No one person can be more bound to do right than another; and yet when it comes to doing wrong it might easily be more serious for you than for Mrs. Pyne or for me."

"I don't see why it should be."

"Because you have a national position, one might even say an international position, and Mrs. Pyne hasn't, and neither have I. If we do wrong, only our own little circles have to know about it, and the harm we can do is limited; but if you do wrong it hurts the whole country."

"I must say I don't see that."

"You're the wife of a man who might be called a national institution—"

"There are just as important men in the country as he."

"Not many—let us say, at a venture, a hundred. Think of what it means to be one of the hundred most conspicuous women among a population of a hundred millions. The responsibility must be tremendous."

"I've never thought of myself as having any particular responsibility—not any more than anybody else."

"But, of course, you have. Whatever you do gets an added significance from the fact that you're Mrs. Howard Brokenshire. When, for example, you came to me that day among the rocks at Newport, your kindness was the more wonderful for the simple reason that you were who you were. We can't get away from those considerations. When you do right, right seems somehow to be made more beautiful; and when you do wrong—"

"I don't think it's fair to put me in a position like that."

"I don't put you in that position. Life does it. You were born to be high up. When you fall, therefore—"

"Don't talk about falling."

"But it would be a fall, wouldn't it? Don't you remember, some ten or twelve years ago, how a Saxon crown princess left her home and her husband? Well, all I mean is that because of her position her story rang through the world. However one might pity unhappiness, or sympathize with a miserable love, there was something in it that degraded her country and her womanhood. I suppose the poor thing's inability to live up to a position of honor was a blow at human nature. Don't you think that that was what we felt? And in your case —"

"You mustn't compare me with her."

"No; I don't—exactly. All I mean is that if—if you do what—what I think you've started out to do—"

She raised her head defiantly.

"And I'm going to."

"Then by the day after to-morrow there will not be a newspaper in the country that won't be detailing the scandal. It will be the talk of every club and every fireside between the Atlantic and the Pacific, and Mexico and Montreal. It will be in the papers of London and Paris and Rome and Berlin, and there'll be a week in which you'll be the most discussed person in the world."

"I've been that already—almost—when Mr. Brokenshire made his attack in the Stock Exchange on—"

"But this would be different. In this case you'd be pointed at—it's what it would amount to—as a woman who had gone over to all those evil forces in civilization that try to break down what the good forces are building up. You'd do like that unhappy crown princess, you'd strike a blow at your country and at all womanhood. There are thousands of poor tempted wives all over Europe and America who'll say: 'Well, if she can do such things—'"

"Oh, stop!"

I stopped. It seemed to me that for the time being I had given her enough to think about. We sat silent, therefore, looking out at the rushing dark. People who drifted back from the dining-car glanced at us, but soon were dozing or absorbed in books.

We were nearing New London when she pointed to one of her bags and asked me if I would mind opening it. I welcomed the request as indicating a return of friendliness. Having extracted a parcel of sandwiches, she unfolded the napkin in which they were wrapped and held them out to me. I took a pâté de foie-gras and followed her example in nibbling it. On my own responsibility I summoned the porter and asked him to bring a bottle of spring-water and two glasses.

"I guess the old lady's feelin' some better," he confided, when he had carried out the order.

We stopped at New London, and went on again. Having eaten three or four sandwiches, I declined any more, folding the remainder in the napkin and stowing them away. The simple meal we had shared together restored something of our old-time confidence.

"I'm going to do it," she sighed, as I put the bag back in its place. "He's—he's somewhere on the train—in the smoking-car, I suppose. He's—he's not to come for me till—till we're getting near the Back Bay Station in Boston."

I brought out my question simply, though I had been pondering it for some time. "Who'll tell Mr. Brokenshire?"

She moved uncomfortably.

"I don't know. I haven't made any arrangements. He's in Newport for one or two nights, seeing to some small changes in the house. I—I had to take the opportunity while he was away." As if with a sudden inspiration she glanced round from staring out into the dark. "Would you do it?"

I shook my head.

"I couldn't. I've never seen a man struck dead, and—"

She swung her chair so as to face me more directly.

"Why," she asked, trembling—"why do you say that?"

"Because, if I told him, it's what I should have to look on at."

She began wringing her hands.

"Oh no, you wouldn't."

"But I should. It would be his death-sentence at the least. It's true he has probably received that already—"

"Oh, what are you saying? What are you talking about?"

"Only of what every one can see. He's a stricken man—you've told me so yourself."

"Yes, but I said it only about Hugh. Lots of men have to go through troubles on account of their children."

"But when they do they can generally get comfort from their wives."

She seemed to stiffen.

"It's not my fault if he can't."

"No, of course not. But the fact remains that he doesn't—and perhaps it's the greatest fact of all. He adores you. His children may give him a great deal of anxiety but that's the sort of thing any father looks for and can endure. Only you're not his child; you're his wife. Moreover, you're the wife whom he worships with a slavish idolatry. Everything that nature and time and the world and wealth have made of him he gathers together and lays it down at your feet, contented if you'll only give him back a smile. You may think it pitiful—"

She shuddered.

"I think it terrible—for me."

"Well, I may think so, too, but it's his life we're talking of. His tenure of that"—I looked at her steadily—"isn't very certain as it is, do you think? You know the condition of his heart—you've told me yourself—and as for his nervous system, we've only to look at his face and his poor eye."

"I didn't do that. It's his whole life—"

"But his whole life culminates in you. It works up to you, and you represent everything he values. When he learns that you've despised his love and dishonored his name—"

Her foot tapped the floor impatiently.

"You mustn't say things like that to me."

"I'm only saying them, dear Mrs. Brokenshire, so that you'll know how they sound. It's what every one else will be saying in a day or two. You can't be what—what you'll be to-morrow, and still keep any one's respect. And so," I hurried on, as she was about to protest, "when he hears what you've done, you won't merely have broken his heart, you'll have killed him just as much as if you'd pulled out a revolver and shot him."

She swung back to the window again. Her foot continued to tap the floor; her fingers twisted and untwisted like writhing living things. I could see her bosom rise and fall rapidly; her breath came in short, hard gasps. When I wasn't expecting it she rounded on me again, with flames in her eyes like those in a small tigress's.

"You're saying all that to frighten me; but—"

"I'm saying it because it's true. If it frightens you—"

"But it doesn't."

"Then I've done neither good nor harm."

"I've a right to be happy."

"Certainly, if you can be happy this way."

"And I can."

"Then there's no more to be said. We can only agree with you. If you can be happy when you've Mr. Brokenshire on your mind, as you must have whether he's alive or dead—and if you can be happy when you've desecrated all the things your people and your country look to a woman in your position to uphold—then I don't think any one will say you nay."

"Well, why shouldn't I be happy?" she demanded, as if I was withholding from her something that was her right. "Other women—"

"Yes, Mrs. Brokenshire, other women besides you have tried the experiment of Anna Karénina—"

194

"What's that?"

I gave her the gist of Tolstoi's romance—the woman who is married to an old man and runs away with a young one, living to see him weary of the position in which she places him, and dying by her own act.

As she listened attentively, I went on before she could object to my parable.

"It all amounts to the same thing. There's no happiness except in right; and no right that doesn't sooner or later—sooner rather than later—end in happiness. You've told me more than once you didn't believe that; and if you don't I can't help it."

I fell back in my seat, because for the moment I was exhausted. It was not merely the actual situation that took the strength out of me, but what I dreaded when the man came for his prize from the smoking-car. I might count on Larry Strangways to aid me then, but as yet he had not recognized my struggle by so much as glancing round.

Nor had I known till this minute how much I cared for the little creature before me, or how deeply I pitied the man she was deserting. I could see her as happier conditions would have made her, and him as he might have become if his nature had not been warped by pride. Any impulse to strike back at him had long ago died within me. It might as well have died, since I never had the nerve to act on it, even when I had the chance.

She turned on me again, with unexpected fierceness.

"It doesn't matter whether I believe all those things or not—now. It's too late. I've left home. I've—I've gone away with him."

Though I felt like a spent prize-fighter forced back into the ring, I raised myself in my chair. I even smiled, dimly, in an effort to be encouraging.

"You've left home and you've gone away; but you won't have gone away with him till—till you've actually joined him."

"I've actually joined him already. His things are there beside that chair." She nodded backward. "By the time we've passed Providence he'll be—he'll be getting ready to come for me."

I said, more significantly than I really understood: "But we haven't passed Providence as yet."

To this she seemingly paid no attention, nor did I give it much myself.

"When he comes," she exclaimed, lyrically, "it will be like a marriage—"

I ventured much as I interrupted.

"No, it will never be like a marriage. There'll be too much that's unholy in it all for anything like a true marriage ever to become possible, not even if death or divorce—and it will probably be the one or the other—were to set you free."

That she found these words arresting I could tell by the stunned way in which she stared.

"Death or divorce!" she echoed, after long waiting. "He—he may divorce me quietly—I hope he will—but—but he won't—he won't die."

"He'll die if you kill him," I declared, grimly. I continued to be grim. "He may die before long, whether you kill him or not—the chances are that he will. But living or dead, as I've said already, he'll stand between you and anything you look for as happiness—after to-night."

She threw herself back, into the depths of her chair and moaned. Luckily there was no one near enough to observe the act. As we talked in low tones we could not be heard above the rattle of the train, and I think I passed as a companion or trained nurse in attendance on a nervous invalid.

"Oh, what's the use?" she exclaimed at last, in a fit of desperation. "I've done it. It's too late. Every one will know I've gone away—even if I get out at Providence."

I am sorry to have to admit that the suggestion of getting out at Providence startled me. I had been so stupid as not to think of it, even when I had made the remark that we had not as yet passed that town. All I had foreseen was the struggle at the end of the journey, when Larry Strangways and I should have to fight for this woman with the powers of darkness, as in medieval legends angels and devils fought over a contested soul.

I took up the idea with an enthusiasm I tried to conceal beneath a smile of engaging sweetness.

"They may know that you've gone away; but they can also know that you've gone away with me."

"With you? You're going to Boston."

"I could wait till to-morrow. If you wanted to get off at Providence I could do it, too."

"But I don't want to. I couldn't let him expect to find me here—and then discover that I wasn't."

"He would be disappointed at that, of course," I reasoned, "but he wouldn't take it as the end of all things. If you got off at Providence there would be nothing irrevocable in that step, whereas there would be in your going on. You could go away with him later, if you found you had to do it; but if you continue to-night you can never come back again. Don't you see? Isn't it worth turning over in your mind a second time—especially as I'm here to help you? If you're meant to be a Madeline Pyne or an Anna Karénina, you'll get another opportunity."

"Oh no, I sha'n't," she sobbed. "If I don't go on to-night, he'll never ask me again."

"He may never ask you again in this way; but isn't it possible that there may eventually be other ways? Don't make me put that into plainer words. Just wait. Let life take charge of it." I seized both her hands. "Darling Mrs. Brokenshire, you don't know yourself. You're too fine to be ruined; you're too exquisite to be just thrown away. Even the hungry, passionate love of the man in the smoking-car must see that and know it. If he comes back here and finds you gone—or imagines that you never came at all—he'll only honor and love you the more, and go on wanting you still. Come with me. Let us go. We can't be far from Providence now. I can take care of you. I know just what we ought to do. I didn't come here to sit beside you of my own free will; but since I am here doesn't it seem to you as if—as if I had been sent?"

As she was sobbing too unrestrainedly to say anything in words, I took the law into my own hands. The porter had already begun dusting the dirt from the passengers who were to descend at Providence on to those who were going to Boston. Making my way up to him, I had the inspiration to say:

"The old lady I'm with isn't quite so well, and we're going to stop here for the night."

He grinned, with a fine show of big white teeth.

"All right, lady; I'll take care of you. Cranky old bunch, ain't she? Handle a good many like that between Boston and Ne' Yawk."

Mrs. Brokenshire made no resistance when I fastened the lighter of her two veils about her head, folding the other and putting it away. Neither did she resist when I drew her cloak about her and put on my own coat. But as the train drew into Providence station and she struggled to her feet in response to my touch on her arm, I was obliged to pull and drag and push her, till she was finally lifted to the platform.

Before leaving the car, however, I took time to glance at the English traveling-cap. I noted then what I had noted throughout the journey. Not once did the head beneath it turn in my direction. Of whatever had happened since leaving the main station in New York Larry Strangways could say that he was wholly unaware.

CHAPTER XVIII

What happened on the train after Mrs. Brokenshire and I had left it I heard from Mr. Strangways. Having got it from him in some detail, I can give it in my own words more easily than in his.

I may be permitted to state here how much and how little of the romance between Mr. Grainger and Mrs. Brokenshire Larry Strangways knew. He knew next to nothing—but he inferred a good deal. From facts I gave him once or twice in hours of my own perplexity he had been able to get light on certain matters which had come under his observation as Mr. Grainger's confidential man, and to which otherwise he would have had no key. He inferred, for instance, that Mrs. Brokenshire wrote daily to her lover, and that occasionally, at long intervals, her lover could safely write to her. He inferred that when their meetings had ended in one place they were taken up discreetly at another, but only with difficulty and danger. He inferred that the man chafed against this restraint, and as he had got out of it with other women, he was planning to get out of it again. I understood that had Mrs. Brokenshire been the only such instance in Stacy Grainger's career Larry Strangways might not have felt impelled to interfere; but seeing from the beginning that his employer "had a weakness," he felt it only right to help me save a woman for whom he knew I cared.

I have never wholly understood why he believed that the situation had worked up to a crisis on that particular day; but having watched the laying of the mine, he could hardly do anything but expect the explosion on the application of the match.

When Mr. Grainger had bidden him that morning go to the station and secure a drawing-room, or, if that was impossible, two parlor-car seats, on the five-o'clock for Boston, he had reasons for following the course of which I have briefly given the lines. No drawing-room was available, because any that was not sold he bought for himself in order to set the stage according to his own ideas. How far he was justified in this will be a matter of opinion. Some may commend him, while others will accuse him of unwarrantable interference. My own judgment being of no importance I hold it in suspense, giving the incidents just as they occurred.

It must be evident that as Mr. Strangways didn't know what was to happen he could have no plan of action. All he could arrange for was that he and I should be on the spot. As it is difficult for guilty lovers to elope while acquaintances are looking on, he was resolved that they should find elopement difficult. For anything else he relied on chance—and on me. Chance favored him in keeping Stacy Grainger out of sight, in putting Mrs. Brokenshire next to me, and in making the action, such as it was, run smoothly. Had I known that he relied on me I should have been more terrified than I actually was, since I was relying on him.

It will be seen, then, that at the moment when Mrs. Brokenshire and I left the train Larry Strangways had but a vague idea of what had taken place. He merely conjectured from the swish of skirts that we had gone. His next idea was, as he phrased it, to make himself scarce on his own account; but in that his efforts miscarried.

Hoping to slip into another car and thus avoid a meeting with the outmanoeuvered lover, he was snapping the clasp of the bag into which he had thrust his cap when he perceived a tall figure enter the car by the forward end. To escape recognition he bent his head, pretending to search for something on the floor. The tall figure passed, but came back again. It was necessary that he should come back, because of the number on the ticket, the ulster, the walking-stick, and the golf-clubs.

What Stacy Grainger saw, of course, was three empty seats, with his secretary sitting in a fourth. The sight of the three empty seats was doubtless puzzling enough, but that of the secretary must have been bewildering. Without turning his head Mr. Strangways knew by his sixth and seventh senses that his employer was comparing the number on his ticket with that of the seat, examining the hand-luggage to make sure it was his own, and otherwise drawing the conclusion that his faculties hadn't left him. For a private secretary who had ventured so far out of his line of duty it was a trying minute; but he turned and glanced upward only on feeling a tap on his shoulder.

"Hello, Strangways! Is it you? What's the meaning of this?"

Strangways rose. As the question had been asked in perplexity rather than in anger, he could answer calmly.

"The meaning of what, sir?"

"Where the deuce are you going? What are you doing here?"

"I'm going to Boston, sir."

"What for? Who told you you could go to Boston?"

The tone began to nettle the young man, who was not accustomed to being spoken to so imperiously before strangers.

"No one told me, sir. I didn't ask permission. I'm my own master. I've left your employ."

"The devil you have! Since when?"

"Since this morning. I couldn't tell you, because when you left the office after I'd given you the tickets you didn't come back."

"And do you call that decent to a man who's— But no matter!" He pointed to the seat next his own. "Where's the—the lady who's been sitting here?"

Mr. Strangways raised his eyebrows innocently, and shook his head.

"I haven't seen any lady, sir."

"What? There must have been a lady here. Was to have got on at One Hundred and Twenty-fifth Street."

"Possibly; I only say I didn't see her. As a matter of fact, I've been reading, and I don't think I looked round during the entire journey. Hadn't we better not speak so loud?" he suggested, in a lower tone. "People are listening to us."

"Oh, let them go to— Now look here, Strangways," he began again, speaking softly, but excitedly, "there must be some explanation to this."

"Of course there must be; only I can't give it. Perhaps the porter could tell us. Shall I call him?"

Mr. Grainger nodded his permission. The colored man with the flashing teeth came up on the broad grin, showing them.

"Yep," he replied, in answer to the question: "they was two ladies in them seats all the way f'um Ne' Yawk."

"Two ladies?" Mr. Grainger cried, incredulously.

"Yes, gen'lemen. Two different ladies. The young one she got in at the Grand Central—fust one in the cyar—and the ole one at a Hundred and Twenty-fifth Street."

"Do you mean to say it was an old lady who got in there?"

"Yep, gen'lemen; ole and cranky. I 'ain't handled 'em no crankier not since I've bin on this beat. Sick, too. They done get off at Providence, though they was booked right through to Boston, because the ole lady she couldn't go no farther."

Mr. Grainger was not a sleuth-hound, but he did what he could in the way of verification.

"Did the young lady wear—wear a veil?"

The porter scratched his head.

"Come to think of it she did—one of them there flowery things"—his forefinger made little whirling designs on his coffee-colored skin—"what makes a kind of pattern-like all over people's face."

Because he was frantically seeking a clue, Mr. Grainger blurted out the foolish question:

"Was she—pretty?"

To answer as a connoisseur and as man to man the African took his time.

"Wa-al, not to say p'ooty, she wasn't—but she'd pa-ss. A little black-eyed thing, an' awful smart. One of 'em trained nusses like—very perlite, but a turr'ble boss you could see she'd be, for all she was so soft-spoken. Had cyare of the ole one, who was what you'd call plumb crazy."

"That will do." The trail seemed not worth following any further. "There's some mistake," he continued, furiously. "She must be in one of the other cars."

Like a collie from the leash he bounded off to make new investigations. In five minutes he was back again, passing up the length of the car and going on to examine those at the other end of the train. His face as he returned was livid; his manner, as far as he dared betray himself before a dozen or twenty spectators, that of a balked wild animal.

"Strangways," he swore, as he dropped to the arm of his seat, "you're going to answer for this."

Strangways replied, composedly:

"I'm ready to answer for anything I know. You can't expect me to be responsible for what I don't know anything about."

He slapped his knee.

"What are you doing in that particular chair? Even if you're going to Boston, why aren't you somewhere else?"

"That's easily explained. You told me to get two tickets by this train. Knowing that I was to travel by it myself I asked for three. I dare say it was stupid of me not to think that the propinquity would be open to objection; but as it's a public conveyance, and there's not generally anything secret or special about a trip of the kind—"

"Why in thunder didn't you get a drawing-room, as I told you to?"

202

"For the reason I've given—there were none to be had. If you could have taken me into your confidence a little—But I suppose that wasn't possible."

To this there was no response, but a series of muttered oaths that bore the same relation to soliloquy as a frenzied lion's growl. For some twenty minutes they sat in the same attitudes, Strangways quiet, watchful, alert, ready for any turn the situation might take, the other man stretched on the arm of his chair, indifferent to comfort, cursing spasmodically, perplexity on his forehead, rage in his eyes, and something that was folly, futility, and helplessness all over him.

Almost no further conversation passed between them till they got out in Boston. In the crowd Strangways endeavored to go off by himself, but found Mr. Grainger constantly beside him. He was beside him when they reached the place where taxicabs were called, and ordered his porter to call one.

"Get in," he said, then.

Larry Strangways protested.

"I'm going to—"

I must be sufficiently unlady-like to give Mr. Grainger's response just as it was spoken, because it strikes me as characteristic of men.

"Oh, hell! Get in. You're coming with me."

Characteristic of men was the rest of the evening. In spite of what had happened—and had not happened—Messrs. Grainger and Strangways partook of an excellent supper together, eating and drinking with appetite, and smoking their cigars with what looked like an air of tranquillity. Though the fury of the balked wild animal returned to Stacy Grainger by fits and starts, it didn't interfere with his relish of his food and only once did it break its bounds. That was when he struck the arm of his chair, saying beneath his breath, and yet audibly enough for his secretary to hear:

"She funked it—damn her!"

Larry Strangways then took it on himself to say:

"I don't know the lady, sir, to whom you refer, nor the reasons she may have had for funking it, but may I advise you for your own peace of mind to withdraw the two concluding syllables?"

A pair of fierce, melancholy eyes rested on him for a second uncomprehendingly.

"All right," the crestfallen lover groaned heavily at last. "I may as well take them back."

Characteristic of women were my experiences while this was happening.

Bundled out into the station at Providence no two poor females could ever have been more forlorn. Standing in the waiting-room with our bags around us I felt like one of those immigrant women, ignorant of the customs and language of the country to which they have come, I had sometimes seen on docks at Halifax. As for Mrs. Brokenshire, she was as little used to the unarranged as if she had been a royalty. Never before had she dropped in this way down upon the unexpected; never before had she been unmet, unwelcomed, and unprepared. She was *bouleversée*—overturned. Were she falling from an aeroplane she could not have been more at a loss as to where she was going to alight. Small wonder was it that she should sit down on one of her own valises and begin to cry distressfully.

That, for the minute, I was obliged to disregard. If she had to cry she must cry. I could hear the train puffing out of the station, and as far as that went she was safe. My first preoccupations had to do with where we were to go.

For this I made inquiries of the porter, who named what he considered to be the two or three best hotels. I went to the ticket-office and put the same question, getting approximately the same answer. Then, seeing a well-dressed man and lady enter the station from a private car, which I could discern outside, I repeated my investigations, explaining that I had come from New York with an invalid lady who had not been well enough to continue the journey. They told me I could make no mistake in going to one of the houses already named by my previous informants; and so, gathering up the hand-luggage and Mrs. Brokenshire, we set forth.

At the hotel we secured an apartment of sitting-room and two bedrooms, registering our names as "Miss Adare and friend." I ordered the daintiest supper the house could provide to be served up-stairs, with a small bottle of champagne to inspirit us; but, unlike the two heroes of the episode, neither of us could do more than taste food and drink. No kidnapped princess in a fairy-tale was ever more lovely or pathetic than Mrs. Brokenshire; no giant ogre more monstrously cruel than myself. Now that it was done, I figured, both in her eyes and in my own, not as a savior, but a capturer.

She had dried her tears, but she had dried them resentfully. As far as possible she didn't look at me, but when she couldn't help it the reproach in her glances almost broke my heart. Though I knew I had acted for the best, she made me feel a bad angel, a marplot, a spoil-sport. I had thwarted a dream that was as full of bliss as it was of terror, and reduced the dramatic to the commonplace. Here she was picking at a cold quail in aspic face to face with me when she might have been... .

I couldn't help seeing myself as she saw me, and when we had finished what was not a repast I put her to bed with more than the humility of a serving-maid. You will think me absurd, but when those tender eyes were turned on me with their silent rebuke, I would gladly have put her back on the train again and hurried her on to destruction. As the dear thing sobbed on her pillow I laid my head beside hers and sobbed with her.

But I couldn't sob very long, as I still had duties to fulfil. It was of little use to have her under my care at Providence unless those who would in the end be most concerned as to her whereabouts were to know the facts—or the approximate facts—from the start. It was a case in which doubt for a night might be doubt for a lifetime; and so when she was sufficiently calm for me to leave her I went down-stairs.

Though I had not referred to it again, I had made a mental note of the fact that Mr. Brokenshire was at Newport. If at Newport I knew he could be nowhere but in one hotel. Within fifteen minutes I was talking to him on the telephone.

He was plainly annoyed at being called to the instrument so late as half past ten. When I said I was Alexandra Adare he replied that he didn't recognize the name.

"I was formerly nursery governess to your daughter, Mrs. Rossiter," I explained. "I'm the woman who's refused as yet to marry your son, Hugh."

"Oh, that person," came the response, uttered wearily.

"Yes, sir; that person. I must apologize for ringing you up so late; but I wanted to tell you that Mrs. Brokenshire is here at Providence with me."

The symptoms of distress came to me in a series of choking sounds over the wire. It was a good half-minute before I got the words:

"What does that mean?"

"It means that Mrs. Brokenshire is perfectly well in physical condition, but she's tired and nervous and overwrought."

I made out that the muffled and strangled voice said:

"I'll motor up to Providence at once. It's now half past ten. I shall be there between one and two. What hotel shall I find you at?"

"Don't come, sir," I pleaded. "I had to tell you we were in Providence, because you could have found that out by asking where the long-distance call had come from; but it's most important to Mrs. Brokenshire that she should have a few days alone."

"I shall judge of that. To what hotel shall I come?"

"I beg and implore you, sir, not to come. Please believe me when I say that it will be better for you in the end. Try to trust me. Mrs. Brokenshire isn't far from a nervous breakdown; but if I can have her to myself for a week or two I believe I could tide her over it."

Reproof and argument followed on this, till at last he yielded, with the words:

"Where are you going?"

Fortunately, I had thought of that.

"To some quiet place in Massachusetts. When we're settled I shall let you know."

He suggested a hotel at Lenox as suitable for such a sojourn.

"She'd rather go where she wouldn't meet people whom she knows. The minute she has decided I shall communicate with you again."

"But I can see you in the morning before you leave?"

The accent was now that of request. The overtone in it was pitiful.

"Oh, don't try to, sir. She wants to get away from every one. It will be so much better for her to do just as she likes. She had got to a point where she had to escape from everything she knew and cared about; and so all of a sudden—only—only to-day—she decided to come with me. She doesn't need a trained nurse, because she's perfectly well. All she wants is some one to be with her—whom she knows she can trust. She hasn't even taken Angélique. She simply begs to be alone."

In the end I made my point, but only after genuine beseeching on his part and much repetition on mine. Having said good-night to him—he actually used the words—I called up Angélique, in order to bring peace to a household in which the mistress's desertion would create some consternation.

Angélique and I might have been called friends. The fact that I spoke French *comme une Française*, as she often flattered me by saying, was a bond between us, and we had the further point of sympathy that we were both devoted to Mrs. Brokenshire. Besides that, there is something in me—I suppose it must be a plebeian streak—which enables me to understand servants and get along with them.

I gave her much the same explanation as I gave to Mr. Brokenshire, though somewhat differently put. In addition I asked her to pack such selections from the simpler examples of Mrs. Brokenshire's wardrobe as the lady might need in a country place, and keep them in readiness to send. Angélique having expressed her relief that Mrs. Brokenshire was safe at a known address, in the company of a responsible attendant—a relief which, so she said, would be shared by the housekeeper, the chef, and the butler, all of whom had spent the evening in painful speculation—we took leave of each other, with our customary mutual compliments.

Though I was so tired by this time that fainting would have been a solace, I called for a Boston paper and began studying the advertisements of country hotels. Having made a selection of these I consulted the manager of our present place of refuge, who strongly commended one of them. Thither I sent a night-letter commandeering the best, after which, with no more than strength to undress, I lay down on a couch in Mrs. Brokenshire's room. When I knew she was sleeping I, too, slept fitfully. About once in an hour I went softly to her bedside, and finding her dozing, if not sound asleep, I went softly back again.

Between four and five we had a little scene. As I approached her bed she looked up and said:

"What are we going to do in the morning?"

Afraid to tell her all I had put in train, I gave my ideas in the form of suggestion.

"No, I sha'n't do that," she said, quietly.

She lay quite still, her cheek embossed on the pillow, and a great stray curl over her left shoulder.

"Then what would you like to do?"

"I should like to go straight back."

"To begin the same old life all over again?"

"To begin to see him all over again."

"Do you think that after last night you can begin to see him in the same old way?"

"I must see him in some way."

"But isn't the way what you've still to discover?" I resolved on a bold stroke. "Wouldn't part of your object in going away for a time be to think out some method of reconciling your feeling for Mr. Grainger with—with your self-respect?"

"My self-respect?" She looked as if she had never heard of such a thing. "What's that got to do with it?"

"Hasn't it got everything to do with it? You can't live without it forever."

"Do you mean that I've been living without it as it is?"

"Isn't that for you to say rather than for me?"

She was silent for a minute, after which she said, fretfully:

"I don't think it's very nice of you to talk to me like that. You've got me here at your mercy, when I might have been—" A long, bubbling sigh, like the aftermath of tears, laid stress on the joys she had foregone. "He'll never forgive me now—never."

"Wouldn't it be better, dear Mrs. Brokenshire," I asked, "to consider whether or not you can ever forgive him?"

She raised herself on her elbow and looked at me. Seated in a low arm-chair beside her bed, in an old-rose-colored kimono, my dark hair hanging down my back, I was not a fascinating object of study, even in the light of one small, distant, shaded bedroom lamp.

"What should I forgive him for?—for loving me?"

"Yes, for loving you—in that way."

"He loves me—"

"So much that he could see you dishonored and disgraced—and shunned by decent people all the rest of your life—just to gratify his own desires. It seems to me you may have to forgive him for that."

"He asked me to do only what I would have done willingly—if it hadn't been for you."

"But he asked you. The responsibility is in that. You didn't make the suggestion; he did."

"He didn't make it till I'd let him see—"

"Too much. Forgive me for saying it, dear Mrs. Brokenshire; but do you think a woman should ever go so far to meet a man as you did?"

"I let him see that I loved him. I did that before I married Mr. Brokenshire."

"You let him see more than that you loved him. You showed him that you didn't know how to live without him."

"But since I didn't know how—"

"Ah, but you should have known. No woman should be so dependent on a man as that."

She fell back again on her pillows.

"It's easy to see you've never been in love."

"I have been in love—and am still; but love is not the most important thing in the world—"

"Then you differ from all the great teachers. They say it is."

"If they do they're not speaking of sexual love."

"What are they speaking of, then?"

"They're speaking of another kind of love, with which the mere sexual has nothing to do. I'm not an ascetic, and I know the sexual has its place. But there's a love that's as much bigger than that as the sky is bigger than I am."

"Yes, but so long as one never sees it—"

I suppose it was her tone of feeble rebellion that roused my spirit and made me speak in a way which I should not otherwise have allowed myself.

"You do see it, darling Mrs. Brokenshire," I declared, more sweetly than I felt. "I'm showing it to you." I rose and stood over her. "What do you suppose I'm prompted by but love? What urges me to stand by Mr. Brokenshire but love? What made me step in between you and Mr. Grainger and save him, as well as you, but love? Love isn't emotion that leaves you weak; it's action that makes you strong. It has to be action, and it has to be right action. There's no love separable from right; and until you grasp that fact you'll always be unhappy. I'm a mere rag in my own person. I've no more character than a hen. But because I've got a wee little hold on right—"

She broke in, peevishly, as she turned away:

"I do wish you'd let me go to sleep."

I got down from my high horse and went back, humbly, to my couch. Scarcely, however, had I lain down, when the voice came again, in childish complaint:

"I think you might have kissed me."

I had never kissed her in my life, nor had she ever shown any sign of permitting me this liberty. Timidly I went back to the bed; timidly I bent over it. But I was not prepared for the sudden intense clinging with which she threw her arms round my neck and drew my face down to hers.

CHAPTER XIX

In the morning Mrs. Brokenshire was difficult again, but I got her into a neat little country inn in Massachusetts by the middle of the afternoon. I had to be like a jailer dragging along a prisoner, but that could not be helped.

On leaving Providence she insisted on spending a few days in Boston, where, so she said, she had friends whom she wished to see. Knowing that Stacy Grainger would be at one of the few hotels of which we had the choice, I couldn't risk a meeting. Her predominating shame, a shame she had no hesitation in confessing, was for having failed him. He would never forgive her, she moaned; he wouldn't love her any more. Not to be loved by him, not to be forgiven, was like death. All she demanded during the early hours of that day was to find him, wherever he had gone, and fling herself at his feet.

Because I didn't allow her to remain in Boston we had what was almost a quarrel, as we jolted over the cobblestones from the southern station to the northern. She was now an outraged queen and now a fiery little termagant. Sparing me neither tears nor reproaches, neither scoldings nor denunciations, she nevertheless followed me obediently. Sitting opposite me in the parlor-car, ignoring the papers and fashion magazines I spread beneath her eyes, she lifted on me the piteous face of an angel whom I had beaten and trampled and enslaved. For this kind of sacrilege I had ceased, however, to be contrite. I was so tired, and had grown so grim, that I could have led her along in handcuffs.

But once out in the fresh, green, northern country the joy of a budding and blossoming world stole into us in spite of all our cares. We couldn't help getting out of our own little round of thought when we saw fields that were carpets of green velvet, or copses of hazelnut and alder coming into leaf, or a farmer sowing the plowed earth with the swing and the stride of the *Semeur*. We couldn't help seeing wider and farther and more hopefully when the sky was an arch of silvery blue overhead, and white clouds drifted across it, and the north into which we were traveling began to fling up masses of rolling hills.

She caught me by the arm.

"Oh, do look at the lambs! The darlings!"

There they were, three or four helpless creatures, shivering in the sharp May wind and apparently struck by the futility of a life which would end in

210

nothing but making chops. The ewes watched them maternally, or stood patiently to be tugged by the full woolly breasts. After that we kept our eyes open for other living things: for horses and cows and calves, for Corots and Constables—with a difference!—on the uplands of farms or in village highways. Once when a foal galloped madly away from the train, kicking up its slender hind legs, my companion actually laughed.

When we got out at the station a robin was singing, the first bird we had heard that year. The note was so full and pure and Eden-like that it caught one's breath. It went with the bronze-green of maples and elms, with the golden westering sunshine, and with the air that was like the distillation of air and yet had a sharp northern tang in it. Driving in the motor of the inn, through the main street of the town, we saw that most of the white houses had a roomy Colonial dignity, and that orchards of apple, cherry, and plum, with acres of small fruit, surrounded them all. Having learned on the train that jam was the staple of the little town's prosperity, we could see jam everywhere. Jam was in the cherry-trees covered with dainty white blossoms, in the plum-trees showing but a flower or two, and in the apple-trees scarcely in bud. Jam was in the long straight lines which we were told represented strawberries, and in the shrubberies of currant. Jam was along the roadsides where the raspberry was clothing its sprawling bines with leaves, and wherever the blueberry gladdened the waste places with its millions of modest bells. Jam is a toothsome, homey thing to which no woman with a housekeeping heart can be insensible. The thought of it did something to bring Mrs. Brokenshire's thoughts back to the simple natural ways she had forsworn, even before reaching the hotel.

The hotel was no more than a farm-house that had expanded itself half a dozen times. We traversed all sorts of narrow halls and climbed all sorts of narrow staircases, till at last we emerged on a corner suite, where the view led us straight to the balcony.

Not that it was an extraordinary view; it was only a peaceful and a noble one. An undulating country held in its folds a scattering of lakes, working up to the lines of the southern New Hampshire hills which closed the horizon to the north. Green was, of course, the note of the landscape, melting into mauve in the mountains and saffron in the sky. Spacing out the perspective a mauve mist rose between the ridges, and a mauve light rested on the three white steeples of the town. The town was perhaps two hundred feet below us and a mile away, nestling in a feathery bower of verdure.

When I joined Mrs. Brokenshire she was grasping the balcony rail, emitting little "Ohs!" and "Ahs!" of ecstasy. She drew long breaths, like a thirsty person drinking. She listened to the calling and answering of birds with face illumined and upturned. It was a bath of the spirit to us both. It was cleansing and healing; it was soothing and restful and corrective, setting what was sane within us free.

Of all this I need say little beyond mentioning the fact that Mrs. Brokenshire, in spite of herself, entered into a period in which her taut nerves relaxed and her over-strained emotions became rested. It was a kind of truce of God to her. She had struggled and suffered so much that she was content for a time to lie still in the everlasting arms and be rocked and comforted. We had the simplest of rooms; we ate the simplest of food; we led the simplest of lives. By day we read and walked and talked a little and thought much; at night we slept soundly. Our fellow-guests were people who did the same, varying the processes with golf and moving pictures. For the most part they were tired people from the neighboring towns, seeking like ourselves a few days' respite from their burdens. Though they came to know who Mrs. Brokenshire was, they respected her privacy, never doing worse than staring after her when she entered the dining-room or walked on the lawns or verandas. I had come to love her so much that it was a joy to me to witness the revival of her spirit, and I looked forward to seeing her restored, not too reluctantly, to her husband.

With him I had, of course, some correspondence. It was an odd correspondence, in which I made my customary *gaffe*. On our first evening at the inn I wrote to him in fulfilment of my promise, beginning, "Dear Mr. Brokenshire," as if I was writing to an equal. The acknowledgment came back: "Miss Alexandra Adare: Dear Madam," putting me back in my place. Accepting the rebuff, I adopted the style in sending him my daily bulletins.

As a matter of fact, my time was largely passed in writing, for I had explanations to make to so many. My acquaintance with Mrs. Brokenshire having been a secret one, I was obliged to confess it to Hugh and Mrs. Rossiter, and even to Angélique. I had, in a measure, to apologize for it, too, setting down Mrs. Brokenshire's selection of my company to an invalid's eccentricity.

So we got through May and into June, my reports to Mr. Brokenshire being each one better than the last. My patient never wrote to him herself, nor to any one. We had, in fact, been a day or two at the inn before she said:

"I wonder what Mr. Brokenshire is thinking?"

It was for me to tell her then that from the beginning I had kept him informed as to where she was, and that he knew I was with her. For a minute or two she stiffened into the *grande dame*, as she occasionally did.

"You'll be good enough in future not to do such things without consulting me," she said, with dignity.

That passed, and when I read to her, as I always did, the occasional notes with which her husband honored me, she listened without comment. It must have been the harder to do that since the lover's pleading ardor could be detected beneath all the cold formality in which he couched his communications.

It was this ardor, as well as something else, that began in the end to make me uneasy. The something else was that Mrs. Brokenshire was writing letters on her own account. Coming in one day from a solitary walk, I found her posting one in the hall of the hotel. A few days later one for her was handed to me at the office, with several of my own. Recognizing Stacy Grainger's writing, I put it back with the words:

"Mrs. Brokenshire will come for her letters herself."

From that time onward she was often at her desk, and I knew when she got her replies by the feverishness of her manner. The truce of God being past, the battle was now on again.

The first sign of it given to me was on a day when Mr. Brokenshire wrote in terms more definite than he had used hitherto. I read the letter aloud to her, as usual. He had been patient, he said, and considerate, which had to be admitted. Now he could deny himself no longer. As it was plain that his wife was better, he should come to her. He named the 20th as the day on which he should appear.

"No, no," she cried, excitedly. "Not till after the twenty-third."

"But why the twenty-third?" I asked, innocently.

"Because I say so. You'll see." Then fearing, apparently, that she had betrayed something she ought to have concealed, she colored and added, lamely, "It will give me a little more time."

I said nothing, but I pondered much. The 23d was no date at all that had anything to do with us. If it had significance it was in plans as to which she had not taken me into her confidence.

So, too, when I heard her making inquiries of the maid who did the rooms as to the location of the Baptist church. "What on earth does she want to know that for?" was the question I not unnaturally asked myself. That she, who never went to church at all, except as an occasional act of high ceremonial for which she took great credit to her soul, was now concerned with the doctrine of baptism by immersion I did not believe. But I hunted up the sacred edifice myself, finding it to be situated on the edge of a daisied mead, slightly out of the town, on a road that might be described as lonely and remote. I came to the conclusion that if any one wanted to carry off in an automobile a lady picking flowers—a sort of *enlèvement de Proserpine*—this would be as good a place as any. How the Pluto of our drama could have come to select it, Heaven only knew.

But I did as I was bid, and wrote to Mr. Brokenshire that once the 23d was passed he would be free to come. After that I watched, wondering whether or not I should have the heart or the nerve to frustrate love a second time, even if I got the chance.

I didn't get the chance precisely, but on the 22nd of June I received a mysterious note. It was typewritten and had neither date nor address nor signature. Its message was simple:

"If Miss Adare will be at the post-office at four o'clock this afternoon she will greatly oblige the writer of these lines and perhaps benefit a person who is dear to her."

The post-office being a tolerably safe place in case of felonious attack, I was on the spot at five minutes before the hour. In that particular town it occupied a corner of a brick building which also gave shelter to the bank and a milliner's establishment. As the village hotel was opposite, I advertised my arrival by studying a display of hats which warranted the attention before going inside to invest in stamps. As I was the only applicant for this necessary of life, the swarthy, undersized young man who served me made kindly efforts at entertainment while "delivering the goods," as he expressed it.

"English, ain't you?"

I said, as usual, that I was a Canadian.

He smiled at his own perspicacity.

"Got your number, didn't I? All you Canucks have the same queer way o' talkin'. Two or three in the jam-factory here—only they're French."

I knew some one had entered behind me, and, turning away from the wicket, I found the person I had expected. Mr. Stacy Grainger, clad jauntily in a gray spring suit, lifted a soft felt hat.

He went to his point without introductory greeting.

"It's good of you to have come. Perhaps we could talk better if we walked up the street. There's no one to know us or to make it awkward for you."

Walking up the street he made his errand clear to me. I had partly guessed it before he said a word. I had guessed it from his pallor, from something indefinably humbled in the way he bore himself, and from the worried light in his romantic eyes. Being so much taller than I, he had to stoop toward me as he talked.

He knew, he said, what had happened on the train. Some of it he had wrung from his secretary, Strangways, and the rest had been written him by Mrs. Brokenshire. He had been so furious at first that he might have been called insane. In order to give himself the pleasure of kicking Strangways out he had refused to accept his resignation, and had I not been a woman he would have sought revenge on me. He had been the more frantic because until getting his first note from Mrs. Brokenshire he hadn't known where she was. To have the person dearest to him in the world swept off the face of the earth after she was actually under his protection was enough to drive a man mad.

Having acquiesced in this, I considered it no harm to add that if I had known the business on which I was setting out I should have hardly dared that day to take the train for Boston. Once on it, however, and in speech with Mrs. Brokenshire, it had seemed that there was no other course before me.

"Quite so," he agreed, somewhat to my surprise. "I see that now. He's not altogether an ass, that fellow Strangways. I've kept him with me, and little by little—" He broke off abruptly to say: "And now the shoe's on the other foot. That's what I wanted to tell you."

I walked on a few paces before getting the force of this figure of speech.

"You mean that Mrs. Brokenshire—"

"Quite so. I see you get what I'd like you to know." He went on, brokenly: "It isn't that I don't want it myself as much as ever. I only see, as I didn't see before, what it would mean to her. If I were to take her at her word—as I must, of course, if she insists on it—"

I had to think hard while we continued to walk on beneath the leafing elms, and the village people watched us two as city folks.

"It's for to-morrow, isn't it?" I asked at last.

He nodded.

"How did you know that?"

"Near the Baptist church?"

"How the deuce do you know? I motored up here last week to spy out the land. That seemed to me the most practicable spot, where we should be least observed—"

We were still walking on when I said, without quite knowing why I did so:

"Why shouldn't you go away at once and leave it all to me?"

"Leave it all to you? And what would you do?"

"I don't know. I should have to think. I could do—something."

"But suppose she's counting on me to come?"

"Then you would have to fail her."

"I couldn't."

"Not even if it was for her good?"

He shook his head.

"Not even if it was for her good. No one who calls himself a gentleman—"

I couldn't help flinging him a scornful smile.

"Isn't it too late to think in terms like that? We've come to a place where such words don't apply. The best we can do is to get out of a difficult situation as wisely as possible, and if you'd just go away and leave it to me—"

"She'd never forgive me. That's what I'd be afraid of."

"There's nothing to be afraid of in doing right," I declared, a little sententiously. "You'll do right in going away. The rest will take care of itself."

We came to the edge of the town, where there was a gate leading into a pasture. Over this gate we leaned and looked down on a valley of orchards and farms. He was sufficiently at ease to take out a cigarette and ask my permission to smoke.

"What would you say of a man who treated you like that?" he asked, presently.

"It wouldn't matter what I said at first, so long as I lived to thank him. That's what she'd do, and she'd do it soon."

"And in the mean time?"

"I don't see that you need think of that. If you do right—"

He groaned aloud.

"Oh, right be hanged!"

"Yes, there you go. But so long as right is hanged wrong will have it all its own way and you'll both get into trouble. Do right now—"

"And leave her in the lurch?"

"You wouldn't be leaving her in the lurch, because you'd be leaving her with me. I know her and can take care of her. If you were just failing her and nothing else—that would be another thing. But I'm here. If you'll only do "what's so obviously right, Mr. Grainger, you can trust me with the rest."

I said this firmly and with an air of competence, though, as a matter of fact, I had no idea of what I should have to do. What I wanted first was to get rid of him. Once alone with her, I knew I should get some kind of inspiration.

He diverted the argument to himself—he wanted her so much, he would have to suffer so cruelly.

"There's no question as to your suffering," I said. "You'll both have to suffer. That can be taken for granted. We're only thinking of the way in which you'll suffer least."

"That's true," he admitted, but slowly and reluctantly.

"I'm not a terribly rigorous moralist," I went on. "I've a lot of sympathy with Paolo and Francesca and with Pelléas and Mélisande. But you can see for yourself that all such instances end unhappily, and when it's happiness you're primarily in search of—"

"Hers—especially," he interposed, with the same deliberation and some of the same unwillingness.

"Well, then, isn't your course clear? She'll never be happy with you if she kills the man she runs away from—"

He withdrew his cigarette and looked at me, wonderingly.

"Kills him? What in thunder do you mean?"

I explained my convictions. Howard Brokenshire wouldn't survive his wife's desertion for a month; he might not survive it for a day. He was a doomed man, even if his wife did not desert him at all. He, Stacy Grainger, was young. Mrs. Brokenshire was young. Wouldn't it be better for them both to wait on life—and on the other possibilities that I didn't care to name more explicitly?

So he wrestled with himself, and incidentally with me, turning back at last toward the village inn—and his motor. While shaking my hand to say good-by he threw off, jerkily:

"I suppose you know my secretary, Strangways, wants to marry you?"

My heart seemed to stop beating.

"He's—he's never said so to me," I managed to return, but more weakly than I could have wished.

"Well he will. He's all right. He's not a fool. I'm taking him with me into some big things; so that if it's the money you're in doubt about—"

I had recovered myself enough to say:

"Oh no; not at all. But if you're in his confidence I beg you to ask him to think no more about it. I'm engaged—or practically engaged—I may say that I'm engaged—to Hugh Brokenshire."

"I see. Then you're making a mistake."

I was moving away from him by this time so that I gave him a little smile.

"If so, the circumstances are such that—that I must go on making it."

"For God's sake don't!" he called after me.

"Oh, but I must," I returned, and so we went our ways.

On going back to our rooms I found poor, dear little Mrs. Brokenshire packing a small straw suit-case. She had selected it as the only thing she could carry in her hand to the place of the *enlèvement*. She was not a packer; she was not an adept in secrecy. As I entered her room she looked at me with the pleading, guilty eyes of a child detected in the act of stealing sweets, and confessing before he is accused.

I saw nothing, of course. I saw nothing that night. I saw nothing the next day. Each one of her helpless, unskilful moves was so plain to me that I could have wept; but I was turning over in my mind what I could do to let her know she was deceived. I was reproaching myself, too, for being so treacherous a confidante. All the great love-heroines had an attendant like me, who bewailed and lamented the steps their mistresses were taking, and yet lent a hand. Here I was, the nurse to this Juliet, the Brangaene to this Isolde, but acting as a counter-agent to all romantic schemes. I cannot say I admired myself; but what was I to do?

To make a long story short I decided to do nothing. You may scorn me, oh, reader, for that; but I came to a place where I saw it would be vain to interfere. Even a child must sometimes be left to fight its own battles and stand face to face with its own fate; and how much more a married woman! It became the more evident to me that this was what I could best do for Mrs. Brokenshire in proportion as I watched the leaden hands and feet with which she carried out her tasks and inferred a leaden heart. A leaden heart is bad enough, but a leaden heart offering itself in vain—what lesson could go home with more effect?

During the forenoon of the 23d each little incident cut me to the quick. It was so naïve, so useless. The poor darling thought she was outwitting me. As if she was stealing it she stowed away her jewelry, and when she could no longer hide the suit-case she murmured something about articles to be cleaned at the village cleaner's. I took this with a feeble joke as to the need of economy, and when she thought she would carry down the things herself I commended the impulse toward exercise. I knew she wouldn't drive, because she didn't want a witness to her acts. As far as I could guess the hour at which Pluto would carry off Proserpine, it would be at five o'clock.

And indeed about half past three I observed unusual signs of agitation. Her door was kept closed, and from behind it came sounds of a final opening and closing of cupboards and drawers, after which she emerged, wearing a dark-blue walking-suit and a hat of the *canotière* style, with a white quill feather at one side. I still made no comment, not even when the wan, wee, touching figure was ready to set forth.

If her first steps were artless the last was more artless still. Instead of going off casually, with an implied intention to come back, she took leave of me with tears and protestations of affection. She had been harsh with me, she confessed, and seemingly indifferent to my tender care, but one day she might have a chance to show me how genuine was her gratitude. In this, too, I saw no more than the commonplace, and a little after four she tripped down the avenue, looking, with her suit-case, like a school-girl.

I allowed her just such a handicap as her speed and mine would have warranted. Even then I made no attempt to overtake her. Having previously got what is called the lay of the land, I knew how I could come to her assistance by taking a short cut. I had hardened my heart by this time, and whatever qualms I had felt before, I was resolved now to spare her no drop of the wormwood that would be for her good.

I cannot describe our respective routes without appending a map, which would scarcely be worth while. It will be enough if I say that she went round the arc of a bow and I cut across by the string. I came thus to a slight eminence, selected in advance, whence I could watch her descent of the hill by which the lower Main Street trails off into the country. I could follow her, too, when she deflected into a small cross-thoroughfare bearing the scented name of Clover Lane, in which there were no houses; and I should still be able to trace her course when she emerged on the quiet country road that would take her to her trysting-place. I had no intention to step in till I could do it at some spot on her homeward way, and thus spare her needless humiliation.

In Clover Lane she was within a few hundred yards of her destination. She had only to turn a corner and she would be in sight of the flowery mead whence she was to be carried off. It was a pretty lane, grass-grown and overhung with lilacs in full bloom, such as you would find on the edge of any New England town. The lilacs shut her in from my view for a good part of the time, but not so constantly that I couldn't be a witness to her soul's tragedy.

Her soul's tragedy came as a surprise to me. Closely as I had lived with her, I was unprepared for any such event. My first hint of it was when her pace through the lane began to slacken, till at last she stopped. That she didn't stop because she was tired I could judge by the fact that, though she stood stock-still, she held the light suit-case in her hand. I couldn't see her face, because I stood under a great elm, some five hundred yards away.

Having paused and reflected for the space of three or four minutes, she went on again, but she went on more slowly. Her light, tripping gait had become a dragging of the feet, while I divined that she was still pondering. As it was nearly five o'clock, she couldn't be afraid of being before her time.

But she stopped again, setting the suit-case down in the middle of the road. She turned then and looked back over the way by which she had come, as if regretting it. Seeing her open her small hand-bag, take out a handkerchief, and put it to her lips, I was sure she was repressing one of her baby-like sobs. My heart yearned over her, but I could only watch her breathlessly.

She went on again—twenty paces, perhaps. Here she seemed to find a seat on a roadside boulder, for she sat down on it, her back being toward me and her figure almost concealed by the wayside growth. I could only wonder at what was passing in her mind. The whole period, of about ten minutes' duration, is filled in my memory with mellow afternoon light and perfumed air and the evening song of birds. When the village clock struck five she bounded up with a start.

Again she took what might have been twenty paces, and again she came to a halt. Dropping the suit-case once more, she clasped her hands as if she was praying. As, to the best of my knowledge, her prayers were confined to a hasty evening and morning ritual in which there was nothing more than a pious, meaningless habit, I could surmise her present extremity. Stacy Grainger was like a god to her. If she renounced him now it would be an act of heroism of which I could hardly believe her capable.

But, apparently, she made up her mind that she couldn't renounce him. If there was an answer to her prayer it was one that prompted her to snatch up her burden again and hurry, with a kind of skimming motion, right to the end of the lane. It was to the end of the lane, but not to the turning into the roadway. Once in the roadway she would see—or she thought she would see —Stacy Grainger and his automobile, and her fate would be sealed.

She had still a chance before her—and from that rutted sandy juncture, with wild roses and wild raspberries in the hedgerows on each side, she reeled back as if she had been struck. I can only think of a person blinded by a flash of lightning who would recoil in just that way.

For a few minutes she was hidden from my view behind the lilacs. When I caught sight of her again she was running like a terrified bird back through Clover Lane and toward the Main Street, which would take her home.

I met her as she was dragging herself up the hill, white, breathless, exhausted. Pretending to take the situation lightly, I called as I approached:

"So you didn't leave the things."

Her answer was to drop the suit-case once again, while, regardless of curious eyes at windows and doors, she flew to throw herself into my arms.

She never explained; I never asked for explanations. I was glad enough to get her back to the hotel, put her to bed, and wait on her hand and foot. She was saved now; Stacy Grainger, too, was saved. Each had deserted the other; each had the same crime to forgive. From that day onward she never spoke his name to me.

But as, that evening, I went to her bedside to say good-night, she drew my face to hers and whispered, cryptically:

"It will be all right now between yourself and Hugh. I know how I can help."

CHAPTER XX

M̲r. Brokenshire arrived on the 26th of June, thus giving us a few days' grace. In the interval Mrs. Brokenshire remained in bed, neither tired nor ill, but white, silent, and withdrawn. Her soul's tragedy had plainly not ended with her skimming retreat through Clover Lane. In the new phase on which it had entered it was creating a woman, possibly a wife, where there had been only a lovely child of arrested development. Slipping in and out of her room, attending quietly to her wants, I was able to note, as never in my life before, the beneficent action of suffering.

Because she was in bed, I folded my tent like the Arab and silently vacated my room in favor of Mr. Brokenshire. I looked for some objection on telling her of this, but she merely bit her lip and said nothing. I had asked the manager to put me in the most distant part of the most distant wing of the hotel, and would have stolen away altogether had it not been for fear that my poor, dear little lady might need me.

As it was, I kept out of sight when Mr. Brokenshire drove up with secretary, valet, and chauffeur, and I contrived to take my meals at hours when there could be no encounter between me and the great personage. If I was wanted I knew I could be sent for; but the 27th passed and no command came.

Once or twice I got a distant view of my enemy, as I began to call him— majestic, noble, stouter, too, and walking with a slight waddle of the hips, which had always marked his carriage and became more noticeable as he increased in bulk. Not having seen him for nearly three months, I observed that his hair and beard were grayer. During those first few days I was never near enough to be able to tell whether or not there was a change for the better or the worse in his facial affliction.

From a chance word with the cadaverous Spellman on the 28th I learned that a sitting-room had been arranged in connection with the two bedrooms Mrs. Brokenshire and I had occupied, and that husband and wife were now taking their repasts in private. Later that day I saw them drive out together, Mrs. Brokenshire no more than a silhouette in the shadows of the limousine. I drew the inference that, however the soul's tragedy was working, it was with some reconciling grace that did what love had never been able to accomplish. Perhaps for her, as for me, there was an appeal in this vain, fatuous, suffering magnate of a coarse world's making that, in spite of everything, touched the springs of pity.

In any case, I was content not to be sent for—and to rest. After a tranquil day or two my own nerves had calmed down and I enjoyed the delight of having nothing on my mind. It was extraordinary how remote I could keep myself while under the same roof with my superiors, especially when they kept themselves remote on their side. I had decided on the 1st of July as the date to which I should remain. If there was no demand for my services by that time I meant to consider myself free to go.

But events were preparing, had long been preparing, which changed my life as, I suppose, they changed to a greater or less degree the majority of lives in the world. It was curious, too, how they arranged themselves, with a neatness of coincidence which weaves my own small drama as a visible thread—visible to me, that is—in the vast tapestry of human history begun so far back as to be time out of mind.

It was the afternoon of Monday the 29th of June, 1914. Having secured a Boston morning paper, I had carried it off to the back veranda, which was my favorite retreat, because nobody else liked it. It was just outside my room, and looked up into a hillside wood, where there were birds and squirrels, and straight bronze pine-trunks wherever the sunlight fell aslant on them. At long intervals, too, a partridge hen came down with her little brood, clucking her low wooden cluck and pecking at tender shoots invisible to me, till she wandered off once more into the hidden depths of the stillness.

But I wasn't watching for the partridge hen that afternoon. I was thrilled by the tale of the assassination of the Archduke Franz Ferdinand and the Duchess of Hohenberg, which had taken place at Sarajevo on the previous day. Millions of other readers, who, no more than I, felt their own destinies involved were being thrilled at the same moment. The judgment trumpet was sounding—only not as we had expected it. There was no blast from the sky—no sudden troop of angels. There was only the soundless vibration of the wire and of the Hertzian waves; there was only the casting of type and the rattling of innumerable reams of paper; and, as the Bible says, the dead could hear the voice, and they that heard it stood still; and the nations were summoned before the Throne "that was set in the midst." I was summoned, with my own people—though I didn't know it was a summons till afterward.

The paper had fallen to my knee when I was startled to see Mr. Brokenshire come round the corner of my retreat. Dressed entirely in white, with no color in his costume save the lavender stripe in his shirt and collar, and the violet of his socks, handkerchief, and tie, he would have been the perfect type of the middle-aged exquisite had it not been for the pitiless distortion of his eye the minute he caught sight of me. That he had not stumbled on me accidentally I judged by the way in which he lifted a Panama of the kind that is said to be made under water and is costlier than the costliest feminine confection by Caroline Ledoux.

I was struggling out of my wicker chair when the uplifted hand forbade me.

"Be good enough to stay where you are," he commanded, but more gently than he had ever spoken to me. "I've some things to say to you."

Too frightened to make a further attempt to move, I looked at him as he drew up a chair similar to my own, which creaked under his weight when he sat down in it. The afternoon being hot, and my veranda lacking air, which was one of the reasons why it was left to me, he mopped his brow with the violet handkerchief, on which an enormous monogram was embroidered in white. I divined his reluctance to begin not only from his long hesitation, but from the renewed contortion of his face. His hand went up to the left cheek as if to hold it in place, though with no success in the effort. When, at last, he spoke there was a stillness in his utterance suggestive of an affection extending now to the lips or the tongue.

"I want you to know how much I appreciate the help you've given to Mrs. Brokenshire during her—her"—he had a difficulty in finding the right word —"during her indisposition," he finished, rather weakly.

"I did no more than I was glad to do," I responded, as weakly as he.

"Exactly; and yet I can't allow such timely aid to go unrewarded."

I was alarmed. Grasping the arms of the chair, I braced myself.

"If you mean money, sir—"

"No; I mean more than money." He, too, braced himself. "I—I withdraw my opposition to your marriage with my son."

The immediate change in my consciousness was in the nature of a dissolving view. The veranda faded away, and the hillside wood. Once more I saw the imaginary dining-room, and myself in a smart little dinner gown seating the guests; once more I saw the white-enameled nursery, and myself in a lace peignoir leaning over the bassinet. As in previous visions of the kind, Hugh was a mere shadow in the background, secondary to the home and the baby.

Secondary to the home and the baby was the fact that my object was accomplished and that my enemy had come to his knees. Indeed, I felt no particular elation from that element in the case; no special sense of victory. Like so many realized ambitions, it seemed a matter of course, now that it had come. Nevertheless, it seemed to me that for my own sake and for the sake of the future I must have a more definite expression of surrender than he had yet given me.

I remembered that Mrs. Brokenshire had said she would help me, and could imagine how. I summoned up everything within me that would rank as force of character, speaking quietly.

"I should be sorry, sir, to have you come to this decision against your better judgment."

"If you'll be kind enough to accept the fact," he said, sharply, "we can leave my manner of reaching it out of the discussion."

In spite of the tone I rallied my resources.

"I don't want to be presumptuous, sir; but if I'm to enter your family I should like to feel sure that you'll receive me whole-heartedly."

"My dear young lady, isn't it assurance enough that I receive you at all? When I bring myself to that—"

"Oh, please don't think I can't appreciate the sacrifice."

"Then what more is to be said?"

"But the sacrifice is the point. No girl wants to become one of a family which has to make such an effort to take her."

There was already a whisper of insecurity in his tone.

"Even so, I can't see why you shouldn't let the effort be our affair. Since we make it on our own responsibility—"

"I don't care anything about the responsibility, sir. All I'm thinking of is that the effort must be made."

"But what did you expect?"

"I haven't said that I expected anything. If I've been of the slightest help to Mrs. Brokenshire I'm happy to let the service be its own reward."

"But I'm not. It isn't my habit to remain under an obligation to any one."

"Nor mine," I said, demurely.

He stared.

"What does that mean? I don't follow you."

"Perhaps not, sir; but I quite follow you. You wish me to understand that, in spite of my deficiencies, you accept me as your son's wife—for the reason that you can't help yourself."

Two sharp hectic spots came out on each cheek-bone.

"Well, what if I do?"

"I'm far too generous to put you in that position. I couldn't take you at a disadvantage, not even for the sake of marrying Hugh."

I was not sure whether he was frightened or angry, but it was the one or the other.

"Do you mean to say that, now—now that I'm ready—"

"That I'm not? Yes, sir. That's what I do mean to say. I told you once that if I loved a man I shouldn't stop to consider the wishes of his relatives; but I've repented of that. I see now that marriage has a wider application than merely to individuals; and I'm not ready to enter any family that doesn't want me."

I looked off into the golden dimnesses of the hillside wood in order not to be a witness of the struggle he was making.

"And suppose"—it was almost a groan—"and suppose I said we—wanted you?"

It was like bending an iron bar; but I gave my strength to it.

"You'd have to say it differently from that, sir."

He spoke hoarsely.

"Differently—in what sense?"

I knew I had him, as Hugh would have expressed it, where I had been trying to get him.

"In the sense that if you want me you must ask me."

He mopped his brow once more.

"I—I have asked you."

"You've said you withdrew your opposition. That's not enough."

Beads or perspiration were again standing on his forehead.

"Then what—what would be—enough?"

"A woman can't marry any one unless she does it as something of a favor."

He drew himself up.

"Do you remember that you're talking to me?"

"Yes, sir; and it's because I do remember it that I have to insist. With anybody else I shouldn't have to be so crude."

Again he put up a struggle, and this time I watched him. If his wife had made the conditions I guessed at, I had nothing to do but sit still. Grasping the arms of his chair, he half rose as if to continue the interview no further, but immediately saw, as I inferred, what that would mean to him. He fell back again into the creaking depths of the chair.

"What do you wish me to say?"

But his stricken aspect touched me. Now that he was prepared to come to his knees, I had no heart to force him down on them. Since I had gained my point, it was foolish to battle on, or try to make the Ethiopian change his skin.

"Oh, sir, you've said it!" I cried, with sudden emotion. I leaned toward him, clasping my hands. "I see you do want me; and since you do I'll—I'll come."

Having made this concession, I became humble and thankful and tactful. I appeased him by saying I was sensible of the honor he did me, that I was happy in the thought that he was to be reconciled with Hugh; and I inquired for Mrs. Brokenshire. Leading up to this question with an air of guilelessness, I got the answer I was watching for in the ashen shade that settled on his face.

I forget what he replied; I was really not listening. I was calling up the scene in which she must have fulfilled her promise of helping Hugh and me. From the something crushed in him, as in the case of a man who knows the worst at last, I gathered that she had made a clean breast of it. It was awesome to think that behind this immaculate white suit with its violet details, behind this pink of the old beau, behind this moneyed authority and this power of dictation to which even the mighty sometimes had to bow, there was a broken heart.

He knew now that the bird he had captured was nothing but a captured bird, and always longing for the forest. That his wife was willing to bear his name and live in his house and submit to his embraces was largely because I had induced her. Whether or not, in spite of his pompousness, he was grateful to me I didn't know; but I guessed that he was not. He could accept such benefits as I had secured him and yet be resentful toward the curious providence that had chosen me in particular as its instrument.

I came out of my meditations in time to hear him say that, Mrs. Brokenshire being as well rested as she was, there would be no further hindrance to their proceeding soon to Newport.

"And I suppose I might go back to my home," I observed, with no other than the best intentions.

He made an attempt to regain the authority he had just forfeited.

"What for?"

"To be married," I explained—"since I am to be married."

"But why should you be married there?"

"Wouldn't it be the most natural thing?"

"It wouldn't be the most natural thing for Hugh."

"A man can be married anywhere; whereas a woman, at such a turning-point in her life, needs a certain backing. I've an uncle and aunt and a great many friends—"

The effort at a faint smile drew up the corner of his mouth and set his face awry.

"You'll excuse me, my dear"—the epithet made me jump—"if I correct you on a point of taste. In being willing that Hugh should marry you I think I must draw the line at anything like parade."

I know my eyebrows went up.

"Parade? Parade—how?"

The painful little smile persisted.

"The ancient Romans, when they went to war, had a custom of bringing back the most conspicuous of their captives and showing them in triumph in the streets—"

I, too, smiled.

"Oh! I understand. But you see, sir, the comparison doesn't hold in this case, because none of my friends would know anything more about Hugh than the fact that he was an American."

The crooked features went back into repose.

"They'd know he was my son."

I continued to smile, but sweetly.

"They'd take it for granted that he was somebody's son—but they wouldn't know anything about you, sir. You'd be quite safe so far as that went. Though

I don't live many hundreds of miles from New York, and we're fairly civilized, I had never so much as heard the name of Brokenshire till Mrs. Rossiter told me it was hers before she was married. You see, then, that there'd be no danger of my leading a captive in triumph. No one I know would give Hugh a second thought beyond being nice to the man I was marrying."

That he was pleased with this explanation I cannot affirm, but he passed it over.

"I think," was his way of responding, "that it will be better if we consider that you belong to us. Till your marriage to Hugh, which I suppose will take place in the autumn, you'll come back with us to Newport. There will be a whole new—how shall I put it?—a whole new phase of life for you to get used to. Hugh will stay with us, and I shall ask my daughter, Mrs. Rossiter, to be your hostess till—"

As, without finishing his sentence, he rose I followed his example. Though knowing in advance how futile would be the attempt to present myself as an equal, I couldn't submit to this calm disposition of my liberty and person without putting up a fight.

"I've a great preference, sir—if you'll allow me—for being married in my own home, among my own people, and in the old parish church in which I was baptized. I really have people and a background; and it's possible that my sisters might come over—"

The hand went up; his tone put an end to discussion.

"I think, my dear Alexandra, that we shall do best in considering that you belong to us. You'll need time to grow accustomed to your new situation. A step backward now might be perilous."

My fight was ended. What could I do? I listened and submitted, while he went on to tell me that Mrs. Brokenshire would wish to see me during the day, that Hugh would be sent for and would probably arrive the next afternoon, and that by the end of the week we should all be settled in Newport. There, whenever I felt I needed instruction, I was not to be ashamed to ask for it. Mrs. Rossiter would explain anything of a social nature that I didn't understand, and he knew I could count on Mrs. Brokenshire's protection.

With a comic inward grimace I swallowed all my pride and thanked him.

As for Mrs. Brokenshire's protection, that was settled when, later in the afternoon, we sat on her balcony and laughed and cried together, and held each other's hands, as young women do when their emotions outrun their power of expression. She called me Alix and begged me to invent a name for her that would combine the dignity of Hugh's stepmother with our standing as friends. I chose Miladi, out of *Les Trois Mousquetaires*, with which she was delighted.

I begged off from dining with them that evening, nominally because I was too upset by all I had lived through in the afternoon, but really for the reason that I couldn't bear the thought of Mr. Brokenshire calling me his dear Alexandra twice in the same day. Once had made my blood run cold. His method of shriveling up a name by merely pronouncing it is something that transcends my power to describe. He had ruined that of Adare with me forever, and now he was completing my confusion at being called after so lovely a creature as our queen. I have always admitted that, with its stately, regal suggestions, Alexandra is no symbol for a plain little body like me; but when Mr. Brokenshire took it on his lips and called me his dear I could have cried out for mercy. So I had my dinner by myself, munching slowly and meditating on what Mr. Brokenshire described as "my new situation."

I was meditating on it still when, in the course of the following afternoon, I was sitting in a retired grove of the hillside wood waiting for Hugh to come and find me. He was to arrive about three and Miladi was to tell him where I was. In our crowded little inn, with its crowded grounds, nooks of privacy were rare.

I had taken the Boston paper with me in order to get further details of the tragedy of Sarajevo. These I found absorbing. They wove themselves in with my thoughts of Hugh and my dreams of our life together. An article on Serbia, which I had found in an old magazine that morning, had given me, too, an understanding of the situation I hadn't had before. Up to that day Serbia had been but a name to me; now I began to see its significance. The story of this brave, patient little people, with its one idea—an *idée fixe* of liberty—began to move me.

Of all the races of Europe the Serbian impressed me as the one that had been most constantly thwarted in its natural ambitions—struck down whenever it attempted to rise. Its patriotic hopes had always been inconvenient to some other nation's patriotic hopes, and so had to be blasted systematically. England, France, Austria, Turkey, Italy, and Russia had taken part at various times in this circumvention, denying the fruits of victory after they had been won. Serbia had been the poor little bastard brother of Europe, kept out of the inheritance of justice and freedom and commerce when others were admitted to a share. For some of them there might have been no great share; but for little Serbia there was none.

It was terrible to me that such wrong could go on, generation after generation, and that there should be no Nemesis. In a measure it contradicted my theory of right. I didn't want any one to suffer, but I asked why there had been no suffering. Of the nations that had knocked Serbia about, hedged her in by restrictions, dismembered her and kept her dismembered, most were prosperous. From Serbia's point of view I couldn't help sympathizing with the hand that had struck down at least one member of the House of Hapsburg; and yet in that tragic act there could be no adequate revenge for centuries of repression. What I wanted I didn't know; I suppose I didn't want anything. I was only wondering—wondering why, if individuals couldn't sin without paying for the sin they had committed, nations should sin and be immune.

Strangely enough, these reflections did not shut out the thought of the lover who was coming up the hill; they blended with it; they made it larger and more vital. I could thank God I was marrying a man whose hand would always be lifted on behalf of right. I didn't know how it could be lifted in the cause of Serbia against the influences represented by Franz Ferdinand; but when one is dreaming one doesn't pause to direct the logical course of one's dreams. Perhaps I was only clutching at whatever I could say for Hugh; and at least I could say that. He was not a strong man in the sense of being fertile in ideas; but he was brave and generous, and where there was injustice his spirit would be among the first to be stirred by it. That conviction made me welcome him when, at last, I saw his stocky figure moving lower down among the pine trunks.

I caught sight of him long before he discovered me, and could make my notes upon him. I could even make my notes upon myself, not wholly with my own approval. I was too business-like, too cool. There was nothing I possessed in the world that I would not have given for a single quickened heart-throb. I would have given it the more when I saw Hugh's pinched face and the furbished-up spring suit he had worn the year before.

It was not the fact that he had worn it the year before that gave me a pang; it was that he must have worn it pretty steadily. I am not observant of men's clothes. Except that I like to see them neat, they are too much alike to be worth noticing. But anything not plainly opulent in Hugh smote me with a sense of guilt. It could so easily be attributed to my fault. I could so easily take it so myself. I did take it so myself. I said as he approached: "This man has suffered. He has suffered on my account. All my life must be given to making it up to him."

I make no attempt to tell how we met. It was much as we had met after other separations, except that when he slipped to the low boulder and took me in his arms it was with a certainty of possession which had never hitherto belonged to him. There was nothing for me but to let myself go, and lie back in his embrace.

I came to myself, as it were, on hearing him whisper, with his face close to mine:

"You witch! You witch! How did you ever manage it?"

I made the necessity for giving him an explanation the excuse for working myself free.

"I didn't manage it. It was Mrs. Brokenshire."

He cried out, incredulously:

"Oh no! Not the madam!"

"Yes, Hugh. It was she. She asked him. She must have begged him. That's all I can tell you about it."

He was even more incredulous.

"Then it must have been on your account rather than on mine; you can bet your sweet life on that!"

"Hugh, darling, she's fond of you. She's fond of you all. If you could only have—"

"We couldn't." For the first time he showed signs of admitting me into the family sense of disgrace. "Did you ever hear how dad came to marry her?"

I said that something had reached me, but one couldn't put the blame for that on her.

"And she's had more pull with him than we've had," he declared, resentfully. "You can see that by the way he's given in to her on this—"

I soothed him on this point, however, and we talked of a general reconciliation. From that we went on to the subject of our married life, of which his father, in the hasty interview of half an hour before, had briefly sketched the conditions. A place was to be found for Hugh in the house of Meek & Brokenshire; his allowance was to be raised to twelve or fifteen thousand a year; we were to have a modest house, or apartment in New York. No date had been fixed for the wedding, so far as Hugh could learn; but it might be in October. We should be granted perhaps a three months' trip abroad, with a return to New York before Christmas.

He gave me these details with an excitement bespeaking intense satisfaction. It was easy to see that, after his ten months' rebellion, he was eager to put his head under the Brokenshire yoke again. His instinct in this was similar to Ethel's and Jack's—only that they had never declared themselves free. I could best compare him to a horse who for one glorious half-hour kicks up his heels and runs away, and yet returns to the stable and the harness as the safest sphere of blessedness. Under the Brokenshire yoke he could live, move, have his being, and enjoy his twelve or fifteen thousand a year, without that onerous responsibility which comes with the exercise of choice. Under the Brokenshire yoke I, too, should be provided for. I should be raised from my lowly estate, be given a position in the world, and, though for a while the fact of the *mésalliance* might tell against me, it would be overcome in my case as in that of Libby Jaynes. His talk was a pæan on our luck.

"All we'll have to do for the rest of our lives, little Alix, will be to get away with our thousand dollars a month. I guess we can do that—what? We sha'n't even have to save, because in the natural course of events—" He left this reference to his father's demise to go on with his hymn of self-congratulation. "But we've pulled it off, haven't we? We've done the trick. Lord! what a relief it is! What do you think I've been living on for the last six weeks? Chocolate and crackers for the most part. Lost thirty pounds in two months. But it's all right now, little Alix. I've got you and I mean to keep you." He asked, suddenly: "How did you come to know the madam so well? I'd never had a hint of it. You do keep some things awful close!"

I made my answer as truthful as I could.

"This was nothing I could tell you, Hugh. Mrs. Brokenshire was sorry for me ever since last year in Newport. She never dared to say anything about it, because she was afraid of your father and the rest of you; but she did pity me —"

"Well, I'll be blowed! I didn't suppose she had it in her. She's always seemed to me like a woman walking in her sleep—"

"She's waking up now. She's beginning to understand that perhaps she hasn't taken the right attitude toward your father; and I think she'd like to begin. It was to work that problem out that she decided to come away with me and live simply for a while... . She wanted to escape from every one, and I was the nearest to no one she could find to take with her; and so— If your sisters or your brother ask you any questions I wish you would tell them that."

We discussed this theme in its various aspects while the afternoon light turned the pine trunks round us into columns of red-gold, and a soft wind soothed us with balsamic smells. Birds flitted and fluted overhead, and now and then a squirrel darted up to challenge us with the peak of its inquisitive sharp little nose. I chose what I thought a favorable moment to bring before Hugh the matter that had been so summarily shelved by his father. I wanted so much to be married among my own people and from what I could call my own home.

His child-like, wide-apart, small blue eyes regarded me with growing astonishment as I made my point clear.

"For Heaven's sake, my sweet little Alix, what do you want that for? Why, we can be married in Newport!"

His emphasis on the word Newport was as if he had said Heaven.

"Yes; but you see, Hugh, darling, Newport means nothing to me—"

"It will jolly well have to if—"

"And my home means such a lot. If you were marrying Lady Cissie Boscobel you'd certainly go to Goldborough for the occasion."

"Ah, but that would be different!"

"Different in what way?"

He colored, and grew confused.

"Well, don't you see?"

"No; I'm afraid I don't."

"Oh yes, you do, little Alix," he smiled, cajolingly. "Don't try to pull my leg. We can't have one of these bang-up weddings, as it is. Of course we can't— and we don't want it. But they'll do the decent thing by us, now that dad has come round at all, and let people see that they stand behind us. If we were to go down there to where you came from—Halifax, or wherever it is—it would put us back ten years with the people we want to keep up with."

I submitted again, because I didn't know what else to do. I submitted, and yet with a rage which was the hotter for being impotent. These people took it so easily for granted that I had no pride, and was entitled to none. They allowed me no more in the way of antecedents than if I had been a new creation on the day when I first met Mrs. Rossiter. They believed in the principle of inequality of birth as firmly as if they had been minor German royalties. My marriage to Hugh might be valid in the eyes of the law, but to them it would always be more or less morganatic. I could only be Duchess of Hohenberg to this young prince; and perhaps not even that. She was noble—*adel*, as they call it—at the least; while I was merely a nursemaid.

But I made another grimace—and swallowed it. I could have broken out with some vicious remark, which would have bewildered poor Hugh beyond expression and made no change in his point of view. Even if it relieved my pent-up bitterness, it would have left me nothing but a nursemaid; and, since I was to marry him, why disturb the peace? And I owed him too much not to marry him; of that I was convinced. He had been kind to me from the first day he knew me; he had been true to me in ways in which few men would have been true. To go back on him now would not be simply a change of mind; it would be an act of cruel treachery. No, I argued; I could do nothing but go on with it. My debt could not be paid in any other way. Besides, I declared to myself, with a catch in the throat, I—I loved him. I had said it so many times that it must be true.

When the minute came to go down the hill and prepare for the little dinner at which I was to be included in the family, my thoughts reverted to the event that had startled the world.

"Isn't this terrible?" I said to Hugh, indicating the paper I carried in my hand.

He looked at me with the mild wondering which always made his expression vacuous.

"Isn't what terrible?"

"Why, the assassinations in Bosnia."

"Oh! I saw there had been something."

"Something!" I cried. "It's one of the most momentous things that have ever happened in history."

"What makes you say that?" he inquired, turning on me the innocent stare of his baby-blue eyes as we sauntered between the pine trunks.

I had to admit that I didn't know, I only felt it in my bones.

"Aren't they always doing something of the sort down there—killing kings and queens, or something?"

"Oh, not like this!" I paused. "You know, Hugh, Serbia is a wonderful little country when you've heard a bit of its story."

"Is it?" He took out a cigarette and lit it.

In the ardor of my sympathy I poured out on him some of the information I had just acquired.

"And we're all responsible," I was finishing; "English, French, Russians, Austrians—"

"We're not responsible—we Americans," he broke in, quietly.

"Oh, I'm not so sure about that. If you inherit the civilization of the races from which you spring you inherit some of their crimes; and you've got to pay for them."

"Not on your life!" he laughed, easily; but in the laugh there was something that cut me more deeply than he knew.

CHAPTER XXI

But once we were settled in Newport, I almost forgot the tragedy of Sarajevo. The world, it seemed to me, had forgotten it, too; it had passed into history. Franz Ferdinand and Sophie Chotek being dead and buried, we had gone on to something else.

Personally I had gone on to the readjustment of my life. I was with Ethel Rossiter as a guest. Guest or retainer, however, made little difference. She treated me just as before—with the same detached, live-and-let-live kindliness that dropped into the old habit of making use of me. I liked that. It kept us on a simple, natural footing. I could see myself writing her notes and answering her telephone calls as long as I lived. Except that now and then, when she thought of it, she called me Alix, instead of Miss Adare, she might still have been paying me so much a month.

"Well, I can't get over father," was the burden of her congratulations to me. "I knew that woman could turn him around her finger; but I didn't suppose she could do it like that. You played your cards well in getting hold of her."

"I didn't play my cards," was my usual defense, "because I had none to play.'"

"Then what on earth brought her over to your side?"

"Life."

"Life—fiddlesticks! It was life with a good deal of help from Alix Adare." She added, on one occasion: "Why didn't you take that young Strangways—frankly, now?"

"Because," I smiled, "I don't believe in polyandry."

"But you're fond of him. That's what beats me! You're fond of one man and you're marrying another; and yet—"

I don't know what color I turned outwardly, but within I was fire. It was the fire of confusion and not of indignation. I felt it safest to let her go on, hazarding no remarks of my own.

"And yet—what?"

"And yet you don't seem like a girl who'd marry for money—you really don't. That's one thing about you."

I screwed up a wan smile.

236

"Thanks."

"So that I'm all in the dark. What you can see in Hugh—"

"What I can see in Hugh is the kindest of men. That's a good deal to say of any one."

"Well, I'll be hanged if I'd marry even the kindest of men if it was for nothing but his kindness."

The Jack Brokenshires were jovially non-committal, letting it go at that. In offering the necessary good wishes Jack contented himself with calling me a sly one; while Pauline, who was mannish and horsey, wrung my hand till she almost pulled it off, remarking that in a family like the Brokenshires the natural principle was, The more, the merrier. Acting, doubtless, on a hint from higher up, they included Hugh and me in a luncheon to some twenty of their cronies, whose shibboleths I didn't understand and among whom I was lost.

As far as I went into general society it was so unobtrusively that I might be said not to have gone at all. I made no sensation as the affianced bride of Hugh Brokenshire. To the great fact of my engagement few people paid any attention, and those who referred to it did so with the air of forgetting it the minute afterward. It came to me with some pain that in his own circle Hugh was regarded more or less as a nonentity. I was a "queer Canadian." Newport presented to me a hard, polished exterior, like a porcelain wall. It was too high to climb over and it afforded no nooks or crevices in which I might find a niche. No one ever offered me the slightest hint of incivility—or of interest.

"It's because they've too much to do and to think of," Mrs. Brokenshire explained to me. "They know too many people already. Their lives are too full. Money means nothing to them, because they've all got so much of it. Quiet good breeding isn't striking enough. Cleverness they don't care anything about—and not even for scandals outside their own close corporation. All the same"—I waited while she formulated her opinion—"all the same, a great deal could be done in Newport—in New York—in Washington—in America at large—if we had the right sort of women."

"And haven't you?"

"No. Our women are—how shall I say?—too small—too parochial—too provincial. They've no national outlook; they've no authority. Few of them know how to use money or to hold high positions. Our men hardly ever turn to them for advice on important things, because they've rarely any to give."

Her remarks showed so much more of the reflecting spirit than I had ever seen in her before, that I was emboldened to ask:

"Then, couldn't you show them how?"

She shook her head.

"No; I'm an American, like the rest. It isn't in me. It's both personal and national. Cissie Boscobel could do it—not because she's clever or has had experience, but because the tradition is there. We've no tradition."

The tradition in Cissie Boscobel became evident on a day in July when she came to sit beside me in the grounds of the Casino. I had gone with Mrs. Rossiter, with whom I had been watching the tennis. When she drifted away with a group of her friends I was left alone. It was then that Lady Cecilia, in tennis things, with her racket in her hand, came across the grass to me. She moved with the splendid careless freedom of women who pass their lives outdoors and yet are trained to drawing-rooms.

She didn't go to her point at once; she was, in fact, a mistress of the introductory. The visits she had made and the people she had met since our last meeting were the theme of her remarks; and now she was staying with the Burkes. She would remain with them for a month, after which she had two or three places to go to on Long Island and in the Catskills. She would have to be at Strath-na-Cloid in September, for the wedding of her sister Janet and the young man in the Inverness Rangers, who would then have got home from India. She would be sorry to leave. She adored America. Americans were such fun. Their houses were so fresh and new. She doted on the multiplicity of bathrooms. It would be so horrid to live at Strath-na-Cloid or Dillingham Hall after the cheeriness of Mrs. Burke's or Mrs. Rossiter's.

Screwing up her greenish cat-like eyes till they were no more than tiny slits with a laugh in them, she said, with her deliciously incisive utterance:

"So you've done it, haven't you?"

"You mean that Mr. Brokenshire has come round."

"You know, that seems to me the most wonderful thing I ever heard of! It's like a miracle isn't it? You've hardly lifted a finger—and yet here it is." She leaned forward, her firm hands grasping the racket that lay across her knees. "I want to tell you how much I admire you. You're splendid! You're not a bit like a Colonial, are you?"

Since she meant well, I mastered my indignation.

"Oh yes, I am. I'm exactly like a Colonial, and very proud of the fact."

"Fancy! And are all Colonials like you?"

"All that aren't a great deal cleverer and better."

"Fancy!" she breathed again. "I must tell them when I go home. They don't know it, you know." She added, in a slight change of key: "I'm so glad Hugh is going to have a wife like you."

It was on my tongue to say, "He'd be much better off with a wife like you"; but I made it:

"What do you think it will do for him?"

"It will bring him out. Hugh is splendid in his way—just as you are—only he needs bringing out, don't you think?"

"He hasn't needed bringing out in the last ten months," I declared, with some emphasis. "See what he's done—"

"And yet he didn't pull it off, did he? You managed that. You'll manage a lot of other things for him, too. I must go back to the others," she continued, getting up. "They're waiting for me to make up the set. But I wanted to tell you I'm—I'm glad—without—without any—any reserves."

I think there were tears in her narrow eyes, as I know there were in my own; but she beat such a hasty retreat that I could not be very sure of it.

Mildred Brokenshire was a surprise to me. I had hardly ever seen her till she sent for me in order to talk about Hugh. I found her lying on a couch in a dim corner of her big, massively furnished room, her face no more than a white pain-pinched spot in the obscurity. After having kissed me she made me sit at a distance, nominally to get the breeze through an open window, but really that I might not have to look at her.

In an unnaturally hollow, tragic voice she said it was a pleasure to her that Hugh should have got at last the woman he loved, especially after having made such a fight for her. Though she didn't know me, she was sure I had fine qualities; otherwise Hugh would not have cared for me as he did. He was a dear boy, and a good wife could make much of him. He lacked initiative in the way that was unfortunately common among rich men's sons, especially in America; but the past winter had shown that he was not deficient in doggedness. She wondered if I loved him as much as he loved me.

There was that in this suffering woman, so far withdrawn from our struggles in the world outside, which prompted me to be as truthful as the circumstances rendered possible.

"I love him enough, dear Miss Brokenshire," I said, with some emotion, "to be eager to give my life to the object of making him happy."

She accepted this in silence. At least it was silence for a time, after which she said, in measured, organ-like tones:

"We can't make other people happy, you know. We can only do our duty—and let their happiness take care of itself. They must make themselves happy! It's a mistake for any of us to feel responsible for more than doing right. "When we do right other people must make the best they can of it."

"I believe that, too," I responded, earnestly—"only that it's sometimes so hard to tell what is right."

There was again an interval of silence. The voice, when it came out of the dimness, might have been that of the Pythian virgin oracle. The utterances I give were not delivered consecutively, but in answer to questions and observations of my own.

"Right, on the whole, is what we've been impelled to do when we've been conscientiously seeking the best way... . Forces catch us, often contradictory and bewildering forces, and carry us to a certain act, or to a certain line of action. Very well, then; be satisfied. Don't go back. Don't torture yourself with questionings. Don't dig up what has already been done. That's done! Nothing can undo it. Accept it as it is. If there's a wrong or a mistake in it life will take care of it... . Life is not a blind impulse, working blindly. It's a beneficent, rectifying power. It's dynamic. It's a perpetual unfolding. It's a fire that utilizes as fuel everything that's cast into it... ."

And yet when I kissed her to say good-by I got the impression that she didn't like me or that she didn't trust me. I was not always liked, but I was generally trusted. The idea that this Brokenshire seeress, this suffering priestess whose whole life was to lie on a couch and think, and think, and think, had reserves in her consciousness on my account was painful. I said so to Hugh that evening.

"Oh, you mustn't take Mildred's gassing too seriously," he advised. "Gets a lot of ideas in her head: but—poor thing—what else can she do? Since she doesn't know anything about real life, she just spins theories on the subject. Whatever you want to know, little Alix, I'll tell you."

"Thanks," I said, dryly, explaining the shiver which ran through me by the fact that we were sitting in the loggia, in the open air.

"Then we'll go in."

"No, no!" I protested. "I like it much better out here."

But he was on his feet.

"We'll go in. I can't have my sweet little Alix taking cold. I'm here to protect her. She must do what I tell her. We'll go in."

And we went in. It was one of the things I was learning, that my kind Hugh would kill me with kindness. It was part of his way of taking possession. If he could help it he wouldn't leave me for an hour unwatched; nor would he let me lift a hand.

"There are servants to do that," he would say. "It's one of the things little Alix will have to get accustomed to."

"I can't get accustomed to doing nothing, Hugh."

"You'll have plenty to do in having a good time."

"Oh, but I must have more than that in life."

"In your old life, perhaps; but everything is to be different now. Don't be afraid, little Alix; you'll learn."

"Learn what? It seems to me you're taking the possibility of ever learning anything away."

This was a joke. Over it he laughed heartily.

"You won't know yourself, little Alix, when I've had you for a year."

Mr. Brokenshire's compliments to me were in a similar vein. He seemed always to be in search of the superior position he had lost on the day we sat looking up into the hillside wood. His dear Alexandra must never forget her social inexperience. In being raised to a higher level I was to watch the manners of those about me. I was to copy them, as people learning French or Italian try to catch an accent which is not that of their mother tongue. They probably do it badly; but that is better than not doing it at all. I could never be an Ethel Rossiter or a Daisy Burke, but I could become an imitation. Imitations being to the house of Brokenshire like paste diamonds or fish-glue pearls, my gratitude for the effort they made in accepting me had to be the more humble.

And yet on occasions I tried to get justice for myself.

"I'm not altogether without knowledge of the world, Mr. Brokenshire," I said, after one of his kindly, condescending lectures. "Not only in Canada, but in England, and to some slight extent abroad, I've had opportunities—"

"Yes, yes; but this is different. You've had opportunities, as you say. But there you were looking on from the outside, while here you'll be living from within."

"Oh, but I wasn't looking on from the outside—"

His hand went up; his pitiful crooked smile was meant to express tolerance. "You'll pardon me, my dear; but we gain nothing by discussing that point. You'll see it yourself when you've been one of us a little longer. Meantime, if you watch the women about you and study them—"

We left it there. I always left it there. But I did begin to see that there was a difference between me and the women whom Hugh and his father wished me to take as my models. I had hitherto not observed this variation in type—I might possibly call it this distinction between national ideals—during my two years under the Stars and Stripes; and I find a difficulty in expressing it, for the reason that to anything I say so many exceptions can be made. The immense class of wage-earning women would be exceptions; mothers and housekeepers would again be exceptions; exceptions would be all women engaged in political or social or philanthropic service to the country; but when this allowance has been made there still remain a multitude of American women economically independent, satisfied to be an incubus on the land. They dress, they entertain, they go to entertainments, they live gracefully. When they can't help it they bear children; but they bear as few as possible. Otherwise they are not much more than pleasing forms of vegetation, idle of body and mind; and the American man, as a rule, loves to have it so.

"The American man," Mrs. Rossiter had said to me once, "likes figurines." Hugh was a rebel to that doctrine, she had added then; but his rebellion had been short-lived. He had come back to the standard of his countrymen. He had chosen me, he used to say, because I was a woman of whom a Socialist might make his star; and now I was to be put in a vitrine.

Canadian women, as a class, are not made for the vitrine. Their instinct is to be workers in the world and mates for men. They have no very high opinion of their privileges; they are not self-analytical. They rarely think of themselves as the birds and flowers of the human race, or as other than creatures to put their shoulders to the wheel in the ways of which God made them mistresses. Not ashamed to know how to bake and brew and mend and sew, they rule the house with a practically French economy. I was brought up in that way; not ignorant of books or of social amenities, but with the assumption that I was in this world to contribute something to it by my usefulness. I hadn't contributed much, Heaven only knows; but the impulse to work was instinctive.

And as Hugh's wife I began to see that I should be lifted high and dry into a sphere where there was nothing to be done. I should dress and I should amuse myself; I should amuse myself and I should dress. It was all Mrs. Rossiter did; it was all Mrs. Brokenshire did—except that to her, poor soul, amusement had become but gall and bitterness. Still, with the large exceptions which I cheerfully concede, it was the American ideal, so far as I could get hold of it; and I began to feel that, in the long run, it would stifle me.

It was a kind of feminine Nirvana. It offered me nothing to strive for, nothing to wait for in hope, nothing to win gloriously. The wife of Larry Strangways, whoever she turned out to be, would have a goal before her, high up and far ahead, with the incentive of lifelong striving. Hugh Brokenshire's wife would have everything done for her, as it was done for Mildred. Like Mildred she would have nothing to do but think and think and think—or train herself to not thinking at all. Little by little I saw myself being steered toward this fate; and, like St. Peter, when I thought thereon I wept.

I had taken to weeping all alone in my pretty room, which looked out on shrubberies and gardens. I should probably have shrubberies and gardens like them some day; so that weeping was the more foolish. Every one considered me fortunate. All my Canadian and English friends spoke of me as a lucky girl, and, in their downright, practical way, said I was "doing very well for myself."

Of course I was—which made it criminal on my part not to take the Brokenshire view of things with equanimity. I tried to. I bent my will to it. I bent my spirit to it. In the end I might have succeeded if the heavenly trumpet had not sounded again, with another blast from Sarajevo.

CHAPTER XXII

As I have already said, I had almost forgotten Sarajevo. The illustrated papers had shown us a large coffin raised high and a small one set low, telling us of unequal rank, even at the Great White Throne. I had a thought for that from time to time; but otherwise Franz Ferdinand and Sophie Chotek were less to me than Cæsar or Napoleon.

But toward the end of July there was a sudden rumbling. It was like that first disquieting low note of the "Rheingold," rising from elemental depths, presaging love and adventure and war and death and defeat and triumph, and the end of the old gods and the burning of their Valhalla. I cannot say that any of us knew its significance; but it was arresting.

"What does it mean?"

I think Cissie Boscobel was the first to ask me that question, to which I could only reply by asking it in my own turn. What did it mean—this ultimatum from Vienna to Belgrade? Did it mean anything? Could it possibly mean what dinner-table diplomats hinted at between a laugh and a look of terror?

Hugh and I were descending the Rossiter lawn on a bright afternoon near the end of July. Cissie, who was passing with some of the Burkes, ran over the grass toward us. Had we seen the papers? Had we read the Austrian note? Could we make anything out of it?

I recall her as an extraordinarily vivid picture against the background of blue sea, in white, with a green-silk tunic embroidered in peacock's feathers, with long jade ear-rings and big jade beads, and a jade-colored plume in a black-lace hat cocked on her flaming hair as she alone knew how to cock it. I merely want to point out here that to Cissie Boscobel and me the questions she asked already possessed a measure of life-and-death importance; while to Hugh they had none at all.

I remember him as he stood aloof from us, strong and stocky and summer-like in his white flannels, a type of that safe and separated America which could afford to look on at Old World tragedies and feel them of no personal concern. To him Cissie Boscobel and I, with anxiety in our eyes and something worse already clutching at our hearts, were but two girls talking of things they didn't understand and of no great interest, anyway.

"Come along, little Alix!" he interrupted, gaily. "Cissie will excuse us. The madam is waiting to motor us over to South Portsmouth, and I don't want to keep her waiting. You know," he explained, proudly, "she thinks this little girl is a peach!"

Cissie ran back to join the Burkes and we continued our way along the Cliff Walk to Mr. Brokenshire's. Hugh had come for me in order that we might have the stroll together.

I gave him my view of the situation as we went along, though in it there was nothing original.

"You see, if Austria attacks Serbia, then Russia must attack Austria; in which case Germany will attack Russia, and France will attack Germany. Then England will certainly have to pitch in."

"But we won't. We shall be out of it."

The complacency of his tone nettled me.

"But I sha'n't be out of it, Hugh."

He laughed.

"You? What could you do, little lightweight?"

"I don't know; but whatever it was I should want to be doing it."

This joke might have been characterized as a screamer. He threw back his head with a loud guffaw.

"Well, of all the little spitfires!" Catching me by the arm, he hugged me to him, as we were hidden in a rocky nook of the path. "Why, you're a regular Amazon! A soldier in your way would be no more than a ninepin in a bowling-alley."

I didn't enter into the spirit of this pleasantry. On the contrary, I concealed my anger in endeavoring to speak with dignity.

"And, what's more, Hugh, than not being out of it myself, I don't see how I could marry a man who was. Of course, no such war will come to pass. It couldn't! The world has gone beyond that sort of madness. We know too well the advantages of peace. But if it should break out—"

"I'll buy you a popgun with the very first shot that's fired."

But in August, when the impossible had happened, when Germany had invaded Belgium, and France had moved to her eastern frontier, and Russia was pouring into Prussia, and English troops were on foreign continental soil for the first time in fifty years, Hugh's indifference grew painful. He was perhaps not more indifferent than any one else with whom I was thrown, but to me he seemed so because he was so near me. He read the papers; he took a sporting interest in the daily events; but it resembled—to my mind at least—the interest of an eighteenth-century farmer's lad excited at a cockfight. It was somewhat in the spirit of "Go it, old boy!" to each side indifferently.

If he took sides at all it was rather on that to which Cissie Boscobel and I were nationally opposed; but this, we agreed, was to tease us. So far as opinions of his own were concerned, he was neutral. He meant by that that he didn't care a jot who lost or who won, so long as America was out of the fray and could eat its bread in safety.

"There are more important things than safety," I said to him, scornfully, one day.

"Such as—"

But when I gave him what seemed to me the truisms of life he was contented to laugh in my face.

Cissie Boscobel was more patient with him than I was. I have always admired in the English that splendid tolerance which allows to others the same liberty of thinking they claim for themselves; but in this instance I had none of it. Hugh was too much a part of myself. When he said, as he was fond of saying, "If Germany gets at poor degenerate old England she'll crumple her up," Lady Cissie could fling him a pitying, confident smile, with no venom in it whatever, while I became bitter or furious.

Fortunately, Mr. Brokenshire was called to New York on business connected with the war, so that his dear Alexandra was delivered for a while from his daily condescensions. Though Hugh didn't say so in actual words, I inferred that the struggle would further enrich the house of Meek & Brokenshire. Of the vast sums it would handle a commission would stick to its fingers, and if the business grew too heavy for the usual staff to deal with Hugh's own energies were to be called into play. His father, he told me, had said so. It would be an eye-opener to Cousin Andrew Brew, he crowed, to see him helping to finance the European War within a year after that slow-witted nut had had the hardihood to refuse him!

In the Brokenshire villa the animation was comparable to a suppressed fever. Mr. Brokenshire came back as often as he could. Thereupon there followed whispered conferences between him and Jack, between him and Jim Rossiter, between him and kindred magnates, between three and four and six and eight of them together, with a ceaseless stream of telegrams, of the purport of which we women knew nothing. We gave dinners and lunches, and bathed at Bailey's, and played tennis at the Casino, and lived in our own little lady-like Paradise, shut out from the interests convulsing the world. Knitting had not yet begun. The Red Cross had barely issued its appeals. America, with the speed of the Franco-Prussian War in mind, was still under the impression that it could hardly give its philanthropic aid before the need for it would be over.

Of all our little coterie Lady Cissie and I alone perhaps took the sense of things to heart. Even with us, it was the heart that acted rather than the intelligence. So far as intelligence went, we were convinced that, once Great Britain lifted her hand, all hostile nations would tremble. That was a matter of course. It amazed us that people round us should talk of our enemy's efficiency. The word was just coming into use, always with the implication that the English were inefficient and unprepared.

That would have made us laugh if those who said such things hadn't said them like Hugh, with detached, undisturbed deliberation, as a matter that was nothing to them. Many of them hoped, and hoped ardently, that the side represented by England, Russia, and France would be victorious; but if it wasn't, America would still be able to sit down to eat and drink, and rise up to play, as we were doing at the moment, while nothing could shake her from her ease.

Owing to our kinship in sentiment, Lady Cissie and I drew closer together. We gave each other bits of information in which no one else would have had an interest. She was getting letters from England; I from England and Canada. Her brother Leatherhead had been ordered to France with his regiment—was probably there. Her brother Rowan, who had been at Sandhurst, had got his commission. The young man her sister Janet was engaged to had sailed with the Rangers for Marseilles and would go at once to the front instead of coming home. If he could get leave the young couple would be married hastily, after which he would return to his duty. My sister Louise wrote that her husband's ship was in the North Sea and that her news of him was meager. The husband of my sister Victoria, who had had a staff appointment at Gibraltar, had been ordered to rejoin his regiment; and he, too, would soon be in Belgium.

From Canada I heard of that impulse toward recruiting which was thrilling the land from the Island of Vancouver, in the Pacific, to that of Cape Breton, in the Atlantic, and in which the multitudes were of one heart and one soul. Men came from farms, factories, and fisheries; they came from banks and shops and mines. They tramped hundreds of miles, from the Yukon, from Ungava, and from Hudson Bay. They arrived in troops or singly, impelled by nothing but that love which passes the love of women—the love of race, the love of country, the love of honor, the love of something vast and intangible and inexplicable, that comes as near as possible to that love of man which is almost the love of God.

I can proudly say that among my countrymen it was this, and it was nothing short of this. They were as far from the fray as their neighbors to the south, and as safe. Belgium and Serbia meant less to most of them than to the people of San Francisco, Chicago, and New York; but a great cause, almost indefinable to thought, meant everything. To that cause they gave themselves —not sparingly or grudgingly, but like Araunah the Jebusite to David the son of Jesse, "as a king gives unto a king."

Men are wonderful to me—all men of all races. They face hardship so cheerfully and dangers so gaily, and death so serenely. This is true of men not only in war, but in peace—of men not only as saints, but as sinners. And among men it seems to me that our Colonial men are in the first rank of the manliest. Frenchman, German, Austrian, Italian, Russian, Englishman, and Turk had each some visible end to gain. They couldn't help going. They couldn't help fighting. Our men had nothing to gain that mortal eyes could see. They have endured, "as seeing Him who is invisible."

They have come from the far ends of the earth, and are still coming—turning their backs on families and business and pleasure and profit and hope. They have counted the world well lost for love—for a true love—a man's love—a redemptive love if ever there was one; for "greater love hath no man than this, that a man lay down his life for his friends."

But when, with my heart flaming, I spoke of this to Lady Cecilia, she was cold. "Fancy!" was the only comment she ever made on the subject. Toward my own intensity of feeling she was courteous; but she plainly felt that in a war in which the honors would be to the professional soldier, and to the English professional soldier first of all, Colonials were out of place. It was somewhat presumptuous of them to volunteer.

She was a splendid character—with British limitations. Among those limitations her attitude toward Colonials was, as I saw things, the first. She rarely spoke of Canadians or Australians; it was always of Colonials, with a delicately disdainful accent on the word impossible to transcribe. Geography, either physical or ethnic, was no more her strong point than it is that of other women; and I think she took Colonials to be a kind of race of aborigines, like the Maoris or the Hottentots—only that by some freak of nature they were white. So, whenever my heart was so hot that I could contain myself no longer, and I poured out my foolish tales of the big things we hoped to do for the empire and the world, the dear thing would merely utter her dazed, "Fancy!" and strike me dumb.

And it all threw me back on the thought of Larry Strangways. Reader, if you suppose that I had forgotten him you are making a mistake. Everything made my heart cry out for him—Hugh's inanity; his father's lumbering dignity; Mildred's sepulchral apothegms, which were deeper than I could fathom and higher than I could scale; Cissie Boscobel's stolid scorn of my country; and Newport's whole attitude of taking no notice of me or mine. Whenever I had minutes of rebellion or stress it was on Larry Strangways I called, with an agonized appeal to him to come to me. It was a purely rhetorical appeal, let me say in passing. As it would never reach him, he could not respond to it; but it relieved my repressed emotions to send it out on the wings of the spirit. It was the only vehicle I could trust; and even that betrayed me—for he came.

He came one hot afternoon about the 20th of August. His card was brought to me by the rosebud Thomas as I was taking a siesta up-stairs.

"Tell Mr. Strangways I shall come down at once," I said to my footman knight; but after he had gone I sat still.

I sat still to estimate my strength. If Larry Strangways made such an appeal to me as I had made to him, should I have the will-power to resist him? I could only reply that I must have it! There was no other way. When Hugh had been so true to me it was impossible to be other than true to him. It was no longer a question of love, but of right: and I couldn't forsake my maxim.

Nevertheless, when I threw off my dressing-gown instinct compelled me to dress at my prettiest. To be sure, my prettiest was only a flowered muslin and a Leghorn hat, in which I resembled the vicar's daughter in a Royal Academy picture; but if I was never to see Larry Strangways again I wanted the vision in his heart to be the most decent possible. As I dressed I owned to myself that I loved him. I had never done so before, because I had never known it— or rather, I had known it from that evening on the train when I had seen nothing but his traveling-cap; only I had strangled the knowledge in my heart. I meant to strangle it again. I should strangle it the minute I went down-stairs. But for this little interval, just while I was fastening my gown and pinning on my hat, it seemed to me of no great harm to let the unfortunate passion come out for a breath in the sunlight.

And yet, after having rehearsed all the romantic speeches I should make in giving him up forever, he never mentioned love to me at all. On the contrary, he had on that gleaming smile which, from the beginning of our acquaintance, was like the flash of a sword held up between him and me. When he came forward from a corner of the long, dim drawing-room all the embarrassment was on my side.

"I suppose you wonder what brings me," were the words he uttered when shaking hands.

I tried to murmur politely that, whatever it was, I was glad to see him—only the words refused to form themselves.

"Can't we go out?" he asked, as I cast about me for chairs. "It's so stuffy in here."

I led the way through the hall, picking up a rose-colored parasol of Mrs. Rossiter's as we passed the umbrella-stand.

"How much money have you got?" he asked, abruptly, as soon as we were on the terrace.

I made an effort to gather my wits from the far fields into which they had wandered.

"Do you mean in ready cash? Or how much do I own in all?"

"How much in all?"

I told him—just a few thousand dollars, the wreckage of what my father had left. My total income, apart from what I earned, was about four hundred dollars a year.

"I want it," he said, as we descended the steps to the lower terrace. "How soon could you let me have it?"

I made the reckoning as we went down the lawn toward the sea. I should have to write to my uncle, who would sell my few bonds and forward me the proceeds. Mr. Strangways himself said that would take a week.

"I'm going to make a small fortune for you," he laughed, in explanation. "All the nations of the earth are beginning to send to us for munitions, and Stacy Grainger is right on the spot with the goods. There'll be a demand for munitions for years to come—"

"Oh, not for years to come!" I exclaimed. "Only till the end of the war."

"'But the end is not by and by,'" he quoted from the Bible. "It's a long way off from by and by—believe me! We're up against the struggle mankind has been getting ready for ever since it's had a history. I don't want just to make money out of it; but, since money's to be made—since we can't help making it—I want you to be in on it."

I didn't thank him, because I had something else on my mind.

"Perhaps you don't know that I'm engaged to Hugh Brokenshire. We're to be married before we move back to New York."

"Yes, I do know it. That's the reason I'm suggesting this. You'll want some money of your own, in order to feel independent. If you don't have it the Brokenshire money will break you down."

I don't know what I said, or whether I was able to say anything. There was something in this practical care-taking interest that moved me more than any love declaration he could have made. He was renouncing me in everything but his protection. That was going with me. That was watching over me. There was no one to watch over me in the whole world with just this sort of devotion.

I suppose we talked. We must have said something as we descended the slope; I must have stammered some sort of appreciation. All I can clearly remember is that, as we reached the steps going down to the Cliff Walk, Hugh was coming up.

I had forgotten that this sort of encounter was possible. I had forgotten Hugh. When I saw his innocent, blank face staring up at us I felt I was confronting my doom.

"Well!" he ejaculated, as though he had caught us in some criminal conspiracy.

As it was for me to explain, I said, limply:

"Mr. Strangways has been good enough to offer to make some money for me, Hugh. Isn't that kind of him?"

Hugh grew slowly crimson. His voice shook with passion. He came up one step.

"Mr. Strangways will be kinder still in minding his own business."

"Oh, Hugh!"

"Don't be offended, Mr. Brokenshire," Larry Strangways said, peaceably. "I merely had the opportunity to advise Miss Adare as to her investments—"

"I shall advise Miss Adare as to her investments. It happens that she's engaged to me!"

"But she's not married to you. An engagement is not a marriage; it's only a preliminary period in which two persons agree to consider whether or not a marriage between them would be possible. Since that's the situation at present, I thought it no harm to tell Miss Adare that if she puts her money into some of the new projects for ammunition that I know about—"

"And I'm sure she's not interested."

Mr. Strangways bowed.

"That will be for her to decide. I understood her to say—"

"Whatever you understood her to say, sir, Miss Adare is not interested! Good afternoon." He nodded to me to come down the steps. "I was just coming over for you. Shall we walk along together?"

I backed away from him toward the stone balustrade.

"But, Hugh, I can't leave Mr. Strangways like this. He's come all the way from New York on purpose to—"

"Then I shall defray his expense and pay him for his time; but if we're going at all, dear—"

At a sign of the eyes from Larry Strangways I mastered my wrath at this insolence, and spoke meekly:

"I didn't know we were going anywhere in particular."

"And you'll excuse me, Mr. Brokenshire," our visitor interrupted, "if I say that I can't be dismissed in this way by any one but Miss Adare herself. You must remember she isn't your wife—that she's still a free agent. Perhaps, if I explain the matter a little further—"

Hugh put up his hand in stately imitation of his father.

"Please! There's no need of that."

"Oh, but there is, Hugh!"

"You see," Mr. Strangways reasoned, "it's more than a question of making money. We shall make money, of course; but that's only incidental. What I'm really asking Miss Adare to do is to help one of the most glorious causes to which mankind has ever given itself—"

I started toward him impulsively.

"Oh! Do you feel like that?"

"Not like that; that's all I feel. I live it! I've no other thought."

It was curious to see how the force of this all-absorbing topic swept Hugh away from the merely personal standpoint.

"And you call yourself an American?" he demanded, hotly.

"I call myself a man. I don't emphasize the American. This thing transcends what we call nationality."

Hugh shouted, somewhat in the tone of a man kicking against the pricks:

"Not what I call nationality! It's got nothing to do with us."

"Ah, but it will have something to do with us! It isn't merely a European struggle; it's a universal one. Sooner or later you'll see mankind divided into just two camps."

Hugh warmed to the discussion.

"Even if we do, it still doesn't follow that we'll all be in your camp."

"That depends on whether we're among those driving forward or those kicking back. The American people has been in the first of these classes hitherto; it remains to be seen whether or not it's there still. But if it isn't as a nation I can tell you that some of us will be there as individuals."

Hugh's tone was one of horror.

"You mean that you'd go and fight?"

"That's about the size of it."

"Then you'd be a traitor to your country for getting her into trouble."

"If I had to choose between being a traitor to my country and a traitor to my manhood I'd take the first. Fortunately, no such alternative will be thrust upon us. Miss Adare pointed out to me once that there couldn't be two right courses, each opposed to the other. Right and rights must be harmonious. If I'm true to myself I'm true to my country; and I can't be true to my country unless I do my 'bit,' as the phrase begins to go, for the good of the human race."

"And you're really going?" I asked, breathlessly.

"As soon as I can arrange things with Mr."—but he remembered he was speaking to a Brokenshire—"as soon as I can arrange things with—with my boss. He's willing to let me go, and to keep my job for me if I come back. He'll take charge of my small funds and of any Miss Adare intrusts to me. He asked me to give her that message. When it's settled I shall start for Canada."

"That'll do you no good," Hugh stated, triumphantly. "They won't enlist Americans there."

Larry Strangways smiled.

"Oh, there are ways! If there's nothing else for it I'll swear in as a Canadian."

"You'd do that!" In different tones the exclamation came from Hugh and me, simultaneously.

I can still see Larry Strangways with his proud, fair head held high.

"I'd do anything rather than not fight. My American birthright is as dear to me as it is to any one; but we've reached a time when such considerations must go by the board. For the matter of that, the more closely we can now identify the Briton and the American, the better it will be for the world."

He explained this at some length. The theme was so engrossing that even

Hugh was willing to listen to the argument. People were talking already of a world federation which would follow the war and unite all the nations in approximate brotherhood. Larry Strangways didn't believe in that as a possibility; at least he didn't believe in it as an immediate possibility. There were just two nations fitted to understand each other and act together, and if they couldn't fraternize and sympathize it was of no use to expect that miracle from races who had nothing in common. Get the United States and the British Empire to stand shoulder to shoulder, and sooner or later the other peoples would line up beside them.

But you must begin at the beginning. Unless you started as an acorn you couldn't be an oak; if you were not willing to be a baby you could never become a man. There must be no more Hague conferences, with their vast programs and ineffective means. The failure of that dream was evident. We must be practical; we mustn't soar beyond the possible. The possible and the practical lay in British and American institutions and commonly understood principles. The world had an asset in them that had never been worked. To work it was the task not primarily of governments, but, first and before everything, of individuals. It was up to the British and American man and woman in their personal lives and opinions.

I interrupted to say that it was up to the American man and woman first of all; that British willingness to co-operate with America was far more ready than any similar sentiment on the American side.

Hugh threw the stress on efficiency. America was so thorough in her methods that she couldn't co-operate with British muddling.

"What is efficiency?" Larry Strangways asked. "It's the best means of doing what you want to do, isn't it? Well, then, efficiency is a matter of your ambitions. There's the efficiency of the watch-dog who loves his master and guards the house, and there's the efficiency of the tiger in the jungle. One has one's choice."

It was not a question, he continued to reason, as to who began this war—whether it was a king or a czar or a kaiser. It was not a question of English and German competition, or of French or Russian aggression, or fear of it. The inquiry went back of all that. It went back beyond modern Europe, beyond the Middle Ages, beyond Rome and Assyria and Egypt. It was a battle of principles rather than of nations—the last great struggle between reason and force—the fight between the instinct of some men to rule other men and the contrary instinct, implanted more or less in all men, that they shall hold up their heads and rule themselves.

It was part of the impulse of the human race to forge ahead and upward. The powers that worked against liberty had been arming themselves, not merely for a generation or a century, but since the beginning of time, for just this trial of strength. The effort would be colossal and it would be culminating; no human being would be spared taking part in it. If America didn't come in of her own accord she would be compelled to come in; and meantime he, Larry Strangways, was going of free will.

He didn't express it in just this way. He put it humbly, colloquially, with touches of slang.

"I've got to be on the job, Miss Adare, and there are no two ways about it," were the words in which he ended. "I've just run down from New York to speak about—about the money; and—and to bid you good-by." He glanced toward Hugh. "Possibly, in view of the fact that I'm so soon to be off—and may not come back, you know," he added, with a laugh—"Mr. Brokenshire won't mind if—if we shake hands."

I can say to Hugh's credit that he gave us a little while together. Going down the steps he had mounted, he called back, over his shoulder:

"I'm going off for a walk, dear. I shall return in exactly fifteen minutes; and I expect you to be ready for me then."

But when we were alone we had little or nothing to say. I recall that quarter of an hour as a period of emotional paralysis. I knew and he knew that each second ticked off an instant that all the rest of our lives we should long for in vain; and yet we didn't know how to make use of it.

We began to wander slowly up the slope. We did it aimlessly, stopping when we were only a few yards away from the steps. We talked about the money. We talked about his going to Canada. We talked about the breaking off, so far as we knew, of all intercourse between Mr. Grainger and Mrs. Brokenshire. But we said nothing about ourselves. We said nothing about anything but what was superficial and trite and lame.

Once or twice Larry Strangways took out his watch and glanced at it, as if to underscore the fact that the sands were slipping away. I kept my face hidden as much as possible beneath the rose-colored parasol. So far as I could judge, he looked over my head. We still had said nothing—there was still nothing we could say—when, beneath the bank of the lawn, and moving back in our direction, we saw the crown of Hugh's Panama.

"Good-by!" Larry Strangways said, then.

"Good-by!"

My hand rested in his without pressure; without pressure his had taken mine. I think his eyes made one last wild, desperate appeal to me but if so I was unable to respond to it.

I don't know how it happened that he turned his back and walked firmly up the lawn. I don't know how it happened that I also turned and took the necessary steps toward Hugh. All I can say is—and I can say it only in this way—all I can say is, I felt that I had died.

That is, I felt that I had died except for one queer, bracing echo which suddenly come back to me. It was in the words Mildred Brokenshire had used, and which, at the time, I had thought too deep for me to understand:

"Life is not a blind impulse working blindly. It is a beneficent rectifying power."

CHAPTER XXIII

As Hugh Brokenshire and I were walking along the Ocean Drive a few days after Larry Strangways had come and gone, the dear lad got some satisfaction from charging me with inconsistency.

"You're certainly talking about England and Canada to-day very differently from what you used to."

"Am I? Well, if it seems so it's because you don't understand the attitude of Canadians toward their mother country. As a country, as a government, England has been magnificently true to us always. It's only between Englishmen and Canadians as individuals that irritation arises, and for that most Canadians don't care. The Englishman snubs and the Canadian grows bumptious. I don't think the Canadian would grow bumptious if the Englishman didn't snub. Both snubbing and bumptiousness are offensive to me; but that, I suppose, is because I'm over-sensitive. And yet one forgets sensitiveness when it comes to anything really national. In that we're one, with as perfect a solidarity as that which binds Oregon to Florida. You'll never find one of us who isn't proud to serve when England gives the orders."

"To be snubbed by her for serving."

"Certainly; to be snubbed by her for serving! It's all we look for; it's all we shall ever get. No one need make any mistake about that. In Canada we're talking of sending fifty thousand troops to the front. We may send five hundred thousand and we shall still be snubbed. But we're not such children as to go into a cause in the hope that some one will give us sweets. We do it for the Cause. We know, too, that it isn't exactly injustice on the English side; it's only ungraciousness."

"Oh, they're long on ungraciousness, all right."

"Yes; they're very long on ungraciousness—"

"Even dad feels that. You should hear him cuss after he's been kotowing to some British celebrity—and given him the best of all he's got—and put him up at the good clubs. They bring him letters in shoals, you know—"

"I'm afraid it has to be admitted that the best-mannered among them are often rude from our transatlantic point of view; and yet the very rudeness is one of the defects of their good qualities. You can no more take the ungraciousness out of the English character than you can take the hardness out of granite; but if granite wasn't hard it wouldn't serve its purposes. We Canadians know that, don't you see? We allow for it in advance, just as you allow for the clumsiness of the elephant for the sake of his strength and sagacity. We're not angels ourselves—neither you Americans nor we Canadians; and yet we like to get the credit for such small merits as we possess."

Hugh whipped off the blossom of a roadside flower as he swung his stick.

"All they give us credit for is money."

"Well, they certainly give you a great deal of credit for that!" I laughed. "They make a golden calf of you. They fall down and worship you, like the children of Israel in the wilderness. When we're as rich as we shall be some day they'll do the same by us."

Within a week my intercourse with Hugh had come to be wholly along international lines. We were no longer merely a man and a woman; we were types; we were points of view. The world-struggle—the time-struggle, as Larry Strangways would have called it—had broken out in us. The interlocking of human destinies had become apparent. As positively as Franz Ferdinand and Sophie Chotek, we had our part in the vast drama. Even Hugh, against all his inclinations to hang back, was obliged to take his share. So lost were we in the theme that, as we tramped along, we had not a thought for the bracing wind, the ruffled seas, the dashing of surf over ledges, or the exquisite, gentle savagery of the rocky flowering uplands, with villas marking the sky-line as they do on the Côte d'Azur.

I was the more willing to discuss the subject since I felt it a kind of mission from Mr. Strangways to carry out the object he had so much at heart. I was to be—so far as so humble a body as I could be it—an interpreter of the one country to the other. I reckoned that if I explained and explained and explained, and didn't let myself grow tired of explaining, some little shade of the distrust which each of the great English-speaking nations has for its fellow might be scrubbed away. I couldn't do much, but the value of all effort is in proportion to the opportunity. So I began with Hugh.

"You see, Hugh, peoples are like people. Each of us has his weak points as well as his strong ones; but we don't necessarily hate each other on that account. You've lived in England, and you know the English rub you up the wrong way. I've lived there, too, and had exactly the same experience. But we go through just that thing with lots of individuals with whom we manage to be very good friends. You and your brother Jack, for instance, don't hit it off so very well; and yet you contrive to be Brokenshires together and uphold the honor of the family."

"I'm a Socialist and Jack's a snob—"

"That's it. Mentally you're the world apart. But, as you've objects in common to work for, you get along fairly well. Now why shouldn't the Englishman and the American do the same? Why should they always see how much they differ instead of how much they are alike? Why should they always underscore each other's faults when by seeing each other's good points they could benefit not only themselves, but the world? If there was an entente, let us say, between the British Empire and the United States—not exactly an alliance, perhaps, if people are afraid of the word—"

He stopped and wheeled round suddenly, suspicion in his small, myosotis-colored eyes.

"Look here, little Alix; isn't this the dope that fresh guy Strangways was handing out the other day?"

I flushed, but I didn't stammer.

"I don't care whether it is or not. Besides, it isn't dope; it's food; it's medicine; it's a remedy for the ills of this poor old civilization. We've got it in our power, we English-speaking peoples—"

"You haven't," he declared, coolly. "Your country would still be the goat."

"Yes," I agreed, "Canada would still be the goat; but we don't mind that. We're used to it. You'll always have a fling at us on one side and England on the other; but we're like the strong, good-natured boy who doesn't resent kicks and cuffs because he knows he can grow and thrive in spite of them."

He put his hand on my arm and spoke in the kindly tone that reminded me of his father.

"My dear little girl, you can drop it. It won't go down. Suppose we keep to the sort of thing you can tackle. You see, when you've married me you'll be an American. Then you'll be out of it."

I was hurt. I was furious. The expression, too, was getting on my nerves. I began to wish I was out of it. Since I couldn't be in it, marriage might prove a Lethe bath, in which I should forget I had anything to do with it. Sheer desperation made me cry out:

"Very well, then, Hugh! If we're to be married, can't we be married quickly? Then I shall have it off my mind."

There was not only a woeful decline of spirit in his response, but a full acceptance of the Brokenshire yoke.

"We can't be married any quicker than dad says. But I'll talk to him."

He made no objection, however, when, a little later, I received from my uncle a draft for my entire fortune and announced my intention of handing the sum over to Mr. Strangways for investment. Hugh probably looked on the amount as too insignificant to talk about; in addition to which some Brokenshire instinct for the profitable may have led him to appreciate a thing so good as to make it folly to say nay to it. The result was that I heard from Larry Strangways, in letters which added nothing to my comfort.

I don't know what I expected him to say; but, whatever it was, he didn't say it. He wasn't curt; his letters were not short. On the contrary, he wrote at length, and brought up subjects that had nothing to do with certificates of stock. But they were all political or international, or related in one way or another to the ideal of his heart—England and America! The British Empire and the United States! The brotherhood of democracies! Why in thunder had the bally world waited so long for the coalition of dominating influences which alone could keep it straight? Why dream of the impossible when the practical had not as yet been tried? Why talk peace, peace, when there was no peace at The Hague, if a full and controlling sympathy could be effected nearer home—let us say at Ottawa? He was going to Canada to enlist; he would start in a few days' time; but he was doing it not merely to fight for the Cause; he was going to be one man, at least, just a straggling democratic scout—one of a forlorn hope, if you chose to call it so—to offer his life to a union of which the human race had the same sort of need as human beings of wedlock.

And in all this there was no reference to me. He might not have loved me; I might not have loved him. I answered the letters in the vein in which they were written, and once or twice showed my replies to Hugh.

"Forget it!" was his ordinary comment. "The American eagle is too wise an old bird to be caught with salt on its tail."

Perhaps it was because Larry Strangways made no appeal to me that I gave myself to forwarding his work with a more enthusiastic zeal. I had to do it quietly, for fear of offending Hugh; but I got my opportunities—that is, I got my opportunities to talk, though I saw I made no impression.

I was only a girl—the queer Canadian who had been Ethel Rossiter's nursery governess and whom the Brokenshire family, for unexplained reasons, had accepted as Hugh's future wife. What could I know about matters at which statesmen had always shied? It was preposterous that I should speak of them; it was presumptuous. Nobody told me that; I saw it in people's eyes.

And I should have seen it in their eyes more plainly if they had been interested. No one was. An entente between the United States and the British Empire might have been an alliance between Bolivia and Beluchistan. It wasn't merely fashionable folk who wouldn't think of it; no one would. I knew plenty of people by this time. I knew townspeople of Newport, and summer residents, and that intermediate group of retired admirals and professors who come in between the two. I knew shop people and I knew servants, all with their stake in the country, their stake in the world. Not a soul among them cared a hang.

And then, threatening to put me entirely out of business, we got the American war refugees and the English visitors. I group them together because they belonged together. They belonged together for the reason that there was nothing each one of them didn't know—by hearsay from some one who knew it by hearsay. The American war refugees had all been in contact with people in England whom they characterized as well informed. The English visitors were well informed because they were English visitors. Some of them told prodigious secrets which they had indirectly from Downing Street. Others gave the reasons why General Isleworth had been superseded in his command, and the part Mrs. Lamingford, that beautiful American, had played in the scandal. From others we learned that Lady Hull, with her baleful charm, was the influence really responsible for the shortage of shells.

War was shown to us by our English visitors not as a mighty, pitiless contest, but as a series of social, sexual, and political intrigues, in which women pulled the strings. I know it was talk; but talk it was. For weeks, for months, we had it with the greater number of our meals. Wherever there were English guests—women of title they often were, or eccentric public men—we had an orgy of tales in which the very entrails of English reputations were torn out. No one was spared—not even the Highest in the Land. All the American could do was to listen open-mouthed; and open-mouthed he listened.

I will say for the English that they have no disloyalty but that of chatter; but the plain American could not be expected to know that. To him the chatter was gospel truth. He has none of that facility for discounting gossip on the great which the Englishman learns with his mother tongue. The American heard it greedily; he was avid for more. He retailed it at dinners and teas, and in that Reading-room which is really a club. Naturally enough! From what our English visitors told us about themselves, their statesmen, their generals, their admirals were footlers at the best, and could, moreover, be described by a vigorous compound Anglo-Saxon word in the Book of Revelations.

And the English papers were no better. All the important ones, weeklies as well as dailies, were sent to Mr. Brokenshire, and copies lay about at Mr. Rossiter's. They sickened me. I stopped reading them. There was good in them, doubtless; but what I chiefly found was a wild tempest of abuse of this party or that party, of this leading man or that leading man, with the effect on the imagination of a ship going down amid the curses and confusion of officers and passengers alike. It may have sounded well in England; very likely it did; but in America it was horrible. I mention it here only because, in this babel of voices, my own faint pipe on behalf of a league of democracies could no more be heard than the tinkle of a sacring bell amid the shrieking and bursting of shells.

I was often tempted to say no more about it and let the world go to pot. Then I thought of Larry Strangways, offering his life for an ideal as to which I was unwilling to speak a word. So I would begin my litany of Bolivia and Beluchistan over again, crooning it into the ears of people, both gentle and simple, who, in the matter of response, might never have heard the names of the two countries I mentioned together.

A few lines from one of Larry Strangways's letters, written from Valcartier, prompted me to persevere in this course:

> People are no more interested here than they are on our side of the border; but it's got to come, for all that. What we need is a public opinion; and a public opinion can only be created by writing and talk. Thank the Lord, you and I can talk if we are not very strong on writing! and talk we must! Bigger streams have risen from smaller springs. The mustard seed is the least of all seeds; but it grows to be the greatest of herbs.

It might have been easier to call forth a responsive spark had we realized that there was a war. But we hadn't—not in the way that the fact came to us afterward. In spite of the taking of Namur, Liège, Maubeuge, the advance on Paris, and the rolling back on the Marne, we had seen no more than chariots and horses of fire in the clouds. It was not only distant, it was phantom-like. We read the papers; we heard of horrors; American war refugees and English visitors alike piled up the agonies, to which we listened eagerly; we saw the moneyed magnates come and go in counsel with Mr. Brokenshire; we knitted and sewed and subscribed to funds; but, so far as vital participation went, Hugh was right in saying we were out of it.

And then a shot fell into our midst, smiting us with awe.

Cissie Boscobel, Hugh, another young man, and I had been playing tennis one September morning on Mrs. Rossiter's courts. The other young man having left for Bailey's Beach, the remaining three of us were sauntering back toward the house when a lad, whom Cissie recognized as belonging to the Burkes' establishment, came running up with a telegram. As it was for Cissie she stood still to read it, while Hugh and I strolled on. Once or twice I glanced back toward her; but she still held the brief lines up before her as if she

262

couldn't make out their meaning.

When she rejoined us, as she presently did, I noticed that her color had died out, though there was otherwise no change in her unless it was in stillness. The question was as to whether we should go to Bailey's or not. I didn't want to go and Hugh declared he wouldn't go without me.

"We'll put it up to Cissie," he said, as we reached the house. "If she goes we'll all go."

"I think I won't go," she answered, quietly; adding, without much change of tone, "Leatherhead's been killed in action."

So there really was a war! Hugh's deep "Oh!" was in Itself like the distant rumble of guns.

CHAPTER XXIV

There was nothing to be done for Lady Cecilia because she took her bereavement with so little fuss. She asked for no sympathy; so far as I ever saw, she shed no tears. If on that particular spot in the neighborhood of Ypres a man had had to fall for his country, she was proud that it had been a Boscobel. She put on a black frock and ordered her maid to take the jade-green plume out of a black hat; but, except that she declined invitations, she went about as usual. As the first person we knew to be touched by the strange new calamity of war, we made a kind of heroine of her, treating her with an almost romantic reverence; but she herself never seemed aware of it. It was my first glimpse of that unflinching British heroism of which I have since seen much, and it impressed me.

We began to dream together of being useful; our difficulty was that we didn't see the way. War had not yet made its definite claims on women and girls, and knitting till our muscles ached was not a sufficient outlet for our energies. Had I been in Cissie's place, I should have gone home at once; but I suspected that, in spite of all her brave words to me, she couldn't quite kill the hope that kept her lingering on.

My own ambitions being distasteful to Hugh, I was obliged to repress them, doing so with the greater regret because some of the courses I suggested would have done him good. They would have utilized the physical strength with which he was blessed, and delivered him from that material well-being to which he returned with the more child-like rejoicing because of having been without it.

"Hugh, dear," I said to him once, "couldn't we be married soon and go over to France or England? Then we should see whether there wasn't something we could do."

"Not on your life, little Alix!" was his laughing response. "Since as Americans we're out of it, out of it we shall stay."

Over replies like this, of which there were many, I was gnashing my teeth helplessly when, all at once, I was called on to see myself as others saw me, so getting a surprise.

The first note of warning came to me in a few words from Ethel Rossiter. I was scribbling her notes one morning as she lay in bed, when it occurred to me to say:

"If I'm going to be married, I suppose I ought to be doing something about clothes."

She murmured, listlessly:

"Oh, I wouldn't be in a hurry about that, if I were you."

I went on writing.

"I haven't been in a hurry, have I? But I shall certainly want some things I haven't got now."

"Then you can get them after you're married. When are you to be married, anyhow?"

As the question was much on my mind, I looked up from my task and said:

"Well—when?"

"Don't you know?"

"No. Do you?"

She shook her head.

"I didn't know but what father had said something about it."

"He hasn't—not a word." I resumed my scribbling. "It's a queer thing for him to have to settle, don't you think? One might have supposed it would have been left to me."

"Oh, you don't know father!" It was as if throwing off something of no importance that she added, "Of course, he can see that you're not in love with Hugh."

Amazed at this reading of my heart, I bent my head to hide my confusion.

"I don't know why you should say that," I stammered at last, "when you can't help seeing I'm quite true to him."

She shrugged her beautiful shoulders, of which one was bare.

"Oh, true! What's the good of that?" She went on, casually: "By the by, do call up Daisy Burke and tell her I sha'n't go to that luncheon of theirs. They're going to have old lady Billing, who's coming to stay at father's; and you don't catch me with that lot except when I can't help it." She reverted to the topic of a minute before. "I don't blame you, of course. I suppose, if I were in your place, it's what I should do myself. It's what I thought you'd try for—you remember, don't you?—as long ago as when we were in Halifax. But naturally enough other people don't—" I failed to learn, however, what other people didn't, because of a second reversion in theme: "Do make up something civil to say to Daisy, and tell her I won't come."

We dropped the subject, chiefly because I was afraid to go on with it; but when I met old Mrs. Billing I received a similar shock. Having gone to Mr. Brokenshire's to pay her my respects, I was told she was on the terrace. As a matter of fact, she was making her way toward the hall, and awkwardly carried a book, a sunshade, and the stump of a cigarette. Dutifully I went forward in the hope of offering my services.

"Get out of my sight!" was her response to my greetings. "I can't bear to look at you."

Brushing past me without further words, she entered the house.

"What did she mean?" I asked of Cissie Boscobel, to whom I heard that Mrs. Billing had given her own account of the incident.

Lady Cecilia was embarrassed.

"Oh, nothing! She's just so very odd."

But I insisted:

"She must have meant something. Had it anything to do with Hugh?"

Reluctantly Lady Cissie let it out. Mrs. Billing had got the idea that I was marrying Hugh for his money; and, though in the past she had not disapproved of this line of action, she had come to think it no road to happiness. Having taken the trouble to give me more than one hint that I should many the man I was in love with she was now disappointed in my character.

"You know how much truth there is in all that, don't you?" I said, evasively.

Lady Cissie did her best to support me, though between her words and her inflection there was a curious lack of correspondence.

"Oh yes—certainly!"

I got the reaction of her thought, however, some minutes later, when she said, apropos of nothing in our conversation:

"Since Janet can't be married this month, I needn't go home for a long time."

But knowing that this suggestion was in the air, I was the better able to interpret Mildred's oracular utterance the next time I sat at the foot of the couch, in the darkened room.

"One can't be true to another," she said, in reply to some feeler of my own, "unless one is true to oneself, and one can't be true to oneself unless one follows the highest of one's instincts."

I said, inwardly: "Ah! Now I know the reason for her distrust of me." Aloud I made it:

"But that throws us back on the question as to what one's highest instincts are."

There was the pause that preceded all her expressions of opinion.

"On the principle that it is more blessed to give than to receive, I suppose our highest promptings are those which urge us to give most of ourselves."

"And when one gives all of oneself that one can dispose of?"

"One has then to consider the importance or the unimportance of what one has to withhold."

Of all the things that had been said to me this was the most disturbing. It had seemed to me hitherto that the essence of my duty lay in marrying Hugh. If I married him, I argued, I should have done my best to make up to him for all he had undergone for my sake. I saw myself as owing him a debt. The refusal to pay it would have implied a kind of moral bankruptcy. Considering myself solvent, and also considering myself honest, I felt I had no choice. Since I could pay, I must pay. The reasoning was the more forcible because I liked Hugh and was grateful to him. I could be tolerably happy with him, and would make him a good wife.

To make him a good wife I had choked back everything I had ever felt for Larry Strangways; I had submitted to all the Brokenshire repressions; I had made myself humble and small before Hugh and his father, and accepted the status of a Libby Jaynes. My heart cried out like any other woman's heart—it cried out for my country in the hour of its stress; it cried out for my home in what I tried to make the hour of my happiness; when it caught me unawares it cried out for the man I loved. But all this I mastered as our Canadian men were mastering their longings and regrets on saying their good-bys. What was to be done was to be done, and done willingly. Willingly I meant to marry Hugh, not because he was the man I would have chosen before all others, but because, when no one else in the world was giving me a thought, he had had the astonishing goodness to choose me. And now—

With Mrs. Brokenshire the situation was different. She believed I was in love with Hugh and that the others were doing me a wrong. Moreover, she informed me one day that I was making my way in Newport. People who noticed me once noticed me again. The men beside whom I sat at the occasional lunches and dinners I attended often spoke of me to the hostess on going away, and there could be no better sign than that. They said that, though I "wasn't long on looks," I had ideas and knew how to express them. She ventured to hope that this kindly opinion might, in the end, soften Mr. Brokenshire.

"Do you mean that he isn't softened as it is?"

She answered, indirectly:

"He's not accustomed to be forced—and he feels I've forced him."

It was her first reference to what she had done for Hugh and me. In its way it gave me permission to say:

"But isn't it a question of the *quid pro quo*? If you granted him something for something he granted you in return—"

But the expression on her face forbade my going on. I have never seen such a parting to human lips, or so haunting, so lost a look in human eyes. It told me everything. It was a confession of all the things she never could have said. "Better is it," says the Book of Ecclesiastes, "that thou shouldest not vow, than that thou shouldest vow and not pay." She had vowed and not paid. She had got her price and hadn't fulfilled her bargain. She couldn't; she never would. It was beyond her. The big moneyed man who at that minute was helping to finance a good part of Europe, who was a power not only in a city or a country, but the world, had been tricked by a woman; and I in my poor little person was the symbol of his discomfiture.

No wonder he found it hard to forgive me! No wonder that whenever I came where he was he treated me to some kindly hint or correction which was no sufficient veil for his scorn! As I had never to my knowledge been hated by any one, it was terrible to feel myself an object of abhorrence to a man of such high standing in the world. Our eyes couldn't meet without my seeing that his passions were seething to the boiling-point. If he could have struck me dead with a look I think he would have done it. And I didn't hate him; I was too sorry for him. I could have liked him if he had let me.

I had, consequently, much to think about. I thought and I prayed. It was not a minute at which to do anything hurriedly. To a spirit so hot as mine it would have been a relief to lash out at them all; but, as I had checked myself hitherto, I checked myself again. I reasoned that if I kept close to right, right would take care of me. Not being a theologian, I felt free to make some closeness of identity between right and God. I might have defined right as God in action, or God as right in conjunction with omnipotence, intelligence, and love; but I had no need for exactness of terms. In keeping near to right I knew I must be near to God: and near to God I could let myself go so far that no power on earth would seem strong enough to save me—and yet I should be saved.

I went on then with a kind of fearlessness. If I was to marry Hugh I was convinced that I should be supported; if not, I was equally convinced that something would hold me back.

"If anything should happen," I said to Cissie Boscobel one day, "I want you to look after Hugh."

The dawn seemed to break over her, though she only said, tremulously:

"Happen—how?"

"I don't know. Perhaps nothing will. But if it does—"

She slipped away, doubtless so as not to hear more.

And then one evening, when I was not thinking especially about it, the Cloud came down on the Mountain; the voice spoke out of it, and my course was made plain.

But before that night I also had received a cablegram. It was from my sister Louise, to say that the *King Arthur*, her husband's ship, had been blown up in the North Sea, and that he was among the lost.

So the call was coming to me more sharply than I had yet heard it. With Lady Cecilia's example in mind, I said little to those about me beyond mentioning the fact. I suppose they showed me as much sympathy as the sweeping away of a mere brother-in-law demanded. They certainly said they were sorry, and hinted that that was what nations let themselves in for when they were so rash as to go to war.

"Think we'd ever expose our fellows like that?" was Hugh's comment. "Not on your life!"

But they didn't make a heroine of me as they did with Lady Cissie; not that I cared about that. I only hoped that the fact that my brother-in-law's name was in all the American accounts of the incident would show them that I belonged to some one, and that some one belonged to me. If it did I never perceived it. Perhaps the loss of a mere captain in the navy was a less gallant occurrence than the death in action of a Lord Leatherhead; perhaps we were already getting used to the toll of war; but, whatever the reason, Lady Cissie was still, to all appearances, the only sufferer. Within a day or two a black dress was my sole reminder that the *King Arthur* had gone down; and, even to Hugh, I made no further reference to the catastrophe.

And then came the evening when, as Larry Strangways said on my telling him about it, "the fat was all in the fire."

It was the occasion of what had become the annual dinner at Mr. Brokenshire's in honor of Mrs. Billing—a splendid function. Nothing short of a splendid function would have satisfied the old lady, who had the gift of making even the great afraid of her. The event was the more magnificent for the reason that, in addition to the mother of the favorite, a number of brother princes of finance, in Newport for conference with our host, were included among the guests. Of these one was staying in the house, one with the Jack Brokenshires, and two at a hotel. I was seated between the two who were at the hotel because they were socially unimportant. Even Mr. Brokenshire had sometimes to extend his domestic hospitality to business friends for the sake of business, when perhaps he should have preferred to show his attentions in clubs.

The chief scene, if I may so call it, was played to the family alone in Mildred's sitting-room, after the guests had gone; but there was a curtain-raiser at the dinner-table before the assembled company. I give bits of the conversation, not because they were important, but because of what they led up to.

We were twenty-four, seated on great Italian chairs, which gave each of us the feeling of being a sovereign on a throne. It took all the men of the establishment, as well as those gathered in from the Jack Brokenshires' and Mrs. Rossiter's, to wait on us, a detail by which in the end I profited. The gold service had been sent down from the vaults in New York, so that the serving-plates were gold, as well as the plates for some of the other courses. Gold vases and bowls held the roses that adorned the table, and gold spoons and forks were under our hands. It was the first time I had ever been able to notice with my own eyes how nearly the rich American can rival the state of kings and emperors.

It goes without saying that all the women had put on their best, and that the jewels were as precious metals in the days of Solomon; they were "nothing accounted of." Diamonds flashed, rubies broke out in fire, and emeralds said unspeakable things all up and down the table; the rows and ropes and circlets of pearls made one think of the gates of Paradise. I was the only one not so bedecked, getting that contrast of simplicity which is the compensation of the poor. The ring Hugh had given me, a sapphire set in diamonds, was my only ornament; and yet the neat austerity of my black evening frock rendered me conspicuous.

It also goes without saying that I had no right to be conspicuous, being the person of least consequence at the board. Mr. Brokenshire not only felt that himself, but he liked me to feel it; and he not only liked me to feel it, but he liked others to see that his great, broad spirit admitted me among his family and friends from noble promptings of tolerance. I was expected to play up to this generosity and to present the foil of humility to the glory of the other guests and the beauty of the table decorations.

In general I did this, and had every intention of doing it again. Nothing but what perhaps were the solecisms of my immediate neighbors caused my efforts to miscarry. I had been informed by Mrs. Brokenshire beforehand that they were socially dull, that one of them was "awful," and that my powers would be taxed to keep them in conversation. My mettle being up, I therefore did my best.

The one who was awful proved to be a Mr. Samuel Russky, whose claim to be present sprang from the fact that he was a member of a house that had the power to lend a great deal of money. He was a big man, of a mingled Slavic and Oriental cast of countenance, and had nothing more awful about him than a tendency to overemphasis. On my right I had Mr. John G. Thorne, whose face at a glance was as guileless as his name till contemplation revealed to you depth beyond depth of that peculiar astuteness of which only the American is master. I am sure that when we sat down to table neither of these gentlemen had any intention of taking a hand in my concerns, and are probably ignorant to this day of ever having done so; but the fact remains.

It begins with my desire to oblige Mrs. Brokenshire by trying to make the dinner a success. Having to lift the heaviest corner, so to speak, I gave myself to the task first with one of my neighbors and then with the other. They responded so well that as early as when the terrapin was reached I was doing it with both. As there was much animation about the table, there was nothing at that time to call attention to our talk.

Naturally, it was about the war. From the war we passed to the attitude of the United States toward the struggle; and from that what could I do but glide to the topics as to which I felt myself a mouthpiece for Larry Strangways? It was a chance. Here were two men obviously of some influence in the country, and neither of them of very strong convictions, so far as I could judge, on any subject but that of floating foreign bonds. As the dust from a butterfly's wing might turn the scale with one or both of them, I endeavored to throw at least that much weight on the side of a British and American entente.

At something I said, Mr. Russky, with the slightest hint of a Yiddish pronunciation, complained that I spoke as if all Americans were "Anglo-Zaxons"; whereas it was well known that the "Anglo-Zaxon" element among them was but a percentage, which was destined to grow less.

"I'm not putting it on that ground," I argued, with some zeal, taking up a point as to which one of Larry Strangways's letters had enlightened me. "I see well enough that the American ideal isn't one of nationality, but of principle. When the federation of the States was completed it was on the basis not of a common Anglo-Saxon origin, but on that of the essential unity of mankind. Mere nationality was left out of the question. All nations were welcomed, with the idea of welding them into one."

"And England," Mr. Russky declared, somewhat more loudly than was necessary for my hearing him, "is still bound up in her Anglo-Zaxondon."

"Not a bit of it!" I returned. "Her spirit is exactly the same as that of this country. Except this country, where is there any other of which the gates and ports and homes and factories have been open to all nations as hers have been? They've landed on her shores in thousands and thousands, without passports and without restraint, welcomed and protected even when they've been taking the bread out of the born Englishman's mouth. Look at the number of foreigners they've been obliged to round up since the war began—for the simple reason that they'd become so many as to be a peril. It's the same not only in the British Islands, but in every part of the British Empire. Always the same reception for all, with liberty for all. My own country, in proportion to its population, is as full of citizens of foreign birth as this is. They've been fathered and mothered from the minute they landed at Halifax. Poles and Ruthenians and Slovaks and Icelanders have been given the same advantages as ourselves. I'm not boasting of this, Mr. Russky. I'm only saying that, though we've never defined the principle in a constitution, our instinct toward mankind is the same as yours."

It was here Mr. Thorne broke in, saying that sympathy in the United States was all for France.

"I can understand that," I said. "You often find in a family that the sympathy of each of the members is for some one outside. But that doesn't keep them from being a family, or from acting in important moments with a family's solidarity."

"And, personally," Mr. Thorne went on, "I don't care for England."

I laughed politely in his face.

"And do you, a business man, say that? I thought business was carried on independently of personal regard. You might conceivably not like Mr. Warren or Mr. Casemente"—I named the two other banker guests—"or even Mr. Brokenshire; but you do business with them as if you loved them, and quite successfully, too. In the same way the Briton and the American might put personal fancies out of the question and co-operate for great ends."

"Ah, but, young lady," Mr. Russky exclaimed, so noisily as to draw attention, "you forget that we're far from the scene of European disputes, and that our wisest course is to keep out of them!"

I fell back again on what I had learned from Larry Strangways.

"But you're not far from the past of mankind. You inherit that as much as any European; and it isn't an inheritance that can be limited geographically." I still quoted one of Larry Strangways's letters, knowing it by heart. "Every Russian and German and Jew and Italian and Scotchman who lands in New York brings a portion of it with him and binds the responsibility of the New World more closely to the sins of the Old. Oceans and continents will not separate us from sins. As we can never run away from our past, Americans must help to expiate what they and their ancestors have done in the countries from which they came. This isn't going to be a local war or a twentieth-century war. It's the struggle of all those who have had to bear the burdens of the world against those who have made them bear them."

"If that was the case," Mr. Russky said, doubtfully, "Americans would be all on one side."

"They will be all on one side—when they see it. The question is, Will they see it soon enough?"

Being so interested I didn't notice that our immediate neighbors were listening, nor did I observe, what Cissie Boscobel told me afterward, that Hugh was dividing disquieting looks between me and his father. I did try to divert Mr. Thorne to giving his attention to Mrs. Burke, who was his neighbor on the right, but I couldn't make him take the hint. It was, in fact, he who said:

"We've too many old grudges against England to keep step with her now."

I smiled engagingly.

"But you've no old grudges against the British Empire, have you?"

"What do you mean?"

"You've no old grudges against Canada, or Australia, or the West Indies, or New Zealand, or the Cape?"

"N-no."

"Nor even against Scotland or Wales or Ireland?"

"N-no."

"You recognize in all those countries a spirit more or less akin to your own, and one with which you can sympathize?"

"Y-yes."

"Then isn't that my point? You speak of England, and you see the southern end of an island between the North Sea and the Atlantic; but that's all you see. You forget Scotland and Ireland and Canada and Australia and South Africa. You think I'm talking of a country three thousand miles away, whereas it comes right up to your doors. It's on the borders of Maine and Michigan and Minnesota, and all along your line. That isn't Canada alone; it's the British Empire. It's the country with which you Americans have more to do than with any other in the world. It's the one you have to think of first. You may like some other better, but you can't get away from having it as your most pressing consideration the minute you pass your own frontiers. That," I declared, with a little laugh, "is what makes my entente important."

"Important for England or for America?" Mr. Russky, as a citizen of the country he thought had most to give, was on his guard.

"Important for the world!" I said, emphatically. "England and America—the British Empire and the United States—are both secondary in what I'm trying to say. I speak of them only as the two that can most easily line up together. When they've done that the rest will follow their lead. It's not to be an offensive and defensive alliance, or directed against any other power. It would be a starting-point, the beginning of world peace. It would also be an instance of what could be accomplished in the long run among all the nations of the world by mutual tolerance and common sense."

As I made a little mock oratorical flourish there was a laugh from our part of the table. Some one sitting opposite called out, "Good!" I distinctly heard Mrs. Billing's cackle of a "Brava!" I ought to say, too, that, afraid of even the appearance of "holding forth," I had kept my tone lowered, addressing myself to my left-hand companion. If others stopped talking and listened it was because of the compulsion of the theme. It was a burning theme. It was burning in hearts and minds that had never given it a conscious thought; and, now that for a minute it was out in the open, it claimed them. True, it was an occasion meant to be kept free from the serious; but even in Newport we were beginning to understand that occasions kept free from the serious were over— perhaps for the rest of our time.

After that the conversation in our neighborhood became general. With the exception of Hugh, who was not far away, every one joined in, aptly or inaptly, as the case might be, with pros and cons and speculations and anecdotes and flashes of wit, and a far deeper interest than I should have predicted. As Mrs. Brokenshire whispered after we regained the drawing-room, it had made the dinner go; and a number of women whom I hadn't known before came up and talked to me.

But all that was only the curtain-raiser. It was not till the family were assembled in Mildred's room up-stairs that the real play began.

CHAPTER XXV

Mildred's big, heavily furnished room was as softly lighted as usual. As usual, she herself, in white, with a rug across her feet, lay on her couch, withdrawn from the rest. She never liked to have any one near her, unless it was Hugh; she never entered into general talk. When others were present she remained silent, as she did on this evening. Whatever passed through her mind she gave out to individuals when she was alone with them.

The rest of the party were scattered about, standing or sitting. There were Jack and Pauline, Jim and Ethel Rossiter, Mrs. Billing, Mrs. Brokenshire, Cissie Boscobel, who was now staying with the Brokenshires, and Hugh. The two banker guests had gone back to the smoking-room. As I entered, Mr. Brokenshire was standing in his customary position of command, a little like a pasha in his seraglio, his back to the empty fireplace. With his handsome head and stately form, he would have been a truly imposing figure had it not been for his increased stoutness and the occasional working of his face.

I had come up-stairs with some elation. The evening might have been called mine. Most of the men, on rejoining us in the drawing-room, had sought a word with me, and those who didn't know me inquired who I was. I could hardly help the hope that Mr. Brokenshire might see I was worth my salt, and that on becoming a member of his family I should bring my contribution.

But on the way up-stairs Hugh gave me a hint that in that I might be mistaken.

"Well, little Alix, you certainly gave poor old dad a shock this time."

"A shock?" I asked, in not unnatural astonishment.

"Your fireworks."

"Fireworks! What on earth do you mean?"

"It's always a shock when fireworks go off too close to you; and especially when it's in church."

As we had reached the door of Mildred's room, I searched my conduct during dinner to see in what I had offended.

It is possible my entry might have passed unnoticed if Mrs. Brokenshire, with the kindest intentions, had not come forward to the threshold and taken me by the hand. As if making a presentation, she led me toward the august figure before the fireplace.

"Our little girl," she said, in the hope of doing me a good turn, "distinguished herself to-night, didn't she?"

He must have been stung to sudden madness by the sight of the two of us together. In general he controlled himself in public. He was often cruel, but with a quiet subtle cruelty to which even the victims often didn't know how to take exception. But to-night the long-gathering fury of passion was incapable of further restraint. Behind it there was all the explosive force of a lifetime of pride, complacence, and self-love. The exquisite creature—a vision of soft rose, with six strings of pearls—who was parading her bargain, as you might say, without having paid for it, excited him to the point of frenzy. I saw later, what I didn't understand at the time, that he was striking at her through me. He was willing enough to strike at me, since I was the nobody who had forced herself into his family; but she was his first aim.

Having looked at me disdainfully, he disdainfully looked away.

"She certainly gave us an exhibition!" he said, with his incisive, whip-lash quietude.

Mrs. Brokenshire dropped my hand.

"Oh, Howard!"

I think she backed away toward the nearest chair. I was vaguely conscious of curious eyes in the dimness about me as I stood alone before my critic.

"I'm sorry if I've done anything wrong, Mr. Brokenshire," I said, meekly. "I didn't mean to."

He looked over my head, speaking casually, as one who takes no interest in the subject.

"All the great stupidities have been committed by people who didn't mean to —but there they are!"

I continued to be meek.

"I didn't know I had been stupid."

"The stupid never do."

"And I don't think I have been," I added, with rising spirit.

Though there was consternation in the room behind me, Mr. Brokenshire merely said:

"Unfortunately, you must let others judge of that."

"But how?" I insisted. "If I have been, wouldn't it be a kindness on your part to tell me in what way?"

He pretended not merely indifference, but reluctance.

"Isn't that obvious?"

"Not to me—and I don't think to any one else."

"What do you call it when one—you compel me to speak frankly—what do you call it when one exposes one's ignorance of—of fundamental things before a roomful of people who've never set eyes on one before?"

Since no one, not even Hugh, was brave enough to stand up for me, I had to do it for myself.

"But I didn't know I had."

"Probably not. It's what I warned you of, if you'll take the trouble to remember. I said—or it amounted to that—that until you'd learned the ways of the people who are generally recognized as *comme il faut*, you'd be wise in keeping yourself—unobtrusive."

"And may I ask whether one becomes obtrusive merely in talking of public affairs?"

"You'll pardon me for giving you a lesson before others; but, since you invite it—"

"Quite so, Mr. Brokenshire, I do invite it."

"Then I can only say that in what we call good society we become obtrusive in talking of things we know nothing about."

"But surely one can set an idea going, even if one hasn't sounded all its depths. And as for the relations between this country and the British Empire —"

"Well-bred women leave such subjects to statesmen."

"Yes; we've done so. We've left them to statesmen and"—I couldn't resist the temptation to say it—"and we've left them to financiers; but we can't look at Europe and be proud of the result. We women, well bred or otherwise, couldn't make things worse even if we were to take a hand; and we might make them better."

He was not moved from his air of slightly bored indifference.

"Then you must wait for women with some knowledge of the subject."

"But, Mr. Brokenshire, I have some knowledge of the subject! Though I'm neither English nor American, I'm both. I've only to shift from one side of my mind to the other to be either. Surely, when it comes to the question of a link between the two countries I love I'm qualified to put in a plea for it."

I think his nerves were set further on edge because I dared to argue the point, though he would probably have been furious if I had not. His tone was still that of a man deigning no more than to fling out an occasional stinging remark.

"As a future member of my family, you're not qualified to make yourself ridiculous before my friends. To take you humorously was the kindest thing they could do."

I saw an opportunity.

"Then wouldn't it be equally kind, sir, if you were to follow their example?"

Mrs. Billing's hen-like crow came out of the obscurity:

"She's got you there!"

The sound incited him. He became not more irritable, but cruder.

"Unhappily, that's beyond my power. I have to blush for my son Hugh."

Hugh spoke out of the darkness, his voice trembling with the fear of his own hardihood in once more braving Jove.

"Oh no, dad! You must take that back."

The father wheeled round in the new direction. He was losing command of the ironic courtesy he secured by his air of indifference, and growing coarser.

"My poor boy! I can't take it back. You're like myself—in that you can only be fooled when you put your trust in a woman."

It was Mrs. Brokenshire's turn:

"Howard—please!"

In the cry there was the confession of the woman who has vowed and not paid, and yet begs to be spared the blame.

Jack Brokenshire sprang to his feet and hurried forward, laying his hand on his father's arm.

"Say, dad—"

But Mr. Brokenshire shook off the hand, refusing to be placated. He looked at his wife, who had risen, confusedly, from her chair and was backing away from him to the other side of the room.

"I said poor Hugh was being fooled by a woman; and he is. He's marrying some one who doesn't care a hang about him and who's in love with another man. He may not be the first in the family to do that, but I merely make the statement that he's doing it."

Hugh leaped forward.

"She's not in love with another man!"

"Ask her."

He clutched me by the wrist.

"You're not, are you?" he pleaded. "Tell father you're not."

I was so sorry for Hugh that I hardly thought of myself. I was benumbed. The suddenness of the attack had been like a blow from behind that stuns you without taking away your consciousness. In any case Mr. Brokenshire gave me no time, for he laughed gratingly.

"She can't do that, my boy, because she is. Everybody knows it. I know it— and Ethel and Mildred and Cissie. They're all here and they can contradict me if I'm saying what isn't so."

"But she may not know it herself," Mrs. Billing croaked. "A girl is often the last to make that discovery."

"Ask her."

Hugh obeyed, still clutching my wrist.

"I'm asking you, little Alix. You're not, are you?"

I could say nothing. Apart from the fact that I didn't knew what to say, I was dumbfounded by the way in which it had all come upon me. The only words that occurred to me were:

"I think Mr. Brokenshire is ill."

Oddly enough. I was convinced of that. It was the one assuaging fact. He might hate me, but he wouldn't have made me the object of this mad-bull rush if he had been in his right mind. He was not in his right mind; he was merely a blood-blinded animal as he went on:

"Ask her again, Hugh. You're the only one she's been able to keep in the dark; but then"—his eyes followed his wife, who was still slowly retreating —"but then that's nothing new. She'll let you believe anything—till she gets you. That's always the game with women of the sort. But once you're fast in her clutches—then, my boy, look out!"

I heard Pauline whisper, "Jack, for Heaven's sake, do something!"

Once more Jack's hand was laid on his parent's arm, with his foolish "Say, dad—"

Once more the restraining hand was shaken off. The cutting tones were addressed to Hugh:

"You see what a hurry she's been in to be married, don't you? How many times has she asked you to do it up quick? She's been afraid that you'd slip through her fingers." He turned toward me. "Don't be alarmed, my dear. We shall keep our word. You've worked hard to capture the position, and I shall not deny that you've been clever in your attacks. You deserve what you've won, and you shall have it. But all in good time. Don't rush. The armies in Europe are showing us that you must intrench yourself where you are if you want, in the end, to push forward. You push a little too hard."

Poor Hugh had gone white. He was twisting my wrist as if he would wring it off, though I felt no pain till afterward.

"Tell me!" he whispered. "Tell me! You're—you're not marrying me for—for my money, are you?"

I could have laughed hysterically.

"Hugh, don't be an idiot!" came, scornfully, from Ethel Rossiter.

I could see her get up, cross the room, and sit down on the edge of Mildred's couch, where the two engaged in a whispered conversation. Jim Rossiter, too, got up and tiptoed his sleek, slim person out of the room. Cissie Boscobel followed him. They talked in low tones at the head of the stairs outside. I found voice at last:

"No, Hugh; I never thought of marrying you for that reason. I was doing it only because it seemed to me right."

Mr. Brokenshire emitted a sound, meant to be a laugh:

"Right! Oh, my God!"

Mrs. Brokenshire was now no more than a pale-rose shadow on the farther side of the room, but she came to my aid:

"She was, Howard. Please believe her. She was, really!"

"Thanks, darling, for the corroboration! It comes well from you. Where there's a question of right you're an authority."

Mrs. Billing's hoarse, prolonged "Ha-a!" implied every shade of comprehension. I saw the pale-rose shadow sink down on a sofa, all in a little heap, like something shot with smokeless powder.

Hugh was twisting my wrist again and whispering:

"Alix, tell me. Speak! What are you marrying me for? What about the other fellow? Is it Strangways? Speak!"

"I've given you the only answer I can, Hugh. If you can't believe in my doing right—"

"What were you in such a hurry for? Was that the reason—what dad says—that you were afraid you wouldn't—hook me?"

I looked him hard in the eye. Though we were speaking in the lowest possible tones, there was a sudden stillness in the room, as though every one was hanging on my answer.

"Have I ever given you cause to suspect me of that?" I asked, after thinking of what I ought to say.

Three words oozed themselves out like three drops of his own blood. They were the distillation of two years' uncertainty:

"Well—sometimes—yes."

Either he dropped my wrist or I released myself. I only remember that I was twisting the sapphire-and-diamond ring on my finger.

"What made you think so?" I asked, dully.

"A hundred things—everything!" He gave a great gasp. "Oh, little Alix!"

Turning away suddenly, he leaned his head against the mantelpiece, while his shoulders heaved.

It came to me that this was the moment to make an end of it all; but I saw Mrs. Rossiter get up from her conference with Mildred and come forward. She did it leisurely, pulling up one shoulder of her décolleté gown as she advanced.

"Hugh, don't be a baby!" she said, in passing. "Father, you ought to be ashamed of yourself!"

If the heavens had fallen my amazement might have been less. She went on in a purely colloquial tone, extricating the lace of her corsage from a spray of diamond flowers as she spoke:

"I'll tell you why she was marrying Hugh. It was for two or three reasons, every one of them to her credit. Any one who knows her and doesn't see that must be an idiot. She was marrying him, first, because he was kind to her. None of the rest of us was, unless it was Mrs. Brokenshire; and she was afraid to show it for fear you'd jump on her, father. The rest of us have treated Alix Adare like brutes. I know I have."

"Oh no!" I protested, though I could scarcely make myself audible.

"But Hugh was nice to her. He was nice to her from the start. And she couldn't forget it. No nice girl would. When he asked her to marry him she felt she had to. And then, when he put up his great big bluff of earning a living—"

"It wasn't a bluff," Hugh contradicted, his face still buried in his hands.

"Well, perhaps it wasn't," she admitted, imperturbably. "If you, father, hadn't driven him to it with your heroics—"

"If you call it heroics that I should express my will—"

"Oh your will! You seem to think that no one's got a will but you. Here we are, all grown up, two of us married, and you still try to keep us as if we were five years old. We're sick of it, and it's time some of us spoke. Jack's afraid to, and Mildred's too good; so it's up to me to say what I think."

Mr. Brokenshire's first shock having passed, he got back something of his lordly manner, into which he threw an infusion of the misunderstood.

"And you've said it sufficiently. When my children turn against me—"

"Nonsense, father! Your children don't do anything of the sort. We're perfect sheep. You drive us wherever you like. But, however much we can stand ourselves, we can't help kicking when you attack some one who doesn't quite belong to us and who's a great deal better than we are."

Mrs. Billing crowed again:

"Brava, Ethel! Never supposed you had the pluck."

Ethel turned her attention to the other side of her corsage.

"Oh, it isn't a question of pluck; it's one of exasperation. Injustice after a while gets on one's nerves. I've had a better chance of knowing Alix Adare than any one; and you can take it from me that, when it comes to a question of breeding, she's the genuine pearl and we're only imitations—all except Mildred."

Both of Mr. Brokenshire's handsome hands went up together. He took a step forward as if to save Mrs. Rossiter from a danger.

"My daughter!"

The pale-rose heap on the other side of the room raised its dainty head.

"It's true, Howard; it's true! Please believe it!"

Ethel went on in her easy way:

"If Alix Adare has made any mistake it's been in ignoring her own wishes—I may say her own heart—in order to be true to us. The Lord knows she can't have respected us much, or failed to see that, judged by her standards, we're as common as grass when you compare it to orchids. But because she is an orchid she couldn't do anything but want to give us back better than she ever got from us; and so—"

"Oh no; it wasn't that!" I tried to interpose.

"It's no dishonor to her not to be in love with Hugh," she pursued, evenly. "She may have thought she was once; but what girl hasn't thought she was in love a dozen times? A fine day in April will make any one think it's summer already; but when June comes they know the difference. It was April when Hugh asked her; and now it's June. I'll confess for her. She is in love with—"

"Please!" I broke in.

She gave me another surprise.

"Do run and get me my fan. It's over by Mildred. There's a love!"

I had to do her bidding. The picture of the room stamped itself on my brain, though I didn't think of it at the time. It seemed rather empty. Jack had retired to one window, where he was smoking a cigarette; Pauline was at another, looking out at the moonlight on the water. Mrs. Billing sat enthroned in the middle, taking a subordinate place for once. Mrs. Brokenshire was on the sofa by the wall. The murmur of Ethel's voice, but no words, reached me as I stooped beside Mildred's couch to pick up the fan.

The invalid took my hand. Her voice had the deep, low murmur of the sea.

"You must forgive my father."

"I do," I was able to say. "I—I like him in spite of everything—"

"And as for my brother, you'll remember what we agreed upon once—that where we can't give all, our first consideration must be the value of what we withhold."

I thanked her and went back with the fan. As I passed Mrs. Billing she snapped at me, with the enigmatic words:

"You're a puss!"

When I drew near to the group by the fireplace, Mrs. Rossiter was saying to Hugh:

"And as for her marrying you for your money—well, you're crazy! I suppose she likes money as well as anybody else; but she would have married you to be loyal. She would have married you two months ago if father had been willing; and if you'd been willing you could now have been in England or France together, trying to do some good. If a woman marries one man when she's in love with another the right or the wrong depends on her motives. Who knows but what I may have done it myself? I don't say I haven't. And so —"

But I had taken off the ring on my way across the room. Having returned the fan to Ethel, I went up to Hugh, who looked round at me over his shoulder.

"Hugh, darling," I said, very softly, "I feel that I ought to give you back this."

He put out his hand mechanically, not thinking of what I was about to offer. On seeing it he drew back his hand quickly, and the ring dropped on the floor. I can hear it still, rolling with a little rattle among the fire-irons.

In making my curtsy to Mr. Brokenshire I raised my eyes to his face. It seemed to me curiously stricken. After all her years of submission Mrs. Rossiter's rebellion must have made him feel like an autocrat dethroned. I repeated my curtsy to Mrs. Billing, who merely stared at me through her lorgnette—to Jack and Pauline, who took no notice, who perhaps didn't see me—to Mrs. Brokenshire, who was again a little rose-colored heap—and to Mildred, who raised her long, white hand.

In the hall outside Cissie Boscobel rose and came toward me.

"You must look after Hugh," I said to her, breathlessly, as I sped on my way.

She did. As I hurried down the stairs I heard her saying:

"No, Hugh, no! She wants to go alone."

POSTSCRIPT

I am writing in the dawn of a May morning in 1917.

Before me lies a sickle of white beach some four or five miles in curve. Beyond that is the Atlantic, a mirror of leaden gray. Woods and fields bank themselves inland; here a dewy pasture, there a stretch of plowed earth recently sown and harrowed; elsewhere a grove of fir or maple or a hazel copse. From a little wooden house on the other side of the crescent of white sand a pillar of pale smoke is going straight up into the windless air. In the woods round me the birds, which have only just arrived from Florida, from the West Indies, from Brazil, are chirruping sleepily. They will doze again presently, to awake with the sunrise into the chorus of full song. Halifax lies some ten or twelve miles to the westward. This house is my uncle's summer residence, which he has lent to my husband and me for the latter's after-cure.

I am used to being up at this hour, or at any hour, owing to my experience in nursing. As a matter of fact, I am restless with the beginning of day, fearing lest my husband may need me. He is in the next room. If he stirs I can hear him. In this room my baby is sleeping in his little bassinet. It is not the bassinet of my dreams, nor is this the white-enameled nursery, nor am I wearing a delicate lace peignoir. It is all much more beautiful than that, because it is as it is. My baby's name is John Howard Brokenshire Strangways, though we shorten it to Broke, which, in the English fashion, we pronounce Brook.

You will see why I wanted to call him by this name; but for that I must hark back to the night when I returned the ring to dear Hugh Brokenshire and fled. It is like a dream to me now, that night; but a dream still vivid enough to recall.

On escaping Hugh and making my way down-stairs I was lucky enough to find Thomas, my rosebud footman knight. Poor lad! The judgment trumpet was sounding for him, as for Franz Ferdinand and Sophie Chotek and the rest of us. He went back to England shortly after that and was killed the next year at the Dardanelles. But there he was for the moment, standing with the wraps of the Rossiter party.

"Thomas, call the motor," I said, hurriedly. "Be quick! I'm going home, alone, and you must come with me. I've things for you to do. Mr. Jack Brokenshire will bring Mrs. Rossiter."

On the way I explained my program to him through the window. I had been called suddenly to New York. There was a train from Boston to that city which would stop at Providence at two. I thought there was one from Newport to Providence about twelve-thirty, and it was now a quarter past eleven. If there was such a train I must take it; if there wasn't, the motor must run me up to Providence, for which there was still time. I should delay only long enough to pack a suit-case. For the use I was making of him and the chauffeur, as well as of the vehicle, I should be responsible to my hosts.

Both the men being my tacitly sworn friends, there was no questioning of my authority. I fell back, therefore, into the depths of the limousine with the first sense of relief I had had since the day I accepted my position with Mrs. Rossiter. Something seemed to roll off me. I realized all at once that I had never, during the whole of the two years, been free from that necessity of picking my steps which one must have in walking on a tight-rope. Now it was delicious. I could have wished that the drive along Ochre Point Avenue had been thirty times as long.

For Hugh I had no feeling of compunction. It was so blissful to be free. Cissie Boscobel, I knew, would make up to him for all I had failed to give, and would give more. Let me say at once that when, a few weeks later, the man Lady Janet Boscobel was engaged to had also been killed at the front, and her parents had begged Cissie to go home, Hugh was her escort on the journey. It was the beginning of an end which I think is in sight, of a healing which no one wishes so eagerly as I.

For the last two years Cissie has been mothering Belgian children somewhere in the neighborhood of Poperinghe, and Hugh has been in the American Ambulance Corps before Verdun. That was Cissie's work, made easier, perhaps, by some recollection he retained of me. When he has a few days' leave—so Ethel Rossiter writes me—he spends it at Goldborough Castle or Strath-na-Cloid. I ran across Cissie when for a time I was helping in first-aid work not far behind the lines at Neuve Chapelle.

I had been taking care of her brother Rowan—Lord Ovingdean, he calls himself now, hesitating to follow his brother as Lord Leatherhead, and using one of his father's other secondary titles—and she had come to see him. I hadn't supposed till then that we were such friends. We talked and talked and talked, and still would have gone on talking. I can understand what she sees in Hugh, though I could never feel it for him with her intensity. I hope her devotion will be rewarded soon, and I think it will.

I had a premonition of this as I drove along Ochre Point Avenue that night. It helped me to the joy of liberty, to rightness of heart. As I threw the things into my suit-case I could have sung. Séraphine, who was up, waiting for her mistress, being also my friend, promised to finish my packing after I had gone, so that Mrs. Rossiter would have nothing to do but send my boxes after me. It couldn't have been half an hour after my arrival at the house before I was ready to drive away again.

I was in the down-stairs hall, going out to the motor, when a great black form appeared in the doorway. My knees shook under me; my happiness came down like a shot bird. Mr. Brokenshire advanced and stood under the many-colored Oriental hall lantern. I clung for support to the pilaster that finished the balustrade of the stairway.

There was gentleness in his voice, in spite of its whip-lash abruptness.

"Where are you going?"

I could hardly reply, my heart pounded with such fright.

"To—to New York, sir."

"What for?"

"Be-because," I faltered. "I want to—to get away."

"Why do you want to get away?"

"For—for every reason."

"But suppose I don't want you to go?"

"I should still have to be gone."

He said in a hoarse whisper:

"I want you to stay—and—and marry Hugh."

I clasped my hands.

"Oh, but how can I?"

"He's willing to forget what you've said—what my daughter Ethel has said; and I'm willing to forget it, too."

"Do you mean as to my being in love with some one else? But I am."

"Not more than you were at the beginning of the evening. You were willing to marry him then."

"But he didn't know then what he's had to learn since. I hoped to have kept it from him always. I may have been wrong—I suppose I was; but I had nothing but good motives."

There was a strange drop in his voice as he said, "I know you hadn't."

I couldn't help taking a step nearer him.

"Oh, do you? Then I'm so glad. I thought—"

He turned slightly away from me, toward a huge ugly fish in a glass case, which Mr. Rossiter believed to be a proof of his sportsmanship and an ornament to the hall.

"I've had great trials," he said, after a pause—"great trials!"

**"I'VE HAD GREAT TRIALS … I'VE ALWAYS BEEN MISJUDGED…
. THEY'VE PUT ME DOWN AS HARD AND PROUD"**

"I know," I agreed, softly.

He walked toward the fish and seemed to be studying it.

"They've—they've—broken me down."

"Oh, don't say that, sir!"

"It's true." His finger outlined the fish's skeleton from head to tail. "The things I said to-night—" He seemed hung up there. He traced the fish's skeleton back from tail to head. "Have we been unkind to you?" he demanded, suddenly, wheeling round in my direction.

I thought it best to speak quite truthfully.

"Not unkind, sir—exactly."

"But what did Ethel mean? She said we'd been brutes to you. Is that true?"

"No, sir; not in my sense. I haven't felt it."

He tapped his foot with the old imperiousness. "Then—what?"

We were so near the fundamentals that again I felt I ought to give him nothing but the facts.

"I suppose Mrs. Rossiter meant that sometimes I should have been glad of a little more sympathy, and always of more—courtesy." I added: "From you, sir, I shouldn't have asked for more than courtesy."

Though only his profile was toward me and the hall was dim, I could see that his face was twitching. "And—and didn't you get it?"

"Do you think I did?"

"I never thought anything about it."

"Exactly; but any one in my position does. Even if we could do without courtesy between equals—and I don't think we can—from the higher to the lower—from you to me, for instance—it's indispensable. I don't remember that I ever complained of it, however. Mrs. Rossiter must have seen it for herself."

"I didn't want you to marry Hugh," he began, again, after a long pause; "but I'd given in about it. I shouldn't have minded it so much if—if my wife—"

He broke off with a distressful, choking sound in the throat, and a twisting of the head, as if he couldn't get his breath. That passed and he began once more.

"I've had great trials…. My wife! … And then the burden of this war…. They think—they think I don't care anything about it but—but just to make money…. I've always been misjudged…. They've put me down as hard and proud, when—"

"I could have liked you, sir," I interrupted, boldly. "I told you so once, and it offended you. But I've never been able to help it. I've always felt that there was something big and fine in you—if you'd only set it free."

His reply to this was to turn away from his contemplation of the fish and say:

"Why don't you come back?"

I was sure it was best to be firm.

"Because I can't, sir. The episode is—is over. I'm sorry, and yet I'm glad. What I'm doing is right. I suppose everything has been right—even what happened between me and Hugh. I don't think it will do him any harm—Cissie Boscobel is there—and it's done me good. It's been a wonderful experience; but it's over. It would be a mistake for me to go back now—a mistake for all of us. Please let me go, sir; and just remember of me that I'm —I'm—grateful."

He regarded me quietly and—if I may say so—curiously. There was something in his look, something broken, something defeated, something, at long last, kind, that made me want to cry.

I was crying inwardly when he turned about, without another word, and walked toward the door.

It must have been the impulse to say a silent good-by to him that sent me slowly down the hall, though I was scarcely aware of moving. He had gone out into the dark and I was under the Oriental lamp, when he suddenly reappeared, coming in my direction rapidly. I would have leaped back if I hadn't refused to show fear. As it was, I stood still. I was only conscious of an overwhelming pity, terror, and amazement as he seized me and kissed me hotly on the brow. Then he was gone.

But it was that kiss which made all the difference in my afterthought of him. It was a confession on his part, too, and a bit of self-revelation. Behind it lay a nature of vast, splendid qualities—strong, noble, dominating, meant to be used for good—all ruined by self-love. Of the Brokenshire family, of whom I am so fond and to whom I owe so much, he was the one toward whom, by some blind, spontaneous, subconscious sympathy of my own, I have been most urgently attracted. If his soul was twisted by passions as his face became twisted by them, too—well, who is there among us of whom something of the sort may not be said; and yet God has patience with us all.

Howard Brokenshire and I were foes, and we fought; but we fought as so many thousands, so many millions, have fought in the short time since that day; we fought as those who, when the veils are suddenly stripped away, when they are helpless on the battle-field after the battle, or on hospital cots lined side by side, recognize one another as men and brethren. And so, when my baby was born I called him after him. I wanted the name as a symbol—not only to myself, but to the Brokenshire family—that there was no bitterness in my heart.

At present let me say that, though pained, I was scarcely surprised to read in the New York papers on the following afternoon that Mr. J. Howard Brokenshire, the eminent financier, had, on the previous evening, been taken with a paralytic seizure while in his motor on the way from his daughter's house to his own. He was conscious when carried indoors, but he had lost the power of speech. The doctors indicated overwork in connection with foreign affairs as the predisposing cause.

From Mrs. Rossiter I heard as each successive shock overtook him. Very pitifully the giant was laid low. Very tenderly—so Ethel has written me—Mrs. Brokenshire has watched over him—and yet, I suppose, with a terrible tragic expectation in her heart, which no one but myself, and perhaps Stacy Grainger, can have shared with her. Howard Brokenshire died on that early morning when his country went to war.

I stayed in New York just long enough to receive my boxes from Newport. On getting out of the train at Halifax Larry Strangways received me in his arms.

And this time I saw no little dining-room, with myself seating the guests; I saw no bassinet and no baby. I saw nothing but him. I knew nothing but him. He was all to me. It was the difference.

And not the least of my surprises, when I came to find out, was the fact that it was Jim Rossiter who had sent him there—Jim Rossiter, whom I had rather despised as a selfish, cat-like person, with not much thought beyond "ridin' and racin'," and pills and medicinal waters. That was true of him; and yet he took the trouble to get into touch with Stacy Grainger—as a Brokenshire only by affinity, he could do it—to use his influence at Washington and Ottawa to get Larry Strangways a week's leave from Princess Patricia's regiment—to watch over my movements in New York and know the train I should take— and wire to Larry Strangways the hour of my arrival. When I think of it I grow maudlin at the thought of the good there is in every one.

We were married within the week at the old church which was once a center for Loyalist refugees from New England, beneath which some of them lie buried, and where I was baptized. When my husband returned to Valcartier I went—to be near him—to Quebec. After he sailed for England I, too, sailed, and met him there. I kept near him in England, taking such nursing training as I could while he trained in other ways. I was not many miles away from him when, in the spring of the next year, he was badly cut up at Bois Grenier, near Neuve Chapelle.

He was one of the two or three Canadians to hold a listening post half-way between the hostile lines, where they could hear the slightest movement of the enemy and signal back. A Maxim swept the dugout at intervals, and now and then a shell burst near them. My husband was wounded in a leg and his right arm was shattered.

When I was permitted to see him at Amiens the arm had been taken off and the doctors were doing what they could to save the leg. Fortunately, they have succeeded; and now he walks with no more than a noticeable limp. He is a captain in Princess Patricia's regiment and a D. S. O.

Later he was taken to the American Women's Hospital, at Paignton, in Devonshire, and there again I had the joy of being near him. I couldn't take care of him—I had not the skill, and perhaps my nerve would have failed me —but I worked in the kitchen and was sometimes allowed to take him his food and feed him. I think the hope, the expectation, of my doing this was what brought him out of the profound silence into which he was plunged when he arrived.

That was the only sign of mental suffering I ever saw in him. For the physical suffering he never seemed to care. But something deep and far off, and beyond the beyond of self-consciousness, seemed to have been reached by what he had seen and heard and done. It was said of Lazarus, after his recall to life by Christ, that he never spoke of what he had experienced in those four days; and I can say as much of my husband.

When his mind reverts to the months in France and Flanders he grows dumb. He grows dumb and his spirit moves away from me. It moves away from me and from everything that is of this world. It is among scenes past speech, past understanding, past imagining. He is Lazarus back in the world, but with secrets in his keeping which no one may learn but those who have learned them where he did.

When he came to Paignton he was far removed from us; but little by little he reapproached. I helped to restore him; and then, when the baby was born, the return to earth was quickened.

To have my baby I went over to Torquay, where I had six quiet contented weeks in a room overlooking the peacock-blue waters of Tor Bay, with the kindly roof that sheltered my husband in the distance. When I had recovered I went to a cottage at Paignton, where, when he left the hospital, he joined me. As the healing of the leg has been so slow, we have been in the lovely Devon country ever since, till, a few weeks ago, the British Government allowed us to cross on the ship that brought the British Commissioners to Washington.

I have just been in to look at him. He is sound asleep, lying on his left side, the coverlet sagging slightly at the shoulder where the right arm is gone. He is getting accustomed to using his left hand, but not rapidly. Meantime he is my other baby; and, in a way, I love to have it so. I can be more to him. In proportion as he needs me the bond is closer.

He is a grave man now. The smile that used to flash like a sword between us is never there any more. When he smiles it is with a long, slow smile that comes from far away—perhaps from life as it was before the war. It is a sweet smile, a brave one, one infinitely touching; and it pierces me to the heart.

He didn't have to forfeit his American citizenship in becoming one of the glorious Princess Pats. They were glad to have him on any terms. He is an American and I am one. I thought I became one without feeling any difference. It seemed to me I had been born one, just as I had been born a subject of the dear old queen. But on the night of our landing in Halifax, a military band came and played the "Star-spangled Banner" before my uncle's door, and I burst into the first tears I had shed since my marriage.

Through everything else I had been upheld; but at the strains of that anthem, and all it implied, I broke down helplessly. When we went to the door and my husband stood to listen to the cheering of my friends, in his khaki with the empty sleeve, and the fine, stirring, noble air was played again, his eyes, as well as mine, were wet.

It recalled to me what he said once when I was allowed to relieve the night nurse and sit beside him at Paignton. He woke in the small hours and smiled at me—his distant, dreamy smile. His only words—words he seemed to bring with him out of the lands of sleep, in which perhaps he lived again what now was past for him—his only words were:

"You know the Stars and Stripes were at Bois Grenier."

"How?" I asked, to humor him, thinking him delirious.

He laughed—the first thing that could be called a laugh since they had brought him there.

"Sewn or my undershirt—over my heart! It will be there again," he added, "floating openly!"

And almost immediately he fell asleep once more.

And, after all, it is to be there again—floating openly. The time-struggle has taken it and will carry it aloft. It has taken other flags, too—flags of Asia; flags of South America; flags of the islands of the seas. As my husband predicted long ago, mankind is divided into just two camps. So be it! God knows I don't want war. I have been too near it, and too closely touched by it, ever to wish again to hear a cannon-shot or see a sword. But I suppose it is all a part of the great War in Heaven.

Michael and his angels are fighting, and the dragon is fighting and his angels. By that I do not mean that all the good is on one side and all the evil on the other. God forbid! There is good and evil on both sides. On both sides doubtless evil is being purged away and the new, true man is coming to his own.

If I think most of the spiritualization of France, and the consecration of the British Empire, and the coming of a new manhood to the United States, it is because these are the countries I know best. I should be sorry, I should be hopeless, were I not to believe that, above bloodshed, and cruelty, and hatred, and lust, and suffering, and all that is abominable, the Holy Ghost is breathing on every nation of mankind.

When it is all over, and we have begun to live again, there will be a great Renaissance. It will be what the word implies—a veritable New Birth. The sword shall be beaten to a plowshare and the spear to a pruning-hook. "Nation shall not lift up sword against nation, neither shall they learn war any more."

So, in this gray light, growing so silvery that as day advances it becomes positively golden, I turn to my Bible. It is extraordinary how comforting the Bible has become in these days when hearts have been lifted up into long-unexplored regions of terror and courage. Men and women who had given up reading it, men and women who have never read it at all, turn its pages with trembling hands and find the wisdom of the ages. And so I read what for the moment have become to me its most strengthening words:

> In your patience possess ye your souls... . There shall be signs in the sun, and in the moon, and in the stars; and upon the earth distress of nations, with perplexity; the sea and the waves roaring; men's hearts failing them for fear, and for looking after those things which are coming on the earth; for the powers of heaven shall be shaken... . And when these things begin to come to pass, then look up, and lift up your heads; for your redemption draweth nigh.

That is what I believe—that through this travail of the New Birth for all mankind redemption is on the way.

It is coming like the sunrise I now see over the ocean. In it are the glories that never were on land or sea. It paints the things which have never entered into the heart of man, but which God has prepared for them that love him. It is the future; it is Heaven. Not a future that no man will live to see; not a Heaven beyond death and the blue sky. It is a future so nigh as to be at the doors; it is the Kingdom of Heaven within us.

Meantime there is saffron pulsating into emerald, and emerald into rose, and rose into lilac, and lilac into pearl, and pearl into the great gray canopy that has hardly as yet been touched with light.

And the great gray ocean is responding a fleck of color here, a hint of glory there; and now, stealing westward, from wavelet to wavelet, stealing and ever stealing, nearer and still more near, a wide, golden pathway, as if some Mighty One were coming straight to me. "Even so, come, LordJesus."

Even so I look up, and lift up my head. Even so I possess my soul in patience.

Even so, too, I think of Mildred Brokenshire's words:

"Life is not a blind impulse, working blindly. It is a beneficent, rectifying power."

THE END

CPSIA information can be obtained
at www.ICGtesting.com
Printed in the USA
LVHW112318170820
663477LV00015B/434

9 783752 381559